Perfect Assumption

A Midas Series Standalone Novel

Tracey Jerald

Copyright © 2021 by **Tracey Jerald**
ISBN: 978-1-7358128-4-7 (eBook)
ISBN: 978-1-7358128-7-8 (Paperback)
Library of Congress Control Number: 2021906000

Tracey Jerald
101 Marketside Avenue, Suite 404-205
Ponte Vedra, FL, 3208
https://www.traceyjerald.com

Editor: One Love Editing (http://oneloveediting.com/)
Proof Edits: Holly Malgieri (https://www.facebook.com/HollysRedHotReviews/)
Cover Design by Tugboat Design (https://www.tugboatdesign.net/)
Photo Credit: Wander Aguiar Model: Zach Bradford
PR & Marketing: Linda Russell - Foreword PR (https://www.forewordpr.com)

For my Musketeers —
who taught me not to make assumptions but how to draw
logical conclusion.

PLAYLIST

Lady Gaga: "The Edge Of Glory"
Sara Bareilles: "King of the Lost Boys"
Foreigner: "Waiting for a Girl like You"
Bret Michaels: "Something to Believe In"
Peter Cetera: "One Good Woman"
Katy Perry: "Wide Awake"
k.d. lang: "Constant Craving"
Kelsea Ballerini: "Machine Heart"
The Goo Goo Dolls: "Iris"
John Mayer: "Say"
David Guetta, Sia: "Let's Love"
Toby Lightman: "Breathe In"
Jeremy Renner: "Live for Now"
Taylor Swift: "gold rush"
Shawn Mendes, Justin Bieber: "Monster"
Sting: "Fields Of Gold"

ALSO BY TRACEY JERALD

Midas Series
Perfect Proposal
Perfect Assumption
Perfect Composition
Perfect Order (Fall 2021)

Amaryllis Series
Free - An amaryllis Prequel (Newsletter Subscribers only)
Free to Dream
Free to Run
Free to Rejoice
Free to Breathe
Free to Believe
Free to Live
Free to Dance
Free to Wish (Fall 2021)

Glacier Adventure Series
Return by Air
Return by Land
Return by Sea

Standalones
Close Match
Ripple Effect
Unconditionally With Me – A With Me in Seattle Novella

THE MIDAS TOUCH

In Greek mythology, Midas, wandering one day in his garden, came across the wise satyr Silenus, who was rather the worse for wear. Midas treated him kindly and returned him to his great companion, the god Dionysus

In return for this, Dionysus granted Midas a wish. The king, not realizing the repercussions of his decision, chose to be given the magical ability to turn any object he touched into solid gold. Simple things, everyday things, Midas took for granted were instantly transformed by his touch into solid gold.

The full consequences of this gift soon became evident. At the barest touch, flowers, fruit, and water turned to gold. Food took on a metallic taste the moment it brushed his lips. Midas became sick of this world he surrounded himself with and sought to relieve himself of it.

Those finding themselves burdened with an abundance of perfection gifted to them by the gods often seek relief to reverse their fortune.

Except when that gift is love. Then, it is a treasure of unfathomable value.

And it's absolutely something you never want to rid yourself of.

WARD

Don't worry. We'll celebrate tomorrow when Carys can be here. Really, I'd rather celebrate when we're all together." I shrug nonchalantly.

"Ward, sweetheart…"

"Mom, it's really okay. I don't mind. It's not Carrie's fault she got stuck working late. Justice waits for no man, woman, or dinner." Flashing my mother a quick grin, I'm mentally doing a fist pump. I wonder how long it will take for me to be able to escape this conversation so I can text the guys that I'm free tonight after all.

"But your birthday is today, Ward." The anguish in my mother's eyes is almost enough for me to buckle under.

I lean down and kiss her cheek before teasing her. "Then you won't mind ordering me a beer at dinner tomorrow?"

She smacks me on the arm. "You're turning seventeen, not twenty-one."

"It's not like I haven't had a drink before, Mom," I remind her. "Here at the house. Not in public. And I'd better not hear about anything about school, or your father and I will be having a serious conversation about letting you go back to boarding school with your friends instead of staying here to go locally. As it was, I

had serious reservations about letting you go away. It's too soon to lose my baby." Her eyes—the same aqua color as my sister's—mist over.

I wrap an arm around her shoulders and pull her close. Tiny and blonde, Mom and Carys share the same coloring, whereas I know if I pull out my dad's old school yearbook, we'd pass for twins. "I love you, Mom."

"I love you too, sweetheart." She wraps her dainty arms around my waist and gives me a quick squeeze. When she goes to move away, I hold her in place because even though I love prep school and the way I live it up when I'm off on my own, there are moments when I miss her, Dad, and home so badly there's an ache that just won't go away.

The breath I release ruffles the top of her hair. I'm about to capitulate and go to dinner with her and Dad without my sister when my phone buzzes. Again.

Shit.

Mom arcs back a bit. "Your friends know you're in town?"

I can feel the heat chasing up my neck. "When I heard Carrie was working late, I figured we weren't going out tonight. I sent them a message."

We stand there for a few moments, not saying anything. Finally, her lips begin to twitch. A smile tugs at my mouth. Her shoulders start to shake. My chest heaves up and down, trying to hold in my own laughter. Finally, we both give in. Mom rests her forehead on my chest as she giggles uncontrollably. "Were you trying to calculate the amount of time it would take for dessert?"

"Crap. I'd only factored on appetizers, salads, and entrees." She slaps me on the stomach. "Ward, language," she chastises. "Yes, ma'am." But I'm grinning.

"Tomorrow night. No plans before or after. I want a family evening." She stresses the word. "I never get to see either of my children anymore. Tonight, go celebrate with your friends."

I drop my arms just a bit and lift her off her feet, spinning my mother in a circle around our large living room on Seventy-Fourth Street before dropping her to her feet with a thud. "Thanks, Mom."

I sprint off to my room, texting along the way, never giving another thought as to what my parents would be doing that night.

When I arrive home that night, there are policemen loitering in the lobby of our building. Uh-oh. Maybe I shouldn't have had that last beer. I use the dongle on my key chain to open the elevator when I'm whirled around.

"Ward Burke?" one of the officers asks.

"Um, yeah?" Shit. Mom and Dad are going to lose their minds that I'm being busted by the cops for underage drinking. I back up a step, hoping he doesn't smell the beer on my breath. I fumble in my pocket for another piece of gum.

His fingers clamp down on my shoulder. "There are some people upstairs looking for you. We'd better head straight there."

"I'm not late for curfew," I protest as he ushers me into the elevator.

His face is completely blank as he presses the button for our floor, but he doesn't let me go. He presses the button next to his shoulder and murmurs, "I have him."

"Let me go." I struggle.

He seems startled that I'm fighting him. "Kid, trust me, this is for your own…"

Ding.

The elevator doors open, and I sprint out into the corridor of dark blue leading right to my front door. My closed front door. "What the hell is going on here?" I bellow.

Whether it's the presence of alcohol in my system or my own fear, I turn to the nearest cop and demand, "Tell me what the hell's going on?"

His face is stoic, but through my buzz, I see a flicker in his eyes. It's sympathy.

I start running and yelling. "Mom? Dad? Carrie?"

Suddenly the front door flies open as I get closer, and I spy my older sister surrounded by more police officers and my godfather. A denial is ripped from me without a single person saying a word. "No!"

Carrie jumps up from her chair and races toward me. She slams up against me to catch me as I fall. Her tiny body can't hold my much taller size, and we both go down to the floor as I repeat over and over, "Mom? Dad?"

"Ward, I have something I have to tell you…" she starts. "No! They were just going out to dinner."

"There was an accident," she tries again.

My head swivels around to my godfather—my father's best friend and my sister's boss. As a federal judge, his stress level is normally high, but he looks like he's aged about twenty years. "Hay- den?" My voice breaks on my plea.

He crosses the room and joins the circle. "I'm here for whatever you need, kids."

"I need you to bring them back." And that's when I break down and cry. I feel Carrie's tears against my shoulder. My hand comes up to clutch her to me.

"I wish I could for both your sakes. But I'll be here to help you."

Three weeks later, we're prisoners in our own home. I sneer, a grown man's reaction to a little boy's terror. Ever since the assets behind our parents' wills have been made public because paperwork had to be filed, we've been tormented by nothing but the popping of flashbulbs any time we try to step from our building. According to my godfather, "Any SOB can pay for a copy of your parents' probate file since it has to be recorded with the state."

It makes things that much worse. Carys's and my faces have been splashed on the front of every trashy news site. There's paparazzi camped out waiting to get pictures of two of the youngest multimillionaires in the United States.

"What the hell are we supposed to do with this?" I shouted at the lawyers' office.

"Calm down, Ward," Hayden tried to soothe me."

"Why? My parents were worth—I'm sorry. What was the amount again?" I ask the probate attorney, whose name I've forgotten seconds after I shook his hand.

"The last time they provided me with a quarterly report, the amount was $476,892,743.51."

"Let's not forget the fifty-one cents," I drawl. "Ward," Carys tries again.

"Carrie, what the hell were they thinking not preparing us for this?" I shout.

"I don't know!" she yells back.

That's when I realize Carys has just as little of an idea of what to do as I do. I just assumed because she was older she had a better handle on things.

I should have known better. No one has any idea how to handle this.

I stride in her direction and haul her into my arms. "We'll get through this, Ward. We have to."

"Yeah, we will."

Though I have no idea how.

CHAPTER ONE

ANGELA

Some of your favorite celebs turn fashion into an art. Leading the fall list of best-dressed is genre-defiant singer, Erzulie. Her style is much like her vocal capability. Not everyone can mix fitted sequins, exaggerated over- sized wool cardigans, and thigh-high leather boots together to make it trendy.

— Eva Henn, Fashion Blogger

This wasn't the future I had planned for myself.

For just a moment, I let my mind wander away from calendars and phones. I tap my fingers against my desk agitatedly, hating I'm ruled by mandates of other people's schedules. I had such amazing plans. I was going to explore every nook and corner of the world until I couldn't absorb any more knowledge.

Then, I'd figure out what I wanted to do with that knowledge.

Now, I'm too terrified to do more but trudge through each and every day.

"Angie? Did you arrange for the cake to be delivered?" My boss,

Carys Burke, pops her head out of the inner sanctum of LLF, LLC, her entertainment law firm, to ask.

I plaster a smile on my face before turning around to face her. "I did. It should be here in about an hour."

"Fantastic. If you could bring it back when it gets here, I'd appreciate it. You know I hate to use you for things like this." Carys steps fully out of the office.

I wave off her concern. "It's what some assistants do for their bosses."

"It's not what my legal assistant does," she stresses. "And I want to let you know I appreciate it."

"I know you do. You take care of all of the people who work for you." Just as the words finish coming from my mouth, the frosted glass doors fly open with such force, I'm surprised they don't shatter.

The wonder boy has arrived. "Good morning, Ward." "Angie." He nods

"Ward!" Carys beams up at her younger brother. Then again, if it's a member of the LLF family, Carys always beams at them in greeting. My lips twitch. Definitely different than the early days when I worked for her.

"Not now, Carys. Do you know what your friend Beckett managed to get himself into this time?" He grabs her under the elbow and drags her away from my desk without a word to me, muttering under his breath.

Carys's smile fades. "Oh, the hell he did!"

Ward's grim "Exactly" is the last thing I hear before the heavy wood door closes on their conversation.

I'm not surprised by the siblings' behavior, nor am I put off by Ward's lack of greeting. Before Ward worked here, he would come to visit his sister, and his eyes would land upon me with something else that had nothing to do with business. He was effusive and sweet until one day he wasn't. And so began the arctic freeze.

I never imagined someone like Ward would ever be interested in a person with my reputation, but it was nice just having someone to talk to for a few minutes who treated me with gentlemanly courtesy.

His charm reminded me of the stories my grandmother would tell me about the way my grandfather wooed her. A brief smile flits across my lips. "Anyway, it was a nice time."

I'm startled when the phone rings. "LLF, this is Angela. How may I direct your call?"

"Nowhere, you goose. Don't you ever leave your cell phone on?" my best friend exclaims.

"Rarely, and only when I know you're calling. To what do I owe the pleasure?"

"Angie," Sula chides me.

"I can't think about it," comes my lightning-quick response. "And I sure as hell refuse to speak of it."

"I'm not asking you to. I just want you to know you're loved. That's all."

"Okay."

"All right." I can tell Sula's gearing up to say more, but I'm rescued by the ringing of the office line.

"Have to go. We'll talk more over the weekend."

Even though I know she's reluctant to let me go, Sula hangs up.

It's a complete comfort to have my daily routine start the exact same way after so many years of battling to be normal. It's just like when a piece of software reloads a file you've lost, I think with satisfaction. Feeling content, I swirl to face my computer and begin scanning the social media sites to determine if any of my boss's clients will be calling to interrupt her already packed day.

Carys Burke might be diminutive in stature, but as a lawyer, she's a barracuda. It's why after striking out on her own only five short years ago—and stealing her now husband, David Lennan, and me from the company we all worked for prior—to start LLF, LLC, we represent some of the biggest musical names in the industry. When I came on board, Carys explained in addition to being legal assistant to both her and David, part of my job is to play watchdog to ensure their antics don't require immediate legal services.

"Now, I get the fun of seeing Ward's name pop up as much as our clients," I mutter as I scroll through my RSS feed. The paparazzi can't get enough of Carys's brother, the man whose luke-warm greeting equates me to well-functioning office furniture. Then again, I'm not so certain what I feel about him either.

Carys would erect a shrine to her baby brother, given the opportunity. David has a much clearer impression of "Winsome Ward," as the tabloids have dubbed him. "He's not quite the man you think he is, Angie. Losing their parents affected both of them; Ward more so. I think he lost his ability to have fun," David let slip one day after Ward snapped at me when one of our favorite clients engaged me in a paper airplane contest with Post-its. There was such disdain in the way Ward brushed aside the pink plane.

Ever since, there's a small part of me that's wanted to inform him that tiny little bit of fun —something I, myself, rarely indulge in

— didn't ruin his three-thousand-dollar suit.

Frowning at the screen, I mutter, "I don't get it." Of all of us who work here at the firm, I never expected Ward to be the most serious, especially considering how fierce Carys is and how efficient David is. Yet, Ward is the one people who saunter through our doors believe should smile, yet I rarely see one on his brooding face.

When I was forced to describe him to Sula after she realized I was now working with him, I begrudgingly said, "He's a modern- day Heathcliff." And it's true, if that's your type. Objectively, Ward Burke is a magnificent-looking man whose sheer masculinity is a magnet for men and women alike. Just not this woman.

Not spotting anything critical on social media to raise any alarms, I decide to let David know the special plans he and Carys have going on later shouldn't be ruined. Grabbing my tablet and coffee, I juggle the two while I tug at the heavy door to what we call the inner sanctum— where David's workspace, our file and confer- ence rooms, and Carys's and Ward's offices are. Just as I manage to get the unwieldy door open a few inches, it comes flying at me.

I stumble, my tablet going in one direction, the coffee in the other. "Well, I hope the tablet isn't destroyed." I bend down to pick it up when a pair of black wingtips appear in my line of sight.

"I think the tablet can be replaced much easier than my suit, don't you think, Angela?"

Crap. Double crap. There isn't a chance I'll receive merely a disdainful look. After all, coffee isn't Post-its. My eyes snap up and meet Ward's infuriated ones. "Sorry. I had no idea you were there."

His mouth open and closes like a guppy. If it was Carys or David, I might have even told him that. But Ward's different. He always has been.

He leans forward, causing me to step back instinctively. "Probably with more difficulty than the tablet. We could have picked one of those up on every corner."

"Can't jet off to London to get a new one made?" I joke feebly.

I only know where his suits are made because they were mentioned in the rags one time. "Winsome Ward" made the headlines the next day along with the model he escorted to dinner.

It was annoying to have to filter out gossip about...whatever Ward is in terms of the structural hierarchy in this firm on top of the normal seedy nonsense about our clients being impregnated by alien babies. Although—my lips barely lift—it did humor David immensely when I showed him that nugget about his wife's ex- boyfriend.

Ward, more disjointed than usual, slides by me and the mess without any thought about who should be responsible for cleaning it up. Calling back over his shoulder, he orders, "Tell Carrie I'll be late."

After the front doors of LLF close behind him, I let out a huge breath before saying, "Like that won't be anything new."

The heavy door swings open cautiously. "Angie, did I hear Ward leave?" Carys asks. Then, "What happened?"

"Ward and I collided. Apparently, my latte caused irreparable damage to his day. He's going to be late to your meeting."

She flits her hand as if it's of no consequence. "That's fine. It means the cake will have more time to get here."

I grit my teeth. But all I say is, "Of course. Do you still want me to bring it in straightaway?"

"No, let's hold it until the status meeting later." We both turn when the phone rings on my desk.

Leaving the mess on the floor just a moment longer, I lift the receiver to my ear. "LLF, LLC. This is Angela. How may I direct your call?"

After hearing from security the cake is on its way up, I inform a gleeful Carys, who ducks inside so I can mop up my coffee disaster.

I briefly mourn the loss of my morning coffee but put it out of my mind and get back to work.

There's too much to be done, too many secrets to keep. Including my own.

Hours later, knee-deep in addressing the emails filled with dramatic complaints filed by the celebrities Carys and Ward represent, I can't help but grumble aloud over the one I just responded to. "The gum wasn't watermelon." As if that was going to be notice- able when the band of men known as "The Rind" left their trade- mark wads of it in the greenroom at the satellite interview they were giving this morning.

Maybe I'll never understand what drives the rich, I think before adjusting my ponytail and diving back in. Every day, I act as an intermediary between celebrities with more cash than sense and people who exploit them to amass piles of it themselves.

"Where did people's humanity disappear to?" Then I realize it likely got stuck somewhere between what happened to me and a band whose signature move is to leave their DNA everywhere they go: bathrooms, bars, and now—apparently— the studio of a nation- ally broadcast satellite show.

"They're just fabulous," I mutter.

"Did you say something, Angela?" His dark voice invades my space for the second time in one day.

Ward Burke has this kind of money. Carys too, I suppose. But the way the two siblings carry their wealth is just different.

Carys has an edge of sharp elegance about her that enhances her personality, adding a level of sophistication to her pixie-like appearance. But Ward, with his contradictory darkness, comes off like he stepped out of the pages of Vogue. He oozes the confidence that comes from wearing three-thousand-dollar suits. It's the kind that's impervious to the hard knocks of life the rest of us mere mortals deal with. It's an awesome arrogance, and all it does is leave me wary.

Maybe because it reminds me of too much.

I open my mouth to say something, to apologize for the accidental mishap earlier, because today of all days, he should be happy, but the thunderclouds chasing across his face change my mind. I'm not even certain he knows I know. "No, I didn't," I reply before I turn back to my email.

With a grunt, he eases through the door, and I return to my work, awaiting the moment I'm summoned into the conference room to deliver a cake.

One Ward knows nothing about. Yet

CHAPTER TWO

WARD

Happy Birthday to one of the world's most eligible bachelors—Ward Burke.

To enumerate the many reasons we wish Ward another year of blessings would take up the entire magazine. Put simply, when compared against other men of his ilk, Ward Burke rises head and shoulders above the rest.

He's drop-dead gorgeous, filthy rich, and smart. His aloofness adds a layer of appeal that makes a person want to claw their way through skin and bone to the man beneath. So far, not a single person has managed it.
— **StellaNova**

There's a tension I can't quite rid between my shoulder blades as the banter swirls around me between the other people in the conference room sitting high above Rockefeller Center. Many floors beneath us, crowds of people are gathering like locusts for their turn around the infamous rink, but insulated high up in the air, two people are making jokes instead of business decisions.

A paper airplane flies past my ear with alarming accuracy. I glare at my older sister before asking pointedly, "Aren't we supposed to be finalizing our scheduling for the next month?"

"Come on, Ward. Lighten up. It's only your birthday." Carys grins.

I only wish I could. The words almost slip past my lips, but I manage to hold them back. It's not my sister's fault I feel wound up tighter than a spring inside a clock; it's mine. After thirteen years, the blame belongs solely to me. Still. Always.

It always will.

"Just because you're now a year older doesn't mean you can turn into a grump." Turning to her husband and our shared senior paralegal, David Lennan, Carys purses her lips. "Did I remember to add a 'no grumpiness' clause to his contract when he became a partner?"

"Sorry, love, but I don't recall that. I can check if you like?" David's eyes twinkle with merriment at his wife before he winks at me.

"You both suck," I declare for no other reason other than the fact their family and I can say that without either of them taking offense.

Carys opens her mouth, likely to make some rude comment, but David reaches over and lays his hand over her mouth. "Don't think about responding, my love. Ward doesn't need those kinds of details."

"Damn right I don't." But watching my sister's eyes turn from amusement to burning fire at her husband's words does make the corners of my mouth twitch. "I should have done that to her when we were younger." I nod at the hand over Carys's mouth.

My sister shoves her husband's hand away before growling, "I'd have bitten you so fast, it would have been… Oh, it sounds like Angie's back!" The mercurial moods Carys is having make me wonder if she's pregnant again.

When I ask that aloud, the horror on her face makes me bark out a laugh. "Why, Carrie, Ben isn't that bad," I tease her in return, some of my good humor returning when I think of my little nephew.

"And right now he can cogitate, move faster than I can, and...ooh! Excellent choice, Angie!"

I whirl around in my chair and freeze at the sight before me.

Angela Fahey may be the most dedicated and loyal assistant I've ever met in my life. She is efficient, organized, and should have left working for my sister to grow her career long ago. Of course, this has nothing to do with the fact she causes so many conflicting emotions to run through my system day after day when I come through the doors of LLF, LLC.

I've wanted her the moment I saw her, and I refuse to do a damn thing about it. I'm scarred enough by loving and losing my parents that I'm afraid I'll make the wrong decision—again. And I'll—again—have to watch someone I love get hurt, or worse.

But despite the logic in my brain, my body reacts to her presence every damn day I see her.

I resent the hell out of her for it.

Despite being pulled up, her thick auburn hair falls in waves past shoulders I've imagined are as creamy-skinned as her perfect heart-shaped face. Intelligent, serious blue eyes, high cheekbones, and a perfect bow mouth round out a face that should be gracing magazine covers instead of answering phones for my sister's—no, our—law firm. If I wasn't bound by an ethical clause Carys added to not do a background check on previous hires, I'd bet a million dollars I easily could afford I would find Angie has a modeling background with her perfectly ramrod straight carriage, those long legs, and the smooth-as-glass face she wears.

But none of her physical attributes are what holds me entranced at the moment. It's what she's holding in her hands.

Damnit, it's a birthday cake.

"You have got to be fucking shitting me," I growl.

"Ward…" David warns.

"What part of 'I don't ever want to celebrate my birthday' do any of you not understand?" I shout at the room at large.

Carys's lip begins to tremble. "Christ," I swear. Shoving myself out of my chair, I bump into Angie, who stumbles backward. The cake she's holding bobbles in her arms before it slides backward and lands against her ample bosom—clearly ruining her blouse and staining her ever-present black suit.

Flashes of what I could do with a macerated cake and icing with this woman pop into my brain. And even though there's nothing in our employee guidelines preventing me from asking her out, I can't act upon any of them as I'm almost certain she's involved with someone—someone who I see too often for my own peace of mind.

A tide of dark fury rises through me. Feeling like the monster I know I am, I slip my hand into my pocket and peel off a few bills. Tossing them onto the table, I fling a hand out. "That should buy you a new outfit to replace the one you just ruined on my sister's behalf. It's the least of what she owes you for pulling this stunt."

I storm to the door and slam it behind me, leaving Carys, David, and Angie in silence behind me. I need to get out of this office—away from anyone or anything who can remind me it's my birthday.

And the anniversary of the day my parents died.

I move with the crowds down by Fifth Avenue, having no particular destination in mind other than escape. It doesn't matter if it's in a crowd; I'm just as alone here if I was sitting back at my condo. If anything, the pain of watching the tourists explore the city I love so much is almost worse as I remember my father lifting me up against the rail surrounding the viewing deck to get a better view of the skaters.

"But why do all these people come in to the city to skate here, Dad?"

"I can't say, Ward." My father handed me a cup of cocoa he bought from a local street vendor. "But it's a good thing they do."

"Why?" I tipped my head back to look up at him.

"It gives people jobs. And jobs mean people have extra money. Around this time of the year, a lot of people don't have money for nice things like you and your sister get."

I'm bumped from the side by a rushing mother who's dragging her children along single file. "Likely to make their time to skate," I observe. But my new position puts me directly in the line of sight of a vendor selling hot chocolate. And suddenly, I want some. I need my parents here today in any way I can have them.

After all, if it wasn't for me, they would be.

After waiting for fifteen minutes on line, my hands wrap around the paper cup. I inhale and the scent brings back even more memories of my childhood. Leaning against the railing, I sip slowly as kids in snowsuits that make them as big as marshmallows try to skate around the rink while some whirl around so fast they're a blur.

I don't know how long I stand there lost in memories of long ago until a familiar head of flame rushes past me.

Angie.

She's close enough I can see her face is set in tight lines, and I know it's my fault. I feel my parents' disapproval settle over me. You aren't living up to the man they raised you to be, Ward, I chastise myself on their behalf. I call out her name, but she doesn't turn around.

I don't know if she heard me as she rounds the corner, but even if she did, I can't say I'm surprised she ignores me. I certainly would have. I was an unmitigated ass and not just to her, but to the only people in the world I give a damn about.

I turn away from the skaters and make my way around the rink to our building. It's time to face my sister's fire and her husband's ice. After I get off the elevator, I enter the door with the engraved Celtic knot sandblasted on the frosted glass doors with the discreet *LLF, LLC* beneath it. "Love, loyalty, friendship. How much damage did I do to mine today?" I murmur before pulling the door toward me.

The wooden doors with the same branding are cracked open. I wince as I hear my sister's choked sobs. "...figured if it was just us..."

"Shh, Carrie. It's Ward. He knows you meant well."

"But what about Angie?" she cries.

"Sending her home for the day was the right thing to do," David reassures her.

Damnit. I shove the door open. Two faces immediately swing in my direction: one hopeful and tear-streaked, the other closed off. The first words out of my mouth are "I'm so sorry." And while I may have overreacted about the cake, I'm really apologizing for causing the death of our parents so many years ago. I'm apologizing again for that. I do that so often, I wonder if Carys realizes how often I do it anymore.

"No, I am. I just wanted to make you smile." Carys tries to do that, but her lips wobble.

I step forward and open my arms. She pulls out of David's arms and rushes into mine before bursting into tears again. I close my eyes against the burning sensation, knowing half of these tears aren't because of a damn cake or me being an ass. They're because of what we lost and will never get back.

No matter what we try to celebrate in life, certain moments are never going to be forgotten. It takes nothing but a word or a touch to ignite the feelings all over again. That's how embedded they are in your brain.

I kiss the crown of Carys's head before I tell my brother-in-law, "I apologize."

He nods. "I appreciate it." He gives his wife a once-over. Realizing Carys and I are in a good place, he announces, "I think I'm going to go get Ben early."

"Then how about I treat everyone to dinner." Carys's head snaps up from my chest at the offer. I hold up a hand. "Not as a birthday celebration. I...can't. Okay?"

"Okay, Ward. I'm sorry too. I just thought they'd..." Her voice trails off when I lay my finger across her lips.

"You don't need to apologize," I tell her firmly.

But I'm the one with one left, and I know it's going to be a whopper. Especially because if what I suspect about her is true, the man she's involved with is going to tear into me for hurting her.

And since he's a client, this could be very, very bad.

Shit.

CHAPTER THREE

ANGELA

Last night, "Winsome Ward" Burke was spotted escorting a woman around Manhattan. The petite blonde wasn't able to be identified, but one can only assume he used his charming smile to suggest dessert in other ways. We'd certainly say yes to dessert with one of the world's most eligible bachelors.
— **Sexy&Social, All the Scandal You Can Handle**

I growl slightly, even as I pick up the colorful article to read it closer. "'Winsome Ward,' my ass. The man is as cold and unfeeling as the wind blowing outside. And for the record, it was his damn sister." Finishing, I fling the garbage news rag aside before pushing my cart away from the rack of magazines where I was searching for the latest edition of the knitting magazine my grandmother used to buy me for my birthday. Instead of finding something comforting, I'm now thinking not so very nice things about the brother of my friend and boss, Carys Burke.

Ward Burke is the complete polar opposite of his sister in every way possible. Tall and dark where she's dainty and blonde, the similarities don't just stop with their looks. In just a few short years, she left the media conglomerate Wildcard Entertainment to build a ferocious reputation as an entertainment lawyer to be reckoned with. And more than that, she's become a trusted friend.

On the other hand, Ward has been with the firm for two years, and I'm still trying to determine if he's doing his best to live up or down to what the gossip rags say about him. Carys claims he's been "Invaluable. You have no idea how much he's taken off my shoulders."

Maybe it's because the man is likely blinded by the flashbulbs of the paparazzi than he does in the office that I can't quite figure it or him out. What I don't appreciate is the way he makes me feel when we're together—ignored, yet with a dangerous rush of emotions I haven't experienced in far too long. Both feelings leave me on edge and generally have me plotting ways to make his life unpleasant for the few hours a day he does spend gracing the office with his presence. Then I mentally kick myself. Ward's a good attorney. I'm being unfair, which is unlike me. I know he meets with most of our clients on the West Coast to alleviate the late hours Carys and David used to work. "I just don't understand why he antagonizes me."

Disgusted with everything, I wheel the cart around the store, grabbing the staples I'm low on in addition to sparingly adding fresh produce. I'm hefting a bag of Idaho potatoes into my wagon when a hand clutches my shoulder. I whirl around in panic before recognizing the face and relaxing. "Hi, Mr. Graham."

His gnarled hand drops back to his cane. "Hello, Angela. How are you doing today? Everything quiet up at your house?"

"Wonderfully so."

When he smiles, his face creases into a million wrinkles. "If you have any problems, you call. I'll be there as fast as I can."

"I'll do just that," I promise.

With a nod, he hobbles away. And I use the few moments before I approach the crowds gathered at the checkout to regain my composure. After making small talk, I burst through the store doors and inhale the air that is uniquely fall, a combination of dampness and smoky air as families everywhere burn fuel to keep their loved ones warm.

I yank up the hood on my vest as I push a cart full of groceries out toward my car. The early November wind doesn't just whip a few lingering leaves in my face, but it also brings along a cold so harsh it makes me tip my head back with a frown. The frozen gray sky is a perfect reflection of my mood, but it doesn't look like a snowstorm is going to roll in.

"I guess that's a small gift," I murmur aloud.

"Did you say something, Angela?" Another one of my grandmother's oldest friends makes her way by using a scooter I've had run over my toes on more than one occasion. She pauses right next to me, and I manage to scoot back just in time to avoid the tires trampling over my poor toes.

Again.

"Just commenting on the weather, Mrs. Burnette." At her frown, I explain, "It's a gift."

"Child, you were living with your grandmother for far too long if you think this weather's a gift."

I can't prevent the slight curve of my lips at her cantankerous mention of my beloved grandmother. "Grandma would have said any day there wasn't snow on the ground that she didn't have to have shoveled was a good day, Mrs. Burnette."

She barks out a laugh that sounds like an old furnace wheezing before it finally pushes out heat. An answering giggle bubbles up. I lift my gloved hands up to tamp it down, which is likely why I don't see Mrs. Burnette slap hers down onto the control panel of her scooter, before flying forward into a display of chrysanthemums.

"Ahh!" she shrieks.

It's a good thing it's so cold out because by the time I get her sorted out and explain what happened to the store clerk who came rushing outside, anything frozen I had in my cart would likely have melted. But as cold as I normally am inside, it warmed me for a moment when Mrs. Burnette cupped my cheek and said, "You're a good girl, Angela. Keep that smile on your face," before she finally made it into the store for her weekly shopping.

If only I could, the world would be a very different place.

Pushing my groceries to my car, I load up the bags and let the car warm up for a few moments before I put it in gear to finish the rest of my errands.

The tiny village of Brewster, located in Putnam County, New York, has a lot of history for only having a population of less than 3,000 year-round residents. Brewster's history dates back to the Revolutionary War where a teenage girl rode through the once-upon-a-time farmland to proclaim, "The British are coming!" from nearby Danbury, Connecticut. Due to its proximity to New York City—made possible by the Walter Brewster donating land for the New York and Harlem railroads to be built—Brewster has become a sought-after address for commuters.

It's sheer happenstance I happen to own a home here, but I'm grateful for this oasis outside the constant pressures of New York City my grandparents left to me as a result of settling here back in the '60s. When I crawled back here with a broken soul and my honor more deeply stained than an antique mirror, this little village sheltered me without question.

Stepping into the Eagle Eye Thrift Store, I call out a hello to the proprietress. Receiving one in return, I wander up and down the racks of the clothes people drop off because they're simply out of season or have a microscopic stain that can easily be hidden. "Ridiculous. This shirt is Tory Burch. I can cover the stain with a pin, and no one will ever notice it." Holding the blouse in the air, I frown at the mere $4 being asked for it before performing a more thorough examination of the item. "Miss Thelma, I'm leaving you a $10 for this shirt!"

She pops her head out with a smile. "Go ahead and leave the money behind the counter, honey. I'm just sorting a few things in the back."

I almost volunteer to help her, but I know her pride is as strong as my grandmother's was. "Not a problem." Just as I lay the $10 near the register, a pin catches my eye in the display case. The clashing jewels make me smile as they remind me of the colors of the walls in the home I've yet to repaint. "Grandma would have loved this," I murmur to myself.

I open my mouth to call out again to ask about the cost, and my breath catches in my throat. There are two men standing outside the enormous bay window, staring agape. I've never seen either of them before in my life, in this town. One elbows the other before they both start talking animatedly, pointing at me.

My heart skips a beat. My hands shake even as I present them both with my back. *I'm supposed to be safe here* is all I can think. I quickly move toward the back of the store and the back entrance where my car's parked. Trying to keep my composure, I call out, "If no one buys that flower pin, let me know."

"Sounds good, Angie. You all set?"

"Yes, ma'am. I am. I'll see you soon." *On a day where I don't feel like I'm drawing everyone's attention.*

Calling out a goodbye, I slip out the door and slide behind the wheel, knowing no matter what, no matter where I go, the truth doesn't matter. It didn't back then. Ten years later, people who recognize me will still believe what they want. And those that do will immediately cast judgment no matter what.

Backing my car out, I make certain I'm not being followed before I head home. "Remember what Grandma said. No one sees you for what you are. They make assumptions based on things out of your control." But repeating her words aloud doesn't prevent the lone tear from escaping down my cheek.

"No, really. I'm fine, Sula."

"You don't sound it." Just as I'm about to protest, she barrels on. "Every time I talk to you, Angie, you sound more and more despondent."

Ursula Moore, my college roommate, is the only person I've kept in contact with since I dropped out the second semester my freshman year. Sula was like a one-man army fighting off the harassing phone calls from students and reporters. But in the end, even after I made the decision to leave, she wouldn't let go of me. She wouldn't let me give in to the edge of despair I felt. And every day of loneliness I've experienced, I've been able to beat back simply by having her in my corner. Never doubting me. Not once.

"I don't know how to describe it," I worry aloud.

"Try" is her quick response.

"Every time something happens and his name is in the press, it's all rehashed. I can't move forward because I'm constantly being forced to look back." I manage to get the words out.

Sula's quiet before she responds. "Do you resent me? Wish I hadn't…"

"No." My voice is firm. Resolute.

"Angie, your life is wasting away."

"It isn't."

"Do you have dreams anymore?" she counters.

I open my mouth and snap it shut. I dream, but they're all nightmares. Memories of days that changed the course of my life. I choose my words carefully. "How much of a life would it have been if I hadn't told the truth?"

"Maybe it could have been different." Sula's voice holds years of heartache. For me. Although she transferred schools, she completed her degree on time and has gone on to set an example of the life I wanted to lead.

The life I should have led.

"And I could have ended up being another damn statistic." The temper my grandmother used to say I was born with, something I buried so deep in the early years she claimed it was like living with a different child, sparks. "Different path, same outcome. I'd still have to deal with the shame, the embarrassment, the disbelief."

Only they'd be private thoughts, not something for everyone in the world to dissect every time they recognize my face.

"Oh, I wish we lived closer. You know I'd take on the world for you." Sula's voice is laced with regret. As a project manager for an international technology company, she's been assigned to a project in Ireland for the next few years.

"And how many times do I have to tell you, you already have."

She hums. "How about we go to the beach house when I'm done with this project? We can go grab pizza in Mystic, wander the shops in Newport—anything you want." Sula's parents have a glorious beach home on the Rhode Island border that's a small slice of heaven.

"That sounds perfect." And some of the tension leaves my body at the thought of a week of relaxing with my best friend, my ride or die.

"I love you, Angie. We'll talk soon."

"Soon, my friend. I love you too." I press End on our call, and my thoughts turn back to that night at college.

"Come on, Angie. You know we'll have a blast," Sula urged.

"It's an upperclassman party, Sula. How on earth are we going to get in?"

I burst out laughing as her temporary disappointment transformed to conniving. "We're pledging with a sorority, Ange. All we have to do is go with our sisters." She announced which sorority was co-hosting the event, and even I had to give her credit. It wasn't a bad idea, especially as we did plan on announcing our commitment to them the following week.

"Future sisters," I corrected her.

"Current, future. You know it's a given. I mean, come on. You're being courted by every damn Alpha, Beta, Chi, Delta on campus!"

"Like you're not." I rolled my eyes. My roommate's combination of ice-blue eyes and black hair was startling in a pixie face. Right now, her full lips were in a pout. "All right! I give in. We'll go!"

Sula's smile spread across her face as she tackled me to my bed. "We're going to have such an unforgettable time!"

"We're going to be lucky not to get thrown out." I laughed.

I shake myself from my reverie. That night was certainly unforgettable as it set off a chain of events that changed the course of my life forever.

I only wish we had been thrown out.

CHAPTER FOUR

WARD

Last night, more than one star was spotted catching Erzulie playing at Terminal 5. According to the manager, her powerful voice blew the doors off the place with her ability to switch seamlessly between the highest soprano and the lowest alto ranges. Broadway cast members from *Queen of the Stars* sang along from their prime spots by the stage. "Moments like that can never be matched. I think even Erzulie was in awe," one concertgoer was overheard to say.

We happen to agree.
— **The Fallen Curtain**

My kingdom to escape my pain.

I'd trade anything, my car, my condo in Tribeca, including and especially every damn dollar to my name, if I could escape the damn farce of perfection that makes up my life and if there was any—*any*—way I could go back in time. Just once. I'd dump everything and sleep in a cardboard box without a single moment of hesitation.

I'd hold her tighter to me. I'd grip his hand.

I'd do anything to never let them go. Never to come home from a stupid-ass party to find them both gone. Dead. I was left with something so completely worthless when compared to my parents' love.

Money.

And still, the more largess I'm granted, the more their blood oozes from wounds that have never closed. Not in ten years. Not ever. To me, it's pretty straightforward: it's their blood money. And the life I have that's based upon it? What right do I have to enjoy it? To cherish it?

Little arms reach up and pound my thigh before demanding, "Again!"

"Of course, my liege." I bow to my two-year-old nephew before I swoop him around in a circle.

He chortles loudly in my ear.

Innocence. I wish I could find my way back to it.

Despite the years, and my often careless callousness, Carys has never given up on me. She's all about the most critical bonds of family: love, loyalty, and friendship. *Not like Carys would have let me*, I think wryly. Once she sets her heart on loving someone, they don't stand a chance. Just look at what happened when she decided David's time was up. My smile spreads as their son starts using me as his personal drum kit.

My personal nightmare led to my sister's dream. It doesn't completely mitigate what happened, but it helps knowing the worst kind of failure had the best outcome. Still, I can't reconcile finding happiness when the two people who gave us everything are gone.

Because of me.

I place Ben back down at his table and chairs. "Listen to me, Ben. Don't be afraid of living, of showing people how much you love them. It's important to do that every single chance you get. It doesn't matter if your buddies think it's cool."

He tilts his head, intent on the sound of my voice.

"I get it. You're going to need to experience everything in life. Do it. Savor it. Don't let a single moment pass you by without trying new things. But remember, every moment with family is precious. Especially ours."

Ben blinks back at me without saying a word. Then he slams his fist down on the table in front of him in frustration.

"I get it, buddy. It's not fair that you have to wait to do all of the things you want to do, but you're lucky."

He frowns in confusion.

"You have two amazing parents who love you. I…love you. And none of that will ever change. You'll never have to worry about growing up hungry or cold. There are so many out there your age who don't have what you do."

He nods, totally getting it. I squat down so we're talking man to man. I love these times when my nephew and I get private time and I can share the most important lessons I've learned with him.

"It's important to be a good man—someone your family can rely on. You don't want to earn a reputation as just the clown or as a jock, you know? I mean, it's good to be both athletic and funny, but they shouldn't define you."

Ben gurgles and lurches forward until he can wrap his arms around my neck. Even though his face is entirely David's, his coloring is just like mine and my father's. The minute he was born and was put into my arms, little Benjamin Burke Lennan found the crack to start the blood flowing to my waste of a heart again.

He gives me a smile with tiny little teeth right before whacking me in the head with his airplane. I'm just grateful this one's made out of foam and not the wood one he used the last time we had a chat. "Listen, kid. And don't let Mom and Dad talk you out of occasionally spoiling yourself if you work hard. If you become a pilot, celebrate. Buy the airplane. Life's too short. In the grand scheme of things, it doesn't cost all that much."

"Life lessons from Uncle Ward should be committed to memory, sweet baby boy." Carys's amused voice startles me. But my smile when I look at her delicate stature is automatic. Then I scowl when she adds, "Then you should check with Momma before you do anything rash like wasteful spending."

Ben abandons me for my sister posthaste, shouting, "Momma, Momma!" as he trudges off on his still-chunky toddler legs.

She leans down, picks him up, and balances him on one hip. "An airplane, Ward? Really? You were doing really well up until then."

I shrug before getting to my feet in my nephew's playroom, careful not to crush any of the toys we've left scattered around. "Come on, Carrie. It's not like he's going to remember."

She narrows her aqua eyes at me. "Do you have any memories of Mom and Dad from when you were Ben's age?"

My sister can't understand the savage pain her simple question causes. It's been thirteen years since the drunk driver ran the light that killed our parents, but for me, every day I live with the fact that if I hadn't been such a selfish bastard intent on impressing the guys, maybe they'd be here spoiling their grandson instead of me.

Due to Carys's insistence back then, I spoke with some of the best psychologists. I've openly expressed my feelings of overwhelming guilt since the moment the officers left this very condo the night they came to inform us of their death. And I've moved on from my adolescent psychologist to the one I visited during college, then law school. Until I managed to find a balance in my life.

For the most part.

There are still moments like these where I stare down into Carys's eyes after being scolded for something amusing where I'm transported back to those moments with my mother before I called the guys to tell them I could make the party the night of my seventeenth birthday.

The night our lives changed forever.

Leaning down, I press a kiss to my sister's forehead and tell her, "So many you would be shocked. That's why I know they would spoil Ben rotten."

The admonishing look falls from Carys's face. It's replaced by one of serenity. "They would, wouldn't they?" She goes to press a kiss to Ben's chubby cheek, which he intercepts, so it lands smack on his lips.

We laugh.

"Yeah. They'd be so proud of the family you've built here, Carrie." I ruffle Ben's hair and then try to do the same to Carys's, but she's fast and avoids my brotherly love by ducking outside the door.

"Ha! I'm too quick. Oomph!" She backs up right into her husband's chest.

David catches my eye before he wraps one arm around his wife and son, using the other hand to ruffle Carys's perfectly styled hair. "David," she screeches in laughter. "Stop!"

"Stop what?"

"Stop ganging up on me with Ward!"

"You might be able to negotiate that, Counselor." He smiles down at her as he lifts their son off her hip onto his own. As he does, he brushes a kiss on her lips. "Hmm, that's a good start." He turns and walks down the hall, calling over his shoulder, "Dinner's ready!"

Carys is staring after her husband and son, unmoving. I loop an arm around her shoulders. "Everything okay?"

"Yeah. Sometimes I just like to count my blessings. You know you're one of them."

"Carys," I begin, but she interrupts me by wrapping her arm around my waist and squeezing.

"Come on. I want to try to get my hands on my baby sometime tonight."

"Your husband or your child?" I deadpan.

"Oh, you." Carys begins tickling my ribs which means I have to retaliate. So, just like when we were kids running up and down the halls of this very home, we arrive at the dinner table out of breath and laughing.

And once again two people are waiting for us with smiles on their faces. Just like our parents did when they were still alive.

Hours later, the elevator opens directly into my penthouse condominium in Tribeca. I move forward without seeing the framed photos on the wall, each one priceless because they were taken by my mother not because of any gallery's assessed value. They're certainly not like the collection of Quentin Blakes I gifted Carys when Ben was born, nor are they like the soul-wrenching Holly Freemans that hang in the gallery down the hall I scored after her first showing at the Met.

Shrugging off my coat, I toss it over the mahogany coat tree before heading into one of the three rooms I use in the ridiculous space I let my Realtor talk me into buying when I went house shopping years ago. "It's perfect for a man with your reputation in the community," she cooed.

"Yeah, what reputation is that?" I wonder aloud as I flick on the lights to my sanctuary—my home office. It's one of two spaces I had a personal hand in every inch of the remodel, likely why I eschew the rest of my home for the comfort I find here. Dropping down onto the chesterfield, I find the remote and flick on the television just in time to catch the lead-in about my former bosses' client XMedia. *"In business news, XMedia's again in the news with a possible merger. With the founder's son, Michael Clarke, now taking his seat on the board of directors, will this resurrect the speculation of assault charges in his past? More news at ten."*

Hitting Mute, I toss the remote in disgust to the side. "Of course it will because you meddling savages will ensure it will."

Having been an unwilling victim of the paparazzi after my parents died, I feel a small spark of compassion for everyone involved in the long-ago situation: the man, the woman, and the individuals who had to make a judgment on their fate. Because no matter what they decided, someone's life was going to be destroyed.

Remembering what it was like for me and Carys after our parents died, being set upon with cameras and microphones every time we tried to leave the condo, I can't help but sneer at the news reporter chattering away on mute. Sure there was a law passed here in 2015 stating paparazzi can't use drones to take pictures of unsuspecting celebrities on their own property, but essentially that's putting the individual under house arrest for what? Being famous? Being an overnight media sensation when they never wanted to be one? Imprisoning them even more than they already were inside their own minds?

At least that's how it felt to me. I can't even presume to imagine what it's like when you're scarred mentally and physically because of fate. The thought propels me to my feet. I quickly fire off a text to my former boss with a quick *Good luck, buddy. You're going to need it.*

His response is the middle finger emoji, which makes me grin before I settle down and flip open my laptop to review the contracts David dropped into my drive for me on Friday.

Soon, I'm muttering aloud, "*Any charges, fees, or royalties payable for music rights or any other rights not covered by this Agreement shall be additional to the Royalties and covered by separate agreement.* Forgot that one, David." I grin, knowing he's going to be annoyed at missing a fairly straightforward clause about covering the use of music outside of the documented agreement, an item that should be standard language in all our contracts. I flag it and make a note to ask if it was excluded for a reason before moving on to the next file.

And with it, I find solace.

CHAPTER FIVE

ANGELA

There are certain things in New York that never seem to change: a hot dog that tastes like no other in the world, the ball coming down on New Year's Eve, and Beckett Miller always wearing his trademark white shirt half-open regardless of the season. Thank God.
— **@PRyanPOfficial**

Every day I feel overwhelmed. Anxious. Fearful.

I haven't been able to let go of these emotions since I left college. Then again, I've been too withdrawn to feel anything else on a regular basis since that time in my life. There have been moments of occasional happiness and joy, but those days are rare.

My stomach churns as the train slows.

It isn't New York that makes me feel that way, but people in general. And this city is filled with too damn many of them on an off day. But I need to work, and the work I do, well, there's no better city for it.

Sliding my hands inside my hood, I gently rub my temples. I can feel the pressure rising already. After listening to the news last night before bed, I'm waiting for all of it to start up again. Some enterprising researcher is going to drag out old media reports—hell, old photos. Each time it comes up, it hits harder and harder. As if it's not bad enough, I'll wake up screaming until I find another way to beat back the memories. Again.

But today, I'm too aware of who I was. Hell, who I am. After all, nothing ever really goes away. You're really just given a personal choice to move past it and survive or fade away. And with what happened to me, I never had the luxury for option two.

On a day like today, I'm hyperaware of everything and everyone. I want to bury my head and scurry home to let the storm unleash around me. Then I remember I caused the storm because I believed in the power of honor and truth. That alone forces me to crawl from my bed and get ready to face the day.

Because if people don't stand up for what they know to be true, how can they change the future?

With a rough sigh, I only wish there was some sign to let me know I acted with honor—something to show me I did the right thing even if the rest of the world believed it was wrong. There wasn't. There never will be. Not a damn thing. And now, as the train crawls along, knowing it's about to start all over, my stomach churns as hard as the train engines.

I wonder if I can escape to someplace remote where I won't be recognized. The problem is I need my job too much. Yes, I own my home outright due to the largess of my grandparents, but there are still bills to pay. Besides, in comparison to what someone with a reputation like mine could be doing, it's both lucrative and challenging every single day. I just wish Carys and her husband would get a wild hair and decide to up and move the whole thing to rural Antarctica. A touch of amusement hits me. *Because there's an untapped entertainment Mecca there.*

Instead, I steel myself when the disembodied voice calls out, "Final stop, Grand Central Station. Please be sure to get all of your belongings, and watch your step."

Lucky me.

I don't move from my seat, unlike the other harried professionals who immediately begin gathering their belongings and filling the aisles. Why? What's the point? To get a better position by the train's doors in order to scurry onto the sweltering underground platform like rats once the cage opens? Instead, I do my best to keep my head averted beneath my wool hood, praying that in a city of nine million people, today I won't be recognized by someone with a camera. That someone won't stop and stare at me before I can get behind the safety of the office doors.

There are worse odds of that happening than me winning the lotto, which is why I don't waste my money.

"Good morning, Angie." David strolls up to my desk an hour after I booted up my computer. He holds out a cup, which I take eagerly. "I texted Carys after I dropped Ben off at daycare, and she declared if I walked into the office without copious amounts of caffeine, I was fired." The glint of light off his platinum wedding band matches the one in his eyes over what he assumes is his wife's hyperbole.

"Brace yourself," I warn him before taking a grateful sip of a delicious latte.

He hitches a hip on the corner of my desk. "What happened this time?" David and I have worked with each other since before Carys started the firm. Back at Wildcard, we were much more cordial and less casual than we are here at LLF. I love the difference. In the beginning, before Carys and David had their son, it wasn't uncommon for all of us to kick back after hours with a drink even as we'd slog away arguing over how Carys should argue a case. We'd order food and debate for hours on end. Fortunately, on those nights, Carys and David insist on my taking a car service home so I wouldn't be subjected to the persistent attention I draw on the metro line. Although we do that more often at their apartment than here at the office these days, if there's a need for me to work late, they insist on protecting me. And each time, it's not the luxury that wraps around me. It's the feeling of being cared for.

I've been recruited any number of times by a lot of different corporations, offered a ton of money to leave, but there's nothing that could make me consider that as an option when I know Carys and David feel I'm a part of their family. And they do everything within their power to protect me.

"We were on a call with Z, and the whole internet went down just as Burke got him to agree to the terms of the new contract."

"How long did it take to come back up?"

"Who says it has?" I arch my brow.

"Oh, holy hell," he groans. "Did I buy enough coffee? Should I make another run?"

"Don't you dare go looking for an escape route," I threaten him.

"If I was going to do that, I'd fake an emergency from daycare."

PERFECT ASSUMPTION · 51

I snort. "Like your wife wouldn't leave this hot mess in your hands to deal with while she got to rush out and handle your son."

He opens his mouth to retort when the door crashes open behind him and tattooed male hotness stands in the doorway. Beckett Miller booms out, "I've been trying to call Carrie all morning. What the hell is going on around here, Dave?" Despite the fact David and Carys have been happily married for two years, David still bristles when he hears his wife's ex-boyfriend's voice. Especially when it's shortening his name to a nickname he utterly detests. And only used by the man in question.

I wave the cup to emphasize my point. "See? Today is turning out to be a complete catastrophe."

David leans closer, ignoring Becks for the moment. "I'll give you a month's pay right now if you go set off the fire alarm to get me out of dealing with him."

My shoulders begin to shake with suppressed laughter. "As tempting as that offer is, no."

"Where the hell is Ward? I know he supposedly works here?" David demands testily.

"Do I look like your brother's keeper?" I ask impudently.

"What you always look like," Becks drawls as he comes closer, "is Aphrodite. Angie, run away with me. Let me treat you in the manner in which you should become accustomed. Remove the agony of this world by fulfilling your heart's desire by becoming my one and only."

David looks ready to spit tenpenny nails into the rock giant's face. Since it would be such a shame to mar such sinfulness on a Monday morning, I wade into this ongoing pissing contest that has lasted for years. "Becks, if I ran away with you, who would help Carrie get the internet back up?"

His bright blue eyes widen comically. "That's what the cable company is for, lovely."

Again, I remind him, "And I'm here to assist with problems. Both Carrie's and David's," emphasizing the end of his name, winning a twitch of a smile from the man in question.

"But not Ward's?" Before I can grit my teeth and reply that yes, my scope of responsibilities now includes supporting Ward Burke as well, Becks snaps his fingers. "If I can't get in to see Carrie, can I pop in to see her little brother?"

"No," I declare resolutely.

"Why not?"

David merely chuckles into his coffee. "I'm not touching this one, Angie. I'd better go check on the internet crisis before someone has to represent my wife for murder one." He nods at Becks before disappearing with the tray of coffee behind the heavy wood doors.

Becks waits until he leaves before he drops any and all pretense of being an annoying prick. His voice is laced with true concern when he asks, "How are you doing today? I tried to call to get through, but with both the work line down and your cell off, I started to get worried, love."

I start to say I'm fine, but Becks just pierces me with a stare. It's odd to count one of the world's most famous rock stars as one of your close friends, but one night well before Carys and David were married, when we were all working late, Becks arrived with another one of his infamous "dramas." The four of us ended up engaging in raucous banter for hours. Becks bemoaned he was becoming the laughingstock of the tabloids.

I tried to hold it in, I really did. But my tongue was loosened by the two beers I'd consumed. I finally pointed a finger at him and chortled before saying, "You never will hold that title. Not as long as I'm alive."

I thought my comment went unnoticed by the megastar until a few days later. He showed up, unsurprisingly without an appointment, but this time he didn't ask to see Carys. Beckett Miller dropped into one of the waiting chairs and stared at me, rubbing his forefinger across his full lips for hours. But he didn't utter a single word.

This unusual behavior lasted several days, and for the longest time, I wondered if he was going to ask me out. I began panicking before the more jaded side of me kicked in. It wouldn't be the first time someone put two and two together and in an effort to boost their notoriety made a half-hearted pass on me.

But he didn't want that either.

It was about a week later when the gladiolus bouquet landed on my desk. I stood, prepared to carry them in to David as Carys often received flowers from her artists, when I heard a cough. Becks was leaning against the door. He merely shook his head before turning around and leaving.

Shaking, I returned to my desk and placed the heavy vase down before opening the card.

For standing tall and holding your head high no matter what can be thrown at you by those bastards—then or now. - BM

With trembling fingers, I put the card in my desk, knowing Beckett Miller just became an ally as much as Sula and Carys were. No judgment over what I'd done, no questions asked. Just support. Something I'd received from so few. Something that the media on one side or the other persistently tries to strip from me.

Back then, the people who believed in me couldn't do anything, and those who didn't turned away. Now, each time I let someone in, it creates a small crack in the armor around my heart that I'm not prepared to defend.

I'm not sure I can afford too many more before all my defenses crumble.

Like right now. Despite the fact he knows his presence irritates David to no end, Becks still rolled out of some bed and made the trek to check on me. I give him a real smile, something I so rarely do it stretches unused muscles in my face. "I am."

"Liar." But Becks's smile takes away the sting of his words.

"I have to be okay, Becks. If I'm not breathing, I'm dying. And if I'm dying, they won." I briefly let my lashes flutter shut. "In my heart, I still believe I did the right thing."

"You did." His voice is full of such conviction, it feels like a warm blanket has been wrapped around my cool skin.

"Do you ever think they'll forget about me?" I wonder aloud. It's my biggest fantasy.

He snorts. "I think there's a bigger chance of me fathering Carrie's next baby."

"You are such a scoundrel." I reach out and slap him on the arm.

He captures my hand between both of his tattooed ones, his head tipping to the side as he contemplates his answer. Finally he says, "Angie, if this was the time before social media and things like Timehops, TikTok, and all that crap, maybe.

Your face might fade out of their minds. But now? Every year, gossipmongers are reminded of what they tittered about last year, the year before. Hell, even five, ten years ago."

"Where were you when Angela Fahey's accusations against the son of XMedia's owner of sexual assault were proved to be unfounded?" I murmur aloud.

"Where were you when Beckett Miller was admitted into rehab for his cocaine addiction?" He recalls his latest negative tabloid sensation—the one that days ago had Ward in a tither.

Our eyes lock over our joined hands. "My beautiful friend, both stories are false. But to the media-hungry world, they're in print."

"Therefore they must be true," I conclude sadly. "I'll never understand how you do it every day."

"Do what?"

"Go out there with such a devil-may-care attitude."

Becks's lips quirk before he turns to fully face me. "Probably because I listen to only about thirty percent of what they have to say about me."

"Becks..."

"And when I land on the front page, I pay Carrie an epic amount of money to handle it for me. Unless it's in good fun."

He winks before concluding, "Then I let it ride. Kind of like calling David 'Dave.'"

I grin. "You're a menace of a good man, Becks."

He contemplates that before nodding. "I like the way that sounds."

"You would."

"Well, now that I've made sure you're smiling, *is* there someone for me to talk with?" His smile turns sheepish.

I prop my hand on my chin. "What did you get into this time? Or should I say who?"

"It's a where, beauty. I was at Redemption. I might have deliberately slammed into some reporters on my way out last night." He lifts his shoulders in a careless shrug that just shows off his custom-made suit. "They may have been holding recording devices."

"You're incorrigible."

"That I am." When his true smile is aimed at me, I understand why half of the population of the globe would love to be in the position I am right now. Beckett Miller is just adorable.

"I've heard Redemption's amazing." I change the topic before Becks gets lost on listing his redeeming qualities.

"I keep offering…" he starts before a rude cough sounds behind us.

And there he is. Dark eyes. Thick hair mussed like he's had a rough night of his own. But at least he made it in before noon, I think a bit uncharitably.

"Did you need something, Becks?" Ward addresses Becks directly after running his eyes up and down me so quickly as if he's confirming I'm properly dressed in my school uniform. Not that I want Ward turning those dark, slumberous eyes my way, but being polite to the person who's responsible for your schedule is considered good form. *Especially when I could make it so booked he doesn't have time to use the restroom.*

Becks narrows his eyes to blast the younger man, but I give him a sharp shake of my head. I don't need the additional attention any day, but most especially not today. "Fine." And I know that's for both me and Ward. "Until later, beauty," Becks advises me as he follows Ward through the heavy wood doors.

I curve my lips at Becks, earning myself a blinding glare from Ward, who turns to open the door. Becks taps his phone and winks. *Right. My cell's off.* I open my desk and pull out my phone. When I turn it on, it immediately starts vibrating in my hand. Then my countenance softens when I see the one from Becks. *Dinner at Carys and David's tonight. We're not taking no for an answer. We'll make certain you get back to your hideaway.*

I hold the phone to my chest for just a moment, grateful that the people I work with actually know who I am and care about what today means to me. Just as the euphoria washes over me, a new text comes in from Sula.

Are you okay? I saw the news about XMedia. Call me as soon as you can.

No, I'm not, I think grimly. *But I really have no choice.* And I make a mental note to call Sula at some point during the day if possible. I send her a quick text back, letting her know I'll contact her later—that we're in crisis mode at work with no internet. Her laughing emoji does much to lift my spirits even as I groan. "What a freaking morning."

The door behind me flies open, and a triumphant Carys comes out. "We have phones! We have internet! Angie, can you please get Zapatta back on the line and apologize profusely before seeing if we can salvage any of this day?"

"You bet, Carys." Shoving my cell to the side, I reboot my computer. Ignoring the quiet buzz, I use our business communication platform, get an outside line, and get Z's representatives back on the line. After abjectly apologizing for the communications breakdown, they get the profanity-loving Grammy-winning artist back on the line.

I can't help but grin when his first word to me is "Fuck."

"Let me get Burke for you."

"Yeah, let's fuckin' do that."

I'm sure we'll enjoy this conversation over dinner tonight. And knowing my friends care enough about me to put aside any small differences they may have to get me through today, I manage to get through the rest of the day with a smile on my face.

Not fear in my heart.

CHAPTER SIX

WARD

Multi-multi-multi (are there enough multis?) millionairess Carys Burke Lennan was spotted arm in arm with her gorgeous husband, David, hurrying away from Rockefeller Center. The two stylish lovebirds were both bundled up in Burberry to ward off the November chill.
— Eva Henn, Fashion Blogger

Alcohol and bitterness. I've swallowed down quite a bit of both. Unfortunately, the combination makes a man less guarded about doing certain things—like making phone calls that have no way of ending well. Or ending business relationships that have taken years to formulate.

All because of a woman.

For years, I stayed away from Angie because she was off-limits. And that limit was placed on me Valentine's Day five years ago.

"I can't thank you enough for coming by, Ward." We were just a couple of steps outside of Carys's office, arm in arm.

When she called me to join her on a conference call with the heavy metal band Mastodon to gauge my interest in becoming her partner, I felt something flow through my veins I hadn't in close to ten years.

Excitement.

"My pleasure. I think things are going to work out beautifully."

She beamed up at me. "I hope so. It will certainly be a change, that's for damn sure." We both laughed.

"How about I take you to lunch? You have to be starving," I cajoled her. It had been too long since I'd spent time with just Carys. And I knew that day she was on edge. After all, it wasn't every day your sister was going to propose.

Carys shook her head. "No can do, today, honey. I'm too busy."

I ran a finger along her cheek and whispered, "I've got a secret for you."

She leaned back. "I bet mine's bigger."

"Not for much longer." We both laughed hysterically because we both knew what was going to happen later on that day if Carys's plans worked out the way she masterminded. And as my sister has proven over the years, she's a dynamo at making plans. "Enjoy your Valentine's Day, sweetheart."

She gave a noncommittal sound as she knew the man she planned on tormenting was watching us both. I strolled past, trying not to give away the game, closing the door between Carys's inner sanctum and the outer office before a chuckle escaped.

And I stilled when I saw her again.

Wild red hair tumbling everywhere. Bright blue eyes that snapped in my direction even as she juggled another phone call. She's my sister's angel and the devil who invades my dreams when I sleep. And according to Carys, she leaves every single night to go home to "her family. She's the most dedicated woman I know, Ward. But if you're asking me to tell you if there's someone in her life, well, that's a conversation you need to have with her. All I'm saying is don't put the spotlight around her. She's vulnerable." Carys hesitated when I asked. So, I took it for the warning it was—Angie wasn't meant for the life we were thrust into.

Angela Fahey. LLF's office gatekeeper, lion tamer, and quite possibly the sexiest woman I've ever seen in my life. And she's completely off-limits. With a brusque nod, I somehow moved past her and toward the glass door. But I managed to get myself together enough to call, "You too," over my shoulder when she wished me a Happy Valentine's Day.

Every damn day I have walk past her quickly and constrain myself to a barely civil "hello" or "good night."

Whereas Beckett Fucking Miller gets to drape himself all over her desk and call her "beauty."

Not that she isn't one. God, she might be the most exquisite woman I've ever seen. But how can Carys warn me off but allow her ex-boyfriend to... I whirl away from the ledge of my balcony, remembering the voicemail I received a few minutes ago.

Hey. If you're not busy, Angie and Becks are joining us for dinner tonight. Stop by. I'm cooking lasagne.

Is she kidding me?

If I wasn't constantly tripping over Angie and Beckett together, I wouldn't have realized they were an item. Despite the gossip about him, even I know Becks can't possibly be with that many women at one time. He'd have a damn heart attack.

That being said, he's no choirboy. "Neither are you, Burke," I admit aloud. But why would Carys allow her precious Angie to be with a man so notorious, we trip over him daily to defend new defamation charges against him? Yet, I'm not good enough. I rub the ache in my chest as I step back into my living space. I begin to compare myself against Beckett Miller.

We're both good-looking, albeit in very different ways. We're both wealthy, as in buy a small country kind of ways. Both educated, though many people don't know that about

Becks. There's only one major distinction between the two of us.

I'm the one who killed our parents.

I have to find out if that's the real reason she warned me away from her precious Angie. Nauseous, I pull my cell out of my pocket and dial my sister's cell.

She greets me cheerfully. "Hey! Are you coming over? I can save you some."

I don't bother responding. "Is the reason you encouraged Angie and Becks's relationship because you hate me because of Mom and Dad?"

Her whispered "What?" is horrified. I hear David ask what's wrong in the background.

I slur, "S'okay, Carrie. Get it. Warned me. Mistakes. Because I was selfish."

"Ward, no. You have it all wrong."

I hang up.

I don't have it wrong. I haven't made a single mistake since I found my whole family destroyed because I made the wrong choice.

CHAPTER SEVEN

ANGELA

Conversation starter: Name two celebrities who would make the cutest babies that aren't currently together. And go!
— **Viego Martinez, Celebrity Blogger**

"Is everything all right?" I ask Carys tentatively. She's standing in the kitchen, holding her phone to her ear. David's holding a sleeping Ben in his lap. Becks has just entered the room with our jackets.

She jerks herself from her inner thoughts. "Fine. Just fine. Are you sure *you're* okay?"

After the dinner we had, I know I have my friends at my back. "I'm going to be fine." I wrap my arms around her tightly. Carys's body bucks a bit when I whisper, "Thank you."

During dinner, we reminisced about some of the more intriguing places we've been directed to by Carys to check out the artists we eventually took on as clients. "What about the time I sent you to the bowling alley near your grandparents' house! Oh, God. Do you remember me asking you to do that when I was out on maternity leave?" Carys couldn't catch her breath, she was laughing so hard.

Becks calmly reached over and smacked her between the shoulders since David was feeding Ben. I grinned before answering, "Yes. Now aren't you glad you asked me to go?"

"They're my best clients! No drama." Carys shot a pointed glance at Becks.

"Well, you never know about those guys. They might surprise you," Becks drawled.

Everyone laughed.

Carys and David were also adamant about stating they didn't care if they had to shove through reporters each day to get to the office. "Hell, most of our clients will take this as a challenge to get their name in the paper by showing up at the office. Don't you dare take it as one. You're already in it too much as it is." Carys stabbed her fork in Becks's direction.

"You're no fun," Becks complained.

She threw a dinner roll at him that bounced off his head.

"How did you two ever manage to date one another?" I wondered aloud.

Carys and David began to laugh like hyenas. Becks rolled his eyes before admitting, "I guess it's okay to let Angie in the know. We never dated. I was Carrie's escort—no more."

"Her escort?" I parrot.

"Yes. That one"—he pointed at David—"wouldn't get his head out of his ass. Carys concocted a scheme to get him to notice her."

"It worked," David growled.

Carys smiled serenely before lifting her wine to her lips. Her eyes collided with mine before bouncing away. "It's too bad Ward couldn't join us for dinner."

I snorted. "Why? So everyone could have indigestion?"

"Don't like my brother?" Carys sounded amused instead of insulted.

"More the other way around. He barely tolerates me. So little, in fact, he can't speak to me in the office. I swear, if they offered grunting as a course online, I'd take it so I could translate him."

Both David and Becks began to choke. Carys rolled her lips inward and pressed them together tightly. My eyes narrowed. "Why do I feel like I'm missing some kind of in-joke?"

"You're not. They're only laughing because it's a language they speak fluently. It's called jackass."

A rush of laughter burst out of me. Carys reached over and squeezed my hand.

Now, feeling her shudder in my arms, I can't help but worry. "Was that about…me?" Could a reporter have got a hold of her cell number? Or worse yet—I shiver—someone from XMedia?

Carys delicately wipes beneath her eyes. "It's nothing for you to worry about. It's just something I have to fix."

"If there's anything I can do to help, please let me know."

"And the same goes for you, Angie. You're not eighteen anymore, trying to prove someone's guilt. You have a bevy of legal power at your back. We're here if you need us."

"The call just came from the doorman, ladies. Angie's car is here," David interrupts us.

I shrug into the coat Becks holds out. The three of them walk me to the door. Just as I'm about to leave, I pause. "Thank you. I couldn't have anticipated this when I woke up today." I try to get my thoughts in order. "It's an honor to call you my friends as well as my colleagues."

Then I race out of the condo before they notice the tears falling down my face.

On the ride back to Brewster, I'm almost lulled to sleep by the hypnotic lights, a full stomach, and warm feelings. That is until my female driver comments to herself in disgust, "God, women like the one who accused that man of rape and lied should be shot. She doesn't realize how hard she made it for the rest of us to come forward."

Yes, I do. I know exactly how hard it is.

Except it wasn't rape. If it was, maybe they would have believed me.

I whisper a quiet "Thank you" when I exit the vehicle before I dash into the sanctuary of my home.

Stripping off my clothes, I race for the shower and begin scrubbing every inch of my body. My skin turns bright pink, and still I scrub harder. I feel like there's slime crawling all over my skin. "And Sula wonders why I don't have dreams?" I blubber. I don't dare. It's a level of vulnerability that lays your soul wide open for someone to heartlessly destroy it. I close my eyes against the spray of water as I duck my head beneath.

"Ms. Fahey, we'd recommend counseling. There's very obviously a problem," the head of the Student Conduct Board called out in a clear, controlled voice.

"Angie-love, you can stay here as long as you need to. One day, you'll move past this," my grandmother reassured me.

"Come here, pumpkin," the gruff voice of my grandfather echoes in my brain as I remember the times when I stood with wet hair in the door of his library. He hugged me and ran a hand through my hair until the sopping, ropey length began to dry.

The invisible chains of the past try to snap around me, to drown the progress I've made in the last ten years as I step from the shower. Determinedly, I recall one of the sessions with my psychologist where he said to me, "You know the truth. You live with the truth, and you have to live your life assuming everyone else believes you as well."

"Do you believe me?" I anxiously awaited the answer.

He hesitated. And in that moment, I was back in that small room. I lived and died a thousand times, until he finally said, "This isn't a place to be judged. I will say, I hope I manage to raise my daughter to be as honorable as you one day."

As the tears began to spill, he handed me a box of tissues. "We've spoken of the support of your grandparents. What about your parents?"

After I blew my nose, I asked, "What about them?"

"Have they been supportive?"

"Certainly."

"That's…"

"Of Michael."

"Excuse me?" The hand he used to take notes, which normally was smoothly elegant, scratched like a needle across a record.

"They went to the media and sold them information about me. I haven't spoken with them in five years now." Even as I slip into my pajamas and a sweatshirt Sula sent me from Ireland, I'm still awed by how calm I was when I admitted that.

Finally, the cold in the room begins to penetrate through me. I quickly wring out my hair and braid it so I don't have to worry about doing much more than brushing it before I race out the door in the morning.

The next morning at the office is unusually somber. At first, I begin to wonder if it's something about me until Carys informs me, "Ward will be out all day, Angie. He's ill. Can you address any scheduled appointments he has? Work the urgent ones in with me if you have to."

I do a quick scan of Ward's calendar. "There's a call with…" I don't even get to finish my sentence before Carys interrupts me to say, "That's fine. Just move it over to me."

I shorten Carys's previous meeting by five minutes and slide the meeting to her schedule. "All set."

"Great." Carys spins on her red-soled heel to head back inside, but something drives me to reach out much the same way she did to me.

"Carys?" She stops midstride but doesn't turn around. I get to my feet. "Is something wrong?"

Her shoulders sag for just a moment before they square off. She turns around, and her face is determined. Her face is completely blank of any emotion. For just a moment, I'm startled because it's just like looking into a mirror. "It's just going to be a brutal day. Brace."

"Right." Since that tells me absolutely nothing, I slip into my own armor and turn around to prepare for battle, uncertain of who the enemy is or what direction they may be coming from.

I'm only all too aware they could come in beautiful packages bearing gifts, much like the Greeks did when they invaded Troy.

CHAPTER EIGHT

WARD

Is there anything more delicious than Beckett Miller? Watching him devour a pretzel covered in mustard on a city street is enough for me to get all hot and bothered. Okay, maybe if his abs were drenched in that mustard. That would be even better.
— **Moore You Want**

"I should kick your ass right now. We both know I easily could," David informs me as he slides into the booth across from me.

I rub a hand across my forehead. The lingering nausea and fogginess when I woke today led me to send an email I would be out of the office. I immediately received a reply from my brother-in-law telling me if I wasn't at the ER, then to haul my ass to our favorite diner within the hour. "Nonnegotiable" was the way he phrased it in his message.

"Yeah. You probably could. Want to start?" I cock my chin out a bit.

"Don't tempt me." He rubs his hand over the scruff on his chin before admitting, "I don't think it's going to surprise you to admit, Becks annoys the fuck out of me sometimes."

I scoff. "Did you seriously drag me away from my perfectly good hangover to discuss this?" I pause as a waitress comes by with mugs of coffee for each of us. "Thanks."

"Thank you," David repeats before turning back to me like a wolf on fresh meat. "Yes."

"Why?"

"Because you made my wife cry. Therefore we're going to discuss why."

"*We* can't."

"Why the hell not?"

My hand slaps down on the table, causing our coffee to leap dangerously close to the lip. "Because I don't think *you* hold our parents' deaths against me. Do you?"

"Do you really think that's what Carys is doing, Ward? Or is that what you're doing to yourself?" David lifts his mug to his lips and takes a drink.

My lips part, but no sound comes out.

"Let me tell you something I realized about your sister within three minutes of meeting her.

"What's that?" I bristle immediately, ready to rise to Carys's defense since I know Carys politely tore into her now husband moments after meeting him.

"She could take over the world if she had a mind to. She's intimidated by no one and nothing. If she doesn't like something, she changes it." A rueful smile lifts David's lips. "How do you think she managed to get my attention?"

"By leaving Wildcard," I fling out.

"No, it was long before that. It was when she was involved with damned Becks. God, I hated him. But worse, I despised her for being splashed on every news magazine at his side." David holds my gaze for a second as if he's trying to tell me something before he starts to doctor his own coffee. Shaking his head, he says, "You're assuming your sister has nefarious reasons for allowing Becks to be friends with Angie."

There's that word again. Friends. I can't prevent my lip from curling.

David chuckles. "These women aren't playing with our hearts or our minds. They're waiting for us to use ours to not hurt them. I hurt Carys first by not realizing she was right in front of me, and again by trying to leave LLF."

I trace the lip of my mug. "Then tell me why I was warned off Angie but Becks has free rein?"

He sighs. "I can't do that."

"Of course not." I scoff.

"No, because it's not my story to tell. Riddle me this. How would you feel if someone who had no idea who you are was speculating about you behind your back?"

"It's a moot point. I know Angie. *And* Becks."

"Right there is your faulty logic, Counselor," David shoots back. "You don't know either of them. Not the way your sister does. Until you spend the time to build the relationship with each of them, you won't understand why Carys encourages their friendship. Stop letting the past rule your present."

My voice is jagged when I whisper, "You have no idea what you're asking me."

"Yes, I do, because your sister has to do the same thing every day. She wakes up, she lives. She goes to sleep all without your parents. And on top of that, she managed to love, be loved, and create love. But you? You're letting your assumptions poison everything about your life."

His words hit directly beneath the arrogance I wear. "I was an ass."

"Trust me, I'm well aware of that. Now, tell me, what set you off?"

With a sigh, I let David in about how when I met Angie the day they got engaged a few years ago, it was like I'd been struck in the heart. I then recount Carys's warning.

He winces. "I'm not certain she meant it like that, Ward. She's...protective...of her."

"And there's Becks."

"Becks... Listen. All I'll say is he's no threat to you, Ward. Not if you're serious. If you're just playing, well, there's plenty of women out there who would jump if you did this." He snaps his fingers.

I can't deny the truth in his words. I wonder what it would be like if Angie anticipated my arrival in the office instead of dismissing it as easily as she does every day.

David coughs to get my attention. "Put more time into the relationships you want if you care about the outcome. That includes your sister, by the way."

My cheeks heat like I'm being scolded by a parent instead of my brother-in-law. "I owe Carys an apology."

"You owe her your life." The easy way he says that makes me realize there are no secrets between them. Not that there should be. "Your sister loves you, Ward. She played the grown-up for you at a time when she should have been able to have curled into a ball and crumbled. Don't ever accuse her of not loving you. That's bullshit and complete disrespect. Plus, your parents would be ashamed of you, and you damn well know it."

With that, David slides out of the booth and strides out of the door, leaving me to think about his words. All of them.

After a while, I drop a couple of twenties on the table for our coffee—more for the time I spent taking up space in the booth—and head for the door.

I owe my sister the respect of a full day of hard work.

And an apology.

When I stride through the doors of LLF after I've showered and dressed, Angie's head snaps up. "Good morning, Ward. I thought you were out all day."

I stop at her desk as I shrug off my coat. "I'm not sure what it was. I felt better after a few hours." *And a good talking-to.* "Did you have a good time last night?"

Her eyes widen until all I see are blue lagoons I could lose myself in. "I…I did. Your sister is a good cook. She…she saved some for you."

"Considering that lasagne recipe was our grandmother's, I hope she would."

"Mother's or father's?" Angie blurts before clarifying, "I never got to ask your sister if it was from your mother or your father's side of the family."

"Too busy joking with everyone?" I toss out, trying to get the lay of the land.

"Too busy stuffing my face. It was so good." A red stain starts to crawl up her cheeks.

"My maternal ancestors thank you. They were Italian," I explain when her brows draw together in confusion.

"But?"

"But what?" I turn around briefly and hang up my coat. When I face Angie again, her finger is drawing pictures in the air.

"You look just like your father, and he's the one who's dark," she accuses.

"And my mother's family is from northern Italy. There's a heavy German influence there which is how Carys got her blonde hair and blue eyes." And there wasn't the ache of a thousand daggers answering this simple question for her.

The puzzlement clears. "Well, wherever that recipe was from, it was delicious. It was a sweet thing for your sister to do."

Now I'm the one who's confused. Then, I realize I may have committed a grievous sin. "Did I miss your birthday?"

Horror must have laced my voice. Angie tries to smother a smile, but a small one escapes. "No."

"Thank God. Even I'm not that asinine."

The arch look she shoots me doesn't inspire confidence. I raise my hands in surrender. "Fair enough. I'll just have to prove it to you. Is there a break in my sister's schedule, by any chance?"

"Did you hit yourself on the head?" she wonders aloud, even as she pulls up the calendar.

"No. Why?"

"You're being affable."

"Let's just say I had a poor morning, and I was reminded about what was important."

Her hand stops moving on the mouse. Her ponytail swishes as her head whips in my direction. Angie demands, "Tell me you didn't pull a Becks before I have to rearrange the schedule."

I choke on air. "Pull a Becks."

"Yes."

"Would you please explain what that means?"

"Did you do something so ridiculous I need to get your sister involved to keep the press from reporting it in a media frenzy so epic, it's going to have its own hashtag by the end of the day? We also call these 9-1-1 situations, in case you were wondering." Angie is poised to execute a series of maneuvers I'm certain she and Carys have practiced many times over.

But the explanation is glorious. And leaves me more confused than ever about the relationship between the titian-haired woman before me and the tattooed rock legend.

"No, Angie. I just need to apologize for being a jackass."

"Oh. Do you need time for begging, or does there need to be pleading for mercy?"

"Excuse me?" I sputter.

Eyes twinkling, she points at the schedule. "I have an opening in ten if you want the next thirty after that. If you need more time than that, you'll have to wait until three."

I bark out a laugh. Without thinking, I lay my hand on top of hers and double-click the block for thirty minutes. "That should be good enough." *I hope.* When Angie doesn't move to finish the appointment, I prompt her. "Angie?"

She jolts as if I've just shocked her with a million bolts of lightning. "Yes. Sorry." Her fingers fly across the keyboard. Seconds later, I get a notice on my phone of the meeting, which means Carys does too.

Quickly tugging the back of Angie's hair, I say, "Thanks," before heading to the doors.

Her faint "No problem" is whispered. I whirl around and find her watching me. Before I cross the threshold behind the heavy doors, I smile again.

She offers me a tremulous one in return before turning to face her desk.

A little voice inside me whispers, *Are you sure about Becks? Because she's awfully affected by you.* Ridiculously cheerful by that thought, I stride through the door and open up my office before heading toward my sister's.

Fifteen minutes later, I feel like I'm in my first-year law class presenting during a mock trial. Carys is sitting behind her desk, fingers steepled while I stammer out an explanation for my behavior. Not that there is one beyond petty jealousy. And my ongoing anger at myself.

Finally, she pushes to her feet in her sky-high heels, still barely bringing her dainty height to my shoulder. "Let me get this right. You got your ego bent out of shape because of something I said over two years ago, and instead of talking to me about why, you've been aloof to everyone in this office."

"I wouldn't say that..." I begin.

"I would," she snaps. "You're just damn lucky it hasn't affected your work, or I'd have rescinded the partner paperwork."

Ouch. I rub my hand over my chest. I walk over to the window where a credenza is placed. "Is that what you want to do?"

"No, damnit. I want to know why you hold me responsible for being your parent after Mom and Dad's deaths!" she yells.

I freeze and face my sister for my execution. "How could I hold you responsible for anything? You're the one who should hold me responsible for them being in that car."

"Ward, you are not responsible for their deaths." Carys stalks up until we're next to each other. She grips both of my arms and shakes me.

"If it wasn't for me...they never should have been in that car." I rush the words out.

"No, the man who was driving that other car never should have been drinking. I swear to you, Ward, I don't blame you." Carys's eyes fill with tears.

"If I'd just said to wait for you, they'd still be alive," I choke out.

"Or we'd all be gone. Did you ever think about that?" At my expression of horror, Carys's eyes begin to leak. She impatiently brushes the tears away. "Ward, you're assuming a lot. You always did. Even as a kid."

I lean against the credenza and shoot her a puzzled look. "What do you mean?"

Carys does the same. "You guessed about everything. You were the worst about birthdays and holidays for surprises. Inevitably, we'd bought you something from one of your lists. That's how you figured out that Santa didn't exist."

I grin. "When was that?"

"You were six. Mom blamed me."

I bark out a laugh before tugging her into my arms. Carys lays her head on my shoulder. I hug her tightly before whispering, "You didn't spoil Santa for me. You didn't ruin anything for me. You gave me everything. I'm just sorry I don't know what to do with it most days."

Her arms squeeze me tight. "You do. You just have to remember something."

"What's that?"

"Stop assuming so much—about people. About life. Most of the time, it's going to end up being completely wrong."

I pull back a bit. "Is that experience talking?"

Her voice is quiet. "It's a word of caution. Assumptions often lead to actions you can't take back."

Long after I leave my sister's office, her words reverberate through my head. I spend so long thinking about them that when I finally leave, Angie's already gone for the weekend.

Damn.

I stand next to her desk and promise myself next week will be different. For all of us.

CHAPTER NINE

ANGELA

Ice, ice, baby! At least that's what Emily Freeman has in store for this season's wedding gowns. Check out her new designs here!
— **Beautiful Today**

"You young women of today just don't get it." An elderly woman approaches me just as I'm about to get off my stop in Brewster.

I'm totally confused. "I'm sorry."

"You young women of today."

Uh-oh. This is the last thing I need after the tumultuous week I've suffered at work. I stand swiftly and move toward the train doors. Fortunately, they open just as I approach them. But that doesn't stop the woman from offering her final opinion just as I step off.

"Stop dressing like tarts if you don't want men to look at you!" she yells after me. Over my shoulder, I see her shake her cane at me as the doors begin to close in her face.

Dress like a tart? I want to laugh. The suits I pair with knee-high flat boots are less seductive than the uniforms the local boarding school wears. Every inch of skin I can cover is wrapped up tight. Gripping the collar of my winter trench tighter around me, I dash up the steps from the train platform so I can get to the lot where I left my car.

Thank God it's the weekend. I need the break from everyone and everything starting now.

Even though I'm trembling from the latest attack on what feels like a perpetual altercation on my soul, I don't bother turning on the heat or the music in the quick six-minute drive to my house. It's taking all my effort to breathe in and to breathe out when all I want to do is to scream.

Some days, I get weary of standing up tall and strong. Am I about to be exploited again? Become an agenda item for the country to dissect in detail over their morning breakfast or dinner discussions? Would I receive more lewd offers for modeling to "repair" my image or offers to tell my side of the story on national "news"? And all I want to do is live somewhere quietly where someone sees my heart, not the scandal.

Because somehow I managed to survive. And that's why it hurts. I bang my hand on the steering wheel in frustration. Due to the love and care of my grandparents, Sula, hell, even my therapist, I'm the one who survived.

What would have happened if they hadn't been called away by their pledge chairman? I wonder not for the millionth time. *What would have happened then?* A shudder runs through me as it always does.

My grandparents' home has become my sanctuary in the years after I abandoned college. It's here I realized I couldn't stay tucked away forever to hide my head from the world after I stood up so valiantly before the Student Conduct Board, no matter what the ramifications were for me or for the university. I'd healed too much to stay tucked away forever. But on the other hand, I couldn't go back to the life I was living before.

I just wish the world at large would let the past die. But like Becks said, in today's age of social media, nothing ever does. And so the assumptions about me go on.

It isn't me screeching on street corners reminding people about the night they spiked my drink with GHB. It isn't me who persistently proclaims year after year Michael and Stephen dragged me up to Stephen's room and were in the process of…of…when their pledge chairman, Jorge, ordered them into the hall, leaving me exposed on the bed.

It was the media—then and now—who swooped in on wings like Hermes to raise me up before sentencing me to hell like Tartarus.

The world would never have known the details of my pain, my shame, if not for them. And despite my impassioned testimony, "John Smith" and "Brian Jones" were exonerated. They submitted hair and blood samples, but of course, there were none. After all, they hadn't got around to *that*.

But I was exposed. I was left there. I was the one touched without consent.

And no one at my university cared.

I stood in a room with my head held high, enduring a lecture about underage drinking from my former university elders with "esteemed" classmates looking on. I was told, "The burden of proof lies on you, Ms. Fahey. Not on the men you are accusing," and was reminded, "There has to have been proof of unwillingness."

And due to the infernal media waiting like locusts outside, my departure from that recitation from hell was well-documented. I just kept walking through the circus despite the intruding questions being flung at me from all directions. For me, there was no going back—not to school, not to the carefree way I lived before. All of that was lost in one night, with a few sips of alcohol.

And knowing that it started with a bad decision reinforced by my peers was hard enough. Knowing I did the right thing and I'd never recover took everything inside me to just to keep moving.

It took me hours to get home that day instead of the mere minutes it took me today. But I did then exactly what I do right now. What I do every day no matter the hour. I race up the stairs to my bedroom and begin stripping out of my clothes. Flinging them aside, I race for the shower so I can scrub away the filthy stares and assumptions.

"I thought it'd be easier over time. When is it finally going to let me go?" I feel the salt of my tears mingle with the shower water as I turn my face into the spray.

And since silence reins, I assume I have my answer.

Never.

Wrapped in my flannel pajamas and a long robe, I head downstairs to find Flower. Not finding the overweight snob in the front sitting room, I pad into the kitchen. Then I roll my eyes at the sight before me.

"I should have tried here first. You do realize your food comes out of a can?"

A grumpy *mrumph* is the only response I get from the cat sprawled across my kitchen stove.

Knowing from past experience that if I try to move her before she's ready, she'll claw me bloody, I leave her while I sort out fresh food and water. "Grandma spoiled you rotten, you ridiculous feline."

Gratefully, she jumps down before performing some maneuver that demonstrates despite her age, she's still agile. She begins to lick herself, uncaring that we're in the kitchen. "Really? How about hygiene, Flower?" I'm already reaching for the wipes to scrub down my stovetop so I can heat up a can of soup when my cell rings.

Flower hisses. She's been like this ever since I got my grandmother a cell phone. I've tried different ringers, I've tried silent. The damn cat must just feel the electrical energy of the phone and hate it. I'd swear if I didn't have a waterproof model, she'd have enjoyed batting it into the sink. Repeatedly.

"Deal with it. It's a phone. Not everyone who calls on it is evil."

Flower obviously disagrees as she prepares to launch herself back up to the counter to attack. I snatch up the phone and glance at the display. Quickly I answer, not only to avoid sanitizing my counter but to not make her wait. "Hi, Carys. Is something wrong?"

"I just wanted to say thank you for being concerned about me earlier today. It was appreciated, Angie. I know I didn't show it at the time, but I hope you know I appreciate the gesture. And not just as your boss. I care about you."

I brace my hips against the cabinet and close my eyes. A smile curves my lips as I recall the warmth in the ostentatious New York living space and homemade lasagne. "I'm not certain you have any idea what it means to know all of you support me. It's certainly not something I ever expected when I applied for a job so long ago."

"I'd love to go back in time—being who I am—and tear apart the people who hurt you. One by one. Slowly."

I manage to bark out a laugh through the tightening of my throat. "And you saying that is exactly why I'll never leave, Carys. Once again, your guiding principles are everything I'll ever need." Carys's business was built on the principles of her parents' marriage: love, loyalty, and friendship. And no one who works or becomes a client of the firm doesn't become a recipient of those tenets.

"There's no dollar value that could fix what my heart has endured. But the time I spend at LLF makes an inroad to it."

Carys is grumbling about not being able to give me a hug and wanting to have me over more often. I interrupt her. "Thank you, Carys. You and David mean a lot to me as well."

"Fair enough. You know, Angie, when I had to step back from my life to raise my brother, I lost a number of my friends. I know it's not the same thing," she hurries on to say. "But I appreciate the loneliness a person can feel when they're at home. And a can of soup seems like the easiest thing to have for dinner."

Gaping, I lift up the can I was just about to open before there's a thud on the counter. "Flower, get down!" I hiss.

"Flower?"

"My grandmother's cat. I inherited her with the house."

"As in as delicate as a…?"

"No. As in my grandmother had an obsession with the movie *Bambi*, and the cat's the right color. I'm only thankful I didn't have black hair, or I shudder to imagine if I would have been named after a skunk instead."

"Forget dinner at my place. I want to meet this animal. They won't let us have animals in our building. They never have."

After tucking my phone under my chin, I hook an arm under the cat. Several irritated hisses from both of us later, I ask, "I forget. How long have you lived there?"

There's a delicate pause before Carys answers, "I was brought home from the hospital to this home. Ward and I grew up here. I can't imagine selling the place where I grew up. It must be the same for you in many ways."

I spin around the tiny kitchen I'm standing in that Grandma was so proud to have redone with butcher-block countertops a few years ago. I pull up a mental image of the orange walls of the sewing room I haven't gotten around to changing, the yellow spare bedroom, the kelly green office. And I realize I only have to change it if I want to. "Yes and no. Nothing is forcing me to let go of the memories, nor is anyone requiring me to keep them. But I'm not certain I'd be able to let go of this home." Leaning forward, I stare into the dark, but I know there's a private yard that has a hot tub—something I insisted on buying to help my grandmother after her hip surgery. There's an exquisite garden and patio made of stonework. And depending on if the trees are leafing, a view of nearby Tonetta Lake. "Maybe you and David can bring Ben out one day to come see the house," I offer.

"We'd love to see it. You know our schedule better than we do. Let me know when works best for you," Carys accepts immediately, warming something I didn't realize was cold deep inside of me.

I hear a cry on her end of the line. "Uh-oh. That sounds like a meltdown in the making."

She lets out a gusty sigh. "This could be anything from a slip in the tub to he forgot a specific toy."

"Poor Ben."

"You mean 'Poor David.' He gets cranky when he forgets SpongeBob to play with." There's obvious laughter in her voice. "I'd better let you go to rescue him."

"See you Monday."

"Bye, Angie."

We each disconnect, and for the first time since my grandmother's death, I feel like doing something we did together every Friday night. I put the can of soup back in the cabinet and pick the phone back up. I dial a number I have memorized as Grandma used to make me call it from the time I was nineteen until she passed when I was twenty-six.

I don't know why I stopped calling.

"Pizza Palace, how can I help you?"

"Yes, I'd like to place an order for delivery."

Like she understands the words, Flower takes off to wait in the bay window near the front door. And I smile as a little piece of my heart settles back into place. Even if tonight it's being handled by cheese, garlic, and oregano.

CHAPTER TEN

ANGELA

XMedia's newest board member, Michael Clarke, was spotted out with his latest date. She has red hair. Yawn. In other news, Less than 2% of the world's population have red hair and blue eyes.
— **Jacques Yves, Celebrity Blogger**

"You and your organizational skills. I thank God every day for it," Carys declares.

"It's certainly saved our asses on more than one occasion," David agrees.

"It was nothing. I was just doing my job," I protest.

We're in our weekly meeting where we go over any open cases and high-profile clients to make certain as a team we're all on the same page. Whereas normally this meeting is fairly routine, today we've actually got quite a bit to go over.

"I disagree. If you hadn't noted where you saved the email containing the verbal agreement with the record label, they'd be out millions right now." Ward smiles warmly at me. Turning away from me, he addresses Carys. "So what do we do now about the fact we had a notarized copy and the label had a different version?"

"Well, with the audio, if they try to go to court, I'll eviscerate them," Carys declares confidently.

Ward chuckles. "I almost hope they do. That would be more fun than watching you explain to Mom and Dad why you *needed* to go see Taylor Swift at Madison Square Garden."

Carys straightens. "It was a *need*, Ward. You just don't understand women at all, do you?"

As the two siblings squabble back and forth, David nudges my arm before murmuring, "This is how it should have been between them from the beginning."

"Would we have got as much work done over the last few years if that was the case?"

David chuckles. "Probably not. But office morale sure would have been better."

Innocently, I ask, "Becks isn't good for that, Dave?"

"And here I thought you were such a nice girl, Angie." David clucks his tongue.

The two of us snicker before turning our attention back to the main attraction in the room. Carys leaps to her feet to make her point about the importance of Taylor Swift's music to the twenty-first century. Ward knits his hands behind his head with an indulgent smile, letting his sister run out of steam before he says, "You might note, I haven't disagreed with you. Now, can you finish grandstanding so we have a chance of getting out of here before midnight? I don't think any of us like the idea of Angie taking a train home late." His eyes cut over to me, and he smiles.

My heart skips a beat in my chest. I'm mesmerized by the look in his eyes. He's...happy. Something's changed, but I can't quite put my finger on it. Ever since last week when he came in late, something's been different. But never so much as right now with the way he's sitting there in his shirtsleeves, tie loosened. He's making my mouth dry up at the mere sight of him. Throwing me completely off-kilter, Ward winks at me before turning his attention back to the legal discussion at hand.

My fingers stop clicking on my laptop keyboard where I'm taking notes. *Why did he do that? What does he mean by that?* Confused, I return my focus back to the meeting and continue to take notes.

It's only Tuesday, and life is out of control in none of the ways I would have expected. Despite my anxiety, the announcement about XMedia didn't produce the normal regurgitation of its new board member's past. *Probably because someone in the media owed them a favor.* Whatever the reason, it doesn't matter. It's given me a small kernel of hope I might be able to move on from my past.

"Since we're here discussing the topic, anything of interest on Becks in the feeds?" Carys asks, pulling me from my internal musings.

Both Ward and David groan in unison. Carys hushes them both. "Angie?"

I pull up the file I maintain on Becks. "What I find hysterical is he sends me the articles I should be concerned about."

"Please. With his contacts, he likely has them in advance of them going to print. Is there anything we need to be worried about?"

I quickly scan the database I developed for monitoring news and paparazzi mentions about Beckett Miller. Not noticing anything, I announce, "Nothing. But the week's still young."

Carys narrows her eyes at me. "Bite your tongue."

Because I'm feeling just a bit sassy, I stick it out and clamp down lightly. "Otay," I warble.

"Anything else?" Carys calls out over our combined laughter. "No? See you all tomorrow."

"Angie? Can I ask you to hold up for a moment?" Ward stops me from leaving the conference room.

"Sure." I relax back in my chair as he makes his way around the room toward me. "What's up?"

"Carys mentioned you're a whiz with our databases a while back."

I straighten. "Did you request something and I forgot about it?"

He ducks his head. "No. I was just too stubborn to ask for it."

"Well...that's ridiculous."

His head twists. "Tell me how you really feel about it."

"Being ridiculous doesn't get the job done, Ward. Then, I end up having more work anyway," I inform him primly.

He presses his lips together, whether to gather his thoughts or to suppress a smile, I don't know. "Do you have time to talk about it now?"

"Sure." I stand up and grab a legal pad and a pen from the center of the table. "What kind of data do you want it to store?"

For the next hour, we discuss the type of data, retrieval types, and retention schedule. Finally, I tap my pen to the notes I've taken. "I don't think this is going to be terribly difficult, Ward. The only item we haven't discussed is how to get the metadata for each file into the system."

"Oh, that's not a problem."

I brighten. "You have it on a spreadsheet."

"No, it's all in my head."

My pen clatters to the table. "Say it ain't so."

"Why? Is that a problem?" Ward's confusion would be fairly cute if I wasn't fighting the urge to strangle him.

I put my head down and start banging it on the pad. Repeatedly.

"Angie? What are you doing?"

"Shh. I'm trying to rid myself of the memory of you saying the data about the hundreds of client files you've worked on since you started working here are stored in your head."

"Well, that's not entirely true," he amends.

I stop beating my head against the table and glance at him hopefully.

"Some of it is on a spreadsheet so I can find the file in my office cabinets."

"You…office….those are supposed to go to off-site storage!" I wail. My head goes back down on the pad.

He pats me on the shoulder. "Shh. It's okay, Angie. I'm sure you'd be able to figure it all out in three or four months if I decided to take off for Fiji."

I flip my head back to mean mug him, not caring one iota if he technically outranks me in the firm hierarchy. Carys signs my paychecks, and she's the one I consider my boss. "If you take off for Fiji before that information is in an orderly system, I'll hunt you down," I vow.

He drops his chin down so his face obscures everything else I see. "Now you're giving me an incentive to do just that very thing."

I slowly sit up before whispering, "What do you mean?"

He reaches out and twists a lock of loose hair around his finger. He gives it a tug. Our faces are so close, I can see the spikes of gold in his dark brown eyes. My breathing accelerates.

Then, Ward does something completely unexpected. He lifts my hand that's somehow managed to clench around the pen again. He brings it up, brushing it across his lips. Once. Twice. Then he makes me a promise that both exhilarates and terrifies me. "I'm not running away until we figure out how to solve this problem."

Somehow, I don't think he's talking about his database issue.

CHAPTER ELEVEN

WARD

Who knew Erzulie has a mole right there? Certainly we didn't until the pictures of her naked showed up in our inbox this morning. All we have to say, Erzulie, is wow! You may never be remembered for your vocal cords after this.
— **StellaNova**

"Is the weekend almost here?" Angie groans as she flings open the outer door.

"What happened?" David asks before I get the chance.

"StellaNova printed an article claiming there's nude pics of Erzulie," Angie tells him.

"And it was such a nice week," I lament.

"I'm debating running away to a land far away filled with nothing but chocolate. Maybe when I get back, I'll be prepared to ruin Carys's week." Angie closes her eyes. Her pink tongue darts out and wets her lips.

Good Christ. My whole body tenses. I push away from the doorjamb of my office and say, "So, let's do it." I approach a stunned Angie and take the file from her hands. "Is the article in here?"

She nods mutely, staring at me as if I've grown two heads. And maybe I have, but my resistance to this woman is wearing thin.

I walk over to David. "Here. Give this to your wife. I'm rescuing our assistant for a while."

"Wait, you are?" Angie splutters.

I place my hand on her shoulder and say with complete seriousness, "Do you want to be here when Carys explodes?"

She shakes her head vigorously. "I'll get my coat. Meet me up front."

I spin to grab my keys when I hear David call my name. He doesn't look up from reading the article. All he asks is, "Bring us back something from La Maison or she might really start lopping off heads."

"Do I look stupid? Wait, don't answer that."

That's when David does look up. He smiles. "No, you don't. You look like someone who's trying to rectify the mistakes he's made over the last two years. Just...don't rush her. Okay?"

"Right." Then I walk through the heavy doors.

Angie's already got on her coat, hat, and gloves. I'm shrugging on my overcoat when we both hear, "Are you kidding me?" screeched.

"Time to go. Now." I grab Angie's hand, and we both dash for the door.

"I feel a little bad for leaving her." She looks over her shoulder.

"She won't be coherent until we get back," I assure her.

"True," she accedes. Then, "Where are we going?"

"I'm taking you to a land filled with chocolate." Then I don't say another word as we descend in the elevator.

"Come on. Give me another hint." Her voice is filled with excitement.

"You just have to trust me." I hold out my arm. I pretend not to notice she hooks her hand in with a slight hesitation before we hurry off in the cold fall air.

Minutes later, we burst through the doors of La Maison du Chocolat on West Forty-Ninth Street. Her breathless "Oh" made the cold walk worth it.

I stand back as Angie slowly admires each and every item in the display cases.

One of the sales associates approaches. "Wonderful to see you, Mr. Burke."

I hold out a hand. "You as well, Jacques. Can you make up an assortment for my sister?"

"Of course. *Soixante trois?*"

I contemplate whether I need to go larger than sixty-three pieces. "That should be fine. Thank you."

"Please help yourself to the coffee in the back." But I'm not listening as I watch Angie's gloved fingers run over a price tag before she tucks them behind her back.

I wait until she's inspecting the packages of dark chocolate *Mendiant* before I lean over her shoulder to ask, "What are you going to indulge in?"

She jumps so high, she practically topples over the entire display. When she rights herself, it's with a hand pressed to the center of her chest. Her expression is accusatory, even a bit scared.

I quickly apologize. "I'm sorry, Angie. I didn't realize you were concentrating so hard."

"No. I…just startle easily when I'm approached from behind. Isn't the smell in here divine?" She inhales deeply.

"You'll soon find out it tastes better."

She shakes her head firmly. "No way. We'd have been in my budget more if we'd stopped off at the M&M store in Times Square."

I step forward until I'm directly in front of her. "Angie, I brought you here to La Maison du Chocolat so *you* could escape. After all, it's called House of Chocolate for a reason."

She cocks her head to the side. "You did this for me."

"I did."

"Why?" Her voice is confused.

Why? "Because…" My voice trails off. I smile down at her, remembering each moment of the last week filled with laughter and good humor. I mentally wince, recalling my irrational jealousy over the last two years. I clasp her smaller hands in mine. "Maybe I just wanted to see you away from the office."

As I lower my head to hers, her lips part on a soft gasp. A breath I feel waft across my lips as I brush a stray lock of her gorgeous hair away from her face. She sways; I catch her closer against my body, where her hands automatically come to rest against my chest.

"Ward." She whispers just my name.

"Do you want me to kiss you, Angie?" I murmur, holding her tucked against my body, away from the prying eyes of the store.

She raises her face a bit more. Her pupils dilate. And just when I'm about to give up hope of tasting her lips against mine, she leans forward until her lips are gently lying against mine. Then she soundlessly says, "Yes."

There's something so tender about this kiss, it makes every other one before it vulgar by comparison. The soft way her lips part, the sweet way her tongue duels against mine, I've never felt anything like it. I feel like I'm holding a wish in my arms, perhaps trying to capture fairy dust in a jar. Maybe it's because I've wanted her for so damn long and she's been in my dreams, haunting me.

I cup my fingers around her face, sliding easily from one kiss into another. I keep each kiss soft, tender, because that's what the moment calls for. I have no doubt this woman has passion buried inside of her, but it isn't for now.

A moan escapes the back of my throat and startles Angie. She wrenches back and almost falls into the display again. Her hand comes up to her mouth, eyes wide. "You just kissed me."

I move to the side of her and whisper in her ear, "Yes." Before she can say anything, I proclaim with a touch of arrogance, "See what the smell of good chocolate inspires me to do?"

Angie's hand drops, and she grins. "Is that what did it?"

"Completely," I lie. "Now, did you find something you want?"

"Everything, and none of it's something I can afford." Before I can offer to buy her something, she reaches past me for a box of dark chocolate candied orange peels. "But these were always bought for special celebrations."

"Were they? And what do you have to celebrate, Ms. Fahey?" I ask as we walk up to the register.

For just a moment, there's a spasm of pain across her face before all the beauty I witnessed during our kiss returns. "Maybe one day I'll tell you."

And in that moment, I begin kicking myself mentally for wasting years, for not talking to my sister. I wish I knew everything about this woman because I have strong feelings it's impacted everything about her that attracts me to her.

Her smile.

Her mind.

And her heart.

"It's strangely quiet," Angie comments as we enter the frosted outer doors of LLF.

"Is that a good thing?" I question as we shed our outerwear.

"Well, either it means Carys handled the situation or..." Just as Angie says those words, the wooden doors behind her fly open.

David emerges, his hair standing up on end. "You're back. Thank God. Erzulie is denying the photos are her. Carys is going to war."

I hold out the milk-chocolate-colored bag. "Give this to our general, and we'll be right in."

"Make it quick. Call in five." David snatches the bag before closing the door behind him.

Angie is already gathering her laptop, pens, and calendar. But I stop her just before she rushes through the door. "Amid everything else we're about to go through, I don't want you to forget." Then I brush my lips across hers. "This changes things."

"Ward..."

"Shh. Not now. Later. Right now, we have to go defend someone who can't defend themselves."

Angie's eyes blaze. I hold the door open. "After you."

She crosses the threshold like her world has been shaken on its axis.

I can only hope so.

CHAPTER TWELVE

ANGELA

Why was the mouthwatering Beckett Miller in such a rush out of Redemption last night? He blew past this reporter without his normally generous smile and wink. There wasn't time to do more than admire him as he walked away. Though that's mighty fine indeed.

— Sexy&Social, All the Scandal You Can Handle

After dealing with Erzulie's chaos until the wee hours of Saturday, I didn't have a chance to speak with Ward before I was pushed into a car to drive me home from the office with a written guarantee from StellaNova we'd have a retraction the next day. I think I might have drooled as I slept in the back of the town car. Flower's lucky I remembered to feed her before I fell face-first onto my bed.

I did manage to get a call into Sula where I thought I'd lost my hearing after. "He *kissed* you!"

"Sula, it was…"

"What? Tell me everything."

I recount the difference in Ward's behavior the last few weeks. "I'm afraid," I blurt out.

"Oh, love, I'd be worried if you weren't."

"You would?" I'm poleaxed by that.

"Angie, you were dragged through hell. You went through something you should never have experienced. And despite your protests, I still hold a hell of a lot of guilt over it."

"You're not the one who slipped me that drug," I explain quietly.

"No, but I'm the one who convinced you we should go to that party."

We're both silent for a long moment while the aftermath of that fateful night filters through each of our minds. Then Sula declares, "You deserve the world. I hope you realize that. But more than that, Ward Burke had better realize it. I don't care how much money he has or how hot he is. If he doesn't, he's going to have to deal with me."

My heart overflows with love for my best friend. "I know you have my back."

"And your front. I may be short, but I can protect something. I'm feisty."

My lips curve. "I don't doubt you for a second. Now, tell me all about Ireland."

I thank God for internet calling as we spend several hours catching up on all things that are happening in both our worlds. We end the conversation with a discussion about what I should wear to the office on Monday. "The black suit. It's the nicest thing you own. And no arguments—we're going shopping the next time I'm in town."

"Who said I was arguing?" I disconnect on her squawking.

Maybe it's time for me to stop allowing the pain of my past to rule my present. I was hurt, but I picked myself up. Wandering over to a picture of my grandparents, I pick it up and vow, "I always assumed I was supposed to pay for what happened to me. But you were right. I've healed, and I realize I'm stronger. I just don't know how far that extends."

With a click, I place the frame back down and move away to finish up preparing for the week.

Monday rolls around quicker than I'd like. I'm sitting at my desk when the door to LLF flies open to reveal Becks. "I should be shocked you're here, but I'm not. What happened this time?" I tease him.

"I need to see Carys. Right away."

I roll my eyes. "What else is new? Carys is swamped today, Becks. And I honestly have no idea where Ward is."

"No, this is urgent. It can't wait."

116 · TRACEY JERALD

"What did the press say this time?" I grin into his handsome face until I notice he's not smiling. "Wait. What's wrong?"

"Nothing. Everything. I don't know. This might be huge."

"How huge?"

"Makes the issue with Erzulie look like an amateur huge."

"You need Carys, then." I lift my phone to call her. But he places his hand on mine to force it down.

"No. No phones. Nothing in writing until…" He lowers his head until his mouth is right against my ear. He whispers something that has me jerking my head back in shock. What he said is so astonishing I can't wrap my mind around it.

My hand comes out from under his and presses against his chest in support. "How are you still standing? How are you not shrieking this to the world yet?" My stomach churns, and bile rises in my throat at the very idea of the agony he must be putting himself through.

He grips my hand. "I'm trying to do the right thing. That's why I came here first. My inclination is to go charging in like a raving lunatic and demand answers, but I can't because of who I am. The reputation I've cultivated. I won't do that until I know for sure. I could be wrong, Angie, and if I am, I could do so much damage. I need you to get Carys out of whatever she's in today. I need your help." Despair laces his voice.

"Oh, my God, Beckett. It can't be true."

He just nods. But it's the flat determination in his eyes that has me jerking into motion.

"Give me a few minutes." This time when I pick up the phone to make a call, he doesn't try to stop me. "Hello, this is Angela, Carys Burke's assistant. No, I'm sorry, she won't be able to make the conference call today with Kristoffer from ten to noon. Does he have any other availability this afternoon? From two to four? I'll shift her schedule around. Thank you." My fingers fly as I immediately begin rearranging Carys's schedule.

I start by moving her conference call with the head of Wildcard Records to later in the day. Next, I call Z's people on the West Coast. "Oh, he's fine with the changes, Angela. He's signing everything. In fact, can we make it tomorrow? That works better since he planned on being in the studio today," his manager, JT, tells me.

I let out a sigh. "That's fantastic. Thanks, JT. I look forward to receiving the updated contract."

Two down. One to go. Crossing my fingers, I call Erzulie's agent at the Neo Agency, asking to speak to Walker Hutnik, only to be told that Walker is out with the "flu." *Likely recovering from the hangover from the ass ripping Carys gave him from the way he handled the media Friday*, I think evilly.

"I'm so sorry to hear that. Ms. Burke had an appointment with him in a few hours. Should we reschedule?" I give Becks a big smile that both relieves and deflates him.

"Does tomorrow at noon work?" comes the nasal voice on the other end.

"No, unfortunately, it does not." Noon is blocked off every day for Carys and David to go visit Ben at daycare.

"Well, then I only have an 8:00 a.m., but I don't think…"

I quickly interrupt. "We'll take that. So kind of Mr. Hutnik to do that considering he's ill." I have little doubt the agent is likely recovering from a scouting trip the night before, but since I can't say that aloud, I wait while his assistant furiously reschedules the appointment. Once I receive confirmation, I move the final appointment on Carys's calendar.

I lock my computer and shove my chair back. "Now, let's go talk to Carys."

Becks just stands there for a moment before he walks up and wraps his strong arms around my shoulder. "Thanks, my friend. Even if this all goes nuclear and I can't stop the media from finding out, thank you for doing what you could today." His throat works convulsively.

I lean back against his arm and reach up and cup his face. My eyes follow the column of ink that covers his neck as he swallows. "You've had my back since the minute you figured out who I was. You've never judged me for being *that* girl when we both know you've had more than your fair share of sexual assault cases thrown at you."

"That's because those were damned bogus. Stupid women who wanted to bang a rock star and then get their picture in the paper. What happened to you was a fucking atrocity," Becks declares heatedly.

"That, right there, is why if Carys can't find a way, you know I'll always have your back. Because you never made a single assumption about me. You never asked what happened. You've always just been there. Now, it's my turn to repay the favor." And for the first time since I left college, I turn into a man's arms and give him a hug. It's appropriate it happens to be one of the people I count as a friend.

Pulling back, I turn away so Becks won't catch me wiping the tears from my eyes. "Now, let's go talk to the brains of this outfit."

Maybe he didn't hear me because he says curiously, "Ward?"

I lift my head and find Ward standing there, his jaw clenched. "What happened? I saw the schedule blow up and was just coming out to talk with you."

"Actually, Becks needs to speak with Carys." Before Ward can offer his normal token protests, I tell him, "This is urgent. We're talking a 9-1-1 situation."

"Ah, shit. What the hell did you do, Miller?" But Ward moves back from the entrance to the inner sanctum.

"It's more like what I just found out. And if it's true, it was a long time ago." And with his hand at my lower back, Becks urges me forward.

I guess I'm going to be a part of this conversation.

Then again, as Carys steps out of her office with David, both their faces wreathed in concern, I need to be. I have to know how I can help my friends and how I can support this business.

And I'll do it any way I can.

"Everyone come in," Carys urges us.

We all file into the conference room, falling hard into the plush leather chairs. All of us except Becks. He makes his way over to the windows and just stares out over the New York skyline, not speaking.

Finally, it's Carys who proclaims, "We didn't pay tickets for this show of brooding male posturing, Becks. Angie rearranged my entire day. Do you mind getting on with it, or should we return to our normal schedule?"

Without turning around, he quietly asks, "How hard would it be to get the DJ Kensington under an NDA?"

"Why do we need to?" David blurts out.

Oh, God. This is going to be awful.

Carys stares at Becks's back, trying to see beyond his question to the meaning beneath. I can practically see her wheels churning as she chooses the precise words she wants to use to question Becks.

Ward, sadly, doesn't bother. He bursts into laconic laughter. "What happened? Did you get yourself in a spot of trouble with a girl young enough to be your daughter?"

Becks whirls around, his fists clenching at his side. His light blue eyes are focused on Ward with pure maleficence.

David, wisely, steps in between the two men, snapping at Ward. "That's enough."

"You're right, David. It is." Carys glares at her brother. "Regardless of whatever has happened, it is our job to protect our client."

"I didn't mean…" Ward starts to protest, but Carys cuts him off with a slash of her hand.

"I believe it's almost time for your lunchtime meeting. We'll take it from here and catch you up upon your return."

Wow. I didn't know it was possible for heat and ice to live in such close proximity without causing some kind of weather phenomenon. But between the anger pulsating between the siblings and the mood that just descended upon the room, there's proof it can happen. I try to shrink into my chair when Ward spits out, "Fine. Just don't let whatever he did get us disbarred."

Before the door closes behind us, I feel the full force of Ward's fury just before he turns and storms out the LLF conference room.

"Becks, just come right out with it," David demands sometime later. "Tell us what happened at Redemption last night that has you pale as a ghost."

He glares at David for a moment before he turns to Carys and blurts, "I saw Paige last night at Redemption."

Carys rolls her lips together for a brief moment. "Your high school sweetheart, Paige? That Paige?"

"Yes, Carrie. That Paige. The same Paige who I found out from Marco happens to be his guest DJ's mother when I asked how she could afford the cover charge to his club. Right before I asked some questions about the up-and-coming artist." His chest visibly shudders. "Carrie, there's every possibility…"

"Maybe Kensington's younger than you think." Carys treads carefully.

I speak up. "If she's the age listed on her website…"

"Oh, God." The pain in Becks's voice is unmasked.

But Carys still asks because she's his lawyer, "And you never before imagined this might be a possibility? Ever?"

"I was seventeen when I took off!" he explodes. "She was younger than me and the damn homecoming queen to boot. God knows, I was determined to get out of there, but if I knew I would have stayed no matter what."

"What do you mean?" David's curiosity raises the tension in the room.

Becks whispers in disbelief to Carys. Awe fills his voice. "You never told him?"

Carys meanwhile shuffles and stacks her notes, avoiding her husband's gaze. Finally, she mutters, "I'm under an NDA. And it wasn't my secret to share."

David's lip curves at the corner. "I know."

"But it is mine." Becks begins describing about his life back in Texas before he hitched a ride as a roadie with a summer music festival after his high school graduation. By the time Becks finishes explaining, Carys has tears in her eyes, and

David has stood and crossed to the window. "This sucks, Becks. There's no other way to say it."

"If the media suspects it, I don't know what it could mean for Kensington's career. It could go either way."

"It's going to sound cold, Becks, but that's show business. If she's serious about it, she'd better learn that now." Carys is brutal but truthful.

"Oh, come on. I've known you for years, Carrie. What's the big deal?"

"Gee, I don't know." She slams her fists on the table. "My reputation? I only represent a certain level of clients."

"She's good. Damn good," Becks boasts.

"And right now, you know I can't take your word for it. And that's business, not personal."

Becks cedes the point. "You always go check out your talent to make sure they're on the up and up."

Carys bites her thumb, conceding, "True."

"Then have someone to go listen to her. Tonight, before she moves on to wherever she's going to," Becks urges.

I pipe up again. "Her website says Milwaukee."

Becks turns pleading eyes on Carys. "If you represent her, Carys, then I have time to talk to Kensington. Build some trust. See if I'm right about my suspicions without a million people wondering why we'd be seen together. You know how these scandal sheets are. They'd speculate we're engaged to be married or something. Fucking ridiculous the way they gossip about my life, but I know I bought that. Christ, if I could just walk up to Paige and ask..." Becks leans forward and drops his head into his hands.

"Why can't you?" David asks, always logical.

"Because I left. And she's moved on with her life," Becks says flatly.

"Ouch," David sympathizes.

Becks nods sharply, but the pain lingers beneath the surface, making me wonder just who this woman was to him beyond his high school sweetheart.

"Regardless, if Kensington is seen coming or leaving here, there won't be the same kind of questions because it would just be a normal day here at the office. Everything is speculated about what happens behind these doors," Carys sums up.

"That's about it. I mean, you're my counsel of record as well as being my friend, Carrie."

"Angie? Do me a favor?" Carys asks.

"Of course."

"Pull as much data as you can on Kensington. See if she's presently being represented by anyone which would through a complete wrench in this. Then find us all something to eat. I suspect this strategy session is going to go long." Carys's voice is full of fire.

"On it. Any preferences?" When no one voices any, I pull up our favorite bistro's online ordering. Knowing everyone's favorites, I don't bother to interrupt the conversation swirling around me. Then I begin gathering as much information as I can on Kensington before printing it out to the discreet printer that Carys had David haul in earlier.

I tune back in when Carys, David, and Becks begin arguing about the best method to make an approach. "I think if she's performing at Redemption, she's going to be infuriated her night's being trampled on. And Marco isn't going to welcome the intrusion," Carys states for at least the fourth time.

"What the hell am I supposed to do, then, Carrie? I need for someone to see what I did. To tell me I'm not fucking crazy," Becks yells.

David stands and places a hand on Becks's shoulder, likely to keep him from yelling at his wife as much as to offer comfort.

And before I can think too much about it, I offer, "I'll do it."

Three sets of incredulous eyes focus on me. "Angie, I know you acted as my eyes and ears for those few events when I was on maternity leave and no one else could make it, but this is entirely different. There's no way for you to prepare for this. It's going to be loud music, inside. Are you sure?" Carys asks me.

Loud music. Inside. Likely dark…

"Sure. Piece of cake." I reach for a glass of water and immediately knock it over on its side.

David curses and races for a roll of towels we keep under a sideboard for messes just like this.

"No, Angie. I can't let you. If a pap happens to snap a pic of you, it could explode into a holy mess. Particularly this week. They could follow you home." Becks's blue eyes sear into mine with undiluted anguish.

And his anguish is what convinces me to do it. "Every morning, I look into the mirror and see the exact same look you're wearing on my own face. I'm awake, I'm breathing, but nothing is what it seems anymore." I reach over and grip his trembling arm through his suit jacket. "You shouldn't be wearing that look at all, let alone permanently. If there's anything I can do to help you, it's my duty to do so."

"It's your responsibility to heal," he counters.

"I've done so much of that because of the people in this room. Because Carys gave me a job, because David teases me like a little sister. Because you, Beckett Miller, were proud of me for standing up for what was right. This is what's right. If I don't talk with her, what's the worst that happens?"

"You could be exposed. You won't have any peace," he reminds me. As if he has to.

"That happens every day I walk out my door." He sucks in a jagged breath. "*I* didn't do anything wrong. *I* stood up for what was right. And how would I live with myself if I could have helped you and I don't? Well, then I'm no better than the people who sat there letting me be judged unfairly."

Becks shoves out of his chair, hauling me up with him. "Hold on...just hold on. This is why we're here together, right? To find a better way?"

"Are you sure?" Now that I've worked up the nerve, it's seeping through me, fueling something I haven't had in far too long.

Courage. It might be fleeting, but it's twinkling in the dark sky of my life, and I'm reaching for it.

"No. It might be wishful thinking."

"Oh, for Christ's sake." David grabs the office phone. "Let's take a break and come at this with a fresh perspective after we get some food and drink in us. There has to be some other way than to do..." David makes a spinning motion with his hands.

The four of us collectively slump in our chairs. Becks lifts a shaking hand to his forehead. "Yeah, good idea, David. I actually feel like I could keep something down now."

David walks around the conference table and holds out a hand to Becks, who takes it warily. "We haven't always been on the same side. But you're a good person, Beckett. We're going to help you find out the answers you need."

Becks opens and closes his mouth repeatedly before he breaks away and moves toward the windows, the show of support overwhelming him.

Now that the initial storm's passed, I decide now's as good a time as any to run downstairs to get our food now that I know we won't be sick the moment we begin to eat it. Leaving the conference room, I see Ward's office is still dark. I frown as I pass by. "You know, we could have used your support today, Ward." My heart aches a bit when I recall the kind, sweet man who kissed me in the middle of a candy-induced dream to the resurgence of the irritable bear from just a few days ago.

I squeeze into the crowded elevator. The moment the doors open, I sprint out when my phone goes off. Slowing my stride, I slip it from my purse and read the message.

Can you grab Ward coffee? He should be back soon. Thanks, C.

"She deserves a medal for dealing with him," I mutter. With that thought in my mind, I pick up my speed so I can get in line at Pret A Manger to grab Ward a latte that wasn't in our original order— a drink he likely doesn't need nor want. But because his sister asked nicely for it, I'll grab it.

Even if this is one I'm tempted to actually throw at him for making an assumption about Becks just like everyone else does.

CHAPTER THIRTEEN

WARD

"Winsome Ward" Burke—who made this site's 'Most Eligible Bachelor' list for the last ten years running—was spotted out with yet another female companion of indeterminate identity today. After a cozy lunch at Le Bernadin, he dashed off, leaving the woman stuck with the bill. Does that make one of the world's richest men playing hard to get or ridiculously cheap? **— Sexy&Social, All the Scandal You Can Handle**

I avoid the penetrating stares from varying people who try to capture my attention while weaving my way through the tables behind the maître d' in the exclusive Le Bernadin in New York. I asked my lunch companion to meet me here because I wanted to avoid feeling on display. Obviously, I made an error in judgment.

It hasn't been my first recently. I doubt it will be my last.

The tinkle of glasses as someone makes a toast reminds me of my mother's lecture before she and my father glided out the door of our family home the night they died. "I know you're going to a party, Ward. Don't do anything that would cause us to be disappointed."

Sorry, Mom. The fact I'm alive and you're not is probably the bigger fuckup in the grand scheme of things, so the fact I had a few beers that night probably wouldn't have made you too mad. I clench my jaw as I stride to the table.

I know what has me pushed close to the edge this late-fall day. It started witnessing Angie so damn comfortable in Becks's arms when I felt like she was like a butterfly ready to flit away in mine when I kissed her—God, was it just last week?

And damnit, I also really didn't want to leave the office wondering what the hell is going on, but once a year I have to meet with this woman. I have no choice. It's one meeting I abhor, but it has to be done. After all, not just my livelihood depends on the outcome of it.

Who knew our grandfather was a financial savant? As I approach the table with a sick feeling, I recall the letter my father left along with his will. *Your grandfather thought it was a fun idea to support one of your deceased relatives who worked at J&J. He also dabbled in other stocks when, and I'm quoting him, 'this newfangled S&P 500 was created.' I remember him bitterly complaining the S&P 500 gave him too much free time, so he began to trade the stocks he amassed. He was a whip-smart man who set up our family for several lifetimes over. He sold J&J and many others long before my father passed away*

PERFECT ASSUMPTION · 133

and I inherited this. Don't worry, the portfolio we've left you is diversified enough that you should be able to live on the interest alone for generations.

Why didn't we tell you? Well, let's be honest. Your mother and I wanted you both to appreciate hard work is important. We didn't want to raise two children who had egos the size of this account.

Carys, Ward, let me be clear. We haven't been entirely altruistic. We didn't live entirely off our own money. Occasionally, we dipped into the fund a wee bit. We purchased our home in New York, cars, both of your educations. We donated a great deal to charities. But we were blessed not because of money, but because we had both of you. Every day, the both of you were our truest wealth, not the number of zeros in the account. Hopefully, you felt that.

Now, I hope we've been with you long enough to explain everything. If not, your mother and I are deeply sorry about the shock this must be. But this will be a comfort to know you never have to worry about your futures. But we want you to remember nothing replaces finding love.

There's nothing that fulfills your soul in quite the same way.

We will always love you both.

The words of his letter whisper through my brain. Despair floods me when my eyes collide with the savvy blue ones of the brunette the maître d' steps back for me to greet. Fortunately, Lynne Bradbury—stock market protégé for Bristol Brogan Houde—embraces the eccentricities of her clients. After enduring ten minutes during our first meeting in her office before I started sweating profusely as she presented my portfolio—pages upon pages of charts and breakdown of numbers that many corporations in America would love to boast about—I abruptly stood and asked, "Have you eaten?"

Lynne, ridiculously astute, shrugged. "I could manage a bite."

It's how we ended up at Le Bernadin without a reservation. And every time since. She no longer calls me to review our portfolio; she just schedules lunch. It softens the blow of this meeting in a way I don't deserve since I earned my money the worst way imaginable.

My parents died for me to inherit it.

Immediately, she stands and holds out her hand. "A pleasure to see you, Ward."

Since I can't return the sentiment, I return her shake before sliding behind her to hold her chair as she reseats herself. "How was your trip to Dubai?" I ask, recalling why our meeting had to be delayed until after my birthday.

"Fruitful. Bristol was pleased. And you? How's your sister?"

"Good. Better now." I think of all the animosity between the two of us we've cleared up. Then I frown, realizing how much I've likely just confused everything again today, but not with her.

Lynne's brow raises, silently prompting me to continue. I decide to share something personal that happened not too long ago. "My nephew, Ben, developed an aversion to peas and decided to decorate her kitchen with them."

A smile tugs at my lips as I reach for the water goblet in front of me. I take a quick drink before asking Lynne, even as her laughter peals out, "Do you share a similar distaste for them?"

"I've been at too many family dinners involving children not to find that amusing. Has she avoided being hit in the face?"

I nod. "But not David. He took a direct hit to the eye. Complained about it the rest of the meal. Carrie told him to suck it up. Completely egged Ben on. Funniest thing I saw in quite a while."

Lynne's about to respond when our waiter comes over to announce today's specials. I glance down at my menu briefly before ignoring the words and the waiter's complicated spiel.

"Do you have any preference?" I ask Lynne, knowing the answer will be the same as always.

"Not at all. I'm not picky about food."

I pluck her menu. "Chef's special for two."

"Wine accompaniment?"

I arch a brow at my companion, who chimes in, "I'm fine with sparkling water."

I hand the waiter our menus. "As am I. Thank you."

"Thank you, Mr. Burke." He scurries off to place our order, giving me and Lynne a few uninterrupted minutes.

"So, is there anything we need to know?"

"There was a ten percent overall increase in the value of the portfolio. I can get into specifics if you want."

My lips part. "You mean to tell me we're worth…more?" Lynne had some ideas for some speculative stocks she wasn't quite certain about at our last meeting. I honestly was hoping it would decrease our portfolio.

"What can I say, Ward? I'm damn good at my job."

"Obviously." A heavy silence lies between us before a rough laugh escapes. I lean forward and place my head in my hands. "Christ, Lynne. What the hell are we supposed to do with more? We could never spend the money we have now in six lifetimes."

"There are a lot of people who would be grateful," she begins.

"Eight hundred and eighty million dollars. I'm just grateful the amount is still speculation." I shudder, thinking about the constant eyes trained on me.

"Just until someone hacks your tax returns." Her voice is cheerful.

"You're such a bright ray of sunshine."

"But I have an idea."

"Does it involve making more money?" There's a note of disgust in my voice I can't quite hide.

"Yes—"

I groan loudly.

"—and no."

I peek out at her from in between my fingers.

"You look ridiculous, for what it's worth," she declares.

I sit back in my chair and smile, really smile, for the first time since I stepped foot in the restaurant. "I thought you were supposed to pander to your clients' egos."

"If that happened, we might need to float you down Fifth Avenue for the Macy's Day Parade in a few weeks."

I press my lips together to hold in my laughter. "Do you want to tell me more about this investment now?"

"No."

"No?" My brows lower to a V. "You want me to just blindly trust you to sink…"

"One hundred million," Lynne announces as if I was going to give her my card to make a run to the nearest ATM.

I can't even mouth the number back at her. My mind can't even wrap around the figure she tossed out so carelessly. This wasn't the lifestyle I grew up with. I lived in Manhattan, yes. I went to private schools, sure. Birthdays and holidays were special, but there weren't keys to a yacht under the Christmas tree. Or even a Jet Ski for that matter. I wholeheartedly support why our parents raised Carys and me under a cloak of normalcy, but for us to have inherited such immense wealth upon their death with no warning still leaves us both reeling. "You're out of your mind," I finally manage to get out.

"I'm not telling you anything because it's part of a Lockwood Industries deal. And Jared suggested you be brought into the pool of investors." Lynne sits back as our waiter leans past her to place a plate between us. "Thank you."

I mutter my thanks. "Oh." Ryan Lockwood is one of the world's youngest billionaires, having inherited his father's shipping empire and grown it exponentially since his death. His husband, Jared Dalton, used to be my boss at Watson, Rubenstein, and Dalton, the firm I left to go work with Carys a few years ago. We're not only fellow Harvard Law grads, albeit different years, but we're neighbors, our condos located in adjoining buildings in Tribeca. "I feel like I'm being set up."

Lynne reaches for a piece of baguette with some kind of fish on it. "You are."

"Tell me this won't involve some kind of media coverage with our names all over the place," I warn her.

"They're not stupid." She rolls her eyes.

"Shit." I reach over and squeeze her hand. "You can say it. I'm not thinking."

"Why would I say *I'm* not thinking, Ward? Especially when that's clearly the problem *you're* having today?"

It takes me a second before I grin at her refusal to parrot my words back at me. "How does your significant other handle your smart mouth?"

"You're assuming I have time for one." A look of amusement enters her eyes.

"Well, if you find one, they should consider themselves damn lucky to find someone like you." And I'm not saying that because the woman seated next to me could drive me and Carys to financial ruin with a click of her fingers.

Lynne rolls her eyes. "Save your charm for someone who will appreciate it, Ward. Now, let me give you your annual indigestion while I talk about your portfolio."

I look longingly at the food in front of me. "I'm really hungry, Lynne. Can I get through a few courses first?"

"No." And Lynne immediately begins talking about stock futures.

By the time I leave Lynne to head back to LLF, I have a vicious headache. It's talking about money. As I walk back to the office, I debate calling my sister and telling her I need the rest of the afternoon off when a text comes in from my brother-in-law.

Just sayin' – Becks, followed by a fireworks emoji.

I type quickly back before picking up my pace. *I'm on my way back.*

Good. Sooner rather than later would be preferable.

Why?

Can't say. It pains me to say it, but it's urgent. Get here, ASAP

Hand the phone back to my brother in law, Becks, I joke.

Ha ha. Funny. This is serious. For once, I'm not inclined to throw him out a window.

D, windows are sealed shut, I remind him.

Good, if the urge should ever arise again, it will hurt more when I finally manage to shove him through it.

I type *LOL* and increase my pace.

Entering the building near Rockefeller Center, I wave to the security guard before jumping onto the elevator. Mentally bracing myself for what I'm about to walk into, I don't realize someone else is already on. Automatically, I press the button to close the door when I hear an out-of-breath voice. "Can you press the button for our floor, Ward?"

Shit. Fuck. No. This is not what I need right now.

Turning slightly, I find Angie in a black coat that does nothing to show off her figure. Then again, I've rarely seen her in anything that has. The dim overhead light from the elevator sets highlights off in her windblown red hair. "Angie. Coming back from lunch?" Even I cringe at how superficial I sound.

"Hardly," she grumbles.

"Leaving it a bit late? Did Becks cause problems again?"

Angie's lips form a moue of confusion. It draws my attention to them. "It constantly amazes me how you can be related to your sister."

"What do you mean?"

But I have no one to blame but myself for her attitude. I step out and hold the door for her, only then realizing her arms are overloaded with a tray full of drinks. "Crap. Let me take those for you."

"Wow. Such a gentleman," she drawls as she passes by. My heart plummets as she treats me to her usual blank mask. "Don't bother yourself." She arrives at our office door and shifts the drinks so she can lift her overloaded arms to fling the door in our direction.

I follow her. "I did offer assistance," I remind her.

She ignores me as she carefully sets down the drinks and bags on the desk. Picking up her desk phone, she presses an extension. "Hey. I have everyone's lunch here. Just give me a moment to get my coat hung up." Disconnecting, she whirls around and hangs up her jacket. On her way back to her desk, she addresses my comment. "Ward, I don't pretend to make more of what happened between us than what it was—a kiss. Maybe it was a spur-of-the-moment thing, maybe you regret it, but that's not what today's about."

"What's happening?" I ignore her reference to our kiss, something I don't want to forget, ever.

"Today, the world's gone mad for a roomful of people I care about. To add to that, I—and everyone in the vicinity—gets blasted with your attitude again? You run hotter and colder than my plumbing."

I wince. "I apologize."

Her laugh is frail. "You're good at that—doing something sweet, saying the right things when you want something, aren't you? But right now, you're making me reconsider taking a chance on the things I fear letting get too close."

While I'm left to find the right words to try to piece together the situation I put myself in with Angie and the one occurring at work, she plucks out a coffee from the tray she was balancing and hands it to me. "Here, your sister ordered this for you," she manages before she gathers the remaining drinks on the tray and two bags and makes her way into the inner sanctum, calling out, her voice husky, "Who's hungry?"

There's a loud round of applause before I hear David grumble, "Thank God. Maybe we can shove something into Becks's mouth to keep his panic under control."

Everyone begins talking over one another, all while I'm still frozen in place, holding a cup of coffee I didn't order picked up by a woman who apparently is beginning to pick up on the feelings I have for her. She's not completely wrong about any of them. I'm struggling with trying to identify them myself, with the harmful knowledge of my past that leaves me feeling that no matter what I do, I may not be good enough for her.

There's only one thing she's wrong about. I'm not feeling a drastic temperature shift in the way I'm beginning to feel about her. The tepidness I feel is about myself.

CHAPTER FOURTEEN

WARD

Prodigy DJ Kensington brought down the house at Redemption last night. If you're smart—and if you have the connections to get in—go listen to her. Holy @^%$ She's a game changer!
— **@PRyanPOfficial**

"Hold on." I slam my cup of coffee down so hard on the conference room table, I'm in danger of crushing the cup. I point a finger in Carys's direction. "Let me sum up this cockamamie plan. You want Angie to go to Redemption—tonight—to hear this miracle-sent DJ Kensington because Becks thinks we should get her under an NDA, why? To potentially sign her as a client?"

"That about sums it up," Carys agrees with a straight face.

"And this is an emergency, why?" I run my fingers through my hair as I pace back and forth.

"Does it really matter at this juncture?" Angie breaks in. She and Becks exchange a complicated glance. There's been more cast around the room since I walked in, causing something unpleasant in me to shift. What exactly was discussed when I was shut out earlier? While I was at lunch? But I ignore those questions for the moment and focus on the immediate why.

"It does, Angela."

Becks shoves his way in. "Well, that's just too damn bad. Because that's what you're going to get."

Frustration eats at me. "Why? I'm a partner in this firm. If anyone should be going to negotiate something legal and it can't be Carys, it should be me. You know, an actual attorney."

Becks scoffs. "I think not."

Ignoring him, I direct my comment to my sister. "Before I agree to this…"

Becks talks right over me. "Because I don't trust you the same way I do them. And it's my right as a client to determine who I discuss my business with." He flings his arm out to encompass the other occupants of the room.

Everyone except for me.

"Wow. Never saw that one coming." I shove my hand through my hair to hide its shaking.

"Christ, Ward. It's just…" But I hold a hand to cut off Beckett. I can't listen to someone scrape my insides any more raw than they are.

But I do have a few questions. "What the hell is the purpose of all this? Why all the secrecy?" *Including from me.*

"The same purpose we built this firm on. We represent quality clients, Ward. If I wanted to continue to represent flash-in-the-pan acts, I could have stayed on at Goathead. Instead, I went to Wildcard."

I open my mouth to argue her point, but she plows on. "As in-house counsel for Goathead—hell, even at Wildcard—I'd often be in a position to meet our artists before I'd be directed to approach them. I could never understand why until I realized it was about brand—the companies I was representing. When I struck out on my own, I kept with the same practice, but there was no one to do that legwork except me and David. I'd have Angie research the hell out of them before we went. Then I'd...why am I going into this? You know the drill. Both of you had to step up to do this when I was out on leave. I made it part of this firm's practice doing what I was taught—to represent solid individuals who have a quality reputation. I want, and wanted, to legally represent people who will change the music industry for decades. What I didn't ask for were constant scandals."

"And yet you brought on Becks."

"And you!" Carys fires back. "Christ, I need to give Angie a raise just for monitoring both your feeds on social media. So, fine. Go if you have to stick your nose in. But taking Angie with you is nonnegotiable. Consider it uptraining her, if you so object to having her there. See? All issues solved."

Angie rolls her eyes when I sigh hugely. "Should I bring my copy of *Black's Law Dictionary* for her to study from?"

"Only if you want it shoved somewhere..." Angie starts to threaten.

"Stow it, both of you. Work together. The two of you can determine if this Kensington is the kind of quality I want to represent." Carys shoots Angie another look that has the redhead nodding.

And me fuming.

"Since when do we require an NDA for a simple conversation? And for the record, the specialty of this firm has always been recording artists," I remind Carys, not bothering to address anyone else in the room since they're not letting me in on the silent messages being passed.

"It's not completely out of the blue, Ward," Carys argues. " Sue me—I'm getting cautious in my old age."

I try to speak, but Carys tramples all over me.

"I'd like to have a conversation with a potentially talented young woman. I'd like to continue to practice the due diligence that built this firm. I may want to have a conversation with her, one which I don't want to be repeated. Is it so odd that before I have that conversation I ask her to sign an NDA? No. Later, I may decide to rep her depending on what I find out. What's throwing you off? The fact she's a DJ or her age?"

I cast eyes in Becks's direction before muttering, "Both."

Carys says airily, "There are more and more artists laying down tracks with famous DJs. Think Frankie Knuckles, Daft Punk, David Guetta. Skrillex. They are considered recording artists since they lay the tracks and would be considered both composers and artists, correct?"

I follow Carys's train of thought—at least on the legal aspect. "It depends on whether they're overlaying the track with their own music. Certainly, we've been structuring our contracts correctly for these scenarios and demanding royalty payouts if appropriate from the recording labels in that case. There's always a liability if an artist is using someone else's music or if they do something live that can't be controlled."

"I'm impressed, brother. You did learn something at Watson, Rubenstein, and Dalton," Carys drawls.

"Kiss my ass, Carrie. Let's tell the real story. You want us to drop everything because he"—I point at Becks—"got up into something with this artist. And now what? Instead of you doing your own scouting, we have Becks's number one fangirl ready to sacrifice herself on the altar of the paparazzi in order to save his skin. Isn't that taking your job responsibilities a bit too far, Angie?"

"I explained that. Angie's looked at other artists for me before. Besides, I turned that part of my life up to *you* when I found out I was having a child. But because *I* can't go, someone who understands the situation has to," Carys yells.

"What situation?" I demand just as loudly.

"That's not for me to tell you," my sister shouts back.

"And you were willing to send Angie in without either of us as backup?" Silence follows my frustrated question. "That's awfully risky, and you know it, Carys. She may be your go-to girl for everything, but despite her loyalty, she's not perfect. So, fine. I'll go and I'll fix whatever it is Becks managed to get himself into this time."

Angie recoils even as Becks shoves himself from his seat and stalks over to where I'm standing. "Watch it. Take all the damn potshots you want at me because I'm unwilling to share everything with you, but leave Angie out of this."

"Damn straight." Carys stands as well. Despite my sister's diminutive height, she's a teeming mass of fury. "I know why you're upset, Ward. Anyone with half a brain in this room has figured it out by now. But that gives you no reason to take potshots at someone who's stepping up for the team out of love, loyalty, and friendship. And if you can't, maybe you need to rethink the contract you signed with this firm."

Carys's words kick me back to the ground where I've barely managed to get back on my feet after a morning where I already felt like I was crawling on my belly. "You don't really mean that," I manage hoarsely.

"I damn well do." Carys holds her stance.

And with those words, I'm transported back to when I was a teenager and I'd fuck up in some way. And as always, I can feel her anger and disappointment washing over me, telling me I've let my sister down. Just like I let my parents down.

Before I can say another word, Angie murmurs, "If you all will excuse me, I need a few moments." She scoots back from the table to stand, but I hold out my hand.

"It's probably best if you stay and I go. Apparently, you've been more productive than I have with the team while I was out this morning."

"Ward…" Angie starts to protest.

I stride to the door and fling it open. Looking back at Angie, I say scathingly, "Just make sure you're properly dressed up for this. I'll pick you up at nine."

Ignoring the murmuring behind me, I storm out of the conference room and head into my office to ruminate upon my sins. The pain I glimpsed in Angie's glorious eyes just before I slammed the door behind me is just another one to add to my list.

"How the hell am I supposed to fix this mess?" I ask the thin air. Once the alcohol hits my lips, I ignore the bitterness I swallow along with burning Scotch whisky.

Hours later, the most I've managed to do is put a sizable dent in the tumbler of Macallan I poured the moment I entered here. I've yet to turn on my computer to do a single piece of work which I know will have David riding my ass about the contracts he needs to send out when there's a knock at my door. Figuring it's him there to do just that, I call out, "Enter."

When David slips inside, I don't bother to move. Instead, I reach for my drink and lift it in a silent offering.

"Nah, I've got to run out to go get Ben."

"I thought Carrie picked him up in the evenings."

"She normally does, but since she spent a good portion of today dealing with Becks, fashion crises, and arranging for an overnight guest, our normal plans have been a bit disrupted." Despite the innocuous words, the undercurrent to them has me lifting the glass to my lips. I'm grateful for the burn down my throat. It eases the one in the pit of my stomach when David says, "Thought you left the prick behind, Ward. Turning over a new leaf."

"So, sue me."

"I think that's one of the many things Carrie was advising Angie to do on their way out the door."

Sliding my feet off my desk, I walk over to the floor-to-ceiling windows overlooking the city. Knowing I owe him some kind of explanation for my behavior today, I start by asking a question. "Is there anything you truly regret? Something that if you could do it again would change the course of your life?"

He moves across the room to stand next to me. "Of course. I would assume everyone does, but since I ended up with your sister, it worked out the way it was supposed to in the end."

"That's not what I meant." Frustrated, I lift the glass to my lips, only to have him place his hand on my wrist.

"Then tell me what you mean. And despite the fact you helped botch my wedding proposal to my wife, you know you're one of my best friends."

A small smirk crosses my face as the story of David and Carys's perfect proposal gone awry comes to the forefront of my mind. Then the light fades as the weight of the world lands on my shoulders once again. "I was late because I had a meeting with our financial advisor today."

David cringes. I wipe a hand over my face. "Yeah, that's how I feel every time I meet with her. I could have gone the rest of my life without knowing about me and Carrie inheriting all of that money if once—just once—my father could tell me he was proud of me."

"And then you came back to find not only were you being asked to do something—"

"—where I still feel like the details are a smoke screen for something more. I'm not an idiot, David. I get I'm being left out of the loop," I conclude.

David nods. "And you know better than anyone that sometimes it has to happen like that. We sign agreements that ultimately dictate the client has the final say. But the real question you have to ask yourself is, do you trust Carys to do what's right—what's legally and morally right—to protect both the clients and employees of this firm?"

My "Yes" comes out so fast, I begin to wonder why I've spent hours picking apart my sister's request. After all, more clients than Becks spend time at Redemption. My muscles begin to relax. "Then why am I still so worked up about this whole thing?"

"Could it be due to the fact you're jealous of the connection between Angie and Becks?" David inquires mildly.

A surge of emotion insidiously begins crawling through me. I choke out a laugh. "Why should I care if our legal assistant has a thing for Beckett Miller after he's been with half the women in the northern hemisphere?"

David's amused eyes meet mine. "First, because despite the fact I'd love nothing better than to believe the trash written about him, you know better than that about Becks. Otherwise, your sister would never have maintained the relationship she has with him over the years."

"Fair point," I give in grudgingly. "And second?"

"Because I've seen the way you look at Angie when you think no one else is watching. So has Carrie."

"She's an attractive woman" is all I reply with.

"And we're not idiots. But if that's all you think about her, good for you for having the common decency not to go there. She faces too much day in and day out for someone like you to…never mind. I've said too much already." David rips the drink from my hands and downs it in a few easy swallows. "Since you made your preference about how your partner for this evening should look to all of us in the conference room, I'm out of here to go get my son. You can pick Angie up at nine at our place." He turns and heads for the door.

"Why not at hers?" I frown.

David barks out a laugh as he grips the door handle. "Because Angie doesn't live in the city, asshole. It almost took an act of God, but Carys got her to agree to stay with us tonight so you're not inconvenienced any more than you have to be. Despite the fact she has a fucking cat to feed." And on those parting words, my brother-in-law flings open the door.

Leaving me with a lot more to think about than my own damn miserable day.

CHAPTER FIFTEEN

ANGELA

Based on last week's online survey, women don't get dressed up because we enjoy it. We do it because of men. Let me tell you, that's a bunch of bullshit. Dress to make yourself feel good. Dress to feel empowered. Do NOT do it because some reprobate wants you to change.
— **Beautiful Today**

"That's not too much?" I ask Irina, private sales associate from Saks, who Carys called ahead to pull dresses for me. What I'm really wondering is if it's too little. The hem of the skirt barely covers parts of me I've been reluctant to allow doctors to examine in the last ten years.

"Darling, if I had your legs, I'd do everything possible to show them off. I mean, look at what it does for your derrière." Without warning, she spins me on the pencil-thin heels she insisted I slip on and spins me so I can catch a glimpse of my rear in the three-way mirror. "I'd climb the Empire State

Building three times a day for a tush like that. What kind of workout do you do?"

"Um, I climb the steps from the metro station to get to my car?"

"It's a gift from God, and you're hiding it in…that?" Her hand flutters to where she hung my serviceable work suit.

"At least I can sit in it."

She opens her mouth before snapping it closed. "That's an excellent point."

I point to an asymmetric pleated dress with a rounded collar in a bronze color. "What about that one?"

Her mask of serenity transforms into one of amusement. "Well, we can certainly try it."

A few moments later, I face the mirror. Even I cringe. "I look like a cross between wrinkled wrapping paper and a sack of potatoes."

Irina bursts into gales of laughter. "That may be the nicest thing I've ever heard anyone say about that dress. And trust me when I say you look the loveliest of anyone I've ever seen wear it. Now, do you trust me to pick out something suitable?"

"No."

She rears back as if I've mortally offended her.

"Well, yes," I recant hesitantly.

She pulls me over to one of the chairs and takes one of my hands in hers. "If you were picking a dress out for yourself, it would be something like this. Why?"

Without thinking, I answer bluntly, "I don't like people noticing me."

"Angela, people are going to notice you regardless of whatever you're wearing." But she squeezes my hand as she says the words. "I do understand what you're trying to say. You're trying not to draw undue attention to yourself."

A sigh of relief escapes me that she understands what I'm getting at. "Yes. That's it."

"Have you thought you may be drawing more attention to yourself because you do not dress as you're expected to?"

Expected to? I laugh cynically. "It doesn't matter how I dress."

"I see." And maybe she does because she quickly flits past a few dresses that make me internally cringe. Her hands stop on a buff-colored, ruched dress. "Come. I think this will work."

"Isn't it a bit…small?" I critically eye the dress which looks like it belongs on a tween, not a woman fast approaching her thirties.

"It stretches" is all Irina says.

Within moments she has me zipped into the body-contour-hugging dress that appeared so tiny on the hanger. With its sheer arms and an exposed back, it's demurely sexy without giving me heart palpitations just by looking at myself in it, let alone imagining a roomful of people seeing me in it.

Hugging every inch of me from my shoulders to just below my knees in a material that almost matches my skin tone, it might be the singular most sinful article of clothing I've ever owned. And while the part of me that's so scarred is cowering in a corner, there's a large part of me that's tempted to ask for a picture of myself in it because I know I've never looked so beautiful.

"Now, this? This is how a woman should feel when she puts on a dress. Powerful and confident."

"Do I get my money back if it doesn't work?" I deadpan. But even I can't help twisting and turning at the way the dress flatters my body without making me feel cheap. My eyes close. I brace. "How much does it cost?"

"Four hundred and ninety-five dollars." Before I can formulate words, Irina's quick to add, "Plus, there's a twenty percent discount."

"Why?" I ask suspiciously, but not ungratefully.

She flips up the inside of one wrist, showing me where a few stitches have come undone. "Since the only one that would fit you is off the mannequin and it was somehow damaged, I have the authority to discount the dress."

I twist and turn a final time. I move over to the chair in the corner of the room and sit, then stand. Finally, a small smile curves my lips. "What do I wear underneath?"

Irina lifts the hanger from the hook discreetly placed on the wall. I thought it was empty before. Now, I notice a small scrap of material hooked over the top. "These." She lifts up the tiniest excuse for a thong I've ever seen.

"And what about here?" I gesture to my chest area.

She frowns. "Is the built-in bra not enough?"

"Well, it's fine. I just...I never..."

Her bejeweled hand squeezes my arm slightly. "You look elegant. Classy, Angela. Why, with a little lingerie tape over your nipples..."

I choke on air. "What kind of tape?"

Her eyes sparkle. "Honey, where have you been living? Mars?"

"No. Brewster."

She tsks as she undoes the zipper. "Let's get you back into your own clothes. Then I'll get you a roll."

"It comes in rolls?" I'm incredulous. My grandmother never talked about this with me.

Compassion crosses Irina's face. "You don't get out much, do you."

"This will be my first dressy night out since my senior prom," I respond honestly.

A myriad of emotions crosses Irina's face. Seconds later, I'm being pulled into her arms, and she murmurs, "Then let's make certain you feel as beautiful as any Cinderella should."

"Things didn't end up so well for her that night," I remind her, sliding out of the dress, amazed it bounces back to its much smaller size.

"They do in the end."

"That's true.

"And really, darling. Isn't that all that matters?"

A new dress, a lecture on lingerie tape, and recommendations on how to do my hair and makeup, I finally escape Saks. I snag a cab and immediately pull out my cell to call Carys.

She answers on the first ring. "How did it go?"

"I found a dress."

"Excellent." She lets out a sigh of relief, causing me to check out my clothes exposed due to my open jacket. Do I really dress so dowdy? Sula's been urging me to go on a shopping expedition for years. I frown in consternation as Irina's words whisper through my mind. I just can't think of them now. They're for later. Much later.

"And I was given my first ever lecture about lingerie tape." The cab driver begins to cough frantically. I frown as I scoot closer to the door, hoping he's not ill. "Apparently, I'm supposed to take pieces of it and place it across my—"

"Oh, my God, Angie! Hold on!" Carys screeches. A moment later I hear a clattering before she's cracking up in my ear. "I had you on speaker because I was feeding Ben, and David walked in. I think I was in such shock you had never heard about tit tape before I could get the words out to tell you."

"They call it…" I sputter.

"Tit tape. Yep," Carys confirms. There's a pause before Carys snaps, "Oh, for the love, David. You've seen me apply it. Deal with me discussing it."

I can't stop the giggle that escapes. "No wonder Irina was so shocked I'd never heard about it before."

"With the kind of clients she sees? I bet she was." Now, Carys is chortling.

"I feel so naive."

"No, you just have been surviving. And it's wrong of people to make assumptions about you based on the way you look."

"How do I look?" *Scared. Frightened.*

"Like a fashion model. An exclusive one at that."

"Um, Carys? Have you been hitting the wine?" Because I don't know who she's talking about, but it's not me.

"You'll see soon enough," she says mysteriously. Then she hangs up.

I throw my phone in my bag and pull out my wallet as the car slows and pulls up outside Carys and David's building. Swiping my card, I approve the payment and leave the driver a tip that will likely shock him as much as the discussion of tit tape did. He deserves it after overhearing even half of that conversation.

I fling open my door with a mumbled "Thanks" before leaping out.

Several hours later, just before Ward is supposed to join us, I finally begin to understand what Carys meant about my looks. And I'm both terrified to the core and exhilarated by the woman reflected in the mirror.

After dragging me into the guest room, oohing and ahhing over my dress, then muttering under her breath about how she wished she had a head of hair like mine, Carys disappeared for a moment, leaving me stunned. She came back, ordered me to strip, and shoved a glass of wine in my hand.

I found it prudent to let her know, "You're terrifying the hell out of me."

She said, "I need to send your clothes to the cleaners so they're ready for work tomorrow. I'll find something for you to sleep in." She moved over to the closet and pulled out a plush robe.

"Phew. I was beginning to get scared." I started unbuttoning my suit jacket before frowning. "Can I have a little privacy for this?"

"Oops. I'm too used to the men around here randomly stripping."

Don't go there, I told myself. But I couldn't not say, "The image of my cordial, funny co-worker in a contest against his two-year-old to strip their clothes at the end of the day is endlessly amusing."

She grinned. "It's not that far from the truth. Now, let me skedaddle for a second. Leave everything on the bed, including intimates."

I quickly changed into the robe. Carys knocked before coming back in. "All set?"

"I am." I nodded to the bundle of clothes. "Just let me know how much I owe you."

She snorted. "Please. We're charging all of this to Becks including your dress."

I shook my head. "No. Not that. It's too much. I won't let a man buy something like that for me."

Carys studied me for a moment. "All right. Not the dress." Then she caught sight of the clock. "We're running late! You have to get into the shower."

She pointed me in the direction of her guest bathroom. "Don't get your hair wet. We don't have time to dry it!"

"Oh, okay?" But I snagged my wine and took a large gulp of a delicious cabernet sauvignon before doing as she dictated.

I now understand why women take hours to get ready for a special night out. Carys sprayed and spritzed me with my head upside down until I was dizzy. Then she twisted my hair, fluffed, and pulled before adding a shield to my head. "Ahh-choo!" I sneeze to the side.

She paused in her merciless attack with an aerosol can. "Too much?"

"I'd have no idea." I reached up and touched my hair only to find it was like a helmet. "Is it supposed to feel like it won't move until next year?"

She nodded and put the can away before turning toward my makeup. That's when I knew my punishment in this life was just beginning. I was plucked, brushed, smeared, and smoothed until I was certain I'd shed a new skin layer. "Look down. Now look up. To the right. God, I'd kill for these lashes."

"I think you're trying to," I muttered.

And the blonde witch just laughed and said, "Just wait until you see the whole effect with the dress."

After allowing me to attach my own tape and slide into the microscopic thong, I wiggled my way into the dress. Carys during that time ran into her own room for shoes and jewelry. "I was thinking less is more..." But she became very quiet, just handing me a pair of large gold hoop earrings and gold sandals with a pencil-thin heel, an ankle strap, and a familiar red sole any female who has read a glossy fashion magazine in the last twenty years recognizes.

"They cost more than the dress," I wheezed before trying to shove them back in her hand.

Carys shook her head and just said, "They're perfect."

And she was right. They are.

In the full-length mirror, my entire appearance has been transformed. Up close, my skin appears translucent, my lips simply glossier. But my eyes have been made to be smokier, more mysterious.

I step back and take in my full appearance.

If you didn't know who I was, I could easily pass for someone else. The thought makes my stomach churn. How much of my own pain have I held on to because I couldn't let go of the past? *And why did I have to realize it long after Grandma was gone?*

I turn away from the woman in the mirror to avoid letting the tears pricking my eyes fall. Carys spent way too many hours working this miracle. Maybe I'll ask her if she would mind helping me with finding my way through makeup and shopping. While I'd love for Sula to be a part of it, it's kind of hard to do that long distance.

"Knock, knock. Ward's going to be here any minute. Are you ready?" Carys peeks her head around the door.

"Because of you, I think I am." A small smile crosses my face. "Could I ask one more favor?"

"Anything."

I reach into the borrowed clutch and pull out my cell phone. "Would you mind taking a picture for me? It might be silly, but all this?" I touch my dress. "It's a pretty big deal for me. I want to share it with my best friend since there's no one else anymore. Well, other than you."

Carys swallows visibly before she says, "I understand better than you think. All I wanted when David and I got married was to share things with my mom."

A moment of shared camaraderie for the most heartbreaking reason passes between us. Then Carys gets her natural spark back by demanding, "Strike a pose."

I do just as the doorbell rings.

My breath catches. Carys and I share a complicated glance before she opens the door behind her. It's time to see if the information we're looking for is out there.

If there's anything to find out at all.

CHAPTER SIXTEEN

WARD

Redemption club owner and man candy Marco Houde has been surprisingly mum about some rumored changes. Akin to asking all guests to strip before entering, we're not certain there's much else to improve on perfection.
— **Viego Martinez, Celebrity Blogger**

"Angie?" I stammer as the slim, elegant redhead meets me in my sister's living room precisely at nine.

"Hello, Ward." Giving me an appraising look, she turns to my sister. "I understand why I needed to go shopping now based on what your brother's wearing."

"Hmm. He cleans up fairly well for a suit." Carys shoots me a quick wink while Angie looks away.

It gives me an opportunity to study her in detail without her notice.

Do I think she's gorgeous? She might be the most stunning woman I've ever seen. I feel my hand tremble on the glass of soda water David handed me when I came in. Whatever machinations women get to when they're together turned this woman from my Angie into this cool, untouchable creature I don't know.

"You look beautiful." It's the truth, but when her flat blue eyes meet mine, I feel like I lost something important by offering up the compliment.

"Thank you. Should we get going?" This woman is exactly what I don't want. She's cold, aloof, standoffish. Then my inner voice taunts me. *This is what you implied you wanted her to be, you bonehead. You can't have it both ways.*

Before I can do something— anything—to put the situation at ease, Carys pipes up. "Your name is on the list, Angie. The doorman will just wave you in when you come back."

Angie turns toward my sister, and for just a moment, the icy veneer melts and the hint of warmth I've seen at the office shines through when she says sincerely, "Thank you."

"No. Thank you." The two have an unspoken conversation before I step forward.

I hold out my arm. "Shall we?"

Barely tucking her fingers inside my elbow, she nods.

Somehow, I have to figure out a way to apologize. But she has no idea that when she walked down the hall toward me, she stole the last of my sanity, and I've been trying to get it back since.

I only hope I can hold on to it long enough for the two of us to talk. Really talk.

We're headed out of downtown toward Fort Washington, and barely a handful of words have passed between us. I open my mouth to say something, anything, but can't string a single sentence together. I make my living with words: reading, writing, hell, arguing them. And yet, I can't find them when I desperately need them to break the tension rising in my Mercedes. I clear my throat. "Have you ever been to Redemption before?"

Angie turns her ridiculously beautiful face from where she's been staring out the window toward me. "No. I've always wondered what it was like after hearing such intriguing stories about it."

I grab hold of the conversation gambit like it's the bottle of Gatorade being shoved at me when I finished running the New York City marathon. "Who mentioned what Redemption's like to you?" It's not like the goings-on inside are state secrets, but most of the people who gain access to the velvet-shrouded nightclub tend to downplay what occurs to keep the mystery intact. Then again, owner Marco Houde rarely lets things stagnate for long. He'd never be able to keep up charging such exorbitant fees otherwise.

Angie's dress rustles against the leather of the seat as she repositions herself. Instead of answering me, she grumbles, "Your sister's a menace."

"Carys?" I ease the car smoothly off Amsterdam Avenue onto Harlem River Drive. "Why do you say that?"

"Because I can't figure out how to lean my head back without either permanently endangering the leather of your seat or jabbing myself in the head," she clarifies.

I stifle the shout of laughter that wants to escape. Her sense of humor is like a beaming ray of sun. "You're not worried about messing up your hair?" Any other woman I've escorted for any sort of event—including my sister—would be more concerned about ensuring they didn't ruin their appearance for their grand entrance. Angie is so oblivious to hers; it's refreshing.

"I think it might take an open flame for me to fear that, and Becks has never mentioned those when he talked this place up."

Becks. Just hearing his name pass her lips makes my hands tighten on the steering wheel. "The two of you are close?" I phrase it as a question instead of the accusation of how she can tremble so hard from my lips and hug him so easily.

"We are," she confirms without saying anything more, increasing my frustration.

"Were you a fan of his?" I glance over at her to find her face scrunched in concentration.

"A fan? I guess. I liked some of his songs, but to be honest we didn't form the bond we have until a few years ago. He's…" Her voice trails off, her face turning back toward the window.

"What?" Anything to keep her talking.

"Different. People make a lot of assumptions about him that just aren't true. I know how that feels," she concludes softly.

I'm about to ask her what she means when I realize even within the confines of the car, she's drifting away. Instead of going down that line of questioning, I decide to yank her back to now. With me.

I figure it might be prudent to brief her about what she can experience once we get inside the club. "If you've never been to Redemption, there are a few rules you should know. First, no cell phones unless you have explicit permission from the owner."

"What? Really?" Her head swivels back around so fast, it sends the gold at her ears dancing. I press my lips together to hide my smile. Carys must have shellacked her hair since it doesn't move an iota with the swift motion.

"Yep. Everyone is scanned—though I'm not certain how. Must be something super high-tech. This includes VIPs—which for tonight's purposes we are." Her lips part, but no sound comes out. I forge on. "If you want, leave yours here in the center console."

I lift my arm as Angie slips hers out of her evening bag and drops it in. After I snap it shut, I drop my arm back down. "I've been to the club numerous times, both with and without clients. When you first step beyond the curtain, there's a moment of darkness that might throw you off."

"Ohh-kay." She drags out the word.

"The staff will be closing one set of soundproof doors and open another in the anteroom. And then it's anything goes."

I can't prevent the smirk at the small squeak in her voice when she asks, "Define 'anything'?"

I shrug beneath my silk shirt. I feel like I'm initiating a virgin to sex for the first time. "Picture the most tactile experience you've ever had and magnify it by a thousand. The lights bounce off crystal chandeliers, the floors shimmer under the lights. The music's loud, but it heats your blood versus destroying your hearing. And every surface that doesn't hold a drink in a public area is covered in velvet."

"Now, I'm anxious to see it," she finally declares after a moment of absorbing everything I've said.

"Let's not forget about the dancers," I tack on smoothly as I turn off 179th Street.

"Dancers?"

"Oh, they're strategically placed. They're, um, meant to charm the guests."

Angie crosses her legs in a dress I thought it would have been a virtual miracle for her to be able to do so in. "Do you mean the half-naked exhibitionists Becks tells me about? The ones with the…instruments…they use on each other?"

"That's one way of putting it." I laugh ruefully. "And here I thought I was going to shock you with that bit of knowledge."

"Gee, thanks for the pep talk, Ward. Like I'm not anxious enough as it is."

I concentrate on driving, recalling when Angie walked into the living room at my sister's.

She stole my breath with her elegant beauty. And all I wanted to do was kick myself in the ass for being so stupid over the last two years. By building an almost insurmountable wall between us that she's turned to Beckett Miller—much like my sister did before my brother-in-law got his head out of his ass.

What is it about that man that makes women like Carys and Angie flock to him? I frown. My jaw locks while I assimilate the fact that Angie—calm, orderly Angie—is sitting next to me dressed like a supermodel because she's willing to step outside of her normal comfort zone to help him out. I finally just outright ask, "What's between you and Becks?"

"What do you mean?" The temperature of her voice has dropped several degrees.

I should heed the warning, but I press on. "I mean, I'm asking you directly. Are you two in some kind of relationship?"

"What makes you ask that?"

"Do you have to answer my question with a question?"

"Do you want me to answer that?" Her voice holds a note of amusement, but I'm not finding much to laugh about.

Finally, I give in. "I've seen the playful way you are with one another. It reminds me of the way he was with Carys. They were together for years," I conclude.

Her sigh is so harsh, I'm surprised it doesn't steam up the windows. But instead of confirming or denying my thoughts, she remains stubbornly silent.

"He's tender with you when he's not that way with his other women."

"Maybe he just likes me instead of playing games with me." Her temper flashes at me.

Instead of focusing on what she said, I latch on to what I want to hear. "Exactly. Beckett Miller *likes* you." My voice is brittle as images of the two of them entwined together flash into my head, and I press down on the gas. Then, just as quickly, I have to slam on the brakes before I almost ram into the car ahead of us. Muttering an "Excuse me," I focus on driving.

Angie whispers something under her breath. I clear my throat before politely asking, "I'm sorry. I didn't quite hear you?"

"You weren't meant to," she snaps.

"What did I say?"

"You have no idea what's going on around you. Yet just like everyone…ugh! There you sit, making assumptions—about me, about your sister."

"Now wait just a damn minute," I bark out. "I didn't make any assumptions about Carys."

"Yes you did, you just don't realize it. And for that matter, you've been making them about Becks."

I snort. "Everyone makes them about Becks."

"Then they should stop! How would you feel if people made them about you?"

Cynically, I wonder what this woman would do if she knew about the gossip rags will likely be printing about her tomorrow morning. Maybe I should warn her? Nah, considering what she does for my sister, she knows the paps are going to be there. Besides, if she's so close to Becks, she knows better. "I'd face it the same way I handle everything else in my life I don't like."

"How's that?" There's true curiosity in her voice.

"I ignore it," I say with determination. Pulling beneath a stoplight, I catch sight of Angie's face. It's pasty white beneath the makeup she's wearing.

"Well, I guess I know why you barely bother to speak to me at work. Ignoring, huh? What did you need in the last few weeks that you actually bothered to pay me any attention let alone kiss me?" she tries to joke, but it's obvious how my careless words have affected her. Her hands are clenched tightly on her bag.

Oh, Christ. "That wasn't what I meant, Angie. I didn't mean you," I rush to say.

"Sure."

"Angie…"

"Light's green, Ward." Her voice is devoid of all emotion.

I'm about to tell her to hell with it, that we're going to sit where we are until she allows me to apologize, when I hear the blare of horns behind me. Cursing, I press the pedal, and we make the rest of the ride in silence.

Pulling up to Redemption's gate, I slow down enough to catch the paleness easing from her skin. I reach over and touch her cheek briefly.

She flinches.

I growl. "Better get used to a mere mortal touching you, not a rock god. We're here."

"Here? Here's a warehouse. Plan on dumping my body in the Hudson?" Her voice drips sarcasm.

I'll take this attitude instead of the pale, shattered woman who's sat next to me for the last five minutes. I nod at the full parking lot as I ease my car forward toward the valet parking. "This isn't a warehouse. Not unless it's a front for a chop shop."

Angie rolls her lips in, refusing to be amused. I try again to charm her using a topic I hope she'll warm to. "Has Becks ever bitched about the cover charge?"

"Oh, only every time he's come here."

"Trust me, he should shut up about it. Just the security alone for the vehicles makes the cost worth it." I pause deliberately. "Now, I've never laid witness to it, but I've heard the catfights in the bathroom also make it imperative."

Angie giggles. "Oh, stop. I was enjoying being pissed at you."

But her small laugh has me entranced. "I think that's the first time I've heard you laugh."

Her face sobers. "Not all of us have a reason to go through life laughing."

"No." I edge the car closer. My hand drops from the wheel and reaches for hers. "Angie, I—"

But before I can apologize for my judgment, something catches her eye. "Ward, I think the man's gesturing you forward."

"Right." I move my hand to the shift and direct the car toward the valet dressed in black with a mulberry shirt. "When you get out, wait for me. I'll come get your arm."

The door opens, but I still hear her mutter, "That's good. I might need help in these shoes. I think Carys is a secret sadist."

I grin even as I slip the valet a bill. Then I walk in front of the car to escort Angie to the front of Redemption. After that car ride, I need to relax for just a bit. At least running this fool's errand for work gives me the chance to do just that.

CHAPTER SEVENTEEN

ANGELA

Did you see the model on #wardburke arm entering #redemption last night? She was SO #beautiful. I immediately spotted him escorting her through the #VIP area wearing this seasons #Louboutins and a dress from #Saks new line. They looked like they were made for one another. #truelove
But will she last more than a minute with the handsome #gagillonaire?
— **CuTEandRich3**

An intimidatingly behemoth of a man greets Ward warmly at the door of Redemption. "Good to see you, man." He leans down and slaps him several times on the back before catching a glimpse of me. "And who is this delicious fireball behind you? Honey, let me get a better look at you so I can be impressed by Ward's taste for once in his depraved life."

I roll my eyes even as Ward gently edges me forward so I'm in the man's full line of sight. "Louie, this is my friend Angie. Angie, Louie Scott. He's the gatekeeper for all that happens behind those curtains." Ward nods toward the floor-to-ceiling crushed-velvet curtains that are pulled back ever so slightly to permit someone entrance to what lies beyond.

I immediately hold out my hand and say, "It's a pleasure to meet you, Mr. Scott. I haven't been out in quite a while, so I expect this will be a novel experience."

He appears flabbergasted for just a moment. I chew my lip and start to draw my hand away. "I apologize. Did I say something wrong?"

Louie captures my hand in both of his before lifting it. Bringing it up to his lips, he murmurs, "You didn't do a damn thing wrong, beautiful. Now, this punk you're with? He's the one who made the massive error. He should have brought you to us sooner."

Ward rolls his eyes. "Here we go."

"I should tell you to fly away, little boy, and let me escort the gorgeous...what does Angie stand for, beautiful?"

Amused at the pained expression on Ward's face, I smile up at Louie before answering, "Angela."

"And here I thought you were going to tell me 'Angel.' Swear, that was going to come right out of my mouth."

"Something was going to come hurling right out of mine," Ward declares.

I have to suppress my laughter because by the annoyance on his face, it's clear it wasn't going to be flowery compliments about my looks. Though to be honest, the dumbfounded expression on his face when I walked in to greet him at Carys's was worth so much more than Louie's smooth lines.

"How about handing over my date so I can, I don't know, take her inside. Maybe so she can see what Redemption is all about?" Ward grumbles. He holds out a hand that is a sign I take to mean I'm to move near him. When I do, Ward doesn't get ridiculously touchy-feely, causing me to relax. That is until Louie jokes, "Be glad Mike isn't here. You know he has a weakness for redheads."

His fingers, which had been lying gently on the center of my back, clench, making my already nervous stomach churn harder. I begin to wobble on my heels. I know I would have toppled over if not for the steadying pressure against my back. If it weren't for the light… My head becomes slightly woozy until I hear Ward say, "I would assume there wouldn't be any problems with one of my oldest friends trying to poach the woman I'm escorting. And if there were, all I'd have to do would be to let you know. Certainly, no one wants to incur any unpleasantness while trying to enjoy themselves inside."

"See that remains the case," Louie orders. His eyes wander up and down me again. "This one's gonna be pure trouble."

For just a moment, I wonder if he recognizes me. I feel a film of moisture form on the back of my neck, but there's no way for me to get to it with the way Carys styled my helmet hair. But in that split second, I realize Louie's not staring at me with derision but male appreciation.

Oh.

I lower my eyes, I hope demurely. "I wouldn't say trouble, exactly."

Ward sighs even as Louie begins to chuckle. "Undiluted trouble. Keep an eye on your woman, Burke."

"A close one. Are we good to pass?"

Confidence returning, I lift my head. Unfortunately when I do, it puts my eyes right in line with Ward's which are burning with something I've never seen before, not even when he kissed me.

More so than any other time since it's occurred, I can't get that kiss out of my mind. Maybe because it's the first time since it happened we're alone together. Or perhaps it's because Ward's not limiting himself to just holding my arm. I can feel the warmth of his fingers as they contract slightly, and despite the armor of touching protecting the tips from dragging across my skin, it still causes chills to race up my exposed skin. I'm both terrified and excited to understand what I'm feeling. And if he's feeling the same way. My heart starts to beat in a rapid staccato.

But now's not the time. Now we have to go find out information that could break the heart of someone I'd lay my life down for.

I'm jolted from my thoughts when Louie says to Ward, "Yep. Try not to corrupt her too much."

Ward guides me toward the curtains that cut off the visual and sound of the club from the waiting throngs of people. As we approach, it's carefully pulled aside. Two scantily clad bodies are standing by doors. Almost by telekinesis, the curtains lower just as the doors open and a flood of sound and lights rush toward us.

It isn't until we're about to cross the threshold Ward touches my cheek to get my attention; I've been so absorbed, I jump slightly. "What is it?"

"Are you ready to be redeemed?" Then a wickedness brightens his normally solemn features. "Angie, before we go any further, I have to say one thing."

I skid to a halt, almost tripping on the wickedly high heels. "Say it."

"No matter what's happened between us, I'm going to try to make it right."

"Ward…" I can't say more past the lump in my throat. I bravely reach up and rub the stubble running along the edge of his face. Heart thundering in my chest, I wonder if he's just as confused by what this is as I am. I try to curve my lips at him for the first time in what feels like forever.

I'm rewarded by him rubbing his thumb along the apple of my cheek before reaching down to take my hand. "I'm going to enjoy every second of watching you experience tonight."

His hand drops, and he takes my elbow. My lips part on a gasp as we step past a couple twisted together on a platform. "Are they dancing or are they…" A gasp of mixed horror and intrigue escape my lips when I realize it could be either.

Ward merely grins but doesn't say either way.

And realizing no one here is going to judge them even if they are doing something borderline illegal, all the tension leaves my body for the first time in ten years. A spark I haven't felt in far too long lights inside me. It's excitement.

I whirl around and demand, "What should we do first?"

He hesitantly reaches for my hand "The first thing we need to do is get you a drink."

"As long as the drink's sealed when it's handed to me," I say firmly.

"You can trust the bartenders, Angie."

"I trust no one, Ward," I tell him truthfully.

Thinking I mean him, he squeezes my fingers. "The night's still young...Angel," he says before leading me further into the bright sparkling light.

We were on the upper deck with our drinks people-watching when I felt my body begin to sway involuntarily. Ward, who had been keeping a protective arm around my lower back, asked, "Do you dance?"

"Not in so many years. It's almost embarrassing."

He plucked the can out of my hand and put it on the high-top table we were next to before taking my hand and leading me down the stairs. "Wait, Ward! Where are we going?" I protested.

"You can't come to Redemption and not dance," he called over his shoulder.

And we danced on the very fringes of the crowded dance floor. There was a crazy-fast beat the DJ laid over an old '80s Hooters song that had us both laughing as Ward tried to swing me out and back, despite my protests. I ended up crashing into him, which was how I saw the man in black. "Whoa. He's incredible," I commented as Ward righted me.

"That's the owner, Marco Houde. Man's ridiculous on a dance floor." The two of us stopped our amateur maneuvers and admired the owner, whose muscular upper body didn't move, but his feet were as fast and nimble as an Irish dancer. Then Ward leaned down until his dark eyes met mine. "Think you can keep up?"

"No way. No how," I declared adamantly.

"Thank God. Neither can I. Let's take a break."

We climbed back upstairs, where I spotted the ladies' room. Ward ran his hand over the sheer material of my arm. "No catfights. This face is too remarkable to have any scratches or bruises on it."

And as I stroll into the ladies' room, I debate if I actually could head back down to the dance floor to take on Marco Houde in a dance competition. Ward's words have me tingling from head to toe with confidence. I give a quick glance around. Realizing there's no one who can see me, I do a quick twirl. Then I laugh when I realize my hair still hasn't moved.

There are no words to describe tonight. I'm humming to myself after leaving the ladies' room despite my disappointment when there wasn't a catfight, though I did spot the well-placed security guard, and I tried my best not to snicker. I try to find Ward amid the people aimlessly wandering when I spot the reason we're even here right in front of me. The guest DJ for the night—Kensington—is talking animatedly to an older woman. She looks just like Becks described her, down to the rainbow-hued braids woven in between her dark hair. And when she shakes her head defiantly, I almost stagger. My heart begins knocking against my ribs.

Because in the light of the club, her eyes from this distance appear to be a pale light blue.

And if I'm having this reaction…

But then something happens that makes my eyes widen. Kensington leans up and presses her full lips—lips I could swear I've seen before—against the older woman's cheek. The woman lays her head against the girl's multi-hued one before they lean in to give each other a quick hug. I whirl around, wondering if Ward processed what I just did or if he's trying to find a way to talk to the DJ before she slides back into the booth for her next set.

Damnit. I can't spot him where I left him. Despite promising me he wasn't going anywhere, he must have slithered off into one of the dark nooks built around the upper deck that overlooks the spectacular dance floor.

Hoping I don't make a mistake by approaching the young woman on my own, I look around for Kensington, but she's already disappeared. *Argh*. Wondering if the woman knows where she might be, I approach her slowly. I frown when I notice she's pointing a little device outward toward the crowd and is looking down at her tablet, frowning. Clearing my voice bravely, I touch her arm gently. "Excuse me."

Her short brown hair whips my way. Behind tortoiseshell glasses are a pair of friendly eyes, despite the seriousness of her features. "May I help you?"

"Umm. I'm really not certain if you're supposed to be recording, but it's my first time here. I know I was told there's no cell phones without approval. I'm guessing that has something to do with no pictures. And I'm not certain if the artist allows for recordings." I wring my hands together, not entirely faking my anxiety.

Her face softens. "Miss…"

"Fahey." Crap. Why did I give her my real name? With all the news circling about XMedia, if she's a reporter, she'll probably figure out who I am in a nanosecond.

"Miss Fahey, this isn't recording equipment."

I frown. "Then do you mind if I ask what you're doing?" When she jerks back in surprise, I rush on to explain, "I work for an entertainment law firm, so I'm kind of freakish about the rights of artists."

She immediately relaxes. "I'm actually testing to make sure the sound is good. The normal person who does this for Austyn isn't here tonight. She likes the music she's written to be heard at a certain level over the music she's mixing over."

"What do you think of the music?" I ask, curious.

She looks around before confessing, "I suppose I should say I love it."

"You don't?"

"Well, I do. But I'm terrified for her. When I think about the fact she cashed out her college fund to do this. And her living here in the city…"

Confusion draws my brows together.

She waves her hand in the air. "I apologize. Consider it a mother's lament over her daughter's teenage rebellion working out so brilliantly."

My eyes pop out of my head. "You mean…Kensington is your daughter?"

"Indeed. And Austyn would be terribly embarrassed, but if you spend a great deal of time in these clubs, you really should wear these." Sliding her hand into her jeans pocket, she pulls out a pair of foam earplugs. "I'm sorry. I should have introduced myself. Dr. Paige Kensington. I'm an audiologist."

Becks's Paige? This can't be possible. "But…" Just as I'm about to ask her more questions, an arm bands around my waist tightly, and I freeze in terror.

A dark room. Spinning. Lights flashing. Music playing.

Someone touching me.

My fight-or-flight instinct kicks in. I begin to struggle with everything inside of me before a furious voice I recognize pierces through the fog of yesterday that I started to sink into. "I realize you were upset before you went into the restroom, *darling*, but I'd have thought you might be over it." Ward's voice is like ice shards next to my ear.

I collapse against him as the past recedes, and shame washes over me. I turn my face away from him.

"I'm sorry. I didn't know it was you. I was advising Dr. Kensington there was no recording in the club," I manage to gasp.

He tugs me next to him. His grip loosens noticeably. "That's club policy, ma'am."

"As Miss Fahey made me aware." Her piercing green eyes stare into mine. *Green, not blue.* Somehow, I dimly manage to note that.

"I'm so sorry for interrupting your work." I'm embarrassed and anxious to scurry away.

Dr. Kensington glares furiously at Ward. "*You* shouldn't be. But right now, I almost wish it did record. No person should ever be terrified like Miss Fahey was. Ever. Are you okay?"

Robotically, I nod. I want to run into the restroom and hide, but I can't. I just can't. Not now. I'll never leave, and I have to. I need to go now. Panic begins to well up inside of me, choking me. My breath comes out in short pants.

What was so beautiful before has turned terrifying. My head swivels from side to side, searching for the monsters hiding in the corners.

Because they're real. I know they are.

"Maybe I'll still speak with Marco." She gives me a woman-to-woman perusal before scooting around us and slides further down the rail. Her arm shoots out back over the balustrade, but her focus remains on us.

I immediately step away from Ward, unable to care what all of this means for Becks. As for me, well, while I got to experience something I never thought I would, I shakily manage, "I'd like to go."

Ward's expression gives nothing away. He simply extends an arm for me to pass him which I do with a wide berth. I shoot a quick look over my shoulder right before we leave. I see Dr. Kensington speaking with the man from the dance floor and gesturing. His head snaps up. I duck my head and slip out the door, unwilling to make a scene.

For the first time, I understand Sula's regrets. Maybe if I hadn't spoken up all those years ago, I would have recovered enough to have lived some sort of a life.

Or maybe, my life would have been that much worse because I wouldn't have my honor to wrap around me when there's nothing else to hold on to and cry.

ANGELA

Conversation starter: Did you catch B.A.D.A.S.S. on TV last night? Who do you call when you hit rock bottom? #lightsoutonbroadway
— **Viego Martinez, Celebrity Blogger**

A short while later, we're ensconced in Ward's Mercedes on our way back to Carys and David's. There's not a lot of space in these luxury vehicles, I think absurdly. I can feel the heat of Ward's body filling the small space without the additional comforts of the seat warmer. And the knowledge that two people can warm a vehicle simply by sitting in it calms one part of my heart while terrifying the damaged part of my soul.

What the hell am I going to do? Do I dare to explain?

The silence between us is oppressive as the miles fly by. But the part of me still shaken from the flashback wonders if it wouldn't have been better for Ward to go alone. I manage to get that much out, causing him to laugh bitterly as he downshifts.

"Do you think so? You likely found out more from just being personable to Dr. Kensington—I assume a relation to the DJ?" I nod but don't offer more. Ward continues. "—than I found out from bluntly asking Louie about whether Kensington was worthwhile to take on as a client when I saw him head back to the office—which is where I disappeared to, by the way. He waylaid me meandering on about how talented she was."

"Oh. I wondered where you were."

Ward makes a sound I can't interpret. "Yeah. So, I figured out I made three major mistakes today." Before I can ask what he means, he immediately launches into, "First, I came into this being a complete jackass, and that started long before we walked into the club."

"I get Becks not letting you in would be a problem; Carys too. I just don't understand what I did that offended you." I try to steer the conversation from where I don't want it to go.

But no luck. Ward doesn't take the gambit. Instead, he plows on. "Second, I scared you. I deeply apologize for that."

I open my mouth, but nothing more than a squeak comes out.

"I mean it, Angie. I am truly sorry. I didn't intend to cause you fear."

My head spins as his word ricochets inside. *Fear, fear, fear.* I lean my head back, uncaring anymore of hurting leather or my hair. "Fear is exhausting."

"Yes, I imagine it is."

After a few moments of silence, I manage to get out a "Thank you." I don't know what to do with his apology other than say that. My head spins as Ward apologized for something that he could have brushed off as playacting as part of our roles. Yet, I couldn't get a real apology for what truly happened. I discreetly dab at wetness on my face. "Most people don't apologize."

His eyes cut over to me, and there's something in them I can't interpret. But his jaw clenches harder. His hands tighten on the steering wheel. "I never intended to...I hope you believe me when I say I'm not the kind of man who would hurt a woman. Any man—and I use the word loosely—who harms a woman should be shot." His eyes flick over.

When I can finally form words, I whisper, "You're guessing."

"And you're not denying it."

Damnit. "It's...I don't..." My shallow breaths are so close together they're almost causing me to hyperventilate. Finally, I manage, "You can't know."

"I do now." If anything, that causes his hands to tighten further. This angry, almost violent contradiction to his previous words soothes me. It reminds me of the reaction my grandfather had when he found out the full truth of the story. Ward Burke, a man who I always thought was lost in his own way, seems to be more righteous than I originally thought. I guess we both made the wrong assumptions about each other.

"Ward?"

"Yes?"

"I think you're going to snap your steering wheel in half." That drags a reluctant smile from his lips just as we pull up at Carys's building. Ward double-parks before jumping out and opening my door. After helping me out and escorting me inside, I blurt out, "You said there were three things."

"I did, didn't I?"

"What is it?" I hold my breath as I ask.

He keeps a respectful distance but leans just his head in. "I wasn't ignoring you. I was ignoring what I was feeling. There's no possible way to ignore you—" He leans back before tacking on the nickname Louie called me earlier. "—Angel."

The warmth that steals through me frightens me. I take a step back and press the button for the elevator. The doors open behind me.

"Angie?"

"Yes?"

He holds out his hand. In it is my cell phone. "I think you might want this? Though honestly, it might be time for an upgrade."

My cheeks flame for multiple reasons. "Thanks for remembering."

His arm drops to his side. "I guess that's it. I'll see you in the office tomorrow."

"See you then." Where maybe if I go back to hiding in a mask on the outside, I can somehow live on the inside. I press the button for the right floor, and finally I'm alone and able to absorb everything that happened.

There was so much good that happened—the shopping, Carys, and the club, well, parts of it—but does it outweigh the fear I felt for that instant? I reach for my phone to ping Sula when I groan aloud. "I can't tell her this."

"Can't tell who what?" comes a voice from the side.

"Oh, my God!" I shriek. Standing at the elevator entrance is Carys. She holds up her cell.

"Ward called. He said you might be upset over something that happened tonight."

I open my mouth to deny it, but nothing can stop the fresh tear that tracks down my cheek. I'm grateful I don't have to say anything to Carys about my past because she already knows it. Prior to my employment background investigation, I gave her a full disclosure of the information any investigation agency would dredge up.

Carys wraps her arms around me and just holds on. And for a few minutes, I absorb the strength in her tiny body. "I wish you knew how remarkable you are, Angie. I don't know how you've managed to stay standing amid the lies."

I open my mouth, and what comes out surprises me. "If I don't stay standing, then I'll fall. Then they won the war I've been fighting all this time."

She squeezes my waist hard before guiding me in the direction of her condo. "Let's get you into a shower so you don't have to sleep on that hair."

I stop. "Carys?"

"Yes?"

"I think I learned some things tonight, which we'll talk about tomorrow at the office. But one thing you should be aware of is your brother thinks I'm together with Becks."

She laughs softly. "Sometimes I wonder if it's these men who want to be with Becks so damn badly. While we adore him, we know better. The man would drive a sane woman mad in under ten minutes."

And after a night of emotions that have spiked up and down, I now add one more to the list. An upward one.

Laughter.

Certain if I close my eyes in this strange room I'll trigger my nightmares, I desperately lie awake searching for anything to keep my mind from going where I can't let it travel. Shoving the covers aside, I get out of bed and make my way over to a seating area closer to the window.

It's 4:30 in the morning. Quickly calculating the time difference, I text Sula. I can't call. I stayed at my boss's last night.

Her reply comes within seconds. *Everything okay?*

Long night at the office. Although Sula knows how close I am with Becks, there's still much that can't be shared due to his attorney-client privilege. *It was a dressy thing.*

I could tell. You looked beautiful. Want details after you've slept some.

Will do. I include a smiley face I don't feel after that.

Her next comment has me choking back a bark of laughter. *Was "Winsome Ward" there?*

God, did you seriously call him that? I demand.

Oh come on, Angie. Don't tell me you didn't realize your boss, who BTW just hit the world's most eligible bachelor list AGAIN, is a hottie?

He's my boss. I try to use that as an excuse.

And?

And I want to tell her that he turns hot and cold more often than a poor, suffering woman going through a change, but I can't. I want to say he's a jerk, but that's not true. My fingers fly, but my thumb hovers over the blue arrow to send her the message in the window.

There's something about him that scares me.

Instead, I use the backspace button to delete the message before lamely sending her a shrug emoji.

As Sula types out a diatribe about Ward, I think about how different he was with me once he put what he thought was the piece of my puzzle in place.

Too bad it won't last, I think wearily. Too bad once he digs up the whole story, I'm sure he'll look at me the way the rest of the world does.

Like I wasn't the victim but the perpetrator.

CHAPTER NINETEEN

WARD

God exists because he created coffee. It's how I write this column day after day.
— **Moore You Want**

There's one more thing I learned tonight. There are worse things in life than death.

It's the way Angie reacted to me. Christ, that tonight tops the list of the worst feeling ever. My stomach still clenches over the anguish lingering on her face when I left her at my sister's.

I sit forward on the sofa in my home office and berate myself again. Maybe if I hadn't acted like such a jackass before… But then I pick apart the events of the evening, from the moment we walked in the door and she held my hand to our time on the dance floor, and realize nothing would have stopped her reaction. "I came up behind her and slid my arm around her waist. It was that millisecond…" Before she started struggling.

I want to hurl.

I managed to catch a glimpse of her broken eyes. *No, not broken. Shattered,* I correct myself. Then for her to inadvertently confirm it... I toss my drink back and let the burn combat the acid trying to crawl its way up my stomach.

It was merely a guess that Angie was a victim of sexual assault. When she confirmed it, I felt an anger so pure course through me, I didn't know how to deal with it. Instead of comforting her, I'm the one who needed reassurance—from her. Knowing nothing about what happened to her, possibly damaging her healing further, this extraordinary woman offered me an olive branch I certainly don't deserve.

"How did I not realize there was something intrinsically wrong all these years?" Then I answer my own question. "Idiot. Because you refused to let yourself get to know her. You took one look at her two years ago and realized she was everything you could ever want—a sexy as fuck, dedicated, family-oriented woman whose loyalty can't be questioned. Unlike your own."

She's everything I've tried so hard to demonstrate to everyone around me over and over that I can be. And tonight, I damaged some of her hard-earned serenity. I don't know how I'm certain of that, but I am. I hate myself even more than I usually do, and that's normally quite a bit.

I lean forward and press the leaded crystal against my forehead. "What happened, Angie? How can I help you? How can I fix this? Us?" I suddenly remember Carys saying Angie was staying at her place tonight because Angie lives outside the city. "Did someone assault you on the train? Goddamn, we have enough money to send a car daily to pick you up." Feeling like I can finally do something, I surge to my feet and make my way to my desk.

But when I try to access Angie's personnel file, I find it's password protected. "Damnit, Carys," I curse my sister, now knowing why it likely is. Reduced to sending Carys an email with my recommendation, I outline my thoughts and mark it as high priority. At the end, I type, *It would have helped to have had some background on our employee so I didn't cause any kind of lasting damage to our working relationship.* Then I press Send.

Let my sister noodle on that one.

"What else can I do?" I ask aloud. Angie does so much for us, it's almost inconceivable. Between me, Carys, and David, every single day she manages the office for three high-functioning legal personnel as well as dealing with the idiosyncrasies of all the celebrities who contact us. She's a consummate professional—excluding the antics Becks normally drags her into.

Airplane fights using Post-its.

Becks making a chain of paperclips between his nose ring and his earring that ran under his arm. And finding no sympathy from Angie when he got it caught on his suit jacket.

Angie daring Becks to go scrub the bathroom while she was taking notes for Carys and me during a conference call for Wildcard only for him to come out with a full face of her makeup.

And for the first time, I find myself laughing aloud when I think of some of them, knowing he did it to put a smile on her otherwise somber face. But Angie? Tonight was the first time I heard her laugh. What would it take to make that happen regularly?

Suddenly, I have an idea.

I wince as I set the alarm on my phone for much earlier than I normally arrive at the office. Angie's always been at our beck and call. Maybe if I grovel while showing my gratitude for everything she does, she'll laugh again.

If not, she can laugh at the fact I'm groveling for anything. Especially for her forgiveness for even momentarily sending her back into the darkness.

"Listen, you have to know who I'm talking about. She's about five nine, gorgeous red hair. Probably orders a massive amount of food every time she comes in," I argue with the counter person.

"Mister, if you knew how many people come through the door who might meet that description," the young girl tries to reason with me.

Desperately, I try to think of another way to get Angie's order when she always knows ours. "Listen, she always orders us the same thing. Croissants, egg sandwiches. Three different kinds of lattes. Well, four if Becks is going to be there," I mutter to myself, or so I think.

"Wait? Are you talking about *Angie*?" the salesperson exclaims.

I close my eyes in relief. "Yes! Then you know what she drinks?"

"If you'd only have said her name." I feel reprimanded by a girl easily ten years younger than me as items begin to race across the register screen in a shorthand computer code known only to those experienced with this kind of software. But I recognize words like "latte" and "skim," which makes me relax. "Angie's the best. Super nice. Even if we're in the middle of a rush, she just steps aside and lets us process everyone else orders. Are you one of the people she works for?" Her head tips to the side quizzically.

"Yes."

"You're lucky to have her. She pointed out a few things that could be changed to make us more efficient just to be nice. I thought our owner was going to genuflect at her feet. He owns a chain of places just like this. Offered her a job on more than one occasion."

Something curdles in my stomach at the idea of Angie ever leaving LLF. Whipping out my credit card, I hand it over to pay for the bill, all the while wondering if Angie was ever interested. Now that I've seen parts of her I never knew existed before last night, I hunger to know more about her.

Even something as stupid as her coffee order.

There's a long period of silence in front of me, so long that I find the girl staring down at my black card with a completely blank expression. "Is there a problem with it?" I flip open my billfold, ready to extract one of a half dozen more just like it.

"Are you *the* Ward Burke?" she whispers incredulously. Her eyes catalogue my face before she begins to flutter her hand in front of her face. "Oh, my God. You *are*."

I wince. "I'd appreciate, for both Angie's sake and mine, if you didn't make a scene."

"I can't believe Angie knows you and never said a word. Every morning, the girls gush about who's trending for the celebrities. And your name is always at the top of it."

I feel myself blushing. Christ, I know it happens, but I still don't get what on earth about my life is so interesting that it *trends*. I cough to clear my throat. "I hope you don't pester Angie with questions about any of the stuff you read." *And I hope to God none of it is true*, I pray silently.

Even though when I was younger I was accepted into certain circles because of the school I attended, those circles widened once the number of zeros after my bank account did. The reality is while Carys and I could both decide to quit working tomorrow and not put a dent in the money we have, that isn't how we were raised. We've both barely touched the interest of the trust fund our parents left to us. I can hear my father's voice inside my head. *"Hard work will bring you lifelong friendships you will cherish more than any amount of money wasting away in a bank account. Remember that, Ward."*

So, while I have the capability to live beyond most people's imagination, I still work hard. I enjoy the company of friends. And beyond anything, I cherish my family. How is that any different from any normal man? I wonder.

The young girl's stammering voice interrupts my thoughts. "No, sir... We wouldn't... Angie's..."

My voice turns almost sinister when I ask, "Angie's what?"

"Angie's special. She always has a kind word for everyone here, compliments for new hairstyles, that kind of thing. She spends time getting to know people." She finishes ringing up my order, and I swiftly sign the touch pad, leaving a large tip. "I feel bad though."

Her words cause me to pause as I'm slipping my card away. "Why's that?"

"Angie's one of the sweetest women I've ever met, but there's a cloud hanging over her."

I'd like to refute the coffee savant's words, but I can't. Instead, I jerk my chin up. "Have a good day..."

"Mara." She points to the pin attached to her apron.

"I appreciate your assistance," I tell her sincerely.

"There's a survey at the bottom," she rushes to inform me. "If you complete it, and it's favorable, I'm entered to win extra time off. I'd appreciate it if you took the time to do that. I could use it around the holidays, Mr. Burke."

Normally I'd throw away the receipt as soon as I expensed the charge, but thinking about Angie, I know she's likely completed every single one. Deliberately, I reach into my pocket and pull out my Mont Blanc and write "Mara" on the receipt before flashing it to her and slipping both the pen and the receipt back into my suit coat.

She beams at me before pointing to the Pick Up sign where I can get our to-go order.

While I'm waiting, I realize I now have more questions about Angie than I do answers—something I wasn't expecting after I came into this little cafe that smells like heaven.

And it appears I can only go to one place to get the answers I want.

CHAPTER TWENTY

ANGELA

Roses are red, Violets are blue. What would you do if Ward Burke bought breakfast for you? One of our loyal readers got this snap of him carrying this tray of drinks and bag of goodies. After zooming in really close, I spy a cup marked with a "C." Could that be for his sister, Carys? Oh, to be adored by one of the world's most eligible bachelors that much.
— **Fab and Delish**

"Here." Carys hands me a cup of steaming coffee when I enter the kitchen the next morning. "You look like you need a pot of this, but we have to get to the office."

"That's okay. It's not your job as my boss to keep me caffeinated."

"No, but as your friend, I'm worried about what last night did to you." The underlying concern in her voice causes me to part my lips to tell her what happened.

To trust.

Fortuitously, David walks into the kitchen at that moment carrying Ben, who looks like a corduroy sausage in his cold-weather gear. "Mama!" he cries, reaching for Carys.

Carys hides her frustration at being interrupted before taking her son into her arms. "Umph! I swear this might keep you warm, but it makes you feel like a small tank." Finding the only bare skin on Ben's neck, Carys begins laying kisses there before pressing them all over his face.

Apparently this is a normal morning ritual, because he starts shrieking. "Daddy, save me!"

I step into the shadows as David recovers his son. Husband and wife exchange a quick kiss and quiet words before David gives me a smile and a "See you at the office to debrief."

I murmur, "Lucky me," before lifting my coffee to my lips.

David grins before disappearing from sight.

"Give me just a moment, Angie." Carys follows them to the door.

I continue to drink my coffee and wonder what it would be like to be loved like that, unconditionally, despite the obstacles I know they overcame to be with one another. Shaking my head, I place my now empty mug on the counter. *It will never happen for you, Angie. There's no one out there who wonders what it's like to love you. They think they already know.*

My head is bowed when Carys comes racing back into the kitchen. "I'm so sorry. I should have warned you mornings around here are a bit hectic."

"That's fine. Besides, it's almost time for me to get going anyway. My boss likes things to be ready when she gets there." My voice is husky even to my own ears.

"Angie, is everything all right? Is there anything you want to tell me about what happened before we go into work?"

How do I explain that the night was nearly perfect? It was everything I could have dreamed of minus those two minutes where reality slipped back in to ruin my life. Again. That what I want was to erase that moment in front of Dr. Kensington, to be anyone but myself? The psychologist I saw for years said one day I might have to explain my past to someone who didn't know about it. I'd laughed in his face and said, "Right now, it's inconceivable anyone doesn't know about it." And yet, it appears that might be the very situation I find myself in. And truly, was one kiss, one night worth risking everything? I open and close my mouth before concluding, "No. If it's important, it will be discussed with everyone."

"Then just give me a moment to get my coat. We'll take a car over this morning. That's what took so long—David and I were arguing about him using the service." There's a loving exasperation in her voice.

Realizing the subject is dropped for now, my humor kicks in. "He's still not used to everything, is he?"

"It's been thirteen years and I'm not used to it. But on a morning like today, I'm grateful my parents left me in a position where I can use the car service this building offers so my husband, son, and trusted *friend*—" I flush up to the roots of my hair as she continues. "—don't have to freeze walking in this obstinate weather. Now, you're right. I do like getting to work early. And I'll bet you someone's going to be camped out there—reporters be damned."

"Becks," I conclude grimly. The two of us exchange wry glances before we make quick work of righting the kitchen. Soon we're heading down the elevator ourselves and requesting a car to head toward Rockefeller Center.

"I must be hallucinating," Carys drawls as we enter the conference room.

I'm in such shock, I can't string two words together. Becks wasn't camped out on our doorstep, but he is inbound. I received a text while we were in the car on the way. I had been furiously typing instructions as Carys rattled them off and asked her to text him back to calm him down.

She did, and Becks—being the soul of patience and decorum—decided sitting on his hands doing nothing wasn't going to work for him. "Because making our life easier is such a priority," I grumbled.

Carys snickered. "I just told him that."

My head snapped up. "You didn't."

"Of course not. He's our biggest client. But oh, the temptation, Angie. The urge is almost overwhelming." We both laughed before Carys asked me to get some food after the morning rush.

"Shut up," Ward responds as he lays out an assortment of pastries on the table. "It wasn't a big deal."

"Are you feeling okay?" Carys asks. Then she whirls to me. "I thought you said there was nothing to worry about."

Before I can say a word, Ward jumps in. "Angie had a bit of a rough night. Cut her some slack. Here." Ward walks directly up to me with a hesitant smile, holding out a cup, my name scrawled on the side. "This is for you."

It's a latte made exactly how I'd order it. "How—" I stammer. I clear my throat and try again. His gaze never wavers. "How did you know what I drink?"

"I asked. They said you always drink the same thing."

He asked? I blink slowly, accepting the drink from his outstretched hand. "Thank you. That was sweet."

From behind me, a perfectly pitched trill of laughter sounds. "Ward? Sweet? Jesus, did Houde pump some kind of herbal essence into the air last night?" Becks saunters into the conference room. As he passes by me, he studies my wan features. His face hardens. "Screw it. I don't care if the damn paps make up secrets to sell about me. Someone better tell me why Angie looks like she didn't sleep a wink."

I open my mouth to answer, but Ward jumps in. "We had a bit of an altercation last night."

Becks growls, "I hope you punched the fucker who got in her face."

"Kind of hard to do that to myself."

"Then allow me." Becks cocks back his arm to throw a punch.

I don't know why I do it, but I jump in front of Ward. Just as Becks's arm starts to swing forward, I fling my coffee at him. His surprise causes him to jump backward as the warm liquid rains down all over his trademark white silk shirt. I yell, "Stop it, Beckett! It's *fine*! I handled it. Okay?"

I feel the eyes of everyone in the room on me as I step forward and shove my finger into a stunned Becks's chest. "And just to let you know, you have *much* bigger issues to be worrying about."

Tension that was starting to leech from his face snaps back. "Why?"

I roll my shoulders before I say, "I could be looking at her right now."

The room goes static at my announcement. Becks swallows hard, pain in his eyes. "You spoke with Kensington, then?"

"No." My words cause Becks's face to deflate. "But I met her mother."

His eyes bug. "Paige? You talked to Paige?"

"She's lovely."

"I can confirm that, though I *still* don't know..." Ward begins.

"Shut up, Ward. I'll fill you in later. Not now," Carys hisses. She gestures for me to continue.

"I'm beginning to get the... Umph."

"Did you get the NDA?" Carys probes gently.

I shake my head in defeat.

"What happened?" Becks's voice is tortured, and I turn away, feeling like I let him down.

Before I can apologize, Becks reaches out a hand and squeezes mine. "No, don't say anything else. Thank you, Angie. I realize it must have been terrifying for you. You have no idea how much I appreciate it."

Chest heaving, lips trembling, I whisper, "It wasn't. It was incredible. Exhilarating. Everything I thought it would be, until—"

"Until it wasn't?" Becks shoots a dirty look behind me. I can only imagine the face Ward must be making because the ink on Becks's neck begins to pulse.

"Something like that." Drained, and in desperate need of caffeine, I head for the door. "I'll be right back."

"Angie." Ward's voice stops me in my tracks.

I whirl around to face him. When I do, something cracks in the air between us. The urge to step back from the lash of it is overwhelming, the intensity is so strong. But I stand my ground. "Yes?"

"If you go downstairs to replace the coffee you threw at Becks stepping in to defend me, I'm going to be royally pissed." Ward moves across the carpeted floor like a sleek panther. Slowly, holding my eyes, he brushes his fingers against mine. Just the tips. A casual movement that could mean anything from comfort to solidarity.

I start but don't move away. I'm frozen in place like a startled doe. Somewhere in the recess of my brain, I hear Carys whisper, "Well, I'll be damned." But I'm too apprehensive of what will happen if I break the moment—from the contradictory emotions of tenderness and anticipation in Ward's eyes.

The tension finally drops when he steps back. Turning to his sister, Ward demands, "Don't you think of finishing this conversation without me. I'll be right back."

"I wouldn't think of it," Carys confirms.

"Especially now," Becks growls.

"Does that mean you're finally reading me in?" Ward demands of Becks.

"I guess I have to," Becks replies petulantly.

Narrowing his eyes just a bit, Ward doesn't say another word to anyone before disappearing out of the office. I almost wish Carys and Becks would fill the air with chatter instead of their intense speculation.

I'm relieved when David strolls into the office. That is until he asks, "What happened? Ward asked me if I'd got my own coffee since he was replacing one for Angie…whoa! Becks, what the hell did you do to deserve to be baptized this morning? And so early?"

Now, no one will stop talking as they catch David up on the morning's events. And when Ward comes in carrying my new coffee, he presents it to me with a courtly bow. "For defending my honor, Angel."

When he stands, I want to hurl this cup at *him*. Especially when Becks demands, "You and you," pointing at the two of us. "Start from the beginning. Tell me what the hell happened last night."

I begin to walk everyone through the night from the moment we entered the doors up to the point where I started speaking with Paige face-to-face. Becks doesn't ask any questions throughout my recitation, but his tattooed hands begin to clench together fiercely as if he's reigning in his emotions.

And they're not good.

"You liked her," Becks finally asks.

I nod. "She was open, gregarious even."

"Until she misunderstood what was happening between Angie and me," Ward interjects.

"Dr. Paige Kensington. Paige always was smart," Becks drawls, anger beginning to chill his blue eyes.

"Watch your tone, Beckett," Ward snaps.

"And, here we go again," Carys sighs before she drops into a chair. "Angie, be a love and see if my brother picked up

PERFECT ASSUMPTION · 223

croissants in his quest to sweeten up all of our moods." Her smile is kind, but her eyes are wicked. She knows by getting me out of the range of male posturing, we might be able to get down to the reason Ward and I were thrown together last night.

After I rifle through the bags, I announce, "Raspberry, chocolate, or plain. What's your preference?"

"All three." I think her response is odd until she takes one of each and proceeds to move around the table, shoving one of each into Ward's, Becks's, and David's mouths respectively.

I can't stop the giggle that bursts out at the sight of them all agog at the tiny firecracker who has a cat-who-ate-the-canary look on her face. My hand comes up to hide my lips, but that's when I notice Ward's smiling at me with a smeared chocolate and powdered sugar smile.

I laugh harder.

Becks whirls around in shock. He's managed to get raspberry caught in his nose ring. I point my finger and try to tell him. "In your…goo in your…" But I end up crouching over as laughter overtakes me.

Carys announces, "I think you're forgiven, Ward."

My head falls back as black wingtips approach my peripheral vision. He crouches down next to me. "Can you forgive me for being a stupid ass, Angie? For being an overall bonehead?"

This close, in the light of day, I'm shocked by what I see in Ward's eyes. It's a reflection of the hell in my own soul. So stunned I am by my discovery, I reach out my hand. He grasps it immediately. "Yes. I can."

He pulls me to my feet. "Then, let's get this meeting started so we can boot Becks out and really get to work. Okay?"

I offer a hesitant smile, which he immediately returns. I don't remember the last time I felt like this. I'm standing on a ledge like a bird ready to take flight or fall straight to the ground.

It's terrifying. But even as I tremble, I know I like it.

CHAPTER TWENTY-ONE

ANGELA

We're running a contest! If you capture a picture of a celebrity out and about the city, then we'll send you all the Sexy&Social gear in our store. Just in time for the holidays. Get out those cameras, ladies. Beckett Miller has been spotted roaming the streets!

— Sexy&Social, All the Scandal You Can Handle

It was a long week. I'm not quite certain how I survived despite Ward putting things back on more than an even keel between us. Despite the fact it's the weekend and this might have been the most draining week I've ever worked for Carys, I hop on a train to return back to the office Saturday morning.

I'm not required to put in any extra hours, but next week will be a logistical nightmare if I leave everything until Monday. Phones will ring, emails will be ignored, and filing will pile up. That will make next week rival this one as one of the most heinous since I started working for LLF. There will be no way to catch up without this quiet time without anyone bombarding me with more work.

It's a perfect plan, I assure myself as I tuck my hair under a battered pink Yankees winter cap my grandpa gave me for Christmas when I was in my teens. Since there won't be any clients there, I dress for my comfort in jeans and a sweater. Grabbing a battered leather bomber jacket, I slip into a pair of comfortable sneakers and race out to my car.

Once on the train, my mind starts to wander as the aboveground phone lines swoop up and down outside the window. One, two, swoop. Three, four, swoop. Repeat. Over and over again until we break for the next stop. *Oh, if only my days would go back to being as predictable as this.* I wonder what it would be like to not be constantly on guard with every part of my soul. I shiver before huddling deeper into my coat against the chill that races through me.

Within the hour, we're pulling into Grand Central Station. I scurry off the train, head down, heading in the direction of the office. A few blocks later, weaving past the mass of people lingering around the plaza, I'm flashing my badge to get past security. I head in the direction of the gilded elevators when the security guard calls out, "Ms. Fahey?"

I stop in my tracks. "Yes?"

"I just wanted to let you know Mr. Burke went up to the office earlier so you weren't alarmed when you went upstairs and found everything unlocked."

I hate myself for the weakness spurned from years of emotional scars that lets me consider, even for half a second, turning around and walking back out the door. But I dig deep and find the core of steel that's forced me to wake up every day for the last ten years. "Thank you for letting me know, Burton. I would have been concerned."

"Not a problem. Call down if you need anything." He turns back to man his desk. I realize as I walk toward the elevators, my heart's pounding, but it's not because I fear being alone with a man in any situation like I used to. I'm just that little bit stronger. I feel my chin raise a little as each step takes me closer to the doors. I wonder if I'll ever be able to face my biggest fear—being alone with a man in a sexual situation.

Any man.

I push the button for the elevator and step inside. Punching the button for our floor, I'm so lost in my thoughts I almost don't get off when the elevator stops. I throw my arm out to prevent the doors from shutting and carrying me back downstairs. "Get yourself together, Angie. You have work to do," I lecture myself before stepping out of the elevator and making my way to the frosted glass door.

Yanking open the door to the outer office, I spy the door to the inner sanctum is wide open. The air is filled with the furious click of fingers on a keyboard. I suppose the right thing to do would be to greet Ward, but part of me hesitates. Despite the way we ended the week, I'm still not sure which Ward Burke I'll be confronted with.

Will he revert to the Ward who ignores me? The Ward who made me twirl during my first night out in ten years? The sweet man who kissed me in a candy store? The same one who sought out my forgiveness mere steps away with a pastry-lover's dream? Or the angry one who has demons locked inside him? He has more sides to him than I suspect his portfolio has ups and downs, and I simply don't have the energy to confront him. Not right now.

Sliding out of my coat and tugging off my cap, I hang them up before I boot up my computer terminal and get to work. *Focus on work, Angie,* I scold myself. *That's what you came in for.*

And opening up the hundreds of unread emails in my inbox, I begin to tackle them one at a time.

Just like I've handled each moment of every day of my life.

I'm doubled over laughing. Z sent an email to Carys wanting to file a complaint against the recording studio for not supplying him pickle juice for him to drink in between takes. "Oh, the complaints of the ego-ridden wealthy."

"Dare I ask what has you so amused?" Ward's voice is laced with amusement, but it still startles me into jumping out of my chair.

"Can't you wear a bell or something?" I protest, pressing my hand to my heart.

He strolls toward my desk, and the closer he gets to me, the more the air seems to be sucked out of the room. Ward Burke in a suit is devastating. But in a pair of worn jeans and an old Harvard Law sweatshirt is something no woman should ever see, not if she wants to ever get sleep ever again in her life. My breath catches somewhere in my throat when he bends over to read the message on my screen. But I think my heart stops completely when he barks out a laugh. "Well, I think Carys has a few options."

"Options?" I repeat numbly.

"About Z?" I must not react fast enough because Ward begins to wave his hand back and forth in front of my face. "Angie, are you okay?"

I give myself a mental shake. "Fine. Just fine. Sorry. I zoned out for a second. What should Carys do?"

230 · TRACEY JERALD

"Well, either she should send him a basket of all things pickled and tell him to deal with it, or she can actually waste his money on sending a legal letter to the studio. Either way, it requires a gentle touch—with a sledgehammer." Ward's fingers drum on the desk next to my mouse.

I imagine his touch would be gentle. I slap my hand over my mouth as if the words had been spoken aloud instead of snaking through my brain. I flush.

He frowns. "Are you okay?"

I clear my throat. "Fine. Just all this talk of pickles made me realize I haven't eaten."

"I was about to order food when I heard you out here. Would you like me to get you something?"

"Oh. You don't need to buy me anything, Ward. I can get my own food." His face falls, and I immediately regret my words. "What were you thinking?" *Breathe, Angie,* I berate myself. *It's not like Ward Burke has shown any further interest in you since that night at Redemption beyond anything more than your typing skills.* The man could have any woman in the world. What would he do with a woman so broken the pieces are scattered to the wind never to be found again?

A hesitant smile crosses his face. "How do you feel about pho on a day like this?"

I lick my lips in anticipation. "That sounds…"

"Yes?"

"Perfect. I love the way the broth is almost a warm oil and salty flavor on my tongue."

Ward makes a choking sound. I blink at him in confusion. "What did I say?"

"Nothing. You're right. What kind of protein do you want?"

Now it's my turn to blush. But I manage to stutter out my order.

It takes a few minutes before Ward calls the order in. "Fifteen minutes. Can you call down to Burton to let him know to clear the delivery guy up?"

"Sure." But when I reach for my wallet, Ward simply says, "Nope."

"Why not?" I demand.

"Because you've been working all day. The firm is paying for this one." His voice brooks no argument.

I drop my wallet back in my bag. "Whatever makes you happy, Ward. I'm certainly not going to get into a dispute—with a lawyer, no less—over something as ridiculous as who's picking up the tab for lunch."

"Then you won't mind when I ask for your company while we consume it either. I mean, you're here. I'm here. It would be ridiculous for us to eat separately when we have to share things like hoisin sauce," he points out.

"Wow, Ward. Now I know why you're such a catch. That logic will get to a woman every time," I joke.

Deadpan, he informs me, "No, that's because I have so much money I could fund the takeover of a small country. Really, I'm a dead bore."

Turning away, I mutter to myself, "Somehow, I doubt that."

When I face him again, a smile is flirting with his lips. "So, lunch? You and me? Maybe we can actually get to talk and get to know one another." Before I can insist there's nothing to know, he shocks me by saying, "This way I can get to know the real you instead of my making assumptions like every other jackass who takes one look at you and genuflect at your feet."

I'm not sure if it's anticipation or anxiety that causes my stomach to clench when I finally give him the answer he's hoping for. "Okay." But when I do, I'm rewarded with a blinding smile that makes my cheeks warm.

Oh, no.

It took me years, but somehow I managed to recover the little that's left of me to function. I'm not planning on offering it up over lunch because I've caught the eye of Ward Burke. He's exactly the kind of man I need to stay far away from:

devastatingly handsome, ridiculously wealthy, and too ingrained in my life.

That is if I ever planned on trusting a man enough with them ever again.

CHAPTER TWENTY-TWO

WARD

How many of your favorite celebs have favorite foods? Probably more than you think.

The entire world knows Brendan Blake would sell his wife's diamond ring for one of Corinna Freeman's blueberry lemon cakes. That is if supermodel Danielle Madison didn't do the deed first. Fortunately neither had to go to such drastic measures for their anniversary dinner last week. When the couple was spotted at their favorite French bistro, a special surprise was waiting for them—the brilliant baker herself! After hugs were exchanged by all, she sliced up their cake before sneaking out the kitchen.

— **Fab and Delish**

"Tell me about your family," I encourage Angie as I use chopsticks to pull long strands of noodles from the warm broth.

Angie, who just swallowed a final bite of bean sprouts, puts down her bowl. Wiping her mouth on the napkin, she begins. "Until last year, I lived with my grandmother. My grandfather passed away a few years before that."

"Did you always live with them?"

"No. I'm just not close with my parents. My grandparents were there for me after things in my life went beyond my control. It was important for me to be there for them later when they needed me as they got older. It's their home I live in outside the city."

"Are you happy there?" I slurp up some more noodles.

"I love it. I could never imagine selling it—not for all the money in the world."

"You sound an awful lot like Carrie right now," I remark.

"Oh? Why's that."

"That's what she said about our parents' home. She felt strongly about wanting to live there."

"And you didn't?"

"The people who made it a home for me weren't there," I declare.

"And the memories were making it worse for you than if you left," Angie guesses intuitively.

I gape at the beautiful woman across from me. We're eating in the boardroom so we don't get any of the pho on either of our desks. "That's exactly it. Everywhere I turned, I felt smothered. How did you know?"

"My grandmother knew she was passing, Ward. She encouraged me to sell the house if the memories overwhelmed me." Her smile is crooked. "Even at her age, I wonder if she would have done that very thing if I wasn't living with her when my grandfather passed."

"I'm sorry for your loss."

"And I for yours." Angie dips her spoon into her broth. "How long has it been?"

"Thirteen years." I pause for a moment since she had just lifted the spoon to her lips. After I'm certain she swallowed, I finish my explanation which hopefully will explain my behavior that I never had a chance to apologize for with Becks's nonsense. "On my birthday."

Angie's spoon clatters into her bowl. "Excuse me?"

"Yes. I'm sorry…" I begin.

"Don't you apologize to me!" Sparks fire from her blue eyes. "What was Carys thinking?"

"Well, when I came back and found her crying—"

"Ouch." Angie winces.

"Yeah. That sums up my feelings pretty well. But she believes wholeheartedly my parents wouldn't want me mourning them forever." What I feel is something I keep to myself.

"Now, I understand your behavior so much more that day. It was very much out of character for you. Cool, distant, yes. Angry?" She shakes her head back and forth.

Her analysis warms something inside me I didn't realize was frozen over. "What did you do with that money?" I ask, suddenly certain she didn't keep it. Because the woman who lives in her grandmother's home, who comes to work in dated but still-elegant clothing, who offered to pay for her share of lunch isn't the kind of woman to take close to five hundred dollars because a cake flopped on her clothes. I'd bet my condo on it.

Angie stands and walks over to the credenza. Opening a drawer, she pulls out the wad of cash I flung at the table. "You mean this money?" She gets closer and holds it out to me.

"What happened with your clothes? The ones that got ruined that day," I clarify.

"They weren't ruined. Not according to my dry cleaner."

"Then at least let me pay for the dry cleaning bill."

"Don't be ridiculous."

"It's only right, Angie. I did cause the incident that soiled them." I choose my words carefully because it wasn't an accident, but I wasn't trying to be malicious. She was collateral damage—something I'll never allow again.

"You. Will. Not. You just paid for lunch." She stomps her foot as she emphasizes her point.

I have to mash my lips together to prevent the grin from spreading across my face.

"Geez, Ward. If I wanted a man to buy me clothes, I'd have taken Becks up on his offer years ago. And he's one of my closest friends."

Just her mention of the other man brings a slight scowl to my face. "How did that come about anyway?"

"What?"

"You and Becks."

She opens and closes her mouth before she blows out a gust of air. Returning to her seat, she picks up her drink. "Becks recognized the real me" is her evasive answer.

"Oh? What's that supposed to mean?" I challenge her.

"Just like him, I'm a lonely misfit. I had planned on leading a very different life, but this is the path I was put on. Maybe that road wasn't meant to be, but how I learned that isn't something I discuss." Her fingers trail over the smooth surface of the wood of the conference room table. She suddenly frowns. "I'll share this because I think you of all people will understand it. People traipse through life treating emotions like they're disposable. And in this world of 24/7 news, of quick-hit attention spans, maybe people think emotions can be recycled. They're not. Some emotions are meant to scar your soul so deeply you don't know what it's like to live without them. They may not be comforting, but they're a part of you." Her eyes lift to mine. "Much as I imagine your parents' death has left that impact on you."

"Yes." It's the only word I can manage.

"Even beyond the things he brought to our attention recently, Becks has been through things like that. Things that changed him irrevocably. He recognized a like-minded person in me because of what happened. He's been the brother I never had—a rock, not a rock god. Other than Sula…"

"Who's that?" I interrupt, craving every bit of knowledge about the beauty in front of me.

"Sula was my freshman-year roommate. We've remained…close doesn't begin to explain it."

"I have friends like that." I'm thinking of the guys from prep school who held on despite my attempt to shove them away.

She nods. "Sula and Becks, they can truly appreciate how badly lies and assumptions did their best to destroy my life." While I recover from the bluntness of her statement, she asks, "Now it's your turn to answer a question."

"All right."

"Why did telling you that matter? Why was it so important for you to understand that after all this time?" Angie wonders.

Leveling a direct look at her, I answer, "Because I've been ridiculously jealous for two years: first of your 'family' that Carrie kept harping on about, then of Becks. I figured it was better to find out the truth from the source instead of relying upon gossip or innuendo if you're involved with anyone."

"Ward..." Angie's obviously flustered.

"Yes?"

"I'm not involved with anyone, but I'm not certain I want to be. I honestly don't know if I can be."

Open. Honest. Direct. And so beautiful that looking at her makes my eyes hurt. Is it any wonder part of me has no problem saying, "That's okay. Why don't you let me know when you are? In the meanwhile, we should work on being friends first. I think that's a good place to start. Don't you?"

"You want to be friends with me? Me?" Her voice trills shrilly.

I shrug nonchalantly. "Why not? It's a great way for us to get to know one another."

Her jaw sags open. Leaning over, I reach for her soup spoon and plunge it into her rapidly cooling pho. "Better eat while the soup's still hot." I lift the spoon to her lips.

She grabs the utensil from my hand. As our fingers brush, a current of electricity races across my skin. I'd give up every dime to my name to feel her hands on my body just to see what kind of charge we'd generate together. If a touch could cause such a reaction, I can only imagine a full touch would be more explosive than an atomic experiment used during Manhattan Project.

Then Angie completely undoes me by wrapping her lips around the spoon, drinking the minuscule amount of broth I had on it before lifting her bowl and toasting me with it and drinking the contents rather like the Beast in a long-ago children's cartoon movie I remember Carys being obsessed with. Even after she puts the bowl back down and I look at her in astonishment, she merely quirks a brow. "I don't hide things like food habits from my friends. I think the best parts of pho are the bean sprouts and the broth. That's why I said no noodles."

Even as I roar with laughter, Angie asks, "So, tell me what's made you decide to work with your sister?"

And I launch into a lengthy explanation about how Carys and I had always wanted to both be lawyers—like our father. "When we got older and she started clerking for a federal judge, I pretty much threw that plan out the window."

"Did you feel like it was a loss of something else in your life? Back then," she qualifies.

I pause. "Do you know you're the first person to ask me that question?"

"Surely not." When I don't respond, Angie's voice holds shock when she asks, "None of your friends did?"

"Back then, my friends were too concerned about drinking and scoring drugs. They were too worried about not being caught by their parents. We were a group of idiots at boarding school who thought we were too cool for any kinds of rules or regulations," I admit wryly.

"And yet, you became a lawyer."

"In the back of mind, I always knew what my future was. I never crossed over the line the way they did. Before, well, I'm sure I gave my family a few gray hairs," I add on when I catch her raised brow. "Especially with the whole underage drinking bit."

She doesn't say anything, so I ask, "What? You weren't a party girl?"

"There wasn't a different kind of law you wanted to go into?" Angie abruptly changes the topic.

I let her. I wipe my hands with the wipe before drying them on a clean napkin. "For me, contracts always fascinated me. I loved closing loopholes. I could spend hours talking about legal liabilities."

"Stimulating lunch conversation, Ward." Angie's smirking at me.

"It's better over dinner; let me assure you." We both chuckle before I become introspective again. "As for Carys, I don't know if things would have been different for her. But she's a phenomenon. I've learned more from her than from any single person I've worked for or from any textbook."

"You would have hated working with her at Wildcard." Angie's statement surprises me.

"Really? I was away at law school the first three years she was at Wildcard, so other than hearing about what a pain in the ass David was, I rarely heard about her time there. Then one day, she declared she was starting the firm."

Angie erupts in laughter. "Yes, David was very aggravating for and to her."

"I didn't recall her mentioning you worked for her then. And considering it was years I listened to her gripe, there wasn't anything about an "Angie" or an "Angela." I don't mention Carys has locked down Angie's file on our office computer like it holds state secrets.

"Carys was well respected and riding a wave to a *much* higher position within the company. But there's a strict no-fraternization policy at Wildcard. And there she was, working with David—day in and day out. It made her very..." Angie

244 · TRACEY JERALD

pauses for a moment while she struggles with finding the right word. She finally settles on, "Remote. Back then she was very much 'Burke' and not 'Carys.'"

"And working for 'Carys' is better?"

"Working for your sister has and always will be a lifesaver. But yes, seeing her this happy has been an incredible pleasure."

I settle back in my chair. "How long did you work for her before all of you left?"

"Maybe a year? I had completed my degree and was looking for a part-time entry-level legal position. Carys and David were working on a big project that involved a charity event for Brendan Blake and required a legal assistant. The rest is history."

"I'm glad it worked out." And I mean that sincerely.

"Me too…oh, God. Is that the time? I still have to finish pulling together Z's pack of pickle preferences before I head out for the day." Angie jumps to her feet. But before she dashes out the conference room, Angie pauses by my chair. And like a butterfly landing for just a moment, her fingers touch my shoulder hesitantly. "I'm glad we got to spend this time talking, Ward."

I hate that the openness, the safety, she felt at Redemption is erased, but glad she made the first move to break the physical barrier between us. With any other woman, I'd reach up and clasp their hand. But with Angie, I know she'd panic. I tip my head back and smile warmly up at her. "Me as well, Angie. We should do it again."

Her smile is hesitant, but I read the sincerity when she says, "I agree. Next time, you should let me pay. Especially since you didn't have to this time. Truly, it wasn't necessary, but it was a nice thing to do." Then she does flutter away.

I sit for a few more moments thinking about everything I learned about my legal assistant today. Food preferences aside, she's thoughtful, kind, and has absolutely no interest in my money. She's interesting and truly observes people.

This lunch ended up being much more than just a way to make amends. It broke through walls I built up around my heart the day my parents died. And maybe, it tore down a few of Angie's.

The question is what the hell I'm going to do about it?

CHAPTER TWENTY-THREE

WARD

The vote is in! Although he's not technically a billionaire (yet), Ward Burke tops your list as world's sexiest billionaire. But we'll let it slide. After all, he has to file taxes just like the rest of us mere mortals. We'll know then whether he attains that ten-digit number. After all, he earned his money the hard way. He inherited it.

— **StellaNova**

I lean against the doorjamb of the conference room while Angie presents the merits of purchasing an additional database to Carys.

"What are the benefits for us, Angie? All of this sounds impressive, but we're a small firm. Isn't it a bit too much?" Carys addresses the same question I was about to interrupt to ask.

"The pricing is different for small business."

"Well, there's that."

"But think of this, Carys. Not only would we be able to import databases like LexisNexis—" Angie names one of the world's providers of legal sources. "—directly into the system to ensure we have current case law, we could directly track the number of times you have to defend against a particular ruling. Think about it." Angie turns and plants her hands on the table in front of her. "You could champion change in entertainment law because you would have statistics to back up your..."

I helpfully supply, "Rants."

Both women's heads whirl in my direction. Angie's cheeks flush while my sister just mean mugs me as I push off the door and move into the room. "Like you both weren't thinking it."

Angie frantically shakes her head. "I would never say..."

"Angie's more tactful than you are, Ward. This is why we let her play with the clients first—you know, so we have some." Carys tosses some of her own back at me.

I move over to one of the chairs and drop into it. Relaxing back, I interlock my fingers behind my head before commenting, "Don't worry. She's rubbing off on me."

Angie gathers her papers together into a neat stack. "Doubtful."

"Haven't I been nicer to Becks as of late?" I chide. Without waiting for an answer, I inform my sister smugly, "I have been."

"That's because all your objections had no merit, Counselor. Now, why are you in here?"

"Because it's past six and your husband called me to ask where the hell you were. He said to tell you to buy the damn database and to put Angie out of her misery." I wink over at Angie, who flushes profusely under my attention.

"He would. He's been listening to her wax poetic about this system for six months," Carys grumbles.

"If you want more information, I can schedule more time," Angie offers.

Carys waves her hand in the air. "No. But don't you dare let them install a single thing while I'm in the office. I can just see it now. It would be the internet disaster part two."

"Yes, Angie. Save us all from my sister having an epic meltdown over problems all businesses deal with every single day—a lack of broadband."

"And that's my cue to leave." Carys stands.

As she rounds the table, she takes the time to slap me upside the head, prompting an involuntary "Ow!" from me.

She kisses the top of my head. "There, is that better?"

"You'd better leave before you don't go home in one piece," I mock.

She laughs on her way out the door, calling out her good-night to Angie. I open my mouth to ask what her plans are for the evening, but she beats me to it. "I know you miss your parents, but you're so lucky to still have your sister."

My whole body locks at her statement. "I've never thought of myself that way."

Our eyes meet across the broad expanse of polished wood. Hers are unguarded for the first time. In them, I drown in depths of undiluted pain and unconscious yearning. For what?

For family? Or, I swallow as I stand to tower over her, for me?

"Have dinner with me?" I manage hoarsely. "I think it's time for me to learn more about my friend. Don't you?"

"What? Ward, we tempted fate once making it out of Redemption unfollowed. I don't particularly feel like being news fodder tomorrow morning." Angie scoops up her papers and clutches them to her chest like a shield.

My mind whirls. Where can I take her where we could avoid being followed? Then a slow smile spreads. "Be ready in fifteen minutes."

"What? Ward, I can't go anywhere like this. I'm dressed for work," she protests.

I round the table cautiously until I'm standing right in front of her. "I think you look perfect just the way you are. And no matter where we go tonight, I'd be proud to have you on my arm."

With the way her cheeks glow, I feel about two inches tall about my idiotic demands for the night we went to Redemption. The reality is I just want Angie.

However I can have her.

I slip inside the back seat of the car with Angie. She frowns up at the driver until I greet him by name. "Hayden, thank you for picking us up this evening."

"My pleasure, Ward. The last time you called for me to do this, I believe you were three sheets to the wind after some law school reunion." His rebuke causes Angie to snicker.

"Way to help me charm the lady," I growl.

"The lady would do well to be aware of your predilection for partying one night a year if things are serious. These law school reunions get quite rowdy. Last year, in fact, Ward booted all over the back of this very car."

I cough the word "Tattletale" into my fist.

Which sets Angie off again.

"Angela Fahey, may I introduce to you our driver for tonight, my godfather, Hayden Wiltshire. He was my father's best friend," I clarify.

"A pleasure to meet you, Mr. Wiltshire," Angie offers.

"Ah, none of that formality with family."

Angie sputters, "But…"

"Make it Hayden while I tell you all the stories you won't read in those trash magazines about my boy here."

So on our drive to a tiny town on the edge of the Connecticut border, Hayden regales Angie with all the antics of my childhood, starting off when I challenged my mother on the belief of Santa Claus up to the day I lost my virginity. "But when he tried to sneak in through the dumbwaiter, I don't know whether his father's first inclination was to be impressed by his brains or to murder him for being so damn idiotic with his safety," Hayden concludes.

Angie, having dropped the barricade she normally wears, eagerly asks me, "What did your father do?"

"Grounded me for a month," I admit ruefully. "After my mother left the room though, he whacked me upside the head for scaring the shit out of them both and asked why I didn't simply ask for the alarm code."

"That's only because you were safe, boy. He sure as hell wouldn't have let you out of your building," Hayden interjects.

"Who says I left the building?" And we all laugh uproariously as we pull up to the curb of a tiny little southwestern cafe. "Let me get your to-go order, Hayden. Then you can pick us up at nine?"

"Works for me. I've got some reading to catch up on."

I open the door and reach for Angie's hand. She blinks rapidly as she exits the vehicle and gets her bearings. "I know where we are. We're in Ridgefield. I live maybe twenty minutes from here."

"I know."

"How?" Her voice holds a wealth of suspicion.

"I asked Carys when I called to make the car arrangements. I figured we would have dinner, and then I'd escort you home. If coming to your door isn't all right with you, I can hang out at the gas station while Hayden drops you off. He'll never tell me anything about your home, what you discuss. Nothing. I swear it, Angie. He's the most trustworthy man I know."

My heart trembles and hopes she'll let me in just a little after I opened up myself. But she merely nods before turning toward the door, not letting me know what path we're taking. "Why do I recognize his name?"

"He's been in the paper some—"

"Oh, lovely."

"—but that's because he's a federal judge." The minute I finish, Angie trips over her own feet.

"You mean to tell me that for the last ninety minutes, you've had a federal judge driving us around?"

I take her elbow and guide her to the cafe's entrance. "Trust me, he wasn't kidding about the law school reunion. I think the only reason he agreed to this was because you were here. He's still pissy about it."

She jerks to a stop. "Ward, can I ask one question?"

"What?"

"Is this a date?" She chews down on her lip.

I pull it out. "Do you want it to be?"

"I...I'd like to try it. I remember what they're like, but the last one wasn't chaperoned."

I clear my throat. "I thought you'd be more comfortable knowing we weren't followed." We approach the black-shirted member of the staff. "Two. Burke."

"Right this way."

As we're escorted to the table, I inform Angie, "There's nothing to worry about. Tonight's nothing more complicated than this."

And I might be hearing things, but after I seat her, I could swear she says, "Oh, yes there is."

CHAPTER TWENTY-FOUR

ANGELA

What happened to the simple art of conversation during a romantic evening between two people? Why does it have to be interrupted by the flash from a camera. Oh, yeah. I wouldn't have a job otherwise.

— Jacques Yves, Celebrity Blogger

Dinner was delicious. Conversation between me and Ward was as lively as the guitar player who stopped at our table. I opened up, telling him small things about me. Like Flower.

"So, you're saying this cat is a threat to your electronic devices?"

"Not just mine. Anyone's. I'm debating a seance or an exorcism."

"Have you wondered if she's just lonely and looking for attention?"

I pretend to give it some thought. "I've wondered if she's a descendant of the competitor's brand," I declare resolutely.

Ward and I share a grin before digging in to our own dishes.

"You talk about your grandparents but not your parents. Are they no longer with you?"

I sip some tea before answering. "I don't have parents. Not anymore."

"Are they part of the cause…"

"They were part of the effect. They chose to betray me rather than stand by me."

Ward's eyes frost over. "I would consider that complacent."

I place my fork down, my appetite gone. "No, you shouldn't."

He holds up his hands, palms up. "Angie, I have to trust you in this situation. I don't want to take the wrong step, make the wrong decision, and harm us."

"What us is there, Ward?"

"I don't know. But I'm curious about the one there could be. Aren't you?"

"I'm tired." The words pop out before I can stop them.

"Of what?"

"Of giving the past the power. I feel…" I glance away to gather my thoughts. Ward doesn't say anything. "My emotions are coming back so fast after being locked away for so long, I feel like I'm speed dating myself. One minute, I'm dating laughter, the next fear. Frustration, sarcasm. And then when I add you to the mix, I get confused." *Terrified.*

"Then don't add me." His voice is soft.

"I…what?" Did he say what I think he said?

"I promised we'd start this off as friends, Angie. I promised I'd *be* your friend. And if it takes a week, a month, or a year, I'm going to show you I can be the friend you need." He pulls out his phone and sends a quick text. Then Ward stands and takes my hand.

I place mine in it. "What's happening?"

"What's happening is it's late. And it's time for you to go home." He drags a single finger along my temple, getting it tangled in a loose lock of my hair. He lifts it to his lips before letting it drop and stepping back. "Go, Hayden's outside waiting to take you home. I'll see you at work tomorrow."

"Thank you, Ward."

"Good night, Angie."

I back away, not out of fear but because of the novel feelings washing over me as his eyes hold mine. I narrowly avoid missing the guitarist and blush to the roots of my hair. "Oops." That's when I turn and head out the door.

And just like promised, Hayden was waiting to take me home.

Alone in the back seat, I relive every moment of dinner. I whip out my phone, ready to text Sula, when Hayden's voice washes over me like a bucket of ice water. "He doesn't know, does he?"

No. Not now. Not when I just had the most perfect evening. I lift tormented eyes to meet Ward's godfather's in the rearview mirror. "No."

His head bobs up and down, but he doesn't say anything else until we pull up at my house. Wildly, I fumble with the handle, but I can't quite get it to open. Hayden turns his head so I can see his profile. "Angela, there is no punishment great enough for what happened to you. I say that not only as a judge, but as Ward's godfather. Anyone worth their legal salt could see the problems with that case."

My forehead hits the cold glass with a thunk. My breathing is jagged.

"Do you think he won't see it the same way?" Hayden presses.

"I want him to see me."

"Then let him in to do just that."

"I'm trying, and I've never wanted to try before him," I admit.

Hayden jumps from the car and opens my door. He holds out his hand to help me from the car. "Just know he'll recognize the truth, Angela." With a quick nod, he slips back inside the car to go back for Ward.

But as I trudge up the front steps to be accosted by Flower, I wonder if Ward will recognize that by being associated with me, I could topple the world as he knows it. He didn't ask for fame, but he also didn't ask for notoriety.

Deciding I need another point of view, I send a text to Sula. *Are you up?*

While I wait for her response, I feed Flower and then scurry upstairs, but the urge to shower, to wash Ward's touch off me fails when I reach my room. Instead, I sink down onto the floor and wait for Sula.

The phone rings.

"What's wrong?" she demands the instant I answer.

My voice hardly a whisper, I ask, "Is it always so scary?"

"What?"

"Feeling."

"If it's done right," she admits.

I tip my head back against my bed and gather my thoughts. "I'm wondering who punished me more for what happened that night. Was it the media or myself? Have I been punishing myself for what those bastards did to me for all these years?"

"If I thought that, I'd have kicked your ass. What's making you call me in the middle of the night questioning yourself."

"Not what. Who."

"Ah. Who is he?"

I muster my courage. "Ward Burke."

"*I. Knew. It*!" I have to pull the phone away Sula screeches so hard in my ear. There's a rustle of sheets as she gets comfortable. "Tell me everything. Is he seriously as…everything as the rags make him out to be?"

"No."

"Oh." Her disappointment is clear.

"He's nothing like the media portrays him and so much more than I could have ever given him credit for."

"Has he kissed you?" Sula's question isn't probing because she's trying to get the skinny on Ward. I know in my heart she's taking the pulse on my well-being.

"Once." My memory immediately calls up the scent of sweet chocolate enveloping us as his lips grazed against mine. "But it might seem crazy."

"What?" she asks eagerly.

"I remember being kissed before everything that happened. But since he figured things out, the way he acts toward me is much more intimate than a kiss. It's like he knows my heart's just coming back to life and he cherishes being along for the ride."

Sula sighs. "That may be the most romantic...hold on. Back up. He figured things out? Everything? He knows what happened at school?"

"Well, no. But after we went to Redemption and my attack there..."

"Stop talking." Sula's voice is no longer dreamy. She's pissed. "You had a panic attack at Redemption? We've talked since that night, Angie!"

"I know! But, I couldn't tell you..."

"Couldn't tell me what?" she snaps.

"It was Ward who set it off." My voice cracks. "Oh, God. What am I trying to do? Why do I think this can be healthy between us?"

"Breathe. Let's talk it out. Please, tell me what happened that night," she pleads.

So I do. When I'm done, she muses, "It wasn't him, sweets. It was simply a flashback. Your doctor said you would have those."

"I was doing fine. I was dancing. Do you know how long it's been since I danced?"

"With or without me?" And that's when I realize that over three thousand miles away, my best friend is crying just as hard as me. "I'm in awe of you every single day for the simple act of getting out of bed. And here you are, ten years later, dancing? You're a bloody miracle."

"Careful, Sula. You're starting to sound Irish." I swipe my fingers across my cheeks.

"Well, I'm about to sound like a prophet. You need to tell him the truth."

As if she were sitting across from me, I hold my hand out to ward off her words. "No. How can I? He already guessed enough."

"Because it's going to fester in between whatever is growing between you both until it breaks you apart. Give it time. You'll know when it's right. But if he's the one your heart wants, you'll feel it's the right thing to do," she predicts.

While the part of me that was raked over the coals so publicly shies away from her words, the part of me that's worked on the side of justice for too many years recognizes the truth in her words. Ward and I can only go so far without him knowing the truth. Hayden inferred as much earlier when he said, *"Just know he'll recognize the truth, Angela."*

"All right. Before this goes much further, I promise you, I'll tell him. But Sula?"

"Yes?"

"What happens if everything changes?"

"No matter what, everything is going to change. That's life. I'm just grateful you're finally living it."

"That's not what I meant."

"I know what you meant. And I don't know, Angie. But I'll always protect you with every resource at my disposal. You know that."

"You always have," I declare loyally.

"No." Her voice is tragic. "If I had, you wouldn't have lost some of the most precious years of your life." Before I can say anything in response, she asks me another question about Ward.

We spend hours talking about my everything and what she declares is her nothing. Because that's what you do with your confidant in the dead of the night when you're scared.

You hold on.

CHAPTER TWENTY-FIVE

ANGELA

Jack Daniels or Cristal? Rumors of a party at Beckett Miller's are surfacing, but the details are unclear. All I know is I wish I was invited regardless of what was served.
— **Viego Martinez, Celebrity Blogger**

"So you went on a date with Ward?"

I glance around furtively. "Shut up, Becks."

"Why? Is it some kind of top secret knowledge? It's about time you enjoyed life even if I expect your name is going to be in the newspapers again."

"No. He knows I have an aversion to it. Just not why."

Dawning comprehension flits across his face. His regal nose dips down at me, the light catching off his nose ring. "He hasn't put it all together?"

I run my fingers through my hair. "Becks, think about it. I was a freshman. Ward was what? A senior in college?"

"Actually, if I remember from dating Carrie, he was in law school by then. I have little doubt this was being talked about, but it's likely due to what happened to them," he muses.

"What do you mean?"

"Nuh-uh. Welcome to the world of mature dating, darling. We don't pass notes in class. If you want to know something about him, ask him yourself."

I crumple up a piece of paper on my desk and pelt him between his light-colored eyes.

"I'm wounded."

"Could you try to do more damage, Angie? It might help keep this a slow week where we could catch up." Ward's amusement over our antics is evident at the smile he shoots our way. He stops at my desk to drop off a fresh cup of coffee that's riddled with hand-drawn warnings symbols marked with "HAWT" in the middle.

I can't resist turning the cup in Ward's direction. I ask innocently, "Is this a temperature warning?"

He flushes. "Apparently some rag got a picture of me out running yesterday and another coming out of Sweom Studios."

Becks slaps his hand on his desk. "Well, that will certainly be interesting for Angie to look at later."

Ward scoffs. "Angie doesn't look at that garbage."

I hide my chuckle beneath a sip of perfectly brewed coffee. Then Carys storms out to join the fray.

"What on earth was Z thinking, Angie. He can't declare a preference on his favorite brand of pickles and not expect that crap not to be picked up by social media."

"This is why I cleared your schedule," I reply calmly.

"Now, I have a freaking pickle crisis on my hands. CEOs of pickle companies are screaming at his agent, who is in turn calling me asking if there's anything we can do." Her eyes narrow at Becks. "Tell me you're just here to give me your normal daily crap and you haven't pulled some shit that's going to make my day worse."

He backs away, appropriately wary. "Nothing. I swear it."

Not taking his word for it, Carys demands, "Angie?"

"Nothing in the feeds, Carys. For once, Becks is clean." I knock on wood as the words pop out of my mouth.

"Thank God for small miracles," Ward mutters.

Carys turns on him like a dog with a new chew toy. "You. Come with me. Just because you're the press's darling with that picture of you shaking your ass near Summit Rock in Central Park yesterday doesn't mean you didn't cause your own hashtag to trend on how many news sites?"

"Two hundred and eighteen," I pipe up.

Ward flushes. "It's not like I ask for it."

Becks slaps him on the shoulder. "None of us do. You'll do well to remember that." He and Carys exchange a complicated look before Becks announces, "And since there's no time for fun here today, I suppose I should head to the financier."

"What? You mean someone's actually doing something with your gobs of money other than throwing parties where no one wore anything but Cristal?" I prop my head on my chin, awaiting his response.

Becks saunters back. "Your information is totally off."

"Really?" Carys's voice is dry.

"Yes. It was Jack Daniels. And I wasn't there." And with that, Becks flings open our doors and saunters out.

The three of us wait until the doors close completely shut before we all burst out into laughter. "Did that really happen? I thought that story had to be complete rock lore," Ward asks.

I nod. "It's a complete nightmare. His place is trashed."

"But he's smiling like he just struck gold." Ward's confusion is obvious.

Carys sighs. "Let's be grateful for the small favors, shall we? And yes, it's true. I try to ignore as many stories about Becks as I can, but even I can't deny the noise ordinance charges I'm having to defend him on. I swear, half of Manhattan was at his home."

"And Becks was nowhere near there," I reiterate.

"Are you serious?" Ward's incredulous.

"Completely. He was down south visiting some family. He came back to find his whole place had been trashed. I thought Carys was going to have to find him a capital defense attorney, but nope. He's smiling."

"So did I. Oh, well. It's back to the grind."

The whistle Ward lets out when it's just the two of us is long and low. My eyes crinkle at the corners. "I know. It's been a crazy few days."

"No, that was because I didn't realize you have to sift through all that crap about our clients every single day. That takes an incredible amount of fortitude."

"No more than being the one on the other side of the camera."

"An interesting theory, Ms. Fahey. Would you like to talk about it more over lunch?"

"Lunch?" I parrot.

"It's the midday meal" is his quick riposte.

I want to say yes with every fiber of my being. Some of that must show on my face because Ward urges me, "Say yes, and I promise it will just be us, Angie. No cameras."

"You can't guarantee that." But my voice caves before I nod my assent.

His smile is mysterious. "Watch me. I'll pick you up at one if that works."

I quickly scan my calendar. "It's perfect."

"This will be too. I'll see you then."

A few minutes to one, Ward appears at my desk. He grabs his coat and mine. When I reach for my purse, he says, "You won't need it."

"But I need my coat?"

"We'll be outside for a few minutes" is the only clue he'll provide me.

He holds out his hand, and it's remarkably easy to slip my hand into his. Sula's words from last night whisper through my mind as his fingers tighten on mine briefly. *No matter what, everything is going to change.* My heart is pounding, but that has everything to do with Ward and nothing to do with what Michael and Stephen did to me that long-ago night at that party.

My soul has been hurt, but not by this man. Not now. And now is where I'm living. It's time to give now a chance to make me feel. I've given the past too much of my time.

We stop in the elevator hallway, and I'm surprised when Ward pushes the Up button. "If you're feeding me, I do believe the food is in the other direction."

"Not today it isn't."

"Now I'm intrigued."

"That was my intention."

"Well played, Mr. Burke."

"Thank you, Ms. Fahey. And if you'll step inside." He holds out his arm for me to precede him onto the elevator. But he doesn't press any buttons.

I open my mouth to ask, but he shakes his head imperceptibly. Instead, he reaches down and lifts the phone out. "Burton? Yes. We're in car three. Thank you."

The elevator jerks a moment. Then, as I stumble up against Ward, it goes soaring to the highest floors of the building. It seems to remain stuck on 24 for quite a while when it slows. Ward smiles down at me. "It's going to be a bit windy."

"What is?" But I don't have long to wait. The elevator opens up to the rooftop.

Ward steps out of the confines of the metal box and tugs me out behind him, pointing through the whipping wind to a small structure set off to the side made of glass. He pulls me behind him as we make our way there.

Once inside, I find myself standing inside an atrium. "What is this place?"

"The owners of the building had it built for summer parties. It's completely climate-controlled." Ward shucks off his overcoat.

I quickly do the same. "You did this for me?"

"Yes."

"How? Why?"

"I called them up to ask if I could use it for lunch, Angie. It wasn't a big deal."

I cock a brow. "Yes, it was."

A crooked grin crosses his face. "Okay. Yes, it was. I wanted to impress you. Did it work? Wait. Don't answer just yet." He fishes his phone from his pocket. After pressing a few buttons, a familiar Hooters song plays over the speakers. "Now, you can answer."

But I can't because I'm pretty certain I just stepped onto a path I never expected to travel, one that leads toward the most dangerous feelings in the world. This path could evoke pain even more fatal to the heart than what I've already suffered.

It's a journey of love.

"I'll be impressed when you tell me what you got us to eat." But I can't prevent my hips from swaying back and forth, losing myself to the perfect emotions I felt that first night out with Ward.

"Later." He takes my hand and swings me out.

I'm not sure if it's my being swept away by the moment, but on top of the world in the light of day, I don't feel petrified as a woman. For the first time, I feel powerful.

CHAPTER TWENTY-SIX

ANGELA

So many celebrities were spotted in the tiny town of Collyer, Connecticut, at their annual fall festival, we had a hard time keeping up with all of them. Evangeline Brogan, the belle of Broadway, was spotted with her family. Her sister, Bristol Brogan-Houde—known by investment bankers everywhere as "Queen of Wall Street"—was close behind with actor husband, Simon Houde.

And who could leave out Marco. Certainly not me.
— @PRyanPOfficial

"Angie, I know we sent a formal letter to Kensington. Have you received any updates? Email, phone calls? Carrier pigeons?" Carys taps a file against the side of her leg.

"Nothing. But you didn't flag it as a priority."

"I should have. She needs to sign it so I can have everything official in her file."

"Agreed. But there's not much more we can do to speed things up."

"I need to do something to distract myself. All I keep thinking about are the what-ifs."

That conversation the day after Ward wooed me on the rooftop with lunch and dancing has sat in my gut like a lead balloon. For now, we're in a holding pattern, and it's making us all anxious which is why I suggested maybe it would be a good time for her brood to escape the city and see what life outside Manhattan is like.

She quickly agreed.

That's how I find myself the weekend before Thanksgiving, awaiting a small convoy of people to arrive at my oasis just outside of the city. Although, it truly is a magnificent day for it. The weather has that perfect bite of cold while the sky is so blue it makes my eyes water to look at it for too long.

I can't help but turn my face toward the wind rustling the last few leaves on the trees as I stand in the yard. Even as I remain motionless, another one flutters to the ground. I track its slow descent with a bittersweet smile on my face. Long ago, my grandfather used to tell me you could tell a lot about people who didn't rest on their laurels. "Putting in a day's hard work is honorable, Angie. Any man or woman who simply earns his living by hanging on the coattails of others isn't someone worthy of you. One day, those are the people who won't care about the nonsense they made up about you."

"But it happened, Grandpa. The only thing they lied about was the outcome," I whispered, afraid I was interpreting his words to believe he, too, didn't believe me.

But that wasn't the case.

It was too soon after everything that had happened to me for me to appreciate the wisdom of his words. And while I can thank him in my heart every single day for believing I would be able to move past the horror to find the beauty in life again, it's not the same as being able to crawl into his lap and hug him.

Just like I did when my life was a mess.

I drag the rake along the ground one last time and admire the large pile. "Ben is going to love this," I declare. For a little boy whose only exposure to the great outdoors has been the times his parents take him to Central Park, I should have thought to tell Carys and David to bring him an extra set of clothing. Rubbing my arms up and down, I quickly move toward the garage to hang up the rake. Then, remembering the corduroy outerwear they had him in to go to daycare, my eyes crinkle. "At least I won't have to worry about him getting cold."

As much as the temperature has begun to plunge overnight, it's warmed significantly at the office. The way Ward's behaving makes me want to fall down in the leaf pile and make angels because I now know they exist. He's like a whole different person. "Or maybe I am," I muse aloud.

Every morning, he greets me with a gentle "Good morning, Angie." Then, he stands there and listens when we both have a moment to talk. We find time for quiet lunches in his office or just moments to chat as we slowly let each other in on small little bits of nothing that mean everything, including laughter.

And each morning I check the feeds, but there's nothing trending about Ward. It's like he's disappeared from the media's notice as Becks—or some other poor soul—becomes their new target.

But yesterday was the incident I have now declared the first LLF Snowball Fight.

I bite my lip, trying to hold in my laugh as I recall how Ward walked into the middle Carys and Becks's blowout over his asinine behavior is drawing more media attention. "These stupid antics have to stop, Beckett! Eventually, I'm going to have to defend one of these cases," Carys yelled up at him, shaking her finger.

His response was to pelt her in the head with a crumpled-up gossip rag that ended up with an all-out paper war, both of them hitting Ward several times in the head before Ward bellowed, "Is this how professionals behave?"

"Apparently today, it is," I drawled.

He whipped around, not realizing I was in the conference room. He opened his mouth to say something when a small piece of paper flew into his mouth. Ward spat it out onto the floor.

By this point, my whole body was shaking with laughter. "I love my job," I proclaimed to the entire room—where no one was listening—as I pushed out of my chair, leaving the three of them to fight it out.

The subtle change between Ward and me was remarked upon by Carys when we spoke yesterday to confirm today was a good day for her family to traipse out to see my home. "Of course it is. I'd truly enjoy the company," I told her.

"Good. You can tell me it's not my business, but..."

Uh-oh. "But what?"

Carys gestured to her guest chair. I dutifully sat down. "I noticed a lot of the frost has melted between you and Ward. I was worried after that night where you helped Becks it would get worse." Her penetrating aqua eyes bore into mine.

I turned my face away to gather my thoughts. "How is it Ward doesn't know who I am, Carys?"

"It was never my place to tell him, Angie. You trusted me with that knowledge. And despite the anxiety that goes through you every time a certain company is mentioned in the media, I truly don't think every person watches you as if you have a scarlet X branded on you. I truly believe many people simply can't help but stare at you because you're exquisitely beautiful." Her voice was gentle.

My hands shook. I clenched them so tightly, my nails dug little half-moons into the palms. "There's no way for you to understand what that kind of media coverage was like," I lashed out.

"Don't I?" My head whipped around to find her hands folded together on her desk. "It wasn't the same kind perverse invasiveness as yours, but it was still a storm we were completely unprepared for."

"After your parents died," I concluded slowly.

"Yes. Ward and I had just inherited a fortune—one which we had no idea about. We were instantaneous millionaires. Christ, if we were selfish, we'd be worth billions at this point."

"I can't even begin to imagine the burden of that kind of money."

Relief crossed Carys's face. "Thank you." At my confusion, she continued. "Not many people appreciate it is a burden. And this wasn't the same kind of thing as picking numbers or scratching off a ticket. It wasn't an unexpected joy to share. We lost the best thing in our lives to acquire fortune. And no one seems to remember that every time they mention us in the media. At the core of who we are, it changed us. Ward especially."

I leaned forward and laid my shaking hand on hers. For just a moment, we were just two people who had survived the worst life can throw at us in the most public way possible. There weren't scandals and degrees separating us. We were just women who knew what it was like to have our pain laid out on page one for everyone to digest on their morning commute.

A whisper of cold races through me, jostling me from my thoughts. "Crap. I don't have much time." Quickly, I dash down the steps and run into the garage to hang up the rake and shed my duck shoes. Closing the garage door, I climb the stairs to the main level to get ready for the arrival of my... I stop in the hallway as the word comes to me. Friends. Somewhere along the way, Carys and David transitioned from being my bosses to being my friends. I don't have to watch what I say around them. I don't have to hide my emotions. I can just be me.

Slowly, I turn towards the mirror hanging in the front hall. Then I take a step forward until I can face the woman staring back at me clearly. For the first time in ten years, I'm not ashamed by the emotions reflecting back at me.

Wariness.

Fear.

And maybe...excitement?

Suddenly, a surge of anger makes me want to hurl the antique mirror across the room. "Damnit, after all this time, don't I deserve to forgive myself? I sacrificed my entire life to tell the truth. If they chose not to believe me, shouldn't they be the ones unable to look in the mirror? I didn't lie," I yell. It's something psychologist after psychologist tried to tell me for years. My grandparents, Sula, they tried to make me believe it. I don't know what changed, but I feel terrified and exhilarated by the realization that maybe they were right.

"I'm entitled to happiness. No one has the prerogative to make me feel fear. No one." With that, I turn and hurry up the stairs to get ready for the first guests I'll ever entertain at my home other than Sula.

"It's charming, Angie" are the first words Carys calls out. Her blonde head immediately ducks into the back seat.

"Thanks." I step out the front door onto the porch and lift a hand. "Need any help?"

David gives a quick wave before he walks around to the trunk. "No. We'll just put Ward to good use."

My heart stutters as another door flies open. "I heard that. No wonder you guys invited me along." Ward's dark hair catches the overhead sunlight as he emerges from the back of the car. "Hey, Angie. I hope you don't mind my tagging along?"

"No, no. Not at all. Welcome." The demons in my head try to take over, cackling about unplanned attacks. I shove them aside. Ward didn't seek me out on his own. He came with his sister, his brother-in-law, and his nephew, for crying out loud. Bravely, I walk down the flagstone steps and reach them at the car just as Carys pulls Ben from his car seat.

Rubbing his little eyes, he blinks a few times before his little mouth forms a perfect O. "Mama. Look, trees!"

Carys smooths a hand up and down his back. "I know, baby. There's lots of trees here."

He squirms to be put down. "Unca Ward. We play?" His question is more of a demand, with the confidence of a little boy who knows he's unequivocally loved.

"I should clarify, Angie, it was Ben who insisted Ward come with us." David slams the trunk. "Ward comes over and both Carys and I disappear."

"Don't pout, David. I seem to recall you and Carrie disappearing while I watched the little bugger this morning." Ward's smile is pure wickedness, his meaning clear.

I blush to the roots of my hair. Carys stomps over to her brother, still holding Ben, and whacks him in the arm. "You're embarrassing Angie. Be nice."

Ben leans over and smashes his hand on Ward's mouth. "Nice, Unca Ward. No time-out. We play." Then Ben flings his arms back high over his head, his delight so obvious all the adults can't help but absorb his enthusiasm. Even me.

"Ben," I call to him. His tiny head whips toward me. "Do you want to jump in some leaves?"

His little body quivers in excitement. "Yes. Puhlease." He tacks on the latter after a stern look from his father.

"Well, I happen to have a pile of them in the backyard and cocoa for after, but only for well-behaved boys..."

"And girls?" Carys pipes in. Even as my jaw falls open in shock, she turns to Ward as they head toward the trunk. "When was the last time we jumped in a pile of leaves?"

"You were in college, and I must have been in middle school." He reaches over and ruffles her hair. "Such a brat, jumping right in the middle of the pile I'd just raked up."

"Wait. I thought you two lived in New York your whole lives?"

David approaches, holding Ben as Carys and Ward unload every possible contraption necessary for a day with a two-year-old. "They did, Angie. But their parents would rent a house very similar to this one to escape the city for weekend trips. Next time you're over, we'll show you the photos," he muses.

"It's true. Rhode Island in the summer, Berkshires in the fall."

"I notice you're leaving out New Hampshire for skiing. Could it be because you spent more time in the snow than skiing on top of it?" Ward drawls.

Carys rolls her eyes before announcing, "I'm not very coordinated."

Ward coughs in his hand. "It sounds an awful lot like you just said 'understatement,'" I call him out.

"Maybe because he did." Carys starts toward him and trips over a bag in the driveway. "Oops."

Ward stabilizes her and Ben. "Some things never change."

We all laugh. "Why don't we drop everything inside, and then we can go check out the leaf pile?" I suggest.

"Leaves!" Ben flings his hands in the air, almost clipping Carys in the jaw. All the adults laugh.

While the laughter dies down, Ward apologizes. "We really should have called along the way to let you know I was tagging along. I'm sorry. I promised you I wouldn't come here without you knowing about it."

If I had a chance to think about Ward at my home, I'd have panicked. But am I sorry to see him so relaxed amid his family where I can learn another new facet to his personality?

"I'm not. Sorry you're here, that is," I blurt out in a rush. My cheeks flame even in the cool air.

His eyes crinkle in the corner. "Good. I'm glad."

Carys screeches like a banshee, breaking our moment. "Okay, Ben. I'll put you down. Stop pulling Mommy's hair."

"Leaves, Mama. Go to leaves. Jump, jump, jump!"

I really try hard not to snicker, but when first David, then Ward succumb, I'm helpless not to join in.

"If one of you dares to say he sounds like me on a bad day at the office, I'll figure out a way to assign you to Becks for the next month. And remember, it's his favorite season— Christmas," Carys threatens.

None of us can hold back our guffaws. But we do make our way inside the house before we immediately head out the back so Ben can do what he came to do—jump in a pile of leaves.

And inside, every time he does, a small part of me which of me which has been chained to the past starts to jump right along with him.

CHAPTER TWENTY-SEVEN

WARD

Conversation starter: What is the one thing you wouldn't do no matter how much money you were offered?
— **Viego Martinez, Celebrity Blogger**

"Again!"

Angie calls back to my nephew, "Are you sure?"

"Puhlease?" Ben begs.

Angie takes off running, her long auburn hair flying out behind her. Just as she takes off to land in the pile of leaves, she lets out a war whoop. My body jerks when her head disappears until the sky rains down with her laughter and leaves. "How was that?"

"You easily outjumped Carrie on that one," David proclaims.

Carys, who pulled herself from the massive leaf pile before Angie took off and was still plucking them from her clothes, turns and sticks her tongue out at her husband. "I'm sure Angie gets more practice."

"Nah. I normally just bag them for recycling." Angie emerges from the leaf pile.

I feel something inside me twist at the way the leaves cling to her hair. *She looks like a woodland nymph, something from the deepest part of my desires, rising from the forest to lead me to salvation.* I shake my head ruefully at my whimsical thoughts as Angie spends a few moments laughing with my sister, helping Carys remove a few hard-to-reach leaves.

After Carys does the same for her, they join us up on the deck. Angie grabs her cup of coffee and takes a drink before making a face. "Ugh. This is ice-cold. Let me go put on a fresh pot."

"Do you mind if we move inside, Angie?" David murmurs. Ben is conked out in his arms, clutching a fistful of leaves in one hand. "It looks like this one went out for a power nap."

"Of course not. Come on in." While David concerns himself with Ben, the rest of us gather up cups and head into Angie's home.

"Why don't you all head into the family room while I get the coffee started? It's down the hall to the right. Try not to let the devil cat trip you. And protect Ben from her at all costs!"

Angie calls out. She points straight ahead to the room we passed on the way in with an enormous bay window overlooking the lake.

David and Carys immediately comply, but I drag my heels in the hall when I spy the neatly framed collage of photos on the wall. Immediately, I'm taken in by the progression of years from the young flame-haired girl with gap teeth to the woman I work with. Leaning closer, I blink in shock. There she is wearing the dress she wore the Valentine's Day my sister got engaged. Only, her arms are wrapped tightly around the date my sister alluded to her having—an elderly couple at a fancy restaurant. "So many stupid assumptions," I murmur. *So much wasted time.*

"About me?" Her voice startles me, and I almost knock the frame off the wall. Her expression holds a mixture of weariness and acceptance.

"I didn't mean anything derogatory, I was just thinking about…" But Angie doesn't let me finish my thought. Instead, her words cause me a great deal of chagrin.

"For years, I've lived with people thinking horrible things about me, Ward. It's nothing new. I know things have changed between us." She tries to move past me with a tray of cups and a new pot of coffee.

I step in front of her to block her path. "Does this have to do with what happened to you?"

Her breath shudders, but her voice is clear. "Yes."

"Will you tell me? I can't promise not to hurt you unless I know."

She tries to edge past me. "I can't discuss this now."

"Angie." I reach out and touch her elbow.

She jerks away, almost upending the tray. "In your entire life, has anyone ever questioned your word? The veracity of your character?" When I don't respond, she continues. "Be grateful, Ward. Because it makes it impossible not to question everything and everyone."

Stepping closer, I whisper, "What kind of monster could hurt you like this?"

"I can't—no, I won't—bring them here today."

"But you'll tell me," I insist.

"Why? Because, I'm your friend? Have I asked you invasive questions? What gives you the right to do the same?"

And although it's the truth, I feel her words like a slap across my face. Suddenly, I can't stay this close to Angie, not after seeing how free she can be. Even now her skin, so ruddy from being outdoors, is paling. Her diamond-bright eyes are losing their luster.

I curse myself roundly before scooting my way around her. This woman has my feelings so muddled I can't think straight. "Tell them—" I nod in the direction of the family room. "—I got a call. I have to go."

"Why?" But before I can answer, she bows her head. "Never mind. You don't have to answer my intrusive questions any more than I have to answer yours."

I observe her for just a moment before I take three long strides that put me back in front of her. Lifting the tray out of her hands, I put it down on a nearby trunk. Catching her trembling hands in mine, I press my lips to the center of her palm. "I need facts, Angie. I don't want to make a mistake with you that could end up harming you—and me. After watching you outside and realizing you're like a fantasy come to life, I'm finding myself impatient for you to catch up. That isn't fair to you because I made you a promise. It doesn't mean I get to rush you just because I'm admitting to myself this is right. I'm afraid of doing or saying the wrong thing that could end up hurting you."

"This is right?" Her lashes blink slowly as she absorbs the impact of my words.

"You. Me. Friends first, remember?" The way the glow spreads back across her face makes me feel like I was granted a boon from some unknown deity.

"But what if I don't want to just be friends?" The words seem to be out of her mouth before her mind realizes what she said because she gasps.

Without knocking any of her precious family photos off the walls, I let her hands go to brace both arms above her head and watch the late-fall sunlight dance across her face before I make a decision. I feel like I'm in a bubble where the rest of the world doesn't exist. I can't hear anything but the pounding of my own heart, the beat of hers. "Stop me if you don't want my lips on yours."

Leaning down, I nuzzle my nose against hers. That's when I feel her arms wrap around my waist. She squeezes me lightly and whispers guilelessly, "Is this the way it's supposed to feel?"

"What?"

"Need."

I pull back so our breath is flowing back and forth between one another's lips—lips that haven't touched yet. Then I answer her honestly, "I don't know. I've never felt anything close to it."

Then I lean my body into hers lightly and tip my head to the side. My lips brush across hers once, twice, before I nip at her lip, seeking entry to her mouth. She almost makes my knees buckle when her lips part and her tongue is there waiting to brush against mine tentatively.

Ruthlessly, I keep my hands where they are, though it wouldn't surprise me if I leave score marks where I'm clutching the wall. I need her to understand there's a rightness here, not just between any man and woman, but between us. Our kiss goes on and on, until I slowly back away by nibbling on her lush lower lip.

I don't want to frighten her again. I can't. She's quickly becoming entwined around my heart, causing parts of it to beat after I thought I'd managed to kill them long ago.

Her head falls forward until it hits my chest. We stand that way for a few moments until Angie whispers, "Unless you really want to go, stay. I promise, we'll talk, Ward. It's just...I haven't figured out how to say everything I need to. You'll be the first." And without another word, the woman I want as my lover ducks beneath my upstretched arm. With one last look back at me, she picks up the coffee server and enters the family room.

I'll be the first what? The first person she's spoken with about this? The first person she's trusted her heart to? My heart pumps frantically. She can't mean...

Or, can she?

I stare blankly out at the dimming light. How did I not notice this has been building up since the moment I first laid eyes on her? The simmering resentment from imagining her with someone else. The burgeoning need. The tension. David said it himself: everyone else has seen this coming. A clawing fear invades me. What happens if she becomes even more woven in my soul and she vanishes from my life—just like my parents did?

Staggering into the room, I sit down. Angie hands me a cup of coffee, which I readily accept. If my hands are shaking when I do, no one else notices but me. And for now, that's okay. No one else needs to know my terror is she's going to disappear from my life once she becomes so entwined in it.

"So, Sula and I snuck out. It was the first major snow of the year here. We totally couldn't resist it. Of course, since we didn't have a sled, we had no idea what we were going to do. Then, she came up with this great idea."

"What did you do?" I take a sip of coffee.

Mistake. Big mistake.

"Cafeteria trays. Grandma had brought a stack of them home from the senior center she worked at to be donated at the thrift shop in town." Angie's smile is both joyful and a bit wicked.

My coffee ends up all over my sweater as I howl with laughter. "Nice. I remember doing something similar, only we stole ours right out of the cafeteria."

Angie leans over and gives me a solid high five.

"That actually works?" Carys demands, a bit truculently.

I snort. "This is what you get for studying all the time."

She sticks her tongue out, and I make a face. We grin before Angie interjects. "Sure does. We almost ended up in the lake." Angie points beyond my shoulder.

"What did your grandmother say?" David asks. Ben woke up a little while ago and is cuddled in his lap.

I'm enthralled by the story, by this unburdened glimpse of Angie. But when she bursts into laughter, I realize it's more than that. It's a damn gift.

"Grandma gave us this disapproving look for about two minutes." Angie lowers her brows and purses her lips. She looks like she just sucked on an overly tart lemon at the same time someone plucked a bit too hard at the groomer's.

"Ooh, show me that look. I need it for when Ben's older," Carys exclaims.

"Or when Ward gets out of line," David drawls.

Smoothing her expression, Angie grins. "But like I said, it was for just for a few moments. Then it was Grandpa roaring like a thundercloud because Grandma wanted to come sledding with us."

We all crack up again.

"My God," I wheeze, unable to catch my breath but not because of the laughter. It's because Angie is transformed.

The late-afternoon sun is streaming through the window and setting her hair on fire. Her smile is wide and unencumbered. *This is what she was meant to be like. Always.* And it makes me want to use every single resource at my disposal to hunt down the people who hurt her and do the same to them until they lose their luster.

And she once again glows.

CHAPTER TWENTY-EIGHT

ANGELA

Jenna Madison was spotted strutting in Dublin wearing the most gorgeous pair of boots. I wanted to scratch her eyes out before I stole them off her feet.
— **Moore You Want**

"Hello?"

"Sula?"

"Hey."

"I just wanted to tell you that you were right."

"About what?"

"About everything."

There's such a long silence on the other end of the line, I wonder if I've hung up on her. I pull the phone away from my ear to check.

"Does this mean you told him and he understands?" she asks carefully.

I stare out across the yard of the home that became my safe haven. "No. It means I know I have to."

"Thank God. What made you come to that conclusion?"

I think back to the last week of subtle pursuit from Ward. "Nothing overwhelming."

"That tells me nothing."

"Coffee every morning. A flower waiting in my chair. Lunch catered in for two in his office from my favorite pizza joint that doesn't deliver. Meeting him out for dinner where he's rented out the entire restaurant."

"Whoa. How did that not make the papers?" Sula's shock is evident.

"He snuck in the back door."

"For a guy who's never been linked with a woman, ever, I'd say he's awfully serious about you. That's a ridiculous amount to spend on a date, Angie."

"I said something similar."

"To which he replied?"

"I was worth it."

"You are," she declares loyally before adding, "But I'm liking the fact he thinks so as well."

My mind drifts, remembering the tiny little Chinese restaurant above Fifth Avenue where Ward was waiting for me with a single yellow rose. He waved off my question like it was nothing. "It's just money. The real treasure is getting to spend time with you."

Sula calling my name yanks me back to our call. My voice is jagged. "Too many years have passed where I let someone else be the judge over my worth. It's time that comes to an end. It's just…"

"What? It's just what, Angie?" Her voice is filled with nerves, likely afraid I'm going to back out.

I'm can't. I'm too far down a path I never thought I'd travel. Inhaling sharply, I ask, "What do I say? How do I tell him I was attacked?"

"You don't tell him anything more than you're comfortable with. Do you hear me? Not one damn thing. You are under no obligation to go into details you don't want to. You only share what you feel is important for Ward to know. And you make him understand the reason you're sharing this is because he's becoming an invaluable part of your life," she stresses, quoting my psychologist.

"He is," I admit.

There's a little war whoop on the other end of the line. My lips kick up a bit as I imagine Sula dancing around her flat. *Her downstairs neighbors must love her*, I think wryly.

After her characteristic exuberance settles down, she whispers, "I'm so proud of you."

"I haven't done it yet," I remind her.

"You will. You're not the kind of person who makes this decision lightly."

"No, I'm not." In fact, the last time I shared this information willingly was with Carys when I applied for the job at Wildcard.

"How do you think he'll react?"

"I have no idea." There's any number of reactions Ward could have. That's what worries me. Then another thought pops into my mind. "I don't know where to have this conversation."

"Hmm, good question. Somewhere you feel safe, somewhere you won't be interrupted. And somewhere you can get help in a heartbeat" is her immediate reply.

"Right." Only one place meets all of that criteria.

I guess I'll have to see what Ward has planned for after hours at work tomorrow night.

CHAPTER TWENTY-NINE

ANGELA

Listen, people, it's snow. Not the damn Apocalypse. You don't need to buy all the chocolate. Save some for the rest of us. **@PRyanPOfficial**

It feels so right, and yet my nerves are overwhelming me.

I've been waiting all day to do this, but the waiting is killing me.

I know the longer I hesitate, the bigger the chance the opportunity is going to vanish—that something could slip in its place. Right now, there's a block of time on Ward's calendar toward the end of our day where we'll be the only ones in the office.

With shaking hands, I block it off, copy the conference room, and mark it as Private.

It's time for me and Ward to finally talk.

It's been less than a week since everyone came to my home, so much has changed between us. Even as I'm helping Carys put out legal fires, I'm constantly bumping up against Ward's calmness and passion. It's like I've been waiting my whole life for a man like this to come into my life. Now that we've spent more time together, the blinders have been swiped from my eyes, and I'm in awe over the man he is. And somehow he wants me.

But will he after he hears what I have to say?

Stomach churning, I reach for the remainder of my lunch to pitch it into the garbage when I recall our late lunch with Carys and David earlier in the week.

"I hate mornings," Ward confessed.

"Which worked out beautifully because this way you can deal with most of our West Coast business." Carys toasted her brother.

"Except for Z." His dark eyes danced at her as he lifted his bottle of sparkling water at her.

Carys groaned. "Don't remind me. Will you please go get a tattoo so he feels he can trust you?"

My soda came flying out of my mouth. "Is that why?" I demanded.

Both Burke siblings nodded before grinning identical smiles. I wondered which parent they inherited them from. But Ward's words pulled me from my thoughts. "Maybe I'm not getting a tattoo just so you *have* to deal with him."

"Cruel. Just plain cruel."

"No, cruel is attempting to sew me a cummerbund to match my prom date's dress," Ward argued.

"I thought that was sweet." Carys pouted.

"If you knew how to sew. Could you, I don't know, maybe have asked someone for help? I looked like I was wearing a diaper by the end of the night."

I'd been in the middle of taking a bite of my salad and managed to jab a kale leaf up my nose with that revelation. "Stop. I beg you both." It actually sounded like "Stahhh. I beh bo ot ooo" between the laughter and since I had shoved a tissue up my nose to stop the bleeding, but the point was made.

Ward winked at me, and he and Carys went back to bickering about clients.

This morning, I found a bouquet of blue larkspur and eucalyptus was delivered to me with a simple card: *Positive energy. I'm here whenever you're ready. - W.* When I took a picture of them and sent it to Sula, she lost her ever-loving mind. Her text back to me read, *The man is mad about you.*

I reach out and touch a delicate bloom. *Maybe. But I know it's certainly true the other way around.*

Any moment where I give myself a spare second to think, I'm fighting a losing battle against myself. "What's the worst that happens?" I whisper. My hands shake. I grip them tightly as the phone bleeps on my desk, indicating an internal call.

I snatch it up. "Yes, Carys?"

"Can you come in here just a moment?

"Be right there."

Grabbing my tablet, I head straight for my boss's office.

When I get there, I'm surprised to find her staring out at the Manhattan skyline. "Is everything okay?"

"I don't know. Is it?"

"What do you mean?"

"You know I'm copied on all conference room requests. And so I know there's a meeting tonight between you and Ward. Angie…" Concern laces her voice as she turns to face me from the window.

"He's become a friend, Carys."

"I think we both know he's become more than that."

I stiffen at her gentle rebuke. "Would you have a problem with that?" *With me?* But I leave that unsaid.

"Of course not. The only issue I would have is my brother not knowing the true extent of what happened so he doesn't inadvertently hurt the both of you."

"That's why I booked the conference room." Now it's my turn to lose myself in the teaming intensity of the city. I move to stand next to her.

"You're telling him?" Carys's voice is laced with shock.

"How can I not?"

"Many wouldn't."

"Then they're fools," I snap. "I learned to live after what happened, but to open my heart again to a man is entirely different. It's not just me who can get hurt." I pause to take a breath before letting it out. "He has to know how I came to be who I really am."

"And that is?" Carys probes gently.

My head whips around. "Me. I may have been broken, but I was restored." My voice comes out strong and firm.

"Carys, you're going to have to deal without either me or Angie for the rest of the day. We're leaving to go somewhere else to finish this conversation." When I whirl around, Ward's leaning against the open doorjamb. His expression is neutral, but his dark eyes are burning with emotion. I recognize protectiveness, and I want to wrap myself in it, luxuriate in the feeling.

Carys holds up a hand. "I wouldn't normally dare intrude this far, Ward, but in this case I am sticking my nose in with good reason."

His expression softens. "I understand."

"I'd like to know where you're going." Before Ward can speak, Carys takes my hand. She squeezes it hard. I return the gesture, appreciating the unspoken support for what I'm about to do. Her voice is thick. "Angie needs to know if she needs to step away from the conversation for any reason, she has people she can reach."

I had already prepared myself to be launched into new stratospheres of emotions with Ward, but watching the love cross over his face before he crosses the room to wrap his sister in a hug flings me higher than I ever expected. But it's his words that throw me closer to love.

"I'm taking her home, Carys. She needs to be in her safe space when we talk."

Carys turns towards me. I nod. "That's a good idea." A great one actually.

"Then both of you, go."

Ward steps aside to let me pass. "I'll meet you at your desk in just a few minutes. I drove in today because we're expecting snow."

"We are?"

He nods. "They're uncertain about the amount, but it should be okay."

Close to two hours later, we're curled in front of the fireplace, watching the television with a frown on both of our faces. "I'm glad I have a two-car garage."

"You know, if I realized the storm of the century was coming, I wouldn't have demanded we drive out here." Ward's words are regretful.

I flutter my hand at him to be quiet. "Three to four inches of snow *an hour*? That can't be right. What the hell *is* thundersnow anyway?"

"Glad you asked, Sam." The newscaster answers my question. "Thundersnow is essentially the same thing as a thunderstorm. Thunder and lightning happen, the same way they do during a thunderstorm. But the air layer closer to the ground has to be warmer than those above it, but still cold enough for it to snow."

"So, Judy, you're saying it will snow as much as it could rain?"

"That's right. People with overhead power lines should take steps now in the event of an emergency. Gather flashlights, extra batteries, battery-powered or hand-cranked radios. Charge all of your cell phones or any emergency devices which require charging. Ensure you know where your first-aid kit is and have easy access to it. And above all, be safe getting home. We know a number of you are commuting right now. Get to your loved ones safely."

I click off the television before facing Ward. "I think you'd better stay here."

"Are you sure?"

"Ward, I'd be devastated if something happened to you on the road. We'll figure it out."

He's pushing buttons on his phone before he holds it up to his ear. "Tell me you both are at home with Ben." He pauses. "Good. No, I'm going to stay here." He lets out a sigh. "I'm certain that Angie isn't going to make me sleep in the car. I'm positive that she has a guest room if nothing else, Carys."

I nod as I jump up and begin to head for the back deck. I stop short as I hear the first crack of thunder. "Ward," I cry out frantically.

"Listen. I have to go. We need to get things ready here. Touch base when you can. I love you." He turns to me. "Tell me what you need me to do."

"Upstairs bedroom on the left. It was my grandparents' room. There's sweatshirts, sweatpants, socks. Get whatever you're comfortable wearing that was my grandfather's." I pant as I bring in the first load of logs.

Grimly, he takes the load from me and begins to stack it next to the fireplace. "Right after I help you. We don't have much time to waste."

I'm about to argue when we both jump due to the light that flashes across the sky. Then small white flakes begin to fall. "God, I hope that suit didn't cost as much as the press reports."

"Doesn't matter at this point, does it?"

"Not really."

"Get a move on, Angie. I have no idea where you keep anything."

Right. We have bigger issues to worry about right now than the cost of Ward's suit. We need to worry about sheltering in place.

CHAPTER THIRTY

ANGELA

Has Ward Burke gone missing, or is he just trapped under the snow with some lucky woman? If so, I'd like to say what we're all thinking. Bitch.
— **Jacques Yves, Celebrity Blogger**

All these years I couldn't ever contemplate intimacy, yet here I am trapped in a house by at least a foot of snow with no power, cozied up in front of a blazing fire with a man who makes every part of me tingle. Flower's as close as she can be near the fire Ward just fed. And I don't feel fear. "Or maybe that's the Baileys hot chocolate warming me up?" I say aloud.

"What is?" Ward asks.

It hasn't been long since we stopped running around. I was shocked to find out Ward Burke was willing but excited to eat a hot dog roasted over an open fire. "Reminds me of the cookouts from when I was a kid. We used to roast them on a grill," he told me enthusiastically.

We nabbed all the cushions and plopped them on the floor directly in front of the stone fireplace like a massive futon. With our backs propped up, we're reclined against the hearth. This way, we're able to gaze out the window at the snow's now gentle fall. But at his words, I push to my feet and wander to stare out to the darkness lit only by the dim light powered by my solar yard lights.

It's time.

I face Ward. I can't have my back to him. Not now, maybe not ever, but certainly not for this. "The entire course of my life changed when I agreed to go to an upperclassmen party with Sula."

Ward doesn't say a word, but his body becomes more alert. He sits up from his relaxed position, placing his drink aside, waiting for me to continue.

"I was drinking a beer. It was stupid—so stupid, accepting an open cup from someone I didn't know. Sula and I figured out it must have been drugged because there's no way I would have left the room without her." Ward starts to speak, but I hold up my hand. "Please, let me get through this? Please," I beseech him.

His jaw tightens, but he doesn't move. Doesn't say a word.

"To this day, I don't know exactly what happened. Whether I just have a different body chemistry than other women or if the wrong dose was used because even though I couldn't react normally by fighting them off while they touched me, I remember everything."

"You said them?" The tic in his jaw becomes more pronounced.

"Yes. I did."

Ward's fists clench. "Will you tell me who?"

I shake my head. "No. Maybe later, but this is difficult enough. Can you understand that?"

"I'll take whatever you're willing to tell me."

Relieved, I whisper, "I need to finish."

"There's more?" His voice comes out as a low growl that wraps around me, shoving away the demons if only for a little while.

Instead of answering him, I find the strength to continue. "I was saved from...from..."

"You weren't raped?" His voice is flat.

"No. But only because they were interrupted by someone else. Sula came searching for me, and we managed to make it home. God, we did everything wrong from that point forward."

"Why do you say that?"

"We never went to the infirmary. I never had my blood tested. I was bruised, but no one took pictures. I hid. I was terrified, Ward. Scared."

"I think anyone in your situation would have been."

"But when I found the courage to try to make things right, no one believed me." I stand in front of Ward, trembling.

"You attempted to press charges?"

"I tried. I also went to the Student Conduct Board. Neither believed me. The only people who have are Sula, my grandparents, your sister, and Becks figured it out." I wrap my arms around myself and look away. I don't mention how his godfather recognized me from the media reports. I just can't. Not now.

Later, I promise myself. Later.

Ward bites off a curse. "That's why you and Becks became so close."

I nod, unable to meet his eyes. "He doesn't know the details of what I shared with you. He just recognized me for being a victim…"

"You're no one's victim. A survivor is much more accurate." Ward's words cause my head to whirl around, mouth agape.

Tears begin to flood my eyes. I blink rapidly to clear them.

He pushes himself until he's sitting on top of the stone hearth. Wearing my grandfather's sweatsuit, he should look ridiculous, but all the change of clothes did was strip him of the facade he shrugs on each day as easily as he pulls on one of his custom-made suits—something I only know because I hung his up to dry in the laundry room earlier. On his face I see his struggle with right and wrong. Much like when I shared my story with my grandparents and his sister. All the illusions I had of him burn away like ash in the crackle of the fire behind him. When he speaks, his voice is low and measured. "What happened to you was revolting—"

I draw in a breath and hold it.

"—but it doesn't define you. It shouldn't. I know for some small-minded people it might. I'm not one of them."

I let out with a whoosh. "I never thought I'd have to explain this to someone because…"

"You didn't think you'd reach the point where it would become an issue?" He stands.

"I never thought it would become an issue with anyone."

I don't move as he approaches me. "You're not afraid of me, are you, Angie?"

"No. I'm not."

"Why? Not that you should be. Nothing's going to happen tonight." He holds out his hand to me when he's a few feet away.

I step the rest of the way toward him, my own outstretched. "I don't fear what I face head-on."

Realization crosses his features as the strength of his fingers grips mine. "It's when someone comes up behind you…"

"That's how one…" I let him tug me closer before I raise my other hand to grip his forearm.

Ward brushes a light kiss over my forehead, against my wet cheeks—when I didn't even know I was crying—before pressing his lips gently against my lips. "Come on. It's time to get some sleep."

He wraps his arm around my shoulder and pulls me to his side. Together we bank the fire and bury ourselves beneath a mass of blankets. For a moment, I blink in the darkness, wondering why he doesn't wrap me in his arms. Didn't what I tell him repel him after all?

Then his voice reminds me not to make assumptions. Not about him. "Take my hand, curl up with my arm, or lay on my heart. I'm right at your side, Angie. It's where I've wanted to be for a long time."

I swallow hard before I reach out in the dark for everything I always wanted but thought I could never have.

The possibility of him.

CHAPTER THIRTY-ONE

ANGELA

We understand most of the tristate area is out of power due to the ridiculous amount of snow. But trust us. We're professionals. Do not use your spare turkey fryer inside.
— **Fab and Delish**

I wake up warm with the smell of bacon sizzling the next morning. And alone in the huddle of blankets. I frown. Was it all a dream?

Then above me, I hear Ward's laugh. "No way, Carrie. There's at least eighteen inches of snow here. We still don't have power. Fortunately, Angie is well prepared with supplies, and we charged our phones. I'm not wasting my battery taking a call from Becks unless it's truly an emergency." There's a pause before a much softer. "She's sleeping still. I'm making breakfast. No, I won't say anything about how last night went. That's Angie's to share."

PERFECT ASSUMPTION · 317

I can't prevent the curve of my lips as I snuggle deeper beneath the warmth of the blankets. Then my jaw drops when I hear him say, "I'm so angry with you for intimidating me away from her two years ago." A pause. "You may have *believed* you had a good reason, but it was Angie's decision to share. And I'll tell you exactly what I told her last night: I *never* want to hear that phrase used in conjunction with her again." He sighs. Finally, "Yeah, you always were smart. I love you too. Yes, I'll be careful."

I wait a few moments until I spy him beneath my lashes moving with a plate of bacon into the kitchen. He comes back with a bowl of scrambled eggs before pouring them into—thank, God—my cast iron and scraping them. "You're handy doing that," I comment, hoping he doesn't startle easily.

Fortunately, he doesn't. "Boy Scout campouts. Plus, Dad would cook on a grill when we'd come out to the Berkshires."

"Really? You were a Boy Scout?" I struggle to sit up.

"Yep, so if you want to relax, I've got this covered if bacon and eggs work for you."

"I'm not moving because I'm offering to help. I'm just not missing a moment of one of the world's most eligible bachelors cooking me breakfast," I drawl. "Especially when he's wearing an eighty-year-old man's sweats."

"See, and I was going to attempt toast."

"Amateur," I scoff, before shoving out of the piles of blankets.

"Where are you going?" Ward calls out.

"I would think as a lawyer you might have heard of a thing called privacy."

"You're going to freeze outside in that. Took me forever to warm up," he warns. He scrapes the pan to get the eggs nice and fluffy.

"You went outside?" I ask, astonished.

"There's no power," he again reminds me.

"Ward, all that means is there's no power. We still have water." To prove my point, I go over to the kitchen sink and turn on the cold water nozzle. "In fact, be grateful for it or I'd be worried about a busted pipe."

"You mean I went outside and..."

"Drew pictures in the snow for no reason? Yes."

I honestly don't know if his face is flushed from cooking so close to the fire or if he's blushing. But I decide to give him a reprieve. "Give me a few minutes and I'll make us something for after the eggs and bacon."

He flaps a hand, and I dart out of sight.

By the time I get back, I have a can of cooking spray and a can of biscuits in my hand. Ward's just scooping the eggs into a bowl. "If you don't mind serving, I'll get these ready. Coffee too."

He pauses, a scoopful of eggs held in midair. "You have coffee?" The hope in his voice is almost too much.

"Oh, Ward. I don't just have coffee—I have good coffee."

"That's just not possible."

"Ye of little faith."

"Actually, when it comes to you, Angie, I don't just believe in faith. I believe in miracles."

He finishes what he's doing, and I carefully lay the biscuits in the pan, making sure they're not directly over the flame. It's a good thing he's walking into the kitchen so he can't tell how much his words affect me.

"Should I cover these with foil?" he yells from the kitchen.

"Yes. And go in the pantry for the white teakettle," I call back.

"Why not the one on the stove?" Ward appears in the doorway.

"'Cause that one's new? I prefer to keep it in good condition."

"Oh. Do you want water in it?"

"As long as you're not going to use the snow from outside," I inform him sweetly.

"Cute. Real cute." He turns back to the kitchen.

"Just remember who's making you coffee!" And after I shout that down the hall, I realize how easy this all seems. Especially the part where I slept in his arms.

Now, if I knew if I could handle the rest without flipping out.

Intimacy.

During his last visit when he was here with his family, I didn't show anyone the second floor. And last night, Ward only saw my grandparents' old room. Today, I give him the full tour, explaining the work I've done on the house since my grandmother passed.

"Why didn't you do any of it before?" He pauses to admire the soft remodel of the hall bath.

"Grandma really wasn't into changing much. The house was very much how she and Grandpa fell in love with it. And I couldn't take that away from her."

"There's not a lot of people in the world who would think like that."

"I'm not a lot of people."

His eyes meet mine in the mirror. "I know."

I wrap my arms around myself before sliding my back against the wall. "Don't be too impressed yet. You haven't seen the rest of the upstairs. I haven't been able to bring myself to change the color of either Grandma's sewing room or Grandpa's library."

"Why would you do that?"

I open the door and step back so Ward can precede me up the three short steps. Before he does, he backs me into the door. "I was taught to never step ahead of a lady through a door."

I bite my lip and lower my eyes.

He tips my chin up. "For the woman you are, I'll go through any door first as long as I know you're right behind me. Then I'll be waiting to take your hand again." He drops a brief kiss on my lips before jogging up the steps.

Oh. I can't formulate any words as he bounds up the stairs.

Then I hear, "Holy hell. Like orange much?"

I grin as I run up to Grandma's sewing room calling out, "Just wait until you see the library."

I have my head on Ward's leg, my back turned away from his stomach, as he reads to me by the battery-operated candle lights I found in my grandfather's office. He arranged the candles strategically so he can view the words in the slim volume easily, but they also afford me the ability to study him without much notice as he speaks softly. It's startling to admit that here, with him, I feel whole for the first time in ten years.

I deliberately dredge up the place where fear has crippled me, pain has flowed through my veins. Instead, I find confusion and anxiety replacing them. They're not born of what happened to me but what's happening to me.

"And then monkeys climbed the stage, wielding swords," Ward whispers excitedly.

I frown. "Monkeys?" I tip the book he's reading down in case my grandfather, in his last days of lucidity, wrote something odd in the margins.

He bounces his leg. "I was making sure I had a captive audience."

"Like that's a problem, I'm sure."

He shifts the book to the side, holding his place. His eyes hold the secrets to a million questions I've never asked because I've been too scared. I don't want to be that way. Not anymore, not with this man. "I don't read for just anyone, Angel."

Dropping a kiss on my nose, he resumes reading some nineteenth-century battle of clashing swords.

I try to focus on the words he's speaking, but I can't. Instead, I think about the ways I've changed since I met Ward Burke. Two years ago, I tried to be polite and nice because he was a part of the LLF family. Constant interaction between the two of us eventually wore away the masks we both hid under: his apathy and my indifference.

"And the monkeys twirled into the prince's arms wearing rainbow-colored tutus encrusted with the gems they fought so valiantly for," Ward interjects a note of joy in his voice.

I burst out laughing. "Busted."

He puts the book on the side table before he reaches for my hand. "Want to talk about what's on your mind? It's not a good sign when I'm trying to impress a woman on our first overnight date and she's losing interest."

My body locks. "Our first overnight date?"

"I know it's a bit unconventional, us being snowbound and all, but I was trying for candlelight and romance. There's no one I can think of who deserves it more." He lifts my hand to his lips and kisses the back gently before laying it on his chest.

I can feel the steady beat of his heart beneath my fingers. I shift so I'm on my knees next to him. From here I could bolt.

Or I could fly.

"Or, it doesn't have to be a date at all." His concern for me is evident.

"Can I ask you a question?" I stretch my hand upward and touch the strength of his jaw. His hands shift restlessly before he ruthlessly stills them.

"Anything."

"Do you see me as different because of what I told you happened to me?" I hold my breath.

"Absolutely." His answer comes so swiftly, I have no time to react. "I want to bury the men who did this to you because somewhere along the way, in between loyalty for your friendship with that ass Becks and eating pho, I realized something significant."

"What's that?" I barely manage to get the words out.

His face is somber. "I feel like your heart may have been created for mine. Now, that's just an assumption, but…"

"Then why are you holding back?"

"Because anyone who has the kind of feelings I do for you doesn't take advantage. That would make me no better than the animals who hurt you in the first place."

My eyes flutter closed. Burning emotion makes its way out and down my cheeks.

"Angel? What is it?" He cups my cheek and brushes away the wetness.

"You. It's just you." And for the first time, I wrap my arms around Ward and kiss him with every pent-up emotion I have.

WARD

In addition to thanking all of our first responders who are on shift during this mess, I'd like to applaud them in advance because they know in just about ten months they're all going to be on duty delivering babies named "Thunder," "Snow," "Fire," or some other sentimental crap. But please, for all that's holy, don't name your child "Toilet Paper." It's bad enough they're going to know their conception date.
— **StellaNova**

This kiss is heaven and hell all wrapped up in a package more precious and valuable than anything I've ever been exposed to. I know the second Angie's lips touch mine, it signifies the end of my bachelor days. It's love without the words, full of tenderness and subdued passion.

It's the type of kiss my parents used to exchange.

It's the kind of kiss I've been waiting to experience because it's soul-binding.

My hands move slowly so they don't startle her. I shift her slightly so she's resting with her back to the arm of our makeshift sofa. Stroking her gently, I begin to accustom her to my touch even as I keep a check on my passion that she stirs up in a heartbeat.

Angie's lips are firm but trembling. A soft moan causes hers to part. I don't immediately rush slipping my tongue into the heat of her mouth. I pull back, even as my arm behind her tightens a bit. "Do you want to take this a bit further, Angel?"

Her hand slides into my hair to pull me back down toward her mouth, but I resist. I lean the weight against hers. "There's no pressure. God, trust me. But, do you want…with me?" Christ, I don't even know how to ask her how she wants more.

A log crackles in the fireplace. But instead of jumping, Angie reaches for my hand before whispering, "I think you're trying to ask me this. Aren't you?" She places it on her ribs, over her bulky sweatshirt.

Just below her breast.

I begin to pant. "Only if you're sure."

Her hand trails around the nape of my neck, and she whispers, "Kiss me, Ward. Kiss me the way I'm hoping you want to."

But I don't, not just yet. I slowly slide my hand upward until my large hand cups the full weight of her breast in my hand. I feel the tremors race through her, but she doesn't shove me away. I quiver a bit when her delicate body arches a bit into mine.

That's when I lean down and touch my lips to hers.

Our tongues fight a duel, sliding against one another. I feel Angie's hands as they restlessly slide over my shoulders and back, trying to find purchase. But I hold myself in check fiercely, limiting myself to touching her over her sweatshirt despite the way her nipples rise prominently through the material to taunt me. My fingers capture one and pinch it slightly, elongating it further.

She makes a soft whimpering sound. Fuck.

Tearing my mouth away, I bury my face in the side of her neck, breathing heavily, "We need to slow down."

"Did I do something wrong?" Her voice is both breathless and confused.

I lift my head and find her pupils almost completely dilated. That wasn't a sound of distress; that was pure enjoyment. I trace a single finger over her breast and around the hardened tip.

She tosses her glorious head back. "Oh, God. Never…"

And that's when it hits me like a bucket of cold ice water. *Never*. This brave, resilient woman I'm holding has never experienced the feelings I'm churning inside of her. *Time to slow down*, I warn myself. I shift Angie forward so she's resting against my chest but still with her back against the arm. "Because I think we need to spend some time acclimating you to my touch," I tell her matter-of-factly.

"Oh. I just don't want…"

I tip her chin up. "Don't want to what?"

"To disappoint you." She blushes to the root of her hair.

"Angie, listen to me. I may have acted like a jackass in our not-so-distant past, but that's because I have my own plate of issues none of which have to do with you."

She chews her lip nervously. "Are you sure?"

I nod decisively.

"Then I'm getting off your lap to start prepping for part two of our overnight date."

She stumbles to her feet before I ask, "What's that?"

"Dinner. And before you make any further assumptions, you should know, I did date before all of this happened to me."

Now, my mind is spinning. Planning. "And how does this one rate?"

She tosses out a saucy wink. "I'll let you know later. I don't want to mess with your ego or anything. Oh, how does foil-packet chicken dinner sound?"

I push to my feet to help her in the kitchen. Grabbing the candles, I follow her. "I can't believe you know how to cook like this."

"I can't believe *you* can." Angie reaches quickly into the fridge and grabs defrosted chicken, veggies, and barbecue sauce. Tossing it all onto the counter, she grabs foil, a cutting board, and a knife.

I lean over the counter and pluck a kiss from her lips. "That's why we're dating."

Before I can back away, she says, "I never expected this."

"From me?"

"From anyone," she admits before she turns away to prepare the food.

But her words resonate deeply with me. She didn't expect this; what else would she not expect?

And then an idea strikes. "How long will these take to cook?"

"It depends. No more than an hour. I might try to clean myself up a bit after I prepare these." Angie's nose scrunches up. "I'd rather be freezing cold but clean."

"That sounds like a great idea. In fact, do you mind if I use the shower first?"

Angie waves her hand. "Be my guest. Upstairs through the guest room where the spare clothes are."

Perfect. That will give me more than enough time to calm the turbulent emotions rioting inside of me and to prepare something special for the woman in front of me.

While Angie's been upstairs, I cleared away our sleeping area and pulled the coffee table back in place. Hoping she'll forgive me for rummaging around, I swiped the candles from her dining room table and a tablecloth and china from the buffet. "God, please let this turn out right," I mutter as I light the last wick. My eyes roam over the setting to make certain I have everything in place. Cup, saucer, teaspoon. Over at the fireplace, I've put the french press, coffee, and teakettle filled with water. Wondering if our dinner's ready, I use the fireplace tongs to nudge a packet to the edge when something in the air changes.

I whirl around and feel like dropping to my knees.

Her hair is towel-dried. It's falling like dark fire over her bare shoulder before it meets the edge of her wide-neck sweater that falls to midthigh. Beneath it, dark leggings wrap around her legs before tucking into a pair of tall, fluffy boots. "I see we had the same idea." She nods to my slightly wrinkled jacket and dress shirt I pulled on with a pair of her grandfather's jeans.

I lean the tongs against the stone before approaching her. "I wanted to give you something you haven't had before."

"What's that?"

The fire crackles at my back, but it's the candlelight that throws gold into her eyes. If I died right now, I'd die a rich man not because of the wealth in my bank account but because of the trust in Angie's eyes when she looks at me. "Potential and endless possibilities."

"I have one more thing to add to that before it will be perfect."

"What's that?"

"Knowledge. I want to know about you, Ward." When I automatically stiffen, she whispers, "Every time we go out, we get closer, but there's still so much I want to know about you. Even the little things like your favorite colors, who chose your name, and your first crush. I want to learn about your favorite drink and your first kiss."

I relax. "Only if I get to know all that about you."

"That's a deal." She holds out her hand. I take it, yank her against me, and brush my lips against hers.

"We'll talk while we eat. As beautiful as you look, I don't want you to get too cold." I escort her to her seat of cushions.

"With the way you're looking at me, I'm not sure it's possible to get cold," she admits.

We're lingering over coffee when Angie asks, "Where has been your favorite vacation?"

"London," I say immediately.

"Why?"

"It was just Dad and me. It was my sixteenth birthday trip, and we did every touristy thing imaginable." I lapse into silence for a moment, remembering the early morning tours, the late dinners, the father-son talks we had on that trip. "It meant so much—then and now. He took two weeks out of his crazy schedule to bring me there. God, when I think about the amount of fish and chips we ate, I still wonder if we came home smelling beer-battered. I'd forgotten how much fun we had. I feel the closest to him right now than I have in a long time." I reach for Angie's hand. "Thank you."

"All I did was ask a question."

"And now I guess it's my turn. Hmm, what shall I ask? How about, what's your favorite type of book to read?"

"Romance," she answers unhesitatingly.

"Really? Reading about…"

"Intimacy?" Angie supplies helpfully, her eyes twinkling.

"Yes. It doesn't bother you."

She shakes her head. "I worked with psychologists for years. I know what my triggers are, Ward, which is why I probably should never have gone with you to Redemption that night, no matter how good the reasons were. The possibilities for them were endless."

"What are they?"

"Dark spaces, loud music, and a stranger grabbing me from behind," she answers immediately. "Certain visuals might do the same, but it's rare."

I hold up a hand. "You said a stranger grabbing you from behind."

She nods, wariness in her eyes.

I push to my feet and hold out my hand. "Do you trust me?"

She stands as well. I know my heart is possibly waiting for hers at the finish line, but this could be a huge step to bring her closer. I whisper, "Will you turn around?"

CHAPTER THIRTY-THREE

ANGELA

Conversation starter: What is the one thing you never gave up on? And you can't say the power coming back on.
— **Viego Martinez, Celebrity Blogger**

"Will you turn around?" Is it possible my heart understands his question before my mind catches up? Because one moment I'm facing him, and the next, I'm facing the big window that overlooks the lake. Anxiety makes my body shudder, wondering what's going to happen next when I mentally give myself a shake.

It's Ward. He's not Mike or Steve. He's not going to hurt me. My lips part, and the cool air, along with any lingering fear, is visible as it leaves me. I stand taller as I wait. When I feel him come up behind me, I feel...complete. While I wait, I cleave to the perfect rightness of it. Like everything has come full circle. Before I searched for fear in every direction, now I seek out Ward.

"Ask me a question," I tell him, my voice strong and true.

"Are you scared?"

"No."

"Why?"

"Because it's you."

"What does that mean?" he demands.

"It's my turn for a question," I say, with my back still to him. His rough expulsion of breath is my only acknowledgement. "We've been in each other's pockets the last few weeks. Between that and this snowstorm, it isn't normal circumstances."

"I'm aware of that."

"Is what you're feeling due to that?" My head twists around, and he's closer than I thought.

His hands come to rest upon my shoulders. His thumbs move back and forth slowly. My breath hitches every time it brushes where there were once bruises. "No. It never has been." He draws his fingers down, scraping them along the center of my back, sending chills racing along my skin. "Now, what did you mean because it's me?"

"Because I wouldn't trust anyone else to touch me like this," I inform him proudly.

Ward nods before he steps away. For a moment I feel the loss so great, my heart feels like it's being ripped from my chest while it's still beating. But then he blows out the first candle, then the other. He quickly shoves the coffee table aside and reassembles our bed of cushions in front of the fire. After spreading a blanket on top of them, he steps until all I can see are his dark eyes.

"Do you know who I am?" He strokes a finger down my cheek.

I lay my hands on his chest. "Yes."

He captures my hand and brings me closer to the fire. I'm just not certain if he's leading me closer to the one we need to stay warm or the one we started together.

For long moments, all Ward does is look at me while he combs his fingers through my hair. His large hands don't try to touch my skin in any way, and I'm confused. So much so, I blurt out, "Are we going to have sex?"

A wry smile touches his lips. He steps forward and places his full lips against my forehead. "No."

Now, I'm really confused. "We're not?"

"Nothing we do will ever be as baseless as sex, Angie. For us, each time, every time, it will be making love. And I plan on making you burn for it long before we take that final step."

Oh. My insides melt. I raise my hands to brace against his flat stomach for purchase as I sway.

"Is that okay?" Now, his thumb sweeps beneath my chin to raise my face up so he can study my features.

The little tugs of passion I've felt for Ward start licking at my heels as I raise my arms to wrap around his neck. Even as I'm nodding, I still give him the words. I suspect he needs them. "I don't know what's going to happen, but I want to be yours."

His head lowers, and his hands gently tug my hair to position my mouth. Drawing my lips beneath his, he still hesitates, doing nothing more than holding me close enough to let me get accustomed to him, the weight of what we're about to do.

Together.

Slowly, I put pressure against the back of his head until our lips meet. I don't close my eyes. I want Ward to know that I see him, feel him, even as his lips graze against mine. A glimmer of alarm tries to rise inside of me, but I set it aside. I want to know what's beyond the fear.

I know Ward's the man who will safely lead me there. I trust him to take me there. I have no doubt in the rightness of this, of him.

And with that, our mouths collide.

I thought I knew what passion was in the few interludes I experienced before my life crashed down around me. Deep down, I somehow thought I understood. I knew nothing, not even from the times Ward swept my mind away with his kisses. His lips part mine. I eagerly meet the thrust of his tongue with mine, stroking and stoking the fire between us.

But it's not just his tongue working magic on me. His fingers dance over mine. He lifts our joined hands, pulling them down between us so I can feel the turgid length of my nipple. So I cup the full weight of my own breast. So I don't fear his touch because it's part of my own. "Ward," I moan. I've never felt so cherished.

He bends his knees slightly so our gazes lock as the back of his hand lays against my heart. I know he can feel the way it's pounding out of control. His voice is rough when he asks, "Are you ready for more, Angel?"

The "Yes" is barely out of my mouth when his mouth crashes down on mine. This time, it's his fingers plucking at my nipples without mine. He rolls them between his thumb and forefinger.

My body arches back. "I've never felt anything like this."

"Tell me." Ward tears his mouth from mine and drops it to the skin exposed by my sweater. His lips are like a brand. Every place he touches sets my skin aflame.

And he wants me to put this into words?

I decide to show him.

I reach up and push his coat off his shoulders. It falls with an almost silent swoosh to the floor. His head snaps up as I begin to tug at the button-down shirt he's wearing. "I can't put this into words."

He hesitates before he unbuttons the top few buttons. Then, he reaches behind him and tugs the shirt over his head. The second it does, an intense arousal suffocates me. It's so profound, I know I have to try to find the words.

"It's like…" I shake my head as I try to gather my thoughts.

Ward's arm bands low and tight around my hips, pulling me close to his hardness. I gasp. His eyes flare. "Does this scare you?"

"Yes. No. Not in the way you mean."

His arm starts to loosen. Hastily, I explain, "I'm not frightened by you. But I'm scared of what you make me feel— this burning ache. I've never felt this way." I drag in a breath while I hope he understands what I'm trying to say.

He closes his eyes, his chest moving up and down rapidly. His lips move silently. "What are you doing?" I whisper.

"Saying a prayer of thanks that someone thought I was worthy of this gift." Ward's eyes open, and the next thing I know, I'm being lifted and laid on our bed by the fire.

Taking both of my hands in one of his, he raises them above my head. Soon my sweater starts to edge up above my waist before it follows the same path. My bra is swiftly divested from my body. I lie unresistingly as Ward begins to drag his fingertips over my arms, worshiping every inch of skin visible to him.

But I can't remain motionless when his seeking mouth drops to my nipple. I moan, frantically twisting beneath him— not out of fear but out of searing pleasure. My hand plunges into his thick dark hair, holding him to my breast. When he switches breasts, I spy the glistening wetness in the firelight.

I feel pride.

I feel passion

This is my choice.

I roll into Ward and tug his face up. Our eyes connect, saying a million words before his mouth comes down hard on mine. His big hands squeeze my breasts as I score my nails down his back.

I want him like I've never dreamed I could want.

His lips continue to tease and taste as his fingers slip to the band of my leggings. Edging in and out, the light touch makes me both comfortable and distinctly agitated before his thumbs hook in and slide my leggings inch by excruciating inch down my legs.

I squirm beneath him. His head snaps up to check on me, his features taut. I sit up and grab his face. "I'm okay."

His face relaxes as he finishes smoothing the tight black material off me. His hand skims up my thigh on his way to lie next to me. "I want this to be everything you ever hoped for."

"It already is," I assure him.

A tender smile crosses his face. "You can't know that yet."

"Yes, I can." I nod frantically.

"Tell me how," he whispers.

"Because it's you. I trust you, Ward. I know you'll make it special for me."

He lays his head against my heart. For long moments, the fire dancing is the only movement. I feel his lips against my skin when he says, "You're damn right I will."

Then Ward drifts his hand carefully between my legs to test my readiness. I arch my hips against his hand. I feel hot, swollen, and wet. I rock myself against his hand, intuition and long-ago memories surfacing. Ward pushes in a finger gently, then stills. His finger rotates, making a come-hither motion that almost has me levitating. I cry out.

He snarls, but the fierceness fuels my blood. I grab him and pull him down on top of me. I want to be electrified by him, the weight of his body, the abrasiveness of his chest hair against my nipples. I wrap my legs around him and hold him as close as I can without accepting him into my body.

But soon. I hope.

Finally, he tears his mouth away. Reaching into his back pocket, he pulls out his wallet. He slips the condom into his mouth until he can shuck his jeans. He rolls away, and I gawk for a second, wondering how he's going to fit, when he asks, "Are you sure, Angie?"

Raising my eyes from where his hands are sheathing up his cock, I whisper, "I've never been more certain of anything in my life."

He doesn't smile. Neither do I. I'm mesmerized by the look in his eyes as he prowls over me. Hitching my leg over his hip, he whispers, "Thank you for trusting me with something so beautiful."

He notches the head of his cock against the core of me. With slow movements, Ward began to move in and out of me.

The strain on his face makes me wrap my legs tighter before sliding my hand down his back. "Ward?"

"Don't!"

I immediately still.

"I don't want to hurt you, Angel. If I go too fast, I could." His words are strained.

He pushes deep, and a whimper escapes my throat—not born of pain, but of pleasure. "Ward, please," I beg.

His pupils dilate. I'm close enough to watch the firelight capture the black eclipsing the brown. "This could hurt," he warns.

"This is torture," I plead.

He pushes his hips forward. Where I expected a never-ending snap of pain, it's so much less and promptly dissipates under the replacement of pleasure that swiftly follows. I moan, tears leaking from the corners of my eyes.

Ward stills. "Why are you crying? Did I hurt you?" His arms are quivering.

"I'm crying because I'm so happy. But, Ward—" I instinctively tighten my arms, my legs, and my internal muscles around him, making him gasp. "Is there more?"

He groans before he shows me there is indeed more.

I urge him closer as he thrusts slowly in and out of me. But it isn't long before the rhythm of his thrusts changes, turning faster, deeper. My hips rise and fall, guided by one of Ward's hands holding mine, the other at my hip. My insides begin to tighten, and my head flails from left to right. I don't know what's happening to me until Ward's lips take mine briefly before his voice demands harshly, "Go over."

And I do. Calling his name, I feel myself explode in my first climax, brought about by my first lover.

Then something beautiful happens.

Ward thrusts hard a few times, and his face twists. He calls out, "Angie!" before he collapses on my chest.

Tears prick my eyes before I start to drift.

Finally, I am whole.

CHAPTER THIRTY-FOUR

WARD

Well, there goes my chance to see Beckett Miller in concert. Please, God, let it be rescheduled when I can make it. I had backstage passes. Crap.
— **Moore You Know**

The wind is whipping outside Angie's living room window, blowing gusts of snow overtop of the roof. It's a miserable night, calling for ruin and misery. Yet, cradled within her arms, I can't believe that to be true.

A warmth hits me square in the chest as I study her glowing face. Slowly, still shy despite everything we've done, she reaches up to push a strand of hair off my forehead. Before it drops away, I turn my head and kiss the center of her palm.

This is a time for her to realize I meant everything I said earlier. She's worth more to me than anything else in my life. She has no idea, but she's the gold that Midas really wanted when he asked Dionysus for a wish.

She's unmeasurable riches beyond compare. There's nothing that could equal the value of her in my life. Ever.

"Are you sore?" I ask in a low rumble.

Her head flops back and forth on the pillow, sending her hair dancing like flames. "Maybe I will be later, but right now, I'm too..." She breaks off in contemplation.

Bracing myself on my forearms, I capture her mouth for a brief kiss. The motion pushes my hips tighter against hers, causing a sweet moan to escape her swollen lips. Tearing my mouth away, I pant, "Too what, Angel?"

"Euphoric maybe?"

"That you were able to be with someone?" I cup her cheek to show my support.

"No, Ward. That when I finally chose to make love with someone, it was you." Her simple words, the directness of them, unman me.

"Angel, there's nothing special about me."

She wiggles her hips, her lips curving against mine. "I beg to differ."

The sauciness makes me bark out a laugh. My forehead drops down to hers. "Every moment I find out something new about you that astonishes me."

Her hands slide up my arms. "And to think, after dinner I thought you might find me perfectly boring by this point."

I slowly pull out, causing her to catch her breath. "Boring is the absolute last thing you ever could be, Ms. Fahey."

I reach for a tissue on the end table and quickly dispense with the condom. Before I can leave our makeshift bed to tend to her, I hear her soft voice murmur, "But I'm afraid I'm not strong enough."

"For what?"

"For..." Angie squares her shoulders much in the same way she does when she's at the office and is about to press her point with one of us. I've always thought it was adorable. Until now when she declares, "For you. I'm afraid I'm not strong enough for you."

I surge to my feet, my jaw clenched. "I can use the bathroom down the hall?" She nods. "Don't move an inch, Angela. I will be taking care of you before we discuss this."

Striding to the bathroom, I quickly dispose of the soiled tissue and wash my hands before reaching for a few washcloths I find neatly stacked on a shelf. Wetting one down with the ice-cold water, I run it over my chest and cock before tossing it into her shower. Dampening a second, I carry it with me back to the living room along with a dry one.

Unsurprisingly, Angie's covered herself up with the blanket. I immediately rip it off.

"Ward!" she screeches, her hands instinctively moving to cover her breasts and mound.

I can't prevent the wicked smile that touches my lips. "No wonder virgins were so prized in ancient times."

"We were sacrificed!" she retorts.

"That too." Sitting down on the side of the bed, I hush her. "This is part of the honor of being the first man you trusted with your body." *Your heart. And if I have my way, I will be the only man to have both.* Somehow, I refrain from saying the words aloud. Slowly, I begin at her neck and run the cold towel over her ample breasts, careful not to aggravate her nipples.

She shivers. I bite back a smile.

I trail the cloth over her stomach, drying her skin with the other, showing her with each touch that men aren't the monsters who hurt her. Certainly not this man. By the time I reach between her legs to clean up the trace evidence of her virginity, Angie's writhing again. Her arms are stretched to the side, fingers clenching the blankets. Her feet slide back and forth, agitated.

Her blue eyes are twin flames burning with a need she's unaccustomed to ask for.

I quickly hurl the cloths to the side and ease my body over hers, letting her know sometimes words aren't needed. When it comes to someone our hearts have linked to, our bodies can talk for us.

And that trust is something beautiful.

My hand smooths up and down her back when I blurt out, "I've made mistakes in my life, too many to name."

"Like what?" Angie trails her fingers over my chest, dragging her fingers through the sweat-dampened curls.

Capturing them, I roll to my back, pulling her along with me. Staring sightlessly up at the ceiling, I begin to admit my shame. "The night of my birthday, when my parents died? I should have been with them."

"Obviously, you weren't."

"No. I managed to convince my mom we should hold off the family celebration until Carrie could join us. I was acting so noble, Angie." I snort, but there's no humor in the sound. "Of course, my mom saw right through me. I ran from the room when I was given the okay to escape the family dinner— something we'd done for as long as I could remember."

"I've heard that's what mothers are supposed to do." There's a note of wistfulness in her voice I can't overlook.

I lift her hand to my lips and press a kiss against the back. "Sometimes I forget you don't have a point of reference for parents."

"Just because my parents were horrid doesn't mean I didn't have support or love, Ward. Quite the opposite, in fact. And since we've..." A blush edges her cheeks.

"We've, what?" I tease because I love watching Angie rise to the bait. For so many years, she's stifled her personality, and I never want her to do that with me.

She ignores my blatant attempt to bait her. Voice thoughtful, she contemplates aloud, "I built a wall around myself to keep the fear away, but instead I kept the love out. The world isn't just made up of just monsters, but I've been too fearful to let them close enough to discern the difference."

I reward her bravery by wrapping her tightly in my arms for long moments, wishing I had a fifth of her courage.

It isn't long before Angie brings us back around to what we were discussing. "What did you do the night your parents died? You said you all were supposed to go out? Where was Carys?"

Her fingers on my skin offer both the strength to go on and the tenderness I've refuted from anyone when this topic has arisen. "I went to a party with the guys who were also home from break."

Angie's hand stills as does my breath. *Here it comes*, I think despondently. The condemnation. "And you said your mom knew you were going out?"

"Sure. She teased me about it before I left. Reminded me I was seventeen, not twenty-one, when she asked me if there was going to be alcohol there. God, I miss the way they used to tease us." My teeth clench at the memory of my mother scolding me while trying not to laugh up into my face.

If she wasn't lying partially on my body, I'm certain I'd have fallen off the bed when Angie murmurs, "That's another thing we have in common, in an odd, screwy kind of way. I don't think my parents ever teased me, or if they did it was so long ago I can't recall it." Then her voice brightens. "But it sounds to me like they loved you the way my grandparents loved me—unconditionally."

"Yes, they did. Did your grandparents always greet you with a hug?"

Her head lifts so watery blue eyes meet mine. "Absolutely."

"Offer words of wisdom you didn't appreciate—then?"

"I wish I had recordings so I could play them back."

And the anguish I've been carrying around for me flows out of me like a dam bursting. "I was a seventeen-year-old shit who wanted to go to a party, Angie. I didn't care my older sister was stuck working for her boss—my godfather. I used it as an excuse to get out of a family night. And what did I get instead?" I cover my eyes with my arm. "Carrie had no idea where I was; neither did the police. Everyone was so damn grateful I was alive. Why? What was it about me and my life that made it so much more important than theirs?" My arm flings out to the side and slams against the mattress in frustration and sadness.

She whispers, "That's not how life works, Ward. Neither the good nor the horrible things that happen to us are dealt out so cavalierly."

"How can you believe that?" My eyes fly open to meet hers, incredulous that she of all people can say something like that.

Her lips curve in the kind of knowing smile sent by gods. It changes the meaning of my life every time I'm the recipient of it. "Because life can't be decided by a single decision of right or wrong. There has to be things like balance and redemption, or who would try to live after a single moment of awfulness? I have to believe that because why did Sula keep me going after that night? Why did my grandparents? Look at the way my life has changed. Isn't that example enough of how life can be redeemed? I guess what I'm trying to say is an outsider would look at your life, maybe even mine, and assume it's perfect when there's really no such thing."

I thread my fingers through hers resting against my heart and squeeze. Angie's voice is husky with tears. "I have to believe that. Otherwise, I'd spend all my time wondering who bestowed the richness of you into my life and what kind of debt I'm going to owe and how awful it will be to pay."

My free arm bands around her, hauling her further up my body so I can bury my face into the base of her throat. For long moments we hold on to one another as the storm outside rages on, adding a background for our mingled tears.

CHAPTER THIRTY-FIVE

ANGELA

Turnover at XMedia is already beginning. Former Executive Vice President of Innovative Solutions, Raquel Laurette, has turned in her resignation to the board of directors. We've obtained a copy of her resignation letter which indicates she's enjoyed her time working with the company, but it's time to move on to new challenges. We wonder if she'll be keeping her balloon package when she leaves, or will newly appointed board director, Michael Clarke, try to block it?
— **StellaNova**

"I don't want to leave you." Ward kisses me again.

"You'll see me tomorrow," I promise, even though I wrap my arms around him to hold him close. Having him here with me the last four days in our own rustic haven has been beyond anything I could have longed for. I rub my cheek along the scruff of his face. "You're going to cause a scandal if you walk into the office like this tomorrow."

He groans. "We could just run away, forget about work."

I shake my head vigorously. "No, we can't. We'd let your sister and David down. And Becks."

"I couldn't care less about Becks."

My carefree laugh echoes across the acre of white snow everywhere but my driveway, which was plowed in the early morning, startling Ward. He woke up shouting, "Are we under attack?" which caused me to laugh in hilarity.

Of course, he had his retribution for me finding humor in his honest mistake.

The sun is shining after days of clouds. It almost hurts my eyes to lean back in his arms, but that may have to do with the fact I really don't want him to leave. If I had my way, we'd stay cocooned in our little world and keep the outside away. But I know better.

Reality always has a way of penetrating its way in.

The next morning, Carys applauds as I enter the office four days after I left it. "Welcome back."

My face flames to the same shade as my hair. "Thanks."

Her smile turns knowing. "Let me guess? You wish you were still stranded?"

"Oh, my God. Do you really want to have this conversation? He's your brother!" I exclaim.

"And you're my friend. Just let me know one thing." She takes my fingers and squeezes them tightly. "Are you happy?"

I try to put the feeling into words. "I didn't know it was possible for my heart to feel like it was shooting off fireworks every moment I breathe."

A second later, Carys is leaping into my arms. I'm still holding her tiny sobbing body when Ward strolls in. He's holding my coffee but stops short when he spots his sister crying. "What's wrong?"

"I don't have the first idea."

"You and you," Carys blubbers. She steps back and blots her eyes.

Ward edges around the front of my desk warily. "Has she lost her mind?"

"It might be the effects of the thundersnow. Who knows if it knocked something out of kilter." Then I turn a horrified look at him. "Oh Lord. You might be in charge of the office."

Even as Ward makes a face, Carys bursts into laughter. "Okay, I get it. I may have overreacted."

"You think? Besides, what happens between me and Angie is between the two of us." Ward punctuates his words by rolling his eyes at his sister.

"Yeah, good luck there, buddy. Angie, I booked lunch for us today so we can catch up."

"Christ," Ward mutters.

My eyes bounce back and forth between the two of them, much like a tennis match.

Then the door is flung open. "My favorite people, I missed you! Being cooped up alone is no way to spend such a dreadful snow. Angie, how did you handle it?" Becks demands.

Ward is immediately in his space. "Who said she was alone?"

The tension level in the outer office rises drastically. Becks's voice is eerily quiet when he asks me, "Angie? Are you okay?"

Suddenly, I'm tired of all of it. I fling up my hands and yell, "I'm fine! Do all of you hear me? I don't mean any offense to anyone, but I want to spend lunch with the man I didn't want to leave my home. I'm sorry, Carys, but I don't feel like talking about it. And Becks, he's my choice. Therefore I'm not only fine, I'm wonderful. What I'm not is going to remain is a victim the rest of my damn life. I refuse."

And just that quickly, the tension dissipates like a balloon that was punctured. Ward plops the two cups of coffee he's holding down on the desk before he leans over and captures my face between his hands. "You know there's a few phrases for what we are to each other." His smile is wicked.

"Don't you dare..." I warn him.

He begins to tick them off in a voice so low only I can hear him. "We can start with the basic boyfriend and girlfriend. Then there's the tidy term 'involved.' But the one I think suits us best is the one you used yourself when you asked for me to slide inside your body the first time."

"Ward," I growl.

"Lovers," he says firmly. "You're my lover, Angie, and I'm yours. And that involves so much more than just our bodies. It involves our minds, our hearts, and our souls." Pressing a kiss to my lips, he snags his cup of coffee before winking at me and heading in the direction of the inner sanctum.

I finally get my wits about me enough to yell, "You'd better hope I don't see too many references to you on the blogger feeds today!"

"It will be made up. Just like always," he calls over his shoulder.

Becks and Carys gape at me. I stack papers together to appear like I'm doing something. When they don't move after a few minutes, I finally ask, "Do you guys need something?"

"I think I need popcorn for that show. Either that or I need to take my husband back home," Carys says faintly.

Becks punches her in the arm good-naturedly before coming over to wrap his arms around me in a fraternal hug. "I couldn't be happier for you," he murmurs against the top of my head.

Carys joins us in our circle before she asks, "Becks, did you need something?"

He squeezes us both before letting us go. "Maybe I just needed that. And, well, to annoy Dave."

Carys rolls her eyes and gestures him inside.

Becks gives me a wink before following her.

But there's a part of me that wonders if he wasn't telling the truth just then. After all, we all need love, the rich, the poor, the famous, and the people who hide in the shadows.

And sometimes if we're blessed, we get a shot at it.

CHAPTER THIRTY-SIX

ANGELA

The Lockwood Industries jet landed at Teterboro Airport before performing a quick turnaround. If billionaire Ryan Lockwood wasn't so completely in love with his husband, lawyer Jared Dalton, he would be fighting "Winsome Ward" to top our Most Eligible List.
— **Sexy&Social, All the Scandal You Can Handle**

I never knew someday I could feel like this. Love is a currency worth more than any item of value in the world. Who knew all the tears I shed, the misery I suffered, could be traded in for something with so much a price can't be placed on it?

These thoughts float through my head while I wait for Ward to finish up with a call with a potential client on the West Coast. In just a few short weeks, I feel stronger. More empowered.

I no longer wonder what would happen if I shared the identity of my attackers with Ward. I close my eyes, recalling the secrets we've shared while lying in each other's arms: his self-flagellation about his parents' deaths, my fears of being known forever as the girl who stood up and failed.

"What devastates me as much is if they did this to me, who else did they do this to?" I whispered to Ward.

"Angel, you can't take that burden on your shoulders."

"Logically, I can't, but every time…" I clamped my lips closed.

"Every time?" he prompted.

"Soon," I promised him. And not just because I need him to know everything before I tell him I've fallen in love with him. Ward's been gently pushing for a night out. "I'm dating the most incredible woman in the world. I want to take you places you've never been."

I'll never be completely comfortable with the media exposure that surrounds Ward, but it's a part of him. And like he's accepted the broken bits of me, I need to do the same for his twisted pieces.

When he enters the conference room a few moments later, he wraps his arms around me. I lean back against his chest. "Good call?"

"It sucked. I have to fly to Bigfork to sign the contracts." His voice is grumbly next to my ear, sending shivers racing across my skin.

"Why do you sound like that's so miserable?" I spin around in his arms to face him.

"Two reasons. The first is we just finished with our own snow that was up to our asses. Do I really want to voluntarily fly to Montana to deal with theirs? It's not like I'll have time to ski. "

"I forgot you ski." I recall the taunting he gave Carys the day they came to the house about her lack of coordination.

"You don't?"

"Let's put it this way, when God was handing out athletic ability, he forgot to give me mine. Dancing is my hard limit."

"So noted." We stand wrapped in each other's arms.

An idea pops into my head. Can I afford to do this— financially and mentally? Quickly, I do a mental assessment. Deciding to go with my gut, I tentatively offer, "Would it be better with company?"

Ward's body jerks. He holds me out at arm's length. "You'd do that? You'd come with me?"

"If you want me there."

"I crave being with you all the time, Angie." His words are blunt, but his touch softens them. "You do realize Bigfork is becoming a winter playground for the rock-and-roll rich and famous?" What he's not saying is more important than what he

364 · TRACEY JERALD

is saying. The press. The very reason I've been reluctant to go out in our own city.

That gives me pause but only for a moment. Then I decide it's time. "Then there should be plenty of others they can amuse themselves with," I say firmly.

I wish I could capture the expression on Ward's face at this very moment—incredulous joy combined with absolute shock. "Not that I'm complaining, but what brought this about?"

"If I don't take the steps to reclaim my freedom, I'll always be letting them win. And they can't have you," I say fiercely.

Ward's mouth is on mine in an instant. There's no buildup to this kiss. It's savage with the way he eats at my lips. I'm woozy by the time he lets me up for air. "I'll take that to mean you want me to come."

"And I want you to be with me in Montana."

We beam at one another. I pull away reluctantly before excitement gets the better of me. "I better go book us tickets. Wow, just think, my first plane ride."

"Nuh-uh. I'll arrange the flight." When I give him a pointed look, he just shakes his head. "Trust me, we'll get there and won't end up in Warsaw."

"Well, at least the clothes I'll be packing would work for either place. When are we leaving?"

"Tomorrow after lunch. I'll go to my place and pack in a few, then do you want to head to your place?" he asks.

I'm thrilled at the idea of being a few days away with Ward where we can be in public doing all the normal things couples do. "Yes. I'll be here waiting."

His dark eyes pierce mine as he reluctantly steps away. "This trip is going to be the beginning of so much, Angie. I can't wait to be with you." Then he slips out of the conference room.

"Me neither." I allow a ridiculous grin to split my face before I gather myself together and tell Carys she'll be without me for a couple of days.

"Teterboro? What airline flies to Montana from Teterboro?" I demand as the car service speeds through the Lincoln Tunnel to carry us beneath the Hudson River to the airport the next night.

"It's a specialty airline." Ward has his body angled toward me, a smug smile on his face.

"It must be, because I've never heard of LockAir. I just hope we're not flying in a propeller plane that has to weigh us before we get on board."

He snickers. "No, you don't need to worry about that."

In the shadowy light of the tunnel, Ward looks like he's bursting with a secret. His five-o'clock shadow just adds another layer of mystery to his gorgeous face. "You're keeping something from me."

His lips curve up just a little more.

"What is it?"

"Nothing bad. I promise."

Unbuckling my seat belt, I slide into the middle seat and rebuckle myself in. "I have ways of making you talk," I say coyly, trying out my rusty flirting skills.

The faintly amused look on his face disappears. In its place is a look so raw, so full of promise, I want time to stop. "All you have to do is ask, and everything I have is yours. My life, my wealth, and especially my heart. Don't you know that, Angie?"

"I don't need your wealth, Ward. But if you're offering the other two, you have to be able to accept everything about mine in return. And that's part of what this weekend is all about."

He crushes me to him. "A large part of me is my wealth," he starts to explain.

"No, it's something you have. Who you are is different," I contradict.

"Thank you." His voice is humble.

"For what?"

"For seeing me—it—like that."

"Anyone who doesn't, doesn't see you."

"I know. And now I appreciate—more than ever—why my parents didn't burden me and Carys with the knowledge of that kind of wealth every day." We pull into Teterboro and collect our bags.

After we check in, we're ushered into a VIP lounge. My head swivels left and right, looking for a sign for LockAir. A flight crew in inky-black suits with gold epaulets shows their badges before making their way past security. I bite a thumbnail. "Are you certain we're not going to be on a small plane?"

Ward takes my hand. "Relax. If I was worried about it, I would have told you last night when you packed for twelve days, not two." He pointedly looks down at his single bag in comparison to my three.

I shoot him a withering glare. "What a great time to mention…"

"Mr. Burke? Ms. Fahey? If you'll both come this way, please." It's one of the crew members in black. I frown.

Ward stands and holds out a hand. I grab a bag, but he takes it from me and puts it back down. "Angie, honey, the crew has it from here."

"Yes, ma'am, Mr. Burke is correct." The young man slings my garment bag and smaller carry-on over his shoulder before he lifts a bag in each hand. "Please follow me."

"Do I look as confused as I feel?" I whisper to Ward as we follow him down a red carpet beneath a plastic shielded archway.

He stops at the end and turns me to face him. "Nope. Now, remember, you can't yell at me."

"Why would I do that?"

"Because, I asked a friend for a favor." Then he leads me beyond the plastic.

And the only plane in front of me is an enormous jet with "Lockwood Industries" painted along the fuselage. I was scared about flying to Montana on a puddle jumper. Why am I suddenly terrified to see the steward carrying our luggage aboard this beast? "Ward?" I have to yell his name to be heard over the planes taking off.

He bends down to be heard. "Your first flight had to be special, Angie. So, I called Ryan Lockwood to see if he was using his plane this weekend."

"You called him up. Just like that?" I snap my fingers, but the sound is lost on the wind.

"I've known him for years, Angie. You'll love him. I used to work for his husband before I came to work for Carys."

"How many other surprises can I expect this trip?"

"How many do you want?"

My mouth falls open at his very serious answer.

Then Ward spurs me into action by saying, "But if it makes you too uncomfortable, I'll have them bring our bags back and we'll head to LaGuardia."

I grab a hold of him and say, "You'd do that for me?"

"In a heartbeat." He reaches for a phone attached to a pole next to where we are standing.

I stop him before he can lift the receiver. "I want to be comfortable with you, Ward. If that means understanding this side of you, then let's get on that plane."

A wicked grin crosses his face before he grabs my hand and we dash for the stairs leading to the sleek black plane.

With a quick layover for fuel and time zone changes, we land at Kalispell Airport in the early afternoon. Ward did have me arrange for an SUV as a rental. So within a few minutes of landing, we're off toward Bigfork when I ask him something that's been stuck in my brain since he said it yesterday. "What did you mean by this is becoming the winter playground for the rock-and-roll rich and famous?"

"There's any number of things Bigfork offers."

"Like what?"

He cuts his eyes off the road for just a second. "Like Kristoffer Wilde for one."

"What? He lives in New York." *And Tennessee and South Carolina*, I add.

"This is his winter getaway. If you want to do serious business with him while he's out of the office, you're coming to Bigfork."

Suddenly, the light dawns. "You're not here to just see an artist, are you?"

"No. Tomorrow is Kris's annual holiday party. Anyone who's anyone in the music business has been invited. This town is going to be teeming with celebrities flying in. And more business deals will be handled in a few short hours than in an entire year."

"All I brought was a little cocktail dress. You told me that's all I would need." Mentally I wonder if I would survive if the car landed in a snowbank because the urge is strong to choke Ward right now.

"Honestly, Angel, that's all you'll need. I'm wearing a sweater and slacks. It's the talent who go all out."

"You realized you saved yourself from certain death, right?"

"Just relax. You're going to love this weekend," he promises as we pull up at the hotel.

"Wow" is all I can manage. Four stories, the clapboard lodge is rustic with snow dusting the cathedral roofline. As we pull under the stone entryway, a valet quickly opens my door.

"I know. I love this place." Ward quickly turns over the keys and comes around for me.

"What about our bags?" I watch as the SUV is driven away.

"They'll bring them up to the room which is right where we should be going."

"Not before I do this." I touch my lips against his briefly. "I'm so happy right now, and that's because of you. There's no way I could feel better than I do right now."

His arm slips around me. "Don't make assumptions, Angie. We have days ahead of us."

I throw my head back and laugh as he leads me into the lobby.

CHAPTER THIRTY-SEVEN

WARD

What do celebrities do when they congregate in the country? They scurry from their city homes to their country homes. But the thing is, they're all in the same place. Do they think we don't know where they are? If they really wanted to disappear, they'd go somewhere they could actually blend in.
— StellaNova

Angie's been introspective since we went downstairs for dinner at the lodge. When I explained my connection to Jared, and Jared to Ryan Lockwood, her only comment was, "I see. I suppose I should have realized you were so close with such influential people."

Maybe taking the jet was a bad idea? "Angie, it's just money. The most I do with mine—ours," I correct myself, "is to donate large amounts of it. In fact, our investment advisor wants us to donate a chunk to a charity Ryan's putting together."

That gets her interest. "Really? To do what?"

I'm glad Lynne finally sent over the information. I'm able to give her a brief rundown of the ways it will help kids who need college scholarships. "I'll be proud to add our money to that," I conclude.

"I'm sure Carys will too."

"I hope so. I committed us for a hundred."

"Thousand? That doesn't sound so bad."

"No. Million."

The chicken wing slips out of her fingers. "One hundred million dollars?" Her voice is weak.

Embarrassed, I admit, "That a little less than ten percent of what we have."

She reaches for her water, and the glass wobbles. "Oh, I'm so sorry."

"Hey. What's wrong?" I capture her hand beneath mine on the table.

"Ward, I had you sleeping in front of a fireplace. In my dead grandfather's clothes, for Christ's sake. And here you are, able to call up a jet at the drop of a hat. You can donate more money than people can dream of making in their lifetime. What on earth are you doing with someone like me?" Her voice cracks.

"Realizing I still have a heart," I shoot back.

"What?"

"Angie, I don't care if it's too soon, but you've given me back the things I lost when my parents died thirteen years ago."

"Ward," she cautions.

"You made me realize I could love. That I could be loved. And the world wasn't going to end if either was going to happen."

Her chest rises and falls as waterfalls of tears cascade down her face. "I want...I need..."

"When you're ready. I already know how you feel."

"That's a pretty damn big assumption, Counselor," she snaps.

"I've got a check big enough for my ego to cash," I joke.

And her tears of panic turn to screeching laughter. If she'd open up that final barrier, she'd never have to feel that panic ever again.

"I swear, you were on my television last night. Sure as the devil, I recognize your hair." The store proprietor follows Angie around the store the next day.

"I can't imagine why, ma'am. I offer no offense."

"None taken. Those earrings are buy two, get one free."

"Thank you." Angie moves away from the kitschy earrings and makes a beeline straight for me. I frown at the fearful intensity on her face. Whatever is wrong, I have to get her out of this store, quickly.

"When are you coming out with your next movie? I was so excited to see that one come on broadcast TV. It has a 93 percent on Rotten Tomatoes, you know," the woman persists.

Angie trips but manages to catch herself before she falls. "Excuse me?"

"You know. That movie where you're the doctor in the emergency room? That's my favorite of all the movies you've been in."

Angie reaches up and touches her dark auburn hair before a faint smile crosses her face. "I think you have me confused with someone else. I'm not an actress."

"You're not?" The store owner's face falls.

"No, ma'am. I'm just a regular citizen."

"Oh. Then those earrings are regular price. I don't discount nothin' during ski season."

Angie regains her aplomb. "That's fine. What about your huckleberry products?"

The two women get into a discussion about the benefits of huckleberry hand lotion while I meander about the store. "What is it that had her so scared?" I mutter to myself. Whatever it is, it's holding her back from being able to tell me how she feels.

I know Angie trusts me with her body, with her mind, and with her soul. But never did I realize the difference of not having a woman's heart until I gave them my own and was left wanting. *How long must I wait until she's able to let go of whatever's holding her back?* I wonder dejectedly. Then I shake myself. I know I'll keep steady on this path, giving her my whole heart until she's ready to join me. There's no other choice.

That's what love is.

"Hey, are you going to buy anything?" Her voice jolts me.

"Hmm? Buy something?"

"Yes, Shepherd of Wealth and Benevolence. Are you acquiring anything to distribute as gifts to individuals as a memento of your trip?" Her teasing makes me realize she's processed any issues she had about my money and dealt with them.

Good. Now I can have a little fun shopping.

"Actually, I do have a place I need to stop. Are you getting hungry?"

"Starved, actually."

"There's a coffee shop on the corner that serves great coffee and huckleberry pie. Want to get us some? I'll grab what I need to and meet you there in twenty minutes."

She rises up on her toes to kiss my mouth. "Deal."

"Angel?"

"Yes?"

"I can see why she mistook you for an actress. You really are that gorgeous."

Angie blushes to the roots of her hair. "Stop. I'm totally not." She ducks out of the store's side door.

"No, you really are." I follow her down the alley between the two stores before I duck into the jeweler's.

I don't spring my purchase on Angie until I see what her outfit for the party at Kristoffer Wilde's consists of. When she steps out of the bathroom, she takes my breath away. The puff sleeves on the black silk dress flows down to show off her small waist and flared hips. "You look stunning."

"It's just a dress, Ward." But the faint flush that accompanies her words lets me know her pleasure.

I step closer and play with one of the curls strategically pulled out from Angie's updo. "This reminds me of the night we went to Redemption."

She bats my hand away. "And that night it took forever with your sister's help and half a pound of hairspray. Tonight's a crapshoot."

My laugh echoes throughout the room until she walks past me to fiddle with her purse. It abruptly dries up when I catch sight of the back of her deceptively demure dress. I swallow hard when I see the cowl that dips down to the middle of her back—silk meeting silk. "Are you sure we have to go to the party?"

She whirls around. "Ward? What is wrong with you?"

"You. That dress. You're incomparable, Angel." Then I slip my hand into my slacks pocket and pull out a square jeweler's box. "I thought I might add a little sparkle to your outfit, but I realize it's going to be dull in comparison. Nothing and no one in that room tonight is going to shine like you, Angela."

She closes her eyes. "Will you put it on me?"

I smile tenderly. "Do you want to look at it first?"

She shakes her head vigorously. Another wisp of hair falls. "No, because it doesn't matter if there's cartoon characters, beads, or sparkly things in that box. You bought a gift thinking of me, not because you had to but because you wanted to make me happy."

"If you'll give me all of you, I'll spend my life doing just that," I vow as I remove the sapphire hoop earrings from the box. Carefully, I undo the ones she's wearing and slip these in. I tuck the pearls away in the box before turning her toward the mirror. With my hands on her shoulders, I whisper, "Go ahead. Open your eyes."

When she does, she finds my eyes in the mirror. "I love them. Thank you."

"You haven't looked at your present," I chastise her.

"You're wrong. I already am."

My heart stretched full to bursting, I slide a hand beneath her arm. I reach around her waist until I can rest it on my favorite part of her body—her heart. "They match your eyes—sparkling and blue."

"They match your heart—generous and overwhelming. I never stood a chance. I never wanted to," she whispers.

I tuck my face against the bare skin of her back and just breathe in her scent. I want to preserve this moment in my mind forever.

We do just that until the alarm on my phone goes off. "It's time to go. Are you ready?"

"Just about."

Moments later, we leave our room to head to Kristoffer Wilde's holiday party.

CHAPTER THIRTY-EIGHT

ANGELA

Tag, you're it! Photos from Kristoffer Wilde's annual holiday get-together are starting to surface and my, oh, my. The guest list was as sexy as it always is. But the shocker was Ward Burke's mysterious redhead. Although no one snapped a photo of her face, there's no doubt she's the same woman he's been seen with in New York.
— **@PRyanPOfficial**

"It's good to see you again, Angela." Kristoffer Wilde shakes my hand warmly.

I choke on my cola. Ward thumps me on the back several times before I shoot him a dirty look. Returning my attention to our host, I say, "It's good to see you, sir, though I'm surprised you remember more than my voice."

"Nonsense. Anyone who helped keep Burke and David from killing each other during those final days was a genuine asset to Wildcard. Are you certain I couldn't tempt you back now that the two of them have worked out their differences?"

PERFECT ASSUMPTION · 383

I'm flattered. "No, sir. My services are still needed, as I'm sure you can imagine. Just because they're married doesn't mean they're never at war."

"Then how about taking a circle around the room with an old man. I'd like to catch up a bit."

Ward's arm, comfortably around my waist, tightens protectively. "I'd enjoy that, Mr. Wilde."

"See, Ward, the lady shows respect when she speaks to me. Why didn't you ever learn that trait?" He scowls at the man I love.

The man I love.

Oh, my God.

"Because you're a constant pain?" Ward says mildly.

"Angela, were you ever unhappy working for me?"

"Umm…" I can't answer that question truthfully because I was completely miserable, but it has nothing to do with the man with the enormous personality in front of me.

Ward narrows his eyes at Kristoffer. "She's happy, Kris."

"Good. Then she can tell me all about it while I introduce her to a few friends who aren't in the business." An unspoken conversation occurs between the two men.

"I'll be fine, Ward. Go do what you came here to do," I encourage him.

His jaw clenches slightly, but he doesn't say anything when I step forward to take Kristoffer's arm.

We're a few steps away when I glance back over my shoulder to find Ward already engrossed in a conversation with the bass player from Nocturne. I tip my head up to meet the hawkish features of the music mega-giant. "Thank you."

"Of course. And none of it was a lie. I do want to hear how Carys and David are getting along. As you know, when I'm normally on the phone with her, she can be very vexing. How is young Benjamin?"

"Adorable." I pause when Kristoffer nods in the direction of the Spine Wrecks. "A few weeks ago, everyone was out at my place north of the city to play in the leaves."

"And did your home fare well in the recent thundersnow?"

"It did." We pause at the outskirts of the room near the steps for the wine cellar. I blurt out the first thing that comes to mind. "How do you handle it?"

"Handle what?"

"The constant media attention?" I hold my breath while I wait for his answer.

"I largely ignore it." He stops a passing waiter and lifts two glasses of champagne. He holds one out.

"No, thank you," I decline politely.

A trace of understanding flashes across his face. He leans slightly closer. "Angela, right there is how you handle the media—by retaining your power in situations where you think you might lose it." He stops a different waiter, who's walking by with a small minibar on a trolley tray. "What are you drinking?"

"Just cola." I watch carefully as the can is freshly popped before it's poured into a crystal glass. Mine is exchanged out.

Kristoffer is silent through the exchange. "Carys always said you were a brilliant employee, Angela. As fast as she was traveling up the ladder, Carys would have brought you and David with her. Nothing in your background would have stopped you from succeeding."

I take a sip of my drink as I contemplate my words. "But would I have stopped myself? I wasn't ready then."

"You are now."

"And now, I don't want to leave. I'm happy."

He tips my glass in understanding before taking his own drink. "You handle vultures by letting the people who love you inside and holding them close. Then nothing will ever... Ah, Kody, Meadow. You made it!" Kristoffer lets me go to greet them both warmly.

A man with reddish-blond hair appears to my left. "We had babysitting issues."

386 · TRACEY JERALD

"That's because you felt the need to lecture Elise on everything that could possibly go wrong." A beautiful brunette fits herself to his side after Kristoffer releases her, and she holds out a hand. "Meadow Laurence. I manage Nature's Song."

"Angela Fahey. I work for an entertainment law firm that does business with Mr. Wilde."

"Angela, after all these years, don't you think you could manage to call me Kristoffer?"

"No. Especially since I'm certain my boss and Becks would kill me."

Kristoffer turns to the others with a pained expression. "See what my life has come to? I can't manage to get this young woman to call me—a quiet, unassuming old man—by his first name."

I snort. I can't help it. Three sets of eyes immediately flash in my direction. "I'm sorry. You were laying it on a bit thick with the 'quiet, unassuming old man' farce."

Kody and Meadow gape at me as I smack down my former boss's boss.

He strokes his silvery beard with a wicked glint in his eye. "Whatever would make you say that?"

"I've heard you curse worse than Becks, and that was during negotiations with my boss only last week!" I exclaim.

"Now, wait just a damn minute, Angie. It was your boss who started that," Kristoffer fires back.

I buff my nails against my dress. "Not from where I was sitting. I believe your exact words to set her off were, 'You can sue my ass all you want. You're not getting another damn dime out of me.'"

A flush rises against his swarthy face. "I may have said something to that effect—"

"Exactly that." I'm enjoying myself.

"Wow, Kris. I see your phone skills haven't improved," Meadow interjects drily. "This reminds me an awful lot of the first time we ever spoke."

"I was under a lot of strain, Meadow Laurence. And don't you offer any lip. You weren't on the phone with Carys at the time."

Meadow whirls excitedly to me. "Carys? You work for Carys? What's she like? I've been compared to her by Kris for years."

"Oh, you'd love her. I do."

"Tell me all about her."

"I'm doomed. What was I thinking introducing the two of you?" Kristoffer groans while Kody laughs.

I hold up a hand to high-five Meadow, which she promptly does.

Ward's scent hits me before I feel his arm slip around me. "I don't know what you were thinking, Kris, but it was a great idea. Kody." He reaches past me and shakes the other man's hand.

"Ward. Good to see you, man. How are you liking the condo?"

"Haven't spent a lot of time there lately."

"Good. If you decide to sell it, let me know. I've got a list of buyers salivating for the chance."

"Wait, Ward. Meadow said she runs Nature's Song—what is that, by the way?"

Meadow opens her mouth, but Ward beats her to the answer. "You're standing in Nature's Song, Angel. As for Kody, he's Laurence Construction. He's one of the best home builders in the United States. He refurbished my condo and developed a bunch of other well-known communities around the country. He and Meadow also did the repairs on this place when it was damaged a few years ago."

My jaw drops because I recall Carys telling me and David how Kristoffer's house had been vandalized but how he lucked out with the most brilliant team to restore his family's getaway. "That was the two of you?" I exclaim.

They both nod, before exchanging looks of such devotion, my heart aches. "I still design custom homes but try to limit my own builds within a certain radius. That is, unless someone like Ward Burke calls."

Ward gives him the finger. "Please. Like you weren't dying to get your hands on a place that big in the city."

"That may or may not be true."

Meadow changes the direction of the conversation. "Do you like working for an entertainment lawyer?" At my nod, she goes on. "I changed careers just a few years ago. Recently, I took over the vacation rental business I originally moved here to work for. It's a crazy story how we both ended up living here, but we both love it."

We continue to chat with the Laurences for a few moments before I glare up at Ward. "Aren't you supposed to be mingling? Making deals?"

"I wanted to check in to make certain you were all right."

I spin away from his arm. "Go conquer the legal world, Ward. I'm going to stand here bugging Meadow about more places to shop…"

"Can I come conquer the legal world with you, Burke?" Kody deadpans. We all chuckle.

Ward brushes a finger along my cheek. "Have fun. I'll be around."

After he walks away, Meadow pounces on me like I'm fresh meat. "I promise to give you the inside scoop about shopping at non-kitschy stores if you'll tell me one thing."

"What's that?"

"Did I interpret what you said right? Do you know Beckett Miller?" Her voice has that slightly high-pitched squeak most women get because they lust after Becks.

"Oh, for the love of God. Standing right here," Kody growls.

Meadow flaps her hand at him "Is he really as gorgeous in person as he is in photos?"

"More so," I confirm.

"Damn," Kody bites out as Meadow lets out a dreamy sigh.

I lift my soda to my lips and catch Kristoffer's eye where he's standing a few feet away talking with another group of people. He lifts his glass in a toast. I lift mine back and mouth, *Thank you, Kristoffer.* Mentally I add, *For everything.*

His face softens as if he knows.

On the balcony that night, clad in only Ward's sweater and a pair of thick socks, I remember Kristoffer's words to me. *You handle vultures by letting the people who love you inside and holding them close.*

It's time to tell Ward the rest of what happened to me. I can't hold back with him anymore. If this means the end of us, then I'll have gained so much from this relationship—the inner certitude of who I am and the kind of man I need to be with me. But inside me, in the heart that's glowing alive, I know that's not the case. He's going to understand.

I hear the door open behind me. "Aren't you freezing?" Ward wraps his arms around me, burying his face in my neck.

"I'm too nervous to be cold."

"Nervous? Why?"

"I never thought I'd ever tell a man I was in love with him before, but tonight I knew for certain I was."

His entire body stills. It's as motionless as the water on the lake in front of me. "What did you say?"

"I said, I love you."

He whirls me around. "Thank God." But just before he kisses me, I place a hand on his chest.

"I'm terrified, Ward. I need to tell you the rest."

"There's more?"

I nod. "There's the who."

CHAPTER THIRTY-NINE

WARD

Michael Clarke made a bold statement at a board of directors meeting about enacting a Code of Business Ethics at XMedia and all subsidiaries. Many will remember Clarke was accused of sexually assaulting a woman during his college years. Is this move prompted on repairing his reputation or true concern for his workforce?
— **StellaNova**

When Angie whispers the names of the two men who abused her in the dark of the night, my arms become immobile. I'm ashamed my first thought is, *Could there be two sets of two men with the same name?* Then I realize the improbability of that, and the pieces begin to fit together in my mind one by one like a puzzle.

Louie's comment. Angie's almost violent physical reaction. Her unwillingness to drink something someone else prepared without watching them. Her desire to spend time alone, almost sheltering herself away from people.

It all collides together and slams into me brutally.

Somehow, someway, the boys of my childhood who I turned to in the worst of days caused a living agony for the woman I love in the prime of hers. My arms slowly slip from around her. Once again, my world has shifted on its axis. I suppress the urge to go out and harm my boyhood friends as she continues on with her explanation.

"Every time Michael Clarke is mentioned in the media, the story manifests itself all over again. I've never felt strong enough to love myself so I could fall in love." Her eyes—in some ways still so innocent—meet mine. "Until now. Until you. But there's a huge price you'll be paying. I've worked so hard all these years to downplay who and what I am. The moment we're seen together, the media will have a field day."

"That's the reason you didn't want to go anywhere?"

"That and I've honestly enjoyed just getting to know you, Ward. I don't need fancy dinners. I'd rather spend the rest of my life with someone who thought to throw a tablecloth over our coffee table. But I know being a part of your life means events like tonight."

"Trust me, nights like tonight are rare."

Angie's laugh is laced with amused cynicism. "Really? I've seen the gossip rags, 'Winsome Ward.'"

I cringe. "Stop. Just stop. Honestly, I spend most of my nights at home reviewing contracts. If I led the life they implied I did, don't you think Carys would have…" Just mentioning my sister's name makes my mind whirl back to the beginning.

Don't play around with her.

"Carys knew." It's a statement, not a question. The warnings, the locked employee files. Was Carys protecting me, Angie, or us both?

"Yes. When I hired on at Wildcard, I accepted the position and then was completing the paperwork for my background check. When I came to the question about whether or not there was anything in my past that could prevent me from being hired, I asked your sister for a meeting, and I told her the whole story."

"What did she say?" How could my sister let me associate with men she suspected were sexual predators, even if by then it was only at the occasional party I saw them at or while clubbing at Redemption? My mind is whirling at the implications of this for all of us.

"I never explicitly told her the names, though it wouldn't surprise me if it came up in my background check. It didn't take Becks long. He recognized me from photos years ago." Angie admits.

A whoosh of air escapes my lungs. "That's why you were so scared in the store shopping."

"Yes. There's been a lot of coverage of XMedia recently. I assumed they had run the photos again. The last thing I want is for anything to hurt you. I'd do anything to protect you."

"No, that's what I'll be doing from now on—protecting you with every available resource I have at my disposal. I don't care if the next six generations of our family are paupers. Goddamned son of a bitch."

"Ward?" Angie's voice is laced with confusion.

I'm not certain if it's because of what I let slip about our future or because of the ferocity of my vow. It doesn't matter. What matters is whether she pushes me away or holds on after what I'm about to tell her next. Swallowing hard, I whisper, "I've known Michael Clarke and Stephen Bellew since I was in grammar school."

Her cry slices through the night air.

"And Angie, I believe you. I believe everything you've told me."

Tears fall out of her eyes and freeze against her cheeks before I can wipe them away. "How can you? They're your *friends*." She spits the last at me.

"Wrong. They were. And from this moment on, no more."

"Ward…"

"Am I going to deny the friendship I shared with them because they carried me through a less than perfect time in my life? No. But I don't care if there's never going to be a plea of guilty or physical evidence. I've held your body against mine during a flashback. Your spirit was both shattered and reborn when you told me what happened." I pull her weeping body against mine. I clutch her tightly against me as I whisper the most important thing. "And I love you. I love you, Angie. The rest of the world can rot in hell—preferably with those two assholes leading the way."

"I love you too. When you said you knew them, I became so afraid."

"Of what?"

She takes in a deep, shuddering breath. "I made an assumption—a wrong one, obviously—that you'd turn away."

"There's no need to be afraid anymore. There's no place you're safer than in my arms. I promise you that."

She hiccups and whispers, "Deep down, I think there's a part of me that might have suspected that."

Thank God. I swing her up in my arms and carry her back inside so we can sit in front of the fire. Tonight's not a night for making love; it's a night for holding on to it.

And for me to figure out how to protect the woman in my arms from any further harm.

My worlds have collided in a way incomprehensible way. I need to immediately sever any and all ties with anyone or anything associated with Mike and Stephen. I have to talk with Carys, but I'm certain she'll have no problem with immediately selling the stock we own in XMedia to start.

"Listen, Carys. I may have thought the money left to us was blood money, but I flat out refuse to own anything related to XMedia."

Angie is asleep in the bedroom of our suite while I'm discussing the sell order I'm about to place with my sister. We're going to take a loss on our shares, but I don't care. Nothing matters but the anger deep in my soul. The few hours I slept hasn't abated it any. If anything, it's bloomed it more.

"Can I ask why?"

"I love her, and I refuse to be associated with anything that will hurt her."

There's silence on the other end of the line. It goes on so long I have to lift my phone to make certain we weren't disconnected. Finally, I call out, "Carys?"

I apparently was on Mute. When the button is pressed, Carys is screaming, "She told you?"

"Yes."

"I want to kill them."

"Get in line." I begin pacing. On my third turn, I jerk to a stop. Angie's standing in the doorway still wrapped in my sweater from last night. Her expression is the picture of vulnerability. "I have to go. Do I have your approval?"

"You'll have it in writing in two minutes. Send it to Lynne to dump all shares. It's about time." Carys slams down the phone in my ear.

I wince as I yank out my earbud.

"Who was on the phone so early?"

"Carys. I needed her approval to do some financial stuff this morning." I walk directly to her and wrap my arms around her waist. "Did you sleep all right?" I know she didn't because I didn't close my eyes, and she tossed and turned in my arms all night.

"Not really." Her head comes to rest on my chest.

"Why not?" Did nightmares follow her into her sleep? Mentally, I run through a list of sleep specialists I know when her words shock me.

"Because you didn't sleep a wink." Angie grabs my hand and leads me back to bed. She slips the button of my jeans through the buttonhole and wriggles the zipper down. She pushes the denim over my hips, and the pants fall to my knees. I kick them off, leaving me clad in only my boxer briefs. "Come lie down for a few more hours with me."

"But I need to…" Before I can tell Angie I need to send an email, she climbs back into the bed and pulls me in with her.

"Sleep. That's what we both need, Ward. Then you can execute whatever evil you and Carys were planning." Trustingly, Angie turns into my arms.

Knowing when I wake I'll be able to start insulating the woman curled up next to me from the evil that has plagued her world for too long has me finally able to close my eyes. Finally, with her slow, warm breath against my neck, I sleep.

And dream of vengeance.

CHAPTER FORTY

ANGELA

What does one celebrity get another for the holidays? No, really, I'm asking.
— **Moore You Want**

Something about Ward's reaction brought out something I hadn't felt in years: justified fury. The way he immediately processed what I told him scared me. There were moments where I could almost feel my words causing him pain, but I didn't understand it until he told me he knew Mike and Stephen. He expected me to turn away—the same way I had of him. *Both of us making assumptions about the other again*, I think ruefully with a shake of my head.

On the flight home, Ward is much quieter than he was on our way to Montana. His fingers are furiously tapping on his keyboard. I finally break in to ask, "Is there anything I can do?"

His head snaps up. "Well, shit."

"Forgot I was here?" Before he can speak, I continue. "Don't worry, I'm not insulted. I am amused though. Is this what you're like all alone at home working on contracts?"

He stretches, his shirt untucking from his jeans, providing me with a glimpse of those perfect Vs on either side of his hips. I want to lean across the aisle and bite them, but if he's busy, I'll save that for later. "Probably. David decided to drop a bunch of stuff in my inbox he needed for tomorrow."

"Let me see," I cajole him. Without waiting for a response, I move over to the couch he dominated for the last hour. After I settle next to him, Ward slides his laptop over in front of me. After scanning the contracts, I declare, "David's evil," before pushing the laptop back in front of the man I love. The man who loves me in return. I want to jump up and down and twirl around in a circle, but I restrain myself. I'm enjoying his confusion too much.

All the years of Ward being a pain in the office are about to come to fruition. Right now.

"What do you mean?" he demands.

"I mean Carys asked for David to explicitly review those contracts. She's trying to have him take on more advanced work. He's sending them to you for a double-check before he sends them back. He's playing you."

"You're shitting me. How in the hell is he getting away with this?" Ward growls.

I curl my nails and rub them against my sweater before blowing on them. "Perhaps if someone wasn't a bit of a control freak in the office..."

"I am not a control freak."

"Oh, my love, you really are."

"Name one time," Ward demands.

I pull his laptop back in front of me and pull up his calendar. There are at least ten meetings scheduled I'm not copied on. "Right here is the perfect example. I need to know about every business meeting you have."

"That's just ridiculous," he splutters.

"Not when I'm the one who sends out the billing to our clients each month. This isn't your old firm where the lawyers did their own billing, Ward. I handle that for everyone in our office. If you don't copy me, I can't bill for your time accurately. Haven't you wondered why your hours are off? And David? He knows you weren't working through me. He's. Playing. You," I conclude with mock sadness.

A mix of horror and admiration flicker across Ward's face. "We have hours on this flight."

"We do."

"Help me."

"Do what?"

"Fix this."

"We can't go back and re-charge clients. That's completely unethical."

"I don't care about that. What I do care about is having leverage over my dear brother-in-law."

"Ahh. Let me get this straight. After two years, you finally want me to help you the way I've always supposed to."

"Please. Do you know how many nights I've brought work home from the office?"

"You know why I'm doing this, right?" I access my own files from Ward's computer and send a copy to his email so I can begin to create a quick database.

"Any reason is a good one, but I'll bite."

"Because Carys's reaction is going to be spectacular. You're both up shit's creek." I cast a quick glance to the side. "You might want to buy earplugs by the gross before we go to work tomorrow."

Ward leans over and presses a kiss on the side of my head. "I swear, I wasn't trying to do anything deliberately wrong."

"Next time, just ask questions, Ward." Then I tune him out, much the same way he did me. When I'm done an hour later, I roll my shoulders and point to the screen. "There you go. Fortunately, I was able to export the data, so it didn't take me all that long. If you look here, I broke down the data for unclaimed meetings versus what was billed and then again what David was supposed to work on that you did charge in. Fortunately, the cost difference isn't ridiculous, so the ass chewing you rightfully should receive from your sister should be fairly minimal."

The way his body collapses next to mine amuses me. "You were that afraid?"

"Of you and my sister, yes."

"Why?"

"Together you're scary. I'm now certain either of you could take over the world. Men should run and hide when you're both on your A game. Don't think I didn't notice the way Kris made you a job offer at the party." His fingers trail down my arm.

Pleased with the compliment, I say, "He does every time we speak on the phone."

"Not interested?"

"Not in the slightest."

"His loss is our gain." He leans in and kisses me. "Thank you. You just saved me hundreds of hours of work. Want to know what I want to be doing instead?"

Before I respond, I save the database, email it to myself, and erase it from Ward's drive. "Why don't you show me instead?"

He yelps, "What the hell did you just do?"

"What? You didn't think I was going to let you keep a hold of that data to eviscerate David, did you? I'll present the information to Carys tomorrow as a discrepancy. This way, we won't have 'World Ward III' at the office." I air quote the play on his name.

Ward grumbles under his breath. I think I hear "punk" and "payback," but I close the laptop lid before tugging my sweater over my head. His eyes grow round when he realizes I only have on a lacy bra beneath the heavy sweater.

He topples me onto my back. "You do realize I was complaining about David, right? You're…"

"I'm what?"

"Everything, Angel. You are my everything." Then Ward lowers his head and kisses me.

Soon contracts, databases, and even the fact we're speeding through the night air is soon forgotten as love is remembered.

Carys's face, red with fury from male duplicity and incompetency moments before, is having a hard time not laughing when I tell her about how I deleted the database in front of Ward on the flight home last night. Her shoulders shake as she whispers, "No more, Angie. I'm going to laugh in their faces instead of yelling at both of them."

"It was brilliant, Carys. Here he was, all ready to say 'nanny-nanny-poo-poo on you' to David."

Her first snicker escapes.

"But no. Erase."

"Oh God. You didn't just delete the file? You erased it?" She slaps the conference room table with her folio in an effort to mask her chortles.

"I don't even think he knows the difference between the two. But getting him to promise to adhere to the rules was the real coup."

"And not because you're together?" Carys plucks the words from my mind.

"Exactly. Look at this." I spin my laptop around.

Her jaw drops. "Three meetings this morning that he's copied you on. My God, if he keeps this up and stops doing my husband's homework, it will be a Christmas miracle."

"Hallelujah!" I shout.

And we're done.

Within thirty seconds, there's a knock on the door. David pops his head in. "What's so funny in here?"

"Your end-of-the-year bonus. Get. Out," Carys growls the minute she spots her husband.

A very smart man, he reads his wife's mood accurately. David doesn't say another word before backing out and closing the door with a snap.

"Now, Angie, since you were the one who so brilliantly pieced this together, what should their punishment be? Because despite how funny it ended up, we could have ended up with some serious problems." Carys sobers up.

She's not wrong. We don't need a reputation for erroneously billing clients, especially the kind of clients we deal with day in and day out.

I'm debating a few ideas in my mind that will keep both David and Ward out of my meticulous filing and bookkeeping when the door flies open unexpectedly. "Ho, ho, ho, darlings. Who else is getting in the holiday spirit?" Becks proclaims. He's wearing a Santa suit fit so well, there can't be a single stitch beneath it.

I drawl, "I can just imagine the headlines tomorrow. 'Who wants to sit on this Santa's lap?'"

"Are you volunteering, Angie?"

"Fuck you, Becks" is yelled by Ward from the vicinity of David's desk.

And then Carys announces, "Ward, David, we're ready for you both now."

"And that's my cue to go," Becks claims.

"Oh, no, Becks. Stay. Please. This impacts you as well." Carys's smile when her brother and husband walk in can only be classified as pure malice. When everyone's seated around the conference table, Carys begins. "Bad boys generally get coal. This season, David, Ward, you both are getting Becks."

They groan unanimously. Becks demands, "What the hell did I do wrong?"

I turn on him. "I'm sure you'll think of something."

He winks, his good mood going unperturbed. "I always do, don't I?"

And that's when Ward says, "Shit."

"'Tis the season, brother. Enjoy your present."

Ward spins in his chair. Instead of angry, his face is relaxed. "Trust me, Carys, I already got my present. If this is the price I have to pay for it, I'll gladly do so."

Sitting here stoically when all I want to do is dive into his lap and declare he's my forever present…oh, shit. Christmas presents. I make a face at Carys and tap my watch insistently.

"Good, now the lot of you get out. Angie and I have an important meeting we have to attend." Once the men disappear, she hurries around my side of the table. "We don't have anything scheduled. I'm off the rest of the day. What's wrong?"

"What the hell do I get the man who can buy himself anything for Christmas?" I ask desperately.

"The same thing I'm getting David. Come shopping with me."

"When?"

"Now."

"We should have done this years ago," Carys declares as she reads a text from David, decides it's not important, and shoves her phone back in her purse. Her aqua eyes are sparkling as we traipse up and down Fifth Avenue.

"Before now, there's no way in hell you'd have dragged my ass out of the office. Oh, excuse me." I bump into yet another tourist as they cut me off to get a better position in front of Saks's windows.

"True. I can't wait for you to see this shop. It's divine."

"Will I be able to afford it?" I ask her.

"Yes."

"Are you sure?"

"David and I have a rule. I can't buy him anything he wouldn't be able to afford for me," Carys tells me as we duck down a side street and head toward Madison Avenue.

"I like that," I declare.

"You and Ward need to put that in place because if I know my brother, he's going to go whack-a-doodle. He always does with us."

"I'll kill him," I say passionlessly.

Carys laughs. "I wish you luck. If you manage to pull it off, David would be grateful. Ben is going to be ridiculously spoiled but not by us."

We approach a nondescript doorway and fling it open. Jogging up a few flights of stairs, we enter a whole new world that's not what I expected when Carys said she had a "perfect idea of what to get Ward." It's the most feminine space I've ever been in. Shrugging off my coat, I take in the gorgeous silks and satins intermingled together. "I feel like I'm in a sexy boudoir," I whisper to Carys, who chuckles.

"Welcome to Pour Vous, Angie. This is what I always get David."

I arch a brow. "Seriously?"

"What does the man really need that he can't or won't buy for himself?" She asks me essentially the same question I've been pondering as we've window-shopped our way through tourists.

"Nothing."

"Exactly. There's only one thing I can give him he really wants."

Remembering the way Ward removed every inch of clothing, not leaving an inch of my skin untouched by his lips, I shiver.

"There's one thing you should know," Carys cautions me.

Uh-oh. I focus on her. She rips my coat out of my arms and hands it to an attendant, with our thanks. Turning to face me, she grabs and holds up two magnificent sets from a random rack—one in a deep blue trimmed in ecru lace and the other reversed. "God, everything's so beautiful. How will I choose?" I wonder how quickly my credit card company will call me to ask me if my card was stolen.

"One way to narrow it down is simple: size. Not everything in the store will fit you, and there are no duplicates based on size."

My eyes widen. "So you mean, if it's not in my size…"

"It never will be. So, let's get you measured and with a salesperson." Carys grabs my hand.

I dig my heels into the carpet. Carys shoots me a quizzical look. "Will you stay with me for that part?" The idea of a stranger touching me still makes my stomach churn, despite the way Ward's fingers and lips have danced over my skin.

But that's Ward.

Carys's eyes soften. "You bet."

Shortly after I'm measured over a silk robe, Carys disappears. An armful of sinfully decadent undergarments is passed to me. I try them all on until I find the one. And if I'm whispering, "Holy shit," what's Ward going to do on Christmas when he gets his gift?

A secret smile crosses my face. I hurriedly redress and head to the register.

I can't wait to find out.

CHAPTER FORTY-ONE

WARD

However you celebrate and whomever you celebrate with, may you find peace tonight.
— **Beautiful Today**

Angie and Carys are laughing in the kitchen like schoolgirls as they FaceTime Angie's best friend, Sula, in Ireland. I spoke with her briefly to wish her a happy holidays. She winked at me before saying, "I bet yours is going to be better, 'Winsome Ward.'"

I almost choked on my drink.

We decided to do Christmas Eve at Angie's, and then we'd meet back at my sister's condo for Christmas dinner. It's not unusual that I haven't decorated a lick for the holidays, but since I've been spending most nights with Angie, I debated having a professional service come in. Angie sneered in disgust when I suggested that. "Ward, decorating for the holidays is supposed to be painful and annoying. Maybe I'd pay someone for outside lights, but inside should be warm. It should feel like family lives there." This was right before she slapped fake garland in my arms and pointed me in the direction of her stairs.

I haven't felt this excited to celebrate the holiday since my parents were alive. When I said as much to Carys earlier when we were in the kitchen, she ducked her head. Guiltily, I turned her against my chest as her shoulders shook. "Crap. I didn't mean the holidays we shared were anything awful, Carrie. It's just…"

"It's just you're in love. And having the woman you love added to our family brings that more to it." Tears streamed down her face even as her smile beamed up at me.

"Yes. I am. I been waiting for her a long time."

Carys hugged me tightly for a long while before moving away. Seeing her and the woman I love now cracking up makes me wish my parents were here. Just once. *Everything I have I'd give away just so you both could meet her. You know that, right?* I lift my glass of eggnog to my lips when a hand clamps down on my shoulder.

I jump, startled to find Hayden grinning down at me with a Santa hat on. Standing, I step into his embrace. "Merry Christmas, you old tattletale. Who the hell invited you?"

His hearty laugh bellows out. "Your sister. And stop complaining. I didn't even tell Angie the stories of you from

Harvard that would have had her screaming from the car, Ward. Really? The streaking? I don't care if you were drunk at the time or not." He clips me upside the head, even all these years later.

"I know. I owe you my education." A very true statement since my godfather stepped in and spoke for me at my disciplinary hearing.

"I'll take the name of your firstborn child."

"Sorry, Hayden. That honor belongs to Mom and Dad when that day comes eventually," I drawl, waiting for his reaction.

The shock that rips across his face is worth everything. I sip on my drink while the man who taught me and my sister to go for the throat in our arguments while we were in diapers struggles to find words. "Angie's the one?"

"She is." I've never been more certain of anything in my life. Resolutely, I go on. "I'd lay down my life for hers. Give up everything I have to protect her heart. The day doesn't work the same unless I'm with her. She's the beginning of everything for me."

His face twists in pride, pleasure, and pain. "It's not going to be an easy road, son."

It dawns on me. "You know."

"I recognized her. The media wasn't just brutal, Ward. They held her up as a champion of women's rights before they savaged her when she lost. She needs a man who's going to stand by her regardless of what the media says about her."

"Fuck the media," I say heatedly.

"You say that now, Ward, but you've always been their darling," Hayden starts.

"And I have enough money to disappear tomorrow and take Angie with me. She's *everything*, Hayden. Get that. Nothing in this world, no one in this family, means more to me than..."

Hayden coughs loudly.

Angie wraps her arm around my waist. "Merry Christmas, Hayden! I didn't know you were coming. Someone forgot to mention it." The daggers she's shooting at me should drop me to the ground dead.

He smooths a hand over her head, and she doesn't flinch. *Such progress*, I think with pride. "What you don't realize, my love, is Hayden's Christmas gift is from all of us and was taken care of by my father. He won't let us buy him anything else."

"Damn right I won't. Stubborn horse's ass," Hayden mutters.

I leave my best friend, Hayden Wiltshire, my football box seats with the understanding he brings my son every weekend he wants to go and they be left to Ward upon your death. They've been paid up for the next one hundred years, you goat. Now, take some time off and have some fun.

I shudder at the memory but dredge up a smile for the woman tucked at my side. "So, you see, Hayden's just here to visit."

Visibly relieved, she smiles brilliantly at my godfather. "Then let me pour you a drink. Eggnog?"

"That would be great." As Angie moves away from us, Hayden comments, "No matter what happens, don't let her go, Ward."

"I wasn't planning on it," I begin. But Hayden's eyes turn on me fiercely.

"She's just starting to bloom."

"I recognize that. What are you trying to say?" My gaze is drawn to where Angie is pouring a glass of eggnog for Hayden.

He steps in front of me, blocking the vision of beauty with his craggy face. "Maybe I'm wrong, but I'm afraid her pain isn't over yet. And I fear for both your hearts if that's the case."

"Christ, Hayden. She loves me."

"Loving someone doesn't mean you won't hurt them. It just means the wounds last longer."

His words cause a deep unease inside of me. I take another sip of my drink to hide my emotion.

"All I'm saying is if she needs time, don't resent it."

"What kind of man do you think I am?"

"Impatient. You always did rattle the presents on Christmas Eve." His voice turns affectionate. "Thank you, Angie."

I was so lost in the myriad of things Hayden gave me to ponder, I didn't even notice Angie approaching. I tuck her against me so her back is protected, and hopefully she can hear the beating of my heart.

After all, I'm beginning to believe it was born to beat for her.

Hours later we're hooting and hollering as David lifts out lacy scraps of nothing from a box. "Just your color, brother. Maybe you should model it for all of us," I taunt as the aqua mesh is quickly buried beneath layers of sparkly tissue paper.

Hayden chokes. "Angie, be a sweetheart and get this old man another drink? With your man making comments like that, it's a good thing I hired a chauffeur for tonight."

"Absolutely, Hayden. Ward, behave yourself," Angie warns.

I grin. "Why? It's so much fun not to."

"Because you never know when you're going to get coal in your stocking," she calls back at me.

"That's for bad boys, Angie," I tease as she hands Hayden his drink.

"And you're claiming you haven't been bad?" One perfectly arched brow raises.

"Nope."

"Nothing that would land you on Santa's naughty list?"

Carys snickers. I glare at my sister. "I'm a freaking saint."

"Right. If that's the case, then you won't have any problem opening your gift." Angie goes over to the tree and pulls out an old-fashioned Christmas stocking and offers it to me.

I narrow my eyes. "This one wasn't labeled before."

"No, it wasn't. I heard all about your gift-shaking tendencies from Carys. Really, Ward? You're thirty years old."

I reach for the gift but hook Angie around the waist, yanking her into my lap, where she falls with a squeal.

The room erupts in laughter. I snatch a quick kiss from Angie before helping her to her feet. She holds out my gift and murmurs, "Merry Christmas. I hope it's what you wanted."

"It's from you. It's going to be perfect." But just for the sake of our audience, I shake the stocking anyway.

Everyone, including Angie, cracks up laughing again.

"I hope there was nothing breakable in there, you bonehead," David calls out. Carys is curled on his lap, watching me with anticipation.

My eyes fly upward to Angie. She quickly shakes her head. "You're fine." Then she holds out her hand, and it's trembling. "But I'm not. Open it already."

I tear into the bright green, then red tissue paper before I find a glittery tissue layer beneath. My breath leaves in a whoosh. I recognize that paper, even if I don't know the store. Now, it's my hands that are hesitant as I pluck away at the tape slowly.

My pulse speeds up when Angie leans down to whisper in my ear, "I happen to know it fits."

Gulp.

I tear into the paper and find Christmas coal.

The dark gray lace on the teddy is so delicate I'm afraid my fingers may puncture it, but I can't resist dancing my fingers over it as I imagine Angie lying on her bed wearing this scrap of nothing while my lips...

My thoughts are rudely interrupted by David demanding, "Hold it up, Ward."

I hold up my middle finger instead. "Asshole."

"See? Like I said, a bad boy. I thought you were supposed to share your gifts," Angie teases.

"Holy freaking snickerdoodle, Angie. This is the most perfect gift I've ever received, but there's no way I'm letting anyone imagine your body in it even for half a second." Immediately after my declaration, I kiss her unabashedly in front of everyone to show my appreciation.

And to give her a preview of what the night ahead will hold.

When I let her up for air, Angie's smile is so bright it easily rivals that of the Christmas tree in the corner. I immediately want to throw my family out so I can fully explore her joy further. But I know we have all night.

If I'm lucky we'll have forever.

"See, this is why I don't require any gifts," Hayden declares, bringing us back into the moment.

"Why's that?" David asks.

"Because, this is what Christmas should be about—being with those you love that you can't live without. I'm just honored you all invited me to be a part of it." Hayden lifts his glass in a toast. "There's nowhere I'd rather be on a cold night like tonight."

We all lift our glasses to toast him back. Then Angie speaks up softly, "And to those who we miss in our hearts. I hope they know how very much they're loved."

We all lift our glasses once again as we think of the ones who aren't with us. A jolt races through me as I realize how appropriate Angie's gift truly is. Clearing my throat, I place my glass to the side. "I think there's one gift left."

Carefully, I fold the present Angie gave me and slip it into the stocking, noting with interest the garters dangling. Stooping down, I place it at my side reverently before reaching inside my jacket pocket and pulling out a square box. "Here, Angel. Let me up."

I shift Angie off my lap before kneeling down next to the chair and hand her the beautifully wrapped gift.

And wait.

Angie slowly undoes the crimson bow before sliding a nail beneath the opalescent paper. Her fingers tremble as she lifts the lid on the rectangular box. Then she lifts the box closer to her face. "Oh, Ward." Her arm not holding the box snakes around my neck to pull me close.

"You didn't open it up," I tease her even as I absorb her scent.

"There's something in it?" Her head jerks back in surprise.

"There's a few somethings."

"What is it?" Carys demands.

"A locket. Hold on, let me get it out." Angie fumble with the pins holding the delicate chain to the satin. "Here it is. It…" Her words halt as she reads the inscription on the back.

My beloved. Always.

The tears are falling so rapidly from Angie's eyes, I can't swipe them away fast enough. I yank her into my arms. "Was this too much?" I struggled to find the balance between giving Angie everything her heart could possibly desire and merely the world. Then I saw the locket as I was roaming around priceless jewels and realized she's wants only one thing from me.

My heart.

Tipping her face back, I whisper, "Open the locket, my love."

"I'm not sure I can. My hands are shaking too hard," she admits.

Carefully, I use my thumbnail to undo the catch. That's when Angie begins to cry. Inside are miniature pictures of the two of us I took using my cell phone: one during our trip to Montana and the other last weekend while we were decorating for Christmas.

"You mean everything to me." Her eyes glow like gems.

And that's my true gift—that she'd say that in front of all the people who matter in my family.

I lean over and brush my lips against hers. "And you're my forever."

Right then, the clock strikes ten times. "Goodness, when did it get to be so late? David, we have to get Ben home and to bed." Carys jumps up from David's lap.

"Then we get to play Santa." He waggles his eyebrows suggestively.

Carys smacks him, but for once I don't chime in. I just can't wait for them all to leave.

I need to hold Angie against me which is right where she belongs.

CHAPTER FORTY-TWO

WARD

Keene Marshall was spotted ducking into HomeGoods on Christmas Eve. It must be domestic bliss.
— **@PRyanPOfficial**

Angie and I stand at the doorway and wave everyone off. But the minute the door closes, I pin her to it. "You do realize what you're standing under," I announce like it wasn't Angie who directed me to hang the mistletoe right in the foyer.

She wraps her arms around my neck. "I do. The question is what are you going to do about it?"

I immediately lower my head and relish the taste of Angie's lips beneath mine. Then before I get too lost in the sensation, I tear my mouth away.

Her eyes open languidly. I immediately lose myself in shining pools of deep blue. It takes me a moment to regain my composure before I drag her into the family room and snatch up my Christmas gift.

A purely feminine smile twitches her lips. "But Ward, I bought this for you."

I growl as I get into her space.

Angie lets a giggle escape.

I brush her hair away from her face before suggesting, "How about you put on the sack of coal you gave me while I turn off the tree and make sure everything's locked up?"

"I think that's an excellent suggestion." Angie rises up on the balls of her feet before snatching the stocking away from me and dashing up the stairs. She darts away before I can capture her in my arms again.

I make quick work of unplugging the tree, making certain the gates Angie laid out are put up so Flower can't knock over the tree due to sheer spite, and checking the front and back locks. Then I make my way up the stairs. There's not a sound as I climb the oak stairs to the second floor and make my way toward Angie's suite of rooms. I knock lightly and wait until I hear, "Come in," before I fling the door open.

But I freeze the moment I see her.

The charcoal-grey lace teddy is held up by sheer force of will. As I numbly approach, I take in the tiny sparkling crystals interwoven around delicate cutouts. The high lift around her hips makes her impossibly long legs appear even longer. And glowing warmly at her neck is the solid gold locket I gave her that she's worrying back and forth along the chain. "You're stunning," I manage, closing the door behind me.

Angie visibly relaxes.

"I don't know what I did so right this year. I was given the best gift in the world." I tug my sweater over my head as I make my way over to her.

Her lips part as I bare my chest to her. That look. I want to sear it onto my brain: innocence and temptation, passion and trust. As she crosses the room on bare feet and slips into my arms, I know I once again believe in Christmas miracles.

I'm holding living proof of it.

I walk Angie backward until her knees bump against the bed. The two of us topple over, and I suck in a breath as her breast pops out from its charcoal wrapping. I cup it as I kiss her hard.

Her fingers rake up the front of my chest, fingers tweaking my nipples much like I do hers. I groan in agony, in pleasure. "Angie, baby. You're going to make me lose control," I warn.

"That was the idea. You're not going to break me, Ward."

Another level of trust handed to me. I tuck the knowledge safely in my heart even as I begin to tug away my Christmas gift because the real present is tucked underneath.

It takes a bit of wiggling on both our parts that sets me more aflame than I already was until her naked skin is touching every inch of mine. I press kisses along her belly, my path the light dusting of reddish curls that cover her core. My fingers follow the path my mouth makes, and soon, Angie's writhing on the bed when I slip one, two fingers inside her and my tongue dances along her clit.

Her breathless gasps permeate the air, but it's her choppy whimpers as she reaches her first climax that drive my own need higher.

I crawl up her still-shivering body, yanking open the drawer where I stashed a box of condoms, and rip it open with my teeth. I quickly roll one on before I hook her leg beneath my elbow. Leaning forward, I catch the look of surprise in her eyes before a heretofore unknown sultriness sets in.

That's when I hear the clock strike midnight.

"Merry Christmas, Angel," I whisper as I slide my cock inside. The sound of her wetness gripping me as I press forward until my pelvic bone rests against her clit makes us both moan. Angie's other leg wraps around my waist as she arches her back.

I begin to thrust and retreat, sliding in slow and easy. Again and again, plunging in and out, driving us both out of our minds. Each and every movement causes the hair to raise on my skin, building the tension in my lower spine.

Angie's tossing her head back and forth, fighting the sensations threatening us both.

"Don't, Angel. Just let go. I've got you. I promise." I drive my hips forward again, faster.

"Kiss me," she begs.

Like she has to ask that twice. I lean forward enough to capture her lips beneath mine. And even as my lower body keeps up its frantic pace, I softly part her lips with my tongue. I stroke mine in and out of her mouth, making her whimper at the dual sensations.

Then, I add a third.

Reaching between us, I graze the side of her clit with my finger lightly. It's sensory overload.

I feel her body clamp down as her climax races over us before her mind catches up enough for her to scream. And it triggers my own. It whips through me like a bolt of lightning.

Gasping, I ride her through the waves of pleasure and aftershocks before I collapse on top of her. I'm splintered into a million pieces. How am I supposed to recover from that? I wonder wearily.

Then I feel her hand pass over my skin before she whispers, "I love you, Ward."

All the pieces of energy that just exploded in every direction whoosh back into my body instantaneously at her words. Struggling to brace myself over her, I nuzzle my nose against hers. "I love you too."

As we settle down to sleep, I immediately begin to count my blessings, namely Angie and my family.

Neither of which has a damn thing to do with money.

CHAPTER FORTY-THREE

ANGELA

Something must be wrong. Beckett Miller held the door for me this morning. When I asked him for a photo, he politely said not today but then paid for my coffee. #strangerthings
— **Jacques Yves, Celebrity Blogger**

"This year is going to be amazing," I tell Sula as I'm getting ready to head into the city. Ward didn't stay with me last night because he received a call from his building super about a busted pipe.

"If the way you're smiling is any indication, it sure as hell is. Damn, Angie, I'm so happy for you." Sula blows her nose into a tissue.

"Are you getting sick?" I worry.

"I'm crying, you fool! My bestie is in love with the most gorgeous man on the planet who happens to be in love with her too! That deserves more than tears. That deserves champagne, but the bleeding stores are closed."

I laugh, carefree and happy. "Oh, Sula. I *do* love him."

She sobs some more. "I want to fly back just to hug him. You know that, right?"

"You'll get to meet him. And I swear, he's as protective of me as you are."

"Damn right. He should be."

"Now, tell me about the construction guy you were seeing. Josef?" I ask eagerly.

She scoffs. "Fecking idiot."

"Sula, you have to come home soon. You're cursing more like a Brit every day," I admonish.

"Fine. Fucking idiot. I went to meet him at the bar the other night, like we planned, only he was there with another woman. Turns out he was dating someone else at the same time."

"Ouch." What else should I say, I wonder. Sula's luck with guys hasn't been the best. But she's held them off for a very good reason.

"I know, right?"

"What did you do?" I gather my purse and shrug into my coat before giving Flower a few treats. I think she's still high on her Christmas catnip because she hasn't taken a swipe at my phone in days.

434 · TRACEY JERALD

"I marched right over to where he was and showed her the photos of him and I."

I'm thankful I'd reached the bottom steps into the basement because her words have me leaning against a wall howling. "Of course you did."

"Damn straight. I'm no man's fool."

Unsaid between us is the word "again." Sula refuses to discuss the man she lost her heart to in the past, and I fully respect that. "What did Josef do?"

A sound of disgust comes out. "Tried to bluff. That is until I showed the date and timestamp of the photos."

"Outstanding. God, I adore you."

"Back at you. Does 'Winsome Ward' have any friends?"

I think back to what he admitted to me on a frigid Montana balcony about Mike and Steve and shudder. "None that are your type." If Sula knew that Ward grew up with the two men who abused me, there's no telling how ballistic she would go in her present mood. That's a conversation best had in person, I decide as I slide into my car.

"Hot, sexy, and rich? Babe, they could be aliens and I could work with that."

I grin as I back my car out of the garage. "I'm going to work now."

"Fine. Keep him wrapped up tight."

"Ward? I will. Thanks." We both crack up at the double entendre.

"Love you, Angie."

"Love you more, Sula." I hang up and focus on driving to the train station.

At the end of the day, Ward is carrying a suitcase and a suit bag as he follows me into the house. "I can't believe they have to go through my library floor to get to the leak," he's still groaning.

"Ward, that's why you have insurance," I point out logically.

"It's not that, Angie. It's one of the few rooms in the whole place I feel like me."

That causes me to pause. "Then why do you own it?"

Sheepishly, he shrugs. "To be honest, I don't know."

We took a car service to the train station where I was dropped off. Then I was followed home. Ward has heaps of boxes and only a few bags he's brought into my home. Kicking off my heels, I grab them and gesture for him to follow me upstairs. "That's a great reason."

"I think I was rebelling after law school," he confides.

"What do you mean?"

"I mean, I had no outlet after my parents died. Buying a ridiculously outrageous condo in Tribeca, completely against everything they taught Carys and me, seemed to be a good way to lash out at them."

I pause on the stairs and consider his words. "Did it work?"

He barks out a bitter laugh. "No. I use three rooms regularly—four if you include the kitchen."

"How many does it have?" I climb the last few steps until I reach the top of the landing.

Ward trips over his own feet.

"Ward, will you let me help you carry something? I don't want you to get hurt." I hold out my hand for him to hand me something.

"God, I just realized you've never been there." His face is incredulous.

"This thing between us—"

"Love?"

I roll my eyes at the droll note in his voice. "Falling in love with you came out of left field, Ward. We're finding out things about one another every single day. I kind of like the newness of that right now."

"So, I didn't completely screw up by not bringing you to see my etchings right off the bat?" he jokes as we enter my suite.

Now it's my turn to roll my eyes as he drops his bag before he hangs up his suits. I call out to him, "Ward, you know if you had brought me to see your etchings, I'd have likely run screaming from your cave."

He steps from my closet, a serious expression on his face. "That's what most of it feels like."

"A cave?" I confirm. At his nod, I ask, "Then why didn't you redecorate?"

"I did. The three rooms I cared about."

"And the kitchen?"

"It's functional."

I can't help giggling. "You're such a man."

"Me man. You woman." He makes apelike sounds as he sheds his suit jacket.

"If the tabloids could see you now, I wonder if they'd name you most-eligible bachelor or most-delusional bachelor," I wonder aloud.

Ward stops joking around and becomes very serious. "I don't care what they call me as long as they stop using the word 'bachelor.' Because I'm very much off the market."

I lick my lips in anticipation as he approaches me. I back up against the long dresser. Ward boosts me up onto it.

And soon I don't care about anything other than what Ward's making me feel.

It isn't until much later when we're both breathing heavily in each other's arms we both hear the plaintive calls of Flower begging for her dinner like she hasn't eaten in a week. For the sake of Ward's laptop and both our cell phones, I find my robe and go feed the diabolical monster. Ward follows me soon after to begin moving the rest of the boxes in from the car while I get dinner ready.

It strikes me when we're eating dinner, curled up together in the living room. I proclaim, "This is my definition of perfect."

He pauses with a bite of chili halfway to his mouth. "What do you mean?"

"We're just sitting here together having dinner, watching TV. It's what people who are comfortable together do."

His spoon drops to his bowl as he absorbs my words.

"I never thought I'd be able to feel like this—that in the darkest part of my soul, I feel every corner is filled with light." I tilt my head up and brush my lips against his chin.

"That's because your confidence has returned."

"At least I'm a lot more than I was before I met you."

He leans down and presses a kiss to my forehead. "You had this deep inside you, Angie. All you were waiting for was the right time to shine."

I consider that. "Maybe."

He smirks and shoves a spoonful of chili into his mouth before groaning. "This is delicious."

"You're remarkably easy." The words escape my mouth before I can stop them.

"And you know me so well, love." He winks.

We tumble against each other, laughing while still balancing our dinner. Flower hisses at us from her spot by the hearth, setting us off again.

This night makes my heart hopeful for more than just the short term.

Maybe, this could be more.

The two weeks Ward spent at my place flew by. Things just clicked for us without interrupting either of our schedules.

More often than not, I'd be on my morning touch base with Sula when Ward would stumble into the kitchen seeking out caffeine. Muttering a haphazard "Good morning," he'd press a kiss upon my lips before stumbling back upstairs.

The first time it happened, it took Sula a good five minutes to lift her jaw back into place. Stammering over his half-naked form, she shrieked, "His body is better than a Greek statue."

"I've only seen the pictures of the statues. I've touched Ward."

"You suck."

"That too," I volunteer helpfully.

Sula makes a face. "That does it. I refuse to date with another lame-ass loser."

While I hold out hope she really means her words, I, of all people, know how deep wounds to the soul can fester.

Now, there's a simple dance to our morning routine and an eagerness to be back at my place at the end of the day.

But the nights? Ward ignites my mind as well as my body.

In between, work has shifted subtly. We enter LLF holding hands before he disappears to get my morning coffee, then leaves it at my desk with a simple kiss to accompany the latte that feels ice-cold in comparison to his warm lips.

But as I scan a brief Carys asked me to review, I realize the biggest change that has occurred is in me. Stretching, I push to my feet and move over to the mirrored frame behind the guest chairs. It's not my appearance; that's the same as always. I tip my head to the side. Is it what Ward said that first night? Has my confidence returned?

With a small jolt, I realize it has when I never gave much thought to the fact I was hiding it. I never noticed before how I'd stifle my opinions during meetings, how I'd hide myself even in a roomful of people I claimed I trusted. Even though I knew I was out of reach of my abusers, I was still the victim.

No more.

Squaring my shoulders, I return to my desk when the phone rings. "LLF, this is Angela. How may I help you?"

"Hey, Angie. It's Becks. Has Carys given me the high sign yet?" His anxiety-ridden voice comes through the line.

"Not yet, hon." Just then, Ward steps out of the inner sanctum. I mouth to him, "Becks." He nods.

"I suppose it's better than a flat-out 'no,'" Becks tries to joke.

"In your case, absolutely. But Ward just walked out. Let me hand you over to him?" I quirk my brow to him.

He nods, holding out his hand.

"Thanks, Angie. I appreciate everything."

Without another word, I pass off the phone receiver to Ward. Listening to Ward calmly reassure Becks that the best thing he can have is patience, but he—Becks—is doing the right thing by keeping calm and staying under the radar, warms me deep inside. "So many changes in such a short time," I murmur as I finish scanning the brief for Carys.

I send it back with a few formatting updates just as Ward hangs up. "What did you mean?" he asks.

"When?"

"While I was on the phone with Becks. You said there were so many changes in such a short time."

I push to my feet and take his hand. Pressing it against the side of my cheek, I assure him, "All of them good."

His fingers slip from beneath mine to comb through my hair. "I came out to tell you my condo's ready."

I can't control the scrunch of my nose but don't say anything.

"I kind of feel the same way. I've become too used to waking up with you beside me." Suddenly, his eyes light. "Why don't you pack a bag and come stay with me for the weekend?"

"Seriously?" My heart begins to pound in excitement. Then I tease, "Be careful, Ward. This is another milestone in this journey we're traveling on."

"I'm willing to risk it. Do you have someone who can feed Flower?"

I nod before confiding, "I think she likes the sitter more than me."

"Why?"

"The sitter leaves her cell phone in the car."

We both snicker. "So then it's settled. Tonight, your place. I'll pack my things up to get them ready to move back. Tomorrow, we'll both head to my home."

"To luxuriate in those three, no, four rooms you use."

"Angie, for you I might branch out to five."

We're grinning at each other like lunatics when Carys comes out with a confused expression on her face. "Angie, why did we change the date on the contract to be two months from now?"

Spinning out of Ward's arms, I explain, "Because the recording label said they refuse to sign until the artist is out of rehab. I have notes from the meeting, but we're responsible for drawing up a short-term contract to cover their medical until that date."

She snaps her fingers. "That's right. I don't know what I would do if I didn't have you here." She disappears behind the heavy wood doors.

"Me neither," Ward whispers into my ear, sending shivers down my spine.

"Then it's a good thing you won't have to find out, isn't it?"

He winks before heading back to work himself. And I send Carys a reminder to draft the second contract.

Then I make a list of all the things I'll need for the weekend at Ward's before I call my cat sitter.

CHAPTER FORTY-FOUR

WARD

Ward Burke and Angela Fahey.

She's the gorgeous redhead. Mystery solved, although everyone here is still in shock over the photo that was emailed to us.

For those who don't remember, Ms. Fahey is the woman who accused XMedia's newest board member, Michael Clarke, of sexual harassment during their college years. As he's been a lifelong friend of Ward Burke's, their relationship is simply astounding. But we say let bygones be bygones. For Ward and Angela to find such obvious happiness, it's obvious past hurts must have been set aside.
— **StellaNova**

We fall into my condo laughing. I had my car picked up and the items transferred earlier in the day so I could assist Angie with her bag. And so she could get the impact of my condo when she enters it for the first time.

It isn't until Angie's eyes widen that I understand why my father would have done anything to appease my mother raising her children as "normal" kids. Having enough money to support families for years means nothing without the right woman at your side.

And Angela Fahey is that woman.

She steps up to one of my prized Holly Freeman photos, her flame-colored hair cascading over her shoulder as she studies the grit and grime of New York City. Her finger taps against her chin as her head takes in the soulless space it's opposite of.

"What are you thinking?" I can't help but ask.

"There's more of you here than you think—decadence and grit entwined together to form a storm of vulnerability."

She's shaken me to my core with that observation.

I wrap my arms around her from behind and inhale her essence. "There are times I miss my family more than others. This is one of them."

Twisting until she faces me, she asks, "Why?"

"Because I've never felt anything close to the way I do about you. You are all the best parts of everything I didn't know to wish for, Angel. And I'd be proud to introduce you to them."

Her eyes soften. Brushing her lips against the stubble against my chin, "I'd like to think both of our families can see us, Ward."

My lips curve. "Well, maybe not when I do this." I bend at the knees and swoop her into my arms.

"Ward!" Angie screeches, pounding on my shoulder. "What about my tour? Don't you want to check on the repairs?"

"Neither is going anywhere," I assure her.

But my heart is. It just soared somewhere stratospheric due to the look in her eyes.

And I really don't want it to come back down.

"There's something profound about the moment your woman steps foot for the first time in your space and sees a side of you that you're both proud and ashamed of," I admit.

Angie's propped next to me, lying on a pillow as I trail my fingers up and down her spine along the silky smooth skin of her back. Her brow furrows. "I still don't get the shame. From what I got to see of it, it's a lovely home—for a family of six."

We both crack up. "That's what I'm talking about. I had no need for a place this size. It's ridiculously ostentatious," I explain.

She shrugs. "So, sell it. Get something smaller that makes you happier."

I roll to my side so I'm fully facing her. "I know I should, but..."

"But what?"

"This is going to sound stupid," I mutter.

"Ward," she warns.

"I feel like my dad's making me do penance here. Like he's saying, 'Well, son. You bought it. Now you live in it.'"

"You're right. That is stupid."

"Thanks for the moral support there, love." I flop over to my back to stare up at my eleven-foot ceiling.

She crawls over to sprawl across my chest. "Ward, your parents *loved* you. If you made a mistake, was there a time while they were alive they didn't forgive you?"

I blink slowly as I feel like everything inside of me I've held as a guiding force for the last thirteen years begins to shift before the armor falls away. "Do you really believe that?"

Her eyes cloud with tears. "Oh, Ward. How would they not? Love doesn't end because of death. All it's doing is taking a break for a little while. At least that's what Grandma used to say."

I swallow over and over to keep the burning moisture trapped. But it's no use. A path of salty liquid falls down my cheeks. "They would have loved you—just as much as I do."

Angie doesn't respond. Then again, she doesn't need to. She just lays her head across the place that's uniquely hers.

My heart.

And like that, we fall asleep not knowing that our love is about to be shaken in ways we never could have imagined.

My phone starts buzzing first. Almost immediately after, Angie's starts pinging. I groan, "It's a Saturday and it's way too early. I officially declare this as a no-work zone." I throw my arm over my eyes even as our phones dance on our respective nightstands.

Angie's rolling away from me despite my best attempts to catch her. Reaching for her cell, she unlocks it to accept a call from Sula. "Too early," she yawns.

"Get to a TV now, babe." Sula's voice, which I've heard be dramatic and outlandish, is inordinately quiet.

Angie's already leaping from the bed and scrambling for my shirt. I snag her phone and bark out, "What is it?"

"Someone sold Angie's identity to the paps, Ward. There's pictures of the two of you entering your building last night. Every trash media news station is reporting it all over the world. And of course, they dug up all sorts of interesting facts about you I wasn't aware of." Sula seethes.

"Goddamnit!" I roar.

"Tell me right now you're not with her because of those two pieces of shit," Sula demands.

But before I can answer, Angie's yanking her phone out of my hands. "I've got to go."

Sula's face marginally relaxes. "I'm here if you need me."

"I know. You always have been," Angie whispers before pressing End. She stands at the foot of my bed clenching her phone so tightly I'm afraid she's going to snap it in two.

I approach her on bare feet, my footfalls not making a sound. When I touch her shoulder like I've done a million times since the first night we made love, she jerks away, her hand raised to strike.

We both freeze.

Then she crumbles against my chest. "Why can't they just leave me alone? Haven't I paid enough in this life for accepting that damn drink?" Her sobs are harsh.

"Shh, baby. You're going to make yourself sick." I stroke my hands over her hair and sides, deliberately avoiding her back.

I'm not certain how long we're together like that. "Let's get some coffee and call Carys. Then we'll figure out how to deal with this. Okay?"

She rubs her nose against the arm of the shirt she's wearing before nodding.

"Besides, you haven't yet seen the fourth room I use yet," I try to get a smile from her. The one I get is a bit forced, but I'll take it. Taking her hand, I lead her down the hall toward my kitchen where a coffee maker I barely know how to operate resides.

Angie drops my hand to tuck herself against me. I let out the breath I didn't even know I was holding. *We're going to get through this*, I think

And that's when I freeze.

Because standing in my foyer is Michael Clarke—my oldest friend and one of Angie's abusers. For years, the guys I knew since prep school treated my place like a crash pad. I can't even count the number of people who've been added to my approved visitor list. And with the elevator entering right into the condo... Before, what the hell did I care? I didn't have anything I cared about, nothing I really believed in. But now, I have everything to protect.

I have Angie, who makes a sound I've only heard from wounded animals on nature programs.

But this isn't TV. This is real life.

My life and that of the woman I love.

CHAPTER FORTY-FIVE

WARD

At the request of XMedia, we've been asked to retract the last part of our previous article.
— **Stella Nova**

"What the hell are you doing here?"

"That's some way to greet an old friend," Mike taunts.

"Get the hell out of my home." I stand in front of Angie to conceal her as much as possible, not that she's protesting. She's huddling behind me, still making that damaged sound.

I think I might be sick.

"Hi, Angie. It's been a while. Why don't you come out from behind Ward and let me see how you've grown up? It's been so many years," he jeers.

Mike's expression is barely concealing a sick lust I want to hide my woman from. But Angie? Even as she shifts to the side, her face is as blank as a doll's mask. The last time I saw her like that was the night I grabbed her from behind at Redemption.

And all the pieces finally fit together. What happened to her at college. Angie's reticence to going out in public. Mike's obsession with red-haired women. "You're the one who leaked the story to the media. You just couldn't let us have our peace," I declare flatly.

But before I can say anything else, I'm interrupted by Mike's predatory laugh. How come I've never noticed the way it sounds before now? It always came off as cocky and confident in my childhood. I open my mouth to speak, but he beats me to it. "I'm glad one of us got to tap that ass, Ward. You're going to have to share how she was with me and Steve when you get over this snit your in."

Angie lets out a beaten sound from somewhere behind me. I reach out a hand, but she adroitly avoids my touch. "Fuck, Angie…"

I never doubted her when she finally was able to share what had happened that night; how could she doubt me now? Then, there was too much pain that threaded through her voice, in the way she held herself as if she expected me to turn away from her. I realize it must be because she's being confronted with one of her attackers so brutally. I repeat myself furiously, "Get the fuck out of my condo."

Mike laughs. "You actually believe her? They didn't at school."

"Why? Did your dad buy off the witnesses or some shit?" I fire back.

Silence greets my response before Mike begins a slow clap. "I'm impressed, Ward. Money made you smart."

"No, if anything it made me bitter," I counter, trying with everything I can to remind Angie of all the wounds she helped heal. "There's a lot more than money out there. I was just too blind to see it."

The most important thing was out there waiting for me. Love.

"I hope your sister sees it that way when I move to block any and all business from going to LLF," he threatens.

"I'll look forward to suing your ass for attempting to do so. I might not give a damn about money the same way you do, but I'll enjoy taking yours." I pause for a moment. "And then I'll enjoy using it to set the story straight about what you did. How long do you think your stock price will hold?"

He glares past me at Angie, who still hasn't spoken a word. "Don't let her cause problems for you, Ward."

"By what? Trying to ruin me? Carys? We both know the two of us could retire tomorrow and never want for a damn thing ever again."

"But could she?" With those words hanging in the air, he turns on his heel and heads to the door. Just as he's about to open it, he addresses Angie. "It was good to renew our acquaintance again, Angie. It's been too long. Next time we shouldn't wait so long." Then he slams out of my condo after flicking my keycard into the hallway, causing a clicking sound in the cavernous room.

The second he leaves, I open my mouth. "Angel." But I hear her footfalls as she dashes away from me. "Shit." I catch a glimpse of her dashing down the hallway toward the master suite. I give her a few moments to get her bearings before following her.

I never should have given her a second.

When I walk in, I immediately declare, "You're not going anywhere." Since I immediately made love to Angie last night, there's nothing for her to repack. I find her scooping up her clothes I'd carelessly tossed on the floor and wedging them into any available space. When her head lifts, a knife pierces my heart, deflating it.

She's shattered.

"I have to go."

"Angie…" I slowly approach her, but the closer I get, the more her trembling intensifies.

"You don't understand how bad it was. They drugged me and touched me, Ward!" she screams.

"You're right. I'll never understand."

"The worst is yet to come," she predicts ominously.

A sick feeling lodges in my stomach. "What do you mean?"

"Now, your friend Mike isn't going to just disappear. He's going to go on the attack. He's going to go tell every scandal sheet I came after him. Again."

"How can you know that?" I wonder aloud.

She makes a desperate mew. "Because every time the rags bring up his past, that's what he says."

A desperate fury I haven't felt since the night my parents died washes over me. "And what do you say when they contact you?"

Her head tilts to the side, sending fiery waves of hair cascading over her shoulder. "What makes you think they do?"

I grit my teeth. "This time, they will. We'll go on the attack first. We'll contact the media. We'll…"

"Do nothing. I'm leaving."

And the sick feeling churns more. "No. Angel, we have to…"

"We? Do 'we' get eviscerated in the media each and every time XMedia's golden boy is mentioned in the news? No. *I* do, Ward. Me." She slaps her hand against her chest.

"But…"

"But what?"

I step closer until I see each and every track from her tears on her face. Since she hasn't shed a single one since I've been in the room, I can only believe she was crying while I was trying to eject Mike out of my condo. Another thing to send him to hell for, I think furiously. "You're not alone anymore. You have an army at your back." Me. I'm there.

Angie closes her eyes. Her body sways, and it leans toward mine instinctively. Just as I'm about to pull her into my arms, her eyes fly open. "I thought I had an army of people at my back the first time too. Then their faith in me broke one by one. You think Sula and I didn't figure out he bought the outcome?" With that, she hauls her bag off the bed.

My anger takes over. I yell, "So, that's it? You're just leaving without giving any of us a chance?"

Angie pauses in the entrance of the doorway. "No, that's not it."

My heart sighs in relief. Too soon, it turns out when she speaks her next words. "Nothing in my life has been perfect—nothing but your love. Maybe that's why it wasn't meant to last."

I'm not certain how she walks down the hall carrying the weight of my heart along with her bag.

I don't move until I hear the condo door close for a second time. Then, I sink into a chair in my room and let the tears come.

After all, Angie taught me it's okay to cry when the pain is overwhelming.

I spent the weekend working frantically to block every move Mike might make. I contact Jared Dalton—my former boss at Watson, Rubenstein, and Dalton—who recommends using his brother-in-law's security and investigation firm to get the information I need.

Sunday night, I receive a file that made me ill after reading it. Literally. I thought I might find some financial data I could use over Mike to prevent him from hurting Angie. Some shady XMedia dealings. Never in my wildest dreams did I think the investigators at Hudson would provide me with the data to screw him in the court of public opinion even if "None of the women in this file are willing to press charges, let alone go to the media. Tragically, for most, their state has a statute of limitations for pressing charges. However, they may still have a civil case should they choose to pursue it. I'd recommend an excellent lawyer," Colby Hunt's email read.

The file showed a direct link between women who had either received hush money after sexual altercations with Michael Clarke or—if they were like Angie and brave enough to press charges—hush money payouts to witnesses. It dated back ten years beginning with the buyout of student and faculty members of Angie's college and members on the Student Conduct Board.

By Monday, I've prepared myself to use everything I printed out in my safe at home to protect the woman I love. But when I walk into the office at 8:00 a.m., she's not there. My heart racing, I walk straight back without our normal morning banter.

Instead of finding her talking with Carys— or God help us, Becks —I find my sister and David poring over a document, frowns on both of their faces. The looks don't change when they spot me. If anything, they intensify. "I take it saying 'good morning' would be an inappropriate greeting?"

Neither says a word as I cross to my office, drop my briefcase, and shrug off my overcoat. Just as I pick up the phone to call Angie, I spot an envelope on my desk.

I drop the handset back into the cradle. My hands begin to shake as I reach for it.

I immediately slit open the back of the envelope.

Her words are brief, but then again, the death of one's soul doesn't have to be drawn out for the effect to be the same.

I know you think I'm strong enough because I pieced together my life. But really, that just makes me weaker, more vulnerable to…everything. I wish I had the strength to fight because the only thing worth fighting for is you.

I told the truth then, and I told you the truth when I said, 'I love you.' Even if no one else believes it, I hope you do.

I do love you, Ward. Despite what you might hear, that part was true. I just need some time to wrap my head around it all happening again.

I'll be back.

~A~

I'm standing there in shock when a knock on my doorframe pulls me from my stupor. "I take it you know what this is about?" Carys waves her own paper in the air.

"I know *everything*." I emphasize the word. Quickly, I give my sister a rundown of what happened Saturday morning and what I've been doing since.

"And now what?" Carys's aqua-colored eyes are burning like flames. My sister is outraged.

I don't reply. I pick up the phone and place a call. "I need the name of the best personal injury lawyer you know.

"Why?"

My chin jerks up, and I find myself staring down into the eyes of a woman who has not only been my sister, but put her life on hold to raise me into the man I am. "Because I intend on recommending to every one of the women on that list they sue the living shit out of Michael Clarke and Stephen Bellew, as well as anyone Clarke paid off for compromising their sexual assault cases. And I'd like to have the name of the lawyer ready. Especially when this hits the media. And we both know it will."

"I'll call you back."

I drop the phone back into the cradle.

Carys taps Angie's resignation letter against her leg for a moment. "I like where this is going. Then what?"

"Then what, what?"

Carys rolls her eyes at me. "How are you going to get Angie back, Ward?"

"She needs to believe she's safe, Carys. And until Mike's been dealt with, she'll never feel that way," I patiently explain.

"I hate that you're right."

"But when that's done..."

"Yes?" There's a note of excitement in her voice.

"No matter where she is, I'm going to find her. After that—well, that's between us." It's time to clear up a few assumptions we've both made, the biggest being that we can exist without the other. It's simple. We can't. Not anymore. Not after we found something so extraordinary, I never thought I'd feel it again.

A future.

Carys studies me for a moment before declaring, "My money's on you, Ward."

I snort. "Considering it's our money, that's not much of a bet."

"Yes it is. Because that means it's everything generations of our family worked for to leave us as a legacy. That's how much I believe in you. I always have, and I know they would too." And with that, Carys turns away.

But she doesn't get out of my office before I swoop her up in my arms. "I never could have done any of this without you, Carrie."

And for long moments, I stand there with one of three women I've ever loved in my arms. And that's when we both hear the bellowing start. "What the hell? Where the hell is Angie?"

Carys sighs. "Becks. I should have guessed."

"I've got this covered," I assure her.

Her eyes rove my face just as Becks makes it to my door. "Oh, goodie. A family moment. How touching. Now, why isn't Angie at her desk with all this bullshit going on in the media? Why aren't you doing something to protect her?" he accuses.

"Beckett, come on in," I invite him formally. Carys slips out, closing the door behind her. Taking a deep breath, I start to explain. "It happened like this…"

CHAPTER FORTY-SIX

ANGELA

Bravo! XMedia stockholders voted out Michael Clarke from the board of directors today after the news hit the media this week alleging payouts to witnesses and victims of sexual assault. While certain criminal charges are pending, a civil suit has been opened by Chase O'Hara, undisputedly the best personal injury lawyer in the nation.

While other victims have spoken to the media, many wonder if Angela Fahey—Michael Clark's first known victim and the first to publicly accuse him—is part of the civil suit. If so, mum's the word. Not surprising considering Ms. Fahey had kept a remarkably low profile until her romance with Ward Burke.
— **StellaNova**

Despite the still frigid temperature of early February, the beach house in Westerly, Rhode Island, that Sula's family lent me without a single question last week has suddenly become confining. I brave the deck overlooking the patio to escape the restrictive feeling growing inside of me. "Not that anyone should be able to call eight thousand square feet confining, right, Flower?" I stroke her fur.

I escaped New York. There's no other way to put it. I left Ward's and drove back to Brewster as fast as I could. Already having one bag packed, I filled as many suitcases as I could, grabbed my laptop and Flower. But before I left the next day, I quickly handwrote out letters. The first was a letter of resignation to Carys, thanking her for being there for me in so many different ways. The second, much shorter but harder to put into words, was a message to Ward.

After dropping them off at the overnight mail office, paying for them to be delivered as soon as possible Monday morning, I hightailed it out of town. I didn't have a destination in mind until I called Sula to let her know I was leaving.

"Angie, go to my parents' place," she argued.

I remember laughing through my tears.

"No, seriously. You know what the place on the beach in Rhode Island is like. Only our family knows about it, and sure as the devil, none of us are going to betray you. The spare key is located beneath the third flowerpot on the right. And once you get there, you can turn off your cell. You've been there before and know there's no cable, no internet. All you have to do is turn off your phone and the whole world will disappear."

"Sula, I have to get food," I start.

"Instacart. In fact, I'm ordering food right now. By the time you get there, you'll be stocked for the next two weeks, love."

I can barely see through my tears, but I point my car north on I-684 and drive.

Pulling up to her family home on Watch Hill—which I've always found the name ironic—despite the shingled cottage being dark, it was as welcoming as every other time I've visited. Spying the mounds of groceries on the front stoop, I send her a text. *There's no way I can thank you for this.*

I immediately get one back. *That's because you don't have to and you know it. Just text me when you're safely inside and I know the heat works.*

After doing those very things, and ignoring a flurry of calls, I power down my phone. "Well, Flower, what do we do next?"

She jumps up next to the fireplace to say, *You could light this.*

I immediately think about Ward and the nights we spent curled in front of the fire during the thundersnow. My knees almost buckle. "No. Not tonight. How about we just go to bed?"

Her tail swooshing, she saunters past me and dashes up the stairs.

I wish I could say I followed her with any sort of enthusiasm. But I know what awaits me in my sleep.

And it isn't sweet dreams.

As the first week passed and I began to recover from the shock and anxiety, anger filled my veins. My heart wept for my hastiness in leaving. I debated sending Ward a letter—an actual paper one—to let him know I was safe. Like I said in my letter to Ward, I fought for myself once. This time I ran to save us both.

But before I do, I need to figure out where I was going.

I also haven't spoken with Sula since that first night. After giving me a few days to regroup, she'd have demanded I turn the car around and fight the way I did the first time, with arguments and interviews. But after years of emotional battery, of feeling so small, where do I find the strength to fight a giant?

Then the whispers of my heart reach my mind as the fog of shame finally clears away. "With the people who love me best. That's how I get through this again."

With a wry smile, I know why I've isolated myself with only the cat for company. Because I had to learn I was never alone, even if I felt that way. I held people away, but I still had

Sula and my grandparents. Now I've added Carys, David, and Ward to that circle.

Ward. God, Ward. Even if he never forgives me for needing this time, I'll never be the same woman I was before him. I will survive what happened to me, but I will never recover from what I feel for Ward Burke.

My days are spent walking up and down the beach and missing Ward. I spend my nights curled up in bed and wondering if I should have had more faith in him. Us. In the pleading promises he made me in his bedroom before I ran. Every day it's getting harder and harder not to dash into town to find a trash magazine or to dig deep to find the bravery to call Ward. Everything in my soul is crying out for him. Maybe if I knew things weren't as bad as I suspect they are... "It's for the best," I tell the purring feline. "The first time I was trying to protect myself. This time, I have to protect him. The things Michael threatened." I shudder, imagining what XMedia could do to LLF. I can't be the one to allow that to happen.

Scooping up the cat, I move into the house to dump her unceremoniously at the door near her food.

The girl I was back then isn't the same as the woman I am now. In ten years, I haven't lived a single day without having this hanging over me. Unless those days were spent with Ward. I meant what I wrote in my letter to him. I want him to be happy.

And with those thoughts, I start off down the beach.

I test my bravery the next day by turning on my phone and listening to voicemails. I save each one from Ward. It doesn't go past my notice that they start to taper off as the week goes off. But before I can get maudlin, Sula calls. I decide to answer it. "Hey."

"Oh, thank God," Sula yells.

My lips curve despite the storm causing the waves to crash up against the bluff. "I can't thank you enough, Sula. I just need time…"

"Angie, time just ran out. You have *no* idea of what you've missed."

Tucking my chin and haunching my shoulders, I hold out a hand. Steady as a rock. "It's okay, Sula. I'm okay. I'm safe, he can't get to me…"

"Angie, he's going down!" she screams. "If you didn't answer, I was going to call the damn Instacart guy to leave a note in your damn groceries! They nailed him. There's proof Michael paid off witnesses—a class E felony. Some as recently as two years ago."

My breath backs up into my lungs. "What?" is all I can manage.

"He's been voted off the board of XMedia."

"That's not possible." I shake my head like she can see me.

"Not only possible, it's hit news all over the world. Stock prices for XMedia are tanking." I suck in a sharp breath as Sula barrels on. "There's a massive civil suit that this bigwig attorney, Chase O'Hara, took on—pro bono—for all of his victims."

"Holy crap." All his victims? "How many are there?"

"So far, dozens have spoken up publicly. But some aren't coming forward." Her jab is pointed, and the aim is true.

Like me. The thought moves insidiously into my mind. Shoving it aside, I whisper, "What started all of this?"

"I don't know."

"What do you mean you don't know. How far back does this go?" I demand.

"Someone, somehow, managed to link him all the way back to bribing students and faculty members on the Student Conduct Board!"

No. My mind immediately rejects the possibility. *It can't be possible.*

Could it?

"Angie, you know what this means? Don't you?" Sula's voice is filled with tears of happiness and relief. "You can do anything. Be anything. Go anywhere. There's no need to live in the shadows anymore." The unspoken words she's not saying are, *There never should have been.*

My mind's whirling. "Are you sure, Sula? How certain are you of this? What about Stephen?"

Then a voice says from behind me. "Why don't you ask me about all of it since I know everything?"

I gasp, frightened, whipping my head around with the phone still to my ear. And there he is, his dark hair a mess from the storm. Or, from long hours of running his fingers through it. He holds up the spare key I replaced. "Tell Sula thanks for letting me know where to find this." It falls harmlessly from his hands.

And along with it, my heart. I wait until the pounding is under control before I state the obvious. "You knew where I was."

"I've known where you were since the Monday after you left my condo."

"How?" My brow furrows.

"I called Sula. After I explained the many ways I planned to fix every goddamned thing that happened, she told me you were safe."

"I was." He flinches. I hastily add. "I mean, I have been. God, I didn't mean to leave you standing there. Come in. Sit down. I know it's a long drive from the city."

He steps forward slowly, uncertain of his welcome. *I did that*, I think achingly. *By running instead of standing by his side—fighting.* I lift the phone to my ear. "I'll call you back." I hang up on a squawking Sula. Tossing the phone to the couch, I start to stand.

He lifts a hand. It freezes me in place. *Oh, God. What if he came just to tell me goodbye?*

"In the beginning, I know I judged you differently than the rest of the world, perhaps. But, I cast judgments nonetheless." he begins.

I remain silent as he crosses in front of me, taking a seat on the antique coffee table, not giving a damn he's dripping water on it. I can feel the heat of his body as his legs surround mine, physical arrogance mingled with emotional need. *By listening with his heart, he taught me we're so alike.* My heart flutters slightly at the memory of his hands showing me the beauty of my own body, the pleasure two lovers can bring each other.

Shared memories flash back and forth between us. He reaches for my hand, and I give it without hesitation. Shock, pleasure, then wretched pain flow across his face. "I thought I knew what it was to hurt, how the heart could die. That was, until the night you trusted me with everything that happened to you."

Tears well in my eyes. "Ward, please, let me explain why I..."

"Then, after trusting me with everything, you were confronted by your demons in my home—after I admitted I knew the monsters who hurt you. I promised you safety in my arms, in my home, in my life. I suppose there was a part of me that wasn't surprised you ran; I was surprised you didn't blame me. So, I knew I needed to make it safe for you to come back."

Dawning comprehension strikes hard. "You. You're the one who found out all the information on—" I still can't say his name aloud, even though Ward and the world knows who *he* is. "—him."

"You're goddamn right I did!" I'm taken aback by his vehemence. Ward seethes, squeezing my fingers hard. "Within hours of you leaving, I sicced one of the best investigation firms in the country on his ass. I thought I'd find crooked deals, things like that. What they discovered was abominable. Repulsive." He swallows hard. "I tried to make it right, and I still didn't hear from you."

"I didn't know. Not until right before you walked in the door."

"Angel, how is that possible?" His voice is laced with disbelief.

"There's no internet here. No cable. This is Sula's parents' getaway."

"What about your phone?"

I let go of his hands and reach for my phone. "I turned it off. The first time I turned it back on was this morning. I only just started deleting voicemails from the paps today. I was burying my head in the sand—well, not literally. I was so afraid it was going to be just like every other time, only it would end up with you being gone. I'm so sorry."

Ward's lips part, but instead of verifying I'm telling him the truth, he chucks the phone to land safely onto the couch. While he does, I drink him in—the lines on his face, the fatigue under his eyes, the weariness that wasn't there the last time I saw him. But the sadness is lifting every second we talk. "So, until I walked through that door…"

"I had no idea about what happened. I just finished talking on the phone for the last fifteen minutes with Sula when you came in." I bite my lip. "What she said is on the news, it's true?"

He nods. "As for Stephen, he's rolling on Michael in order to not be charged as an accomplice. He's trying to get his sentence reduced to the same as the others who took bribes so it appears better for the lawsuits. It won't work."

It won't work. I close my eyes in relief.

"Angie? I want you to know something." Ward reaches for my hand.

My eyes fly open, and I find he's braced his elbows on his knees. "What's that?"

"Even if you never come back, you were worth the fight." He reaches forward and touches my cheek gently.

The warm saltiness of a tear leaks out. He uses his thumb to wipe it away. I throw myself forward and wrap my arms around his neck, heedless of the damp coat he's wearing. "You fought for me in a way no one ever has."

He surges upward, pulling me into his arms. "And I always will. I love you, Angela."

Humbled, I still in his arms. "Despite my leaving?"

"Maybe because you did," he muses. "You did the wrong thing, but for all the right reasons."

Hoping he understands, I start to explain, "I was trying—"

"To protect your family." At my start, his tired eyes crinkle at the corners. "While it would have been simpler for us to fight with you waiting at home every night, I think you needed this time to heal from that blow and put it where it belongs."

"It's in the past. It won't ever come between us. Not ever again," I vow.

"It never was to me. Just remember that when things get rough, okay?" Ward tucks a strand of loose hair behind my ear.

And it's that simple gesture, something he's done a thousand times, that frees me. I burst into tears even as I press my lips to his. Our kiss removes recriminations and replaces them with yearning. Before long, we're stretched out on the couch, side by side, as the sun starts to stream in the floor-to-ceiling windows.

"The storm's over," I whisper.

He pushes up on one elbow and peers down at me. A tingle flows through me when he says, "No, it's not. Ours is just beginning. Are you ready for that?"

I slide my hand up and over his chest to tug him down. His dark eyes flare when I whisper against his lips, "It sounds perfect."

WARD

"How does it look?" Angie asks anxiously.

"Remarkable," I reassure her.

"That's the only kind of work I do," Kitty says cockily. Becks's favorite tattoo artist is doing this tiny design as a favor to him.

The heart Angie's having tattooed on her back where she bruised from her attack eleven years ago is being replaced with something much more inspirational—a mash-up of the lyrics of Erzulie's new number one single and words that each of her "family" chose to remind her of how far she's come along her personal journey:

Sula: *Resilient*

Carys: *Trustworthy*

David: *Confident*

Becks: *Appreciative*

And mine: *Fearless*

I debated love, but once I knew the lyrics of Erzulie's single was being used to bind all of our words together in a heart, I knew I didn't need to. It would have been redundant. I lean closer to read them as Kitty finishes the final "e" in my word. *You will survive if you keep love alive.*

"It's like the song was written for us," Angie murmurs. She holds out her hand straight.

I squat in front of her. "Maybe it was."

Angie's lips curve upward. I'm just about to lean forward and press mine against them when Kitty announces, "Done. Angie, do you want to see it before I seal it up?"

Angie leaps up from her prone position and follows Kitty to the full-length mirror. Taking another in her hand, she lifts it up and studies her back from every angle. "It's perfect."

"No," I counter softly. "That's you."

Angie's eyes promise me the world, and I'm going to hold her to it.

And then I'm humbled to a peasant when Angie leans over to hug Kitty and says, "Thank you. Now, when I see that spot, all I'll think of is love."

People think fortune comes from the number of dollars and cents in a bank account. They're wrong. It's when someone you're uncontrollably in love with returns that love with a healthy dose of trust. That's when you're truly wealthy.

Kitty blinks hard before squeezing Angie tightly. "Let's get you finished so you two can skedaddle."

We take care of the payment, a very large tip, and aftercare products. Then we're outside in the cool February air. I squeeze Angie's fingers through her gloves. "Where to now?"

Angie's about to open her mouth when a paparazzi comes up and snaps our photo. Right next to us. "Great shot, Ward and Angie. Say, who got the ink?" The kid winks before dashing off with his prize photo.

I growl, debating whether or not to take off after him to smash the camera to smithereens. Angie reaches over and lays her hand across my heart. "Ward, let them take all the photos they want. Even if they were to guess, make all the assumptions they could possibly make, they're still not going to get it right about us. Right?" Angie's eyes are filled with laughter.

She's absolutely right.

I cup her face with my left hand, feeling the cool band of metal beneath my glove. The feeling is exciting and thrilling as I've only been wearing it for three days.

Three perfect days.

And so far, no one's cottoned on to the fact except our small family who was present.

"Let's go home," she suggests.

"I love that idea," I growl.

Within minutes, we're at our new condo—a space that's closer to Carys and David. The three-bedroom, three-bath unit has the warmth of our weekend place in Brewster with floor-to-ceiling windows, a study I completely remodeled before we moved in, and a kitchen my wife loves using during the week. Flower plunks herself in front of the postwar-era windows every single morning before we leave for work, ignoring us in her sunlit bliss.

That night, I reverently kiss around Angie's new tattoo, worshiping it, worshiping her. "Every single day, I love you more."

Her hair cascades forward, hiding her face, but nothing hides the strength in her words. "Not as much as I will always love you, Ward." She twists her head to the side. I catch the deep pools of blue reflecting all the emotion in her soul.

It's everything.

I lean forward and press my lips directly beneath the word *love* before I twist her against me. Then I tug her down against my lips so I can show her.

Like I intend to every day.

The next morning as we're sharing breakfast, both of our cell phones start going off, and we groan simultaneously. "And this is why we didn't go away right now," Angie singsongs.

"We didn't go somewhere because you want to go somewhere cold, but you don't want to freeze," I counter.

She makes a sound of agreement. Then she freezes. "Ward. We need to go. Right now. Can we get a cab?"

"We can do better than that." I use the kitchen phone and make arrangements for a car to be waiting.

I grab Angie's arm, and the two of us hurry to get downstairs to the car that's waiting to take us both to the office. After we're both settled inside, I ask her, "Did our wedding finally break?"

She shakes her head, sending flame-colored waves everywhere. "No. Oh, God. Ward, we just need to get there as quickly as possible."

I scowl. "This isn't exactly post-wedded-bliss behavior."

She shoves her phone beneath my nose.

Shit.

I lean forward and inform the driver, "Rockefeller Center, please. And hurry."

"Yes, sir."

I curve my arm around Angie's shoulder as she begins to scan all of the alerts coming in. Just then, my phone rings. Glancing at the caller ID, I immediately tell Carys, "We're on our way in."

Her relief is evident. "Thank God. I can't handle this without the two of you. Is Angie okay?"

I glance down at my wife, who's snarling at her phone. "She's gearing up for battle."

Carys says, "It's nice when a husband and wife have things in common," before hanging up.

I grin before I slip my phone into my pocket. Then to distract my wife's fury, I spend the thirty minutes it takes me and Angie to get to the office by kissing her and reminding her that she is everything her new ink says she is.

Therefore, she's ready to fight alongside the rest of us for one of our friends.

I take one last look at Angie's phone and curse roundly. "They never stop, do they?"

"No. But you said it yourself. It's simpler if we fight together," Angie reminds me.

And not caring if a million paps are taking shots, I lean over and kiss her, causing her to drop her phone to her lap.

The screen flashes off on the alert that drove us to leave our home so rapidly.

Rumors are swirling around Grammy-Award-winning artist Beckett Miller.

How long has he known that a composition he wrote long ago resulted in a melody of a different sort – the nine-month variety that wore adorable booties?

And what does his new woman have to say about it?
— **StellaNova**

SNEAK PEEK

If you can't take time to enjoy the scenery while you're dining, well, you're not opening up all your senses. Even if you are simply reheating leftovers at home, make every meal an experience. Pretend your favorite celebrity is dining with you. Set the table. Interact with one another. Embrace the experience.
— **Fab and Delish**

November – nine months later

"It's good to see you." I hold my hand out to the dark-haired Broadway actor.

"You as well, Beckett." Simon Houde holds up a finger, and the hovering waiter comes rushing over to our table. "Something to drink?"

"Just some sparkling water." At Simon's arched brow, I toss him a careless smile. "Somehow I have a feeling I'm going to need my wits about me for this conversation." The reality about my life is I don't indulge in any vice to a degree that I'd become addicted to it. Not booze, not drugs, and due to my parents, I'll never enjoy a woman to the degree I'll lose myself in her. Not after the way my parents ruined my life.

Or the woman I abandoned to have it.

Simon and I exchange quips about his wife, who is my longtime financier, while the waiter is fetching my drink. "I consider myself a fairly knowledgeable man."

"I would agree."

I lean forward to make my point. "But when your wife starts in on the importance of diversifying my portfolio to include alternative energy futures, I swear I feel like I'm back in high school, man. I have to ask, does she talk like this at home?"

Simon bursts out laughing just as the waiter arrives. I lean back in my chair as my drink is poured. When the waiter steps away to the far corner of the private room we're in, Simon responds, "Sometimes, she talks to Alex like this. And sure, we'll talk about our finances. But after all these years, she knows better than to loop me in on a conversation about energy futures."

I lift my glass in a toast. "To your wife, one of the most crazy-brilliant women I know."

He does the same. We both take a quick sip, and then he declares, "Now, the biggest coup—aside from you agreeing to do the music score by the end of this lunch, of course—would be finding out if some smart, savvy woman has sunk her claws into you, Beckett."

Immediately, I shake my head. "Not going to happen."

"You can't tell me you play the field as much as the tabloids say. You'd be dead."

"And you would have had an affair nine times over with your favorite leading lady—who happens to be your wife's sister," I retort.

"True. Hey, speaking of which, let's look at the menu. I have to find something completely noxious for lunch."

I smirk. "Why? You and Evangeline have a kissing scene to practice later?" I make smooching noises in his direction.

"Tragically, yes. But let's order before we talk business." Simon calls the waiter over.

I lift my menu. "I'll take the halibut."

"And I'll take the tilapia. Extra cilantro."

The waiter clears his throat before clarifying, "Extra cilantro, Mr. Houde?"

The waiter is swallowing repeatedly—like he's trying not to choke over the very idea. I rescue him by shaking my glass. "That's all…Charles. And perhaps some more of the sparkling water when you have a moment?"

"Yes, sir. Right away." He scuttles off.

Simon pouts for just a moment. "I was going to tell him to add onions."

"You were going to give yourself heartburn. Now, let's talk business." Before Simon can say anything, I rattle off names. "ABBA, the Who, Paul Simon, Elton John, Alanis Morrissette, just to name a few. It's been done."

"But see, I believe you can dream up something that's next-level," he argues.

"You flatter me and I think give me too much credit."

"Evangeline doesn't think so either. We're so certain of what you're going to be able to produce, Beckett, we're willing to step away from any commitments next spring. That gives you close to nine months to come up with the book."

My heart starts pounding in my chest. "And you? What about you?"

"I'm so certain that you can do this, I want to talk Bristol into financing it."

Christ. I just clench my jaw. "And if I say no?"

"Then we'll figure something else out. But Beckett, you have a story to tell. What it is, we're not certain."

"You're giving me too much credit. I'm not even sure if I know what it is yet."

He flashes a smile that makes him look remarkably like his brother for just a second. "You know what you need to do?"

"What's that?" I ask.

"You need to fall in love."

"That is the very last thing that will ever happen in my life, Simon. I'll agree to do the music without a contract first. Trust me."

He bobbles his glass "Excuse me?"

I open my mouth to repeat what I said, but his hand slashes through the air. "That's complete and utter bullshit, Beckett. You have one of the biggest hearts of any guy I've ever met. You're funny, not all that bad-looking…"

"Are you planning on writing my online dating profile? Because if you are, be certain to mention I'm filthy rich due to your wife."

He flicks me off. "So, I don't get it. Is it the gold diggers? I mean, Bris knows some great—"

"I refuse to fall in love." My voice, devoid of emotion, is more potent for its absence of feeling.

"Care to share the reasons?"

"There's just one." I hold his gaze steadily when he finally lifts his eyes to mine.

"Oh, hell. There was a woman once, wasn't there? And you're not over it?"

I try to dodge the question with one of my own. "Must we keep talking about this?"

"With the ridiculous nondisclosure agreement you insisted your lawyer have me sign? Yes."

A flicker of amusement cuts through the memories of my life in Texas Simon has unwittingly aroused. My lawyer, Carys Burke, essentially threatened to cut off Simon's balls if he so much as breathes a word about our negotiation to anyone. "It's more because it's unfinished business. Maybe I need it to remain that way," I muse.

"You left someone behind?" he guesses.

"I never let her know I'd be leaving so suddenly. Never told her I'd never be back. Then, one night, I ran into one of her brothers at a club after one of my shows." The sick feeling of seeing Jesse Kensington washes over me. I reach for my water and take a sip.

"What happened then?"

"I asked how she was. He mentioned she had a beautiful daughter. And I felt those words like a punch to my gut."

"Beckett, how old were you when you left her?"

"Eighteen."

Buy Perfect Composition Today on Amazon/KU!

ACKNOWLEDGMENTS

If there's one life lesson my father taught me, don't take people at face value. Be certain about who you accept into your circle of trust — whether that's professionally or personally.

I have an amazing circle.

It starts with my husband, Nathan. Nate, "To infinity and beyond," isn't quite long enough, but I suppose the words will have to do. I love you so much.

To our son, we've raised you to look at the world with compassion and without judgement.

To my mother, who has grown stronger as the years past.

Jen, for being my person. For the nudges, no shoves, when I was afraid to take the next steps. For fighting, for living, for making me do the same.

For my Meows. You don't believe in the word assumption simply because you wait for the truth when the time is right. And I love all of you for it.

To Sandra Depukat, from One Love Editing, for not making the assumption that you couldn't push me harder. I'm a better writer for it.

To Holly Malgieri, from Holly's Red Hot Reviews, a.k.a. my twin, assume away, my friend. You're typically right anyway!

To Deborah Bradseth, Tugboat Designs. you add that extra golden touch to every book!

To photographer Wander Aguiar, Andrey Bahia, and model Zach Bradford, I adore all of you! Thank you so much!

To Gel, at Tempting Illustrations, thank you for the magical touch you bring to each story!

To the fantastic team at Foreword PR, thank you for everything you do! Trust me, I don't take a single thing for granted.

Linda Russell, assume all the sloppy words start here. We both know I'm not sure if I'd be typing this if it weren't for you. Love you more.

To my Musketeers. Yeah, that rabbit hole is wide open just waiting for us. But let's not assume anything. #eyeroll

To Susan Henn, Amy Rhodes, and Dawn Hurst, I don't know what I would do without any of you!

For the love and laughter in Tracey's Tribe, every day is made more amazing because of you!

And especially to the readers and bloggers who take the time to enjoy my books, thank you.

ABOUT THE AUTHOR

Tracey Jerald knew she was meant to be a writer when she would rewrite the ending of books in her head when she was a young girl growing up in southern Connecticut. It wasn't long before she was typing alternate endings and extended epilogues "just for fun".

After college in Florida, where she obtained a degree in Criminal Justice, Tracey traded the world of law and order for IT. Her work for a world-wide internet startup transferred her to Northern Virginia where she met her husband in what many call their own happily ever after. They have one son.

When she's not busy with her family or writing, Tracey can be found in her home in north Florida drinking coffee, reading, training for a runDisney event, or feeding her addiction to HGTV.

Connect with her on her website (https://www.traceyjerald.com) for all social media links, bonus scenes, and upcoming news.

Made in the USA
Middletown, DE
23 May 2022

66095927R00285